THE NIGHT SPARROW

ALSO BY SHELLY SANDERS

Daughters of the Occupation

THE NIGHT SPARROW

Shelly Sanders

HARPER ⬤ PERENNIAL

NEW YORK • LONDON • TORONTO • SYDNEY • NEW DELHI • AUCKLAND

HARPER PERENNIAL

First published in Canada in 2025 by HarperCollins Publishers Ltd.

FIRST US EDITION
Library of Congress Cataloging-in-Publication Data
Names: Sanders, Shelly, 1964- author. Title: The night sparrow : a novel / Shelly Sanders. Description: First U.S. edition. | New York, NY : Harper Perennial, 2025. Identifiers: LCCN 2024043336 | ISBN 9780063319219 (trade paperback) | ISBN 9780063319226 (ebook) Subjects: LCSH: World War, 1939-1945--Soviet Union--Fiction. | World War, 1939-1945--Soviet Union--Participation, Female--Fiction. | Snipers--Soviet Union--Fiction. | Hitler, Adolf,1889-1945--Assassination attempts--Fiction. | LCGFT: Historical fiction. | Novels. Classification: LCC PR9199.4.S34 N54 2025 | DDC 813/.6--dc23/eng/20240920

LC record available at https://lccn.loc.gov/2024043336

ISBN 978-0-06-331921-9 (pbk.)

25 26 27 28 29 LBC 5 4 3 2 1

For Alia, who lifts my spirits every day

THE NIGHT SPARROW

1

Let's get ourselves into gear, stand up to the Nazis and drive them
back.

—YULIA ZHUKOVA, RED ARMY SNIPER

Seelow, Germany

April 1945

E lena Bruskina lay on her stomach, finger poised on the trigger
of her rifle though she couldn't see her own hand in the chilly
darkness. It was almost five o'clock in the morning and she
was entrenched in the front line with the rest of her snipers' platoon,
ready to attack the German Wehrmacht troops. But when more than
a hundred Red Army anti-aircraft searchlights suddenly beamed
overhead, turning night into day, her fingers clenched the stock of
her rifle in alarm. The shafts of light were supposed to temporarily
blind the enemy's frontline soldiers and draw attention to their positions. Instead, the eclipsing glare boomeranged off the thick plumes
of artillery smoke and dust, silhouetting Elena and her 1st Belorussian
Front comrades in sharp, bright lines.

Instead of stealthy hunters, we're well-lit targets, she thought, incensed. Then, adding insult to injury, she couldn't see anything but
spots. While the enemy's eyesight was enhanced, the Red Army's
vision was inferior because of its own searchlights.

She blinked twice to make her eyes water and felt the ground-
shaking howl of Katyushas, multiple rocket launchers, bombarding

the enemy's front. And mortar bombs detonating, with hazy blurs that amassed over the trails of white smoke left by the Katyushas. And Red Army ground-attack Shturmovik planes squealing overhead, with air gunners opening fire at the German front line. They flew at such a low altitude, Elena's hair whooshed from the draft.

She covered her ears with the collars of her greatcoat to blot out the deafening noise. It sounded like a multitude of thunderstorms. Like the world was on fire. She opened her mouth to equalize the pressure on her eardrums. Gaped at the flocks of birds emerging through the artillery storm, fluttering madly in all directions.

Then German anti-aircraft rounds began striking with a relentless force, decreasing the already limited visibility. Elena quivered at her stricken comrades' piercing cries.

"Advance!" Lieutenant General Purkayev shouted. His usually crisp voice was barely audible, as if he was speaking through a tunnel.

Elena rose slightly to a crawl position. Her hands and knees sank into the swampy ground. "Chava, where are you?" she yelled to her shooting partner, to be heard over the bullets and bombs.

She felt a tap on her shoulder. Turned and saw Chava's dirt-stained face.

"Right behind you," Chava shouted.

They exchanged knowing looks before venturing forward into the smoky abyss.

The boggy smell of mud drenched her nose, and the uneven, marshy land was hard to traverse with patches of sludge, dirty snow, and wet brown grass. In the distance, Elena heard Soviet tanks grinding through the mud. This was bad. They were supposed to be closer, the tanks and anti-tank guns, to support the infantry's offensive.

It's Küstrin all over again, Elena panicked, recalling their most recent, interminable conflict. We're going to be here for months. We may never get past Seelow Heights. I may never see Berlin. She rubbed her inflamed eyes across the sleeve of her jacket.

Beneath the fusillade of ammunition, she and Chava clambered across the mire to their platoon comrades, Zina and Raya, in a foxhole twenty-five meters to their right. Through a gap in the smoke, she saw a broad swath of steep hills looming in front of them. Seelow Heights. Eighteen versts, twenty kilometers of hills, she recalled from the map she'd committed to memory. She pictured Wehrmacht soldiers lurking in the distant peaks. Standing their ground like wolves.

Be invisible.

Her commander's stern voice, from sniper training, rose in her head.

"This is a good spot to entrench," she called out, when they'd reached Zina and Raya.

Raya shook her head and cupped her hands around her square jaw. "I think we should go farther," she hollered.

Elena squinted to see through the fog of smoke. Where? All she saw were fields and the hills where the enemy was positioned. Not one stand of bushes or trees except at the perimeter of the meadow.

"We're still a long way from the enemy's front line," Zina shouted. Her crimson eyebrows arched with impatience.

"It's too risky," Elena argued. "The visibility is terrible, there are enemy gunners looking down on us from the heights, and it doesn't look like this smoke will clear anytime soon."

"That's exactly why we should move up," Zina protested. "The smoke is perfect for hiding."

"For the enemy too." Chava pointed in the direction of the hills. "Elena's right. We should stay, entrench in foxholes right here, take out any Fritzes trying to breach our front lines."

"We'll cover more ground if we spread out," Raya pressed.

"I don't think it's a good idea—"

"We'd be like sitting ducks," Zina interrupted Elena, "the four of us in one place."

In answer, their comrades in the Belorussian Front started to launch more batches of Katyusha rockets. The enemy responded with anti-aircraft rounds. At once, the smoke thickened to opaque black and gray clouds.

Raya and Zina sprinted towards the ridge, vanishing in the haze.

On instinct, Elena bolted forward. From the moment she'd entered the sniper training school, she'd been close to Raya and Zina. The thought of being separated was intolerable.

Chava grabbed her arm. "Let them go. They know what they're doing."

But I feel safer when we're all together, Elena wanted to say. Because they're better snipers than us. She was ashamed of her fears. Especially now, when the end was so near, when they were just sixty-five versts from Berlin.

You can't avoid what is meant to happen. Her mother's prescient words engulfed her thoughts. *Feel the fear and do it anyway.* She shook her arm from Chava's grasp. She extracted her spade, plunged it into the damp soil, and began excavating a foxhole as the torrent of rockets and bullets continued overhead. Digging, at least, gave her a semblance of control over her own destiny; the hole she created would protect her from the enemy's fire.

Once she and Chava had dug to their waists, the mud changed to an impenetrable frozen crust.

"This is as deep as it gets," Chava said.

Elena nodded wearily and squatted in her foxhole. She scanned the area for signs of the enemy. In her peripheral vision, she caught glimpses of Soviet comrades, on foot, moving furtively over the battlefield.

As the sky brightened to an overcast milky white, Soviet planes sprayed Wehrmacht troops with bullets. It sounded like a congregation of drums. The Germans retaliated with grenades and machine-gun blasts. A German Panzerfaust grenade whirred through the air, exploding twenty meters to the left of the girls.

"Look . . . the enemy . . . thirty degrees," Chava said, her voice breaking up in the commotion.

Elena peered through her binoculars. There they were. Two Fritzes in foxholes getting ready to launch more hand grenades. "I'll take . . . left."

"On three," Chava said.

Elena shot. Missed. She crept sideways, irked by her incompetence under pressure.

Chava took her Fritz in one shot.

Elena prickled as Chava shifted towards her. There was no way she was going to let her partner take out her target. Again. She aimed from her new position, held her breath, and pulled the trigger. At the exact same time Chava fired. The Fritz toppled backwards.

"Your bullet took him down," Chava said, coolly.

Elena looked at her. "How do you know?"

"Because I didn't load a bullet."

"Are you crazy?" Elena said, stunned. "You know I'm not nearly as good a shot as you."

Chava inclined her head. "What I know is you have the skill, you just need more practice."

"Not here, not now," Elena protested. "What if I'd missed?"

"I knew you wouldn't," Chava replied.

Elena wavered between shame and elation. She had two years of experience as a sniper on the front, yet her sister-in-arms felt the need to boost her confidence as if she were back in training, as a cadet. She caught Chava's eager gaze and understood that her comrade had only been trying to help prove her merit. Still, the truth was impossible to ignore—there was a blurred line between friendship and pity.

By dusk, the storm of artillery finally waned. Elena and Chava had advanced over the ridge after taking out a nest of machine gunners.

As the smoke lifted like a veil, Elena was overcome by the sight of Red Army soldiers strewn across the pitted field. Thousands.

"I don't understand," she said.

"What?" said Chava.

"It was supposed to be a surprise attack, but the enemy didn't seem surprised at all."

"Maybe they're better prepared than we thought."

"Or maybe someone told—"

"Don't come any closer!" a familiar voice cried out, shrill, terrified.

"Raya," Elena and Chava whispered, in unison.

"*Kommunistisches Schwein.*"

The German's taunting voice was a stab in Elena's throat. This was all wrong. Zina and Raya were too cunning to be cornered by the enemy. Still, it had been hours since they'd rushed ahead and there hadn't been any sign of their comrades.

". . . *Russische Huren* . . . Russian whores."

"We have to find them," Elena said.

"We will. But . . ." Chava's voice trailed off.

Elena heard what Chava didn't say. She ignored the niggling voice in her head telling her to stay put, and motioned for them to move quickly in the direction of the voices. And as she crept forward, she knew this could be her final action.

2

It would seem we will never break through to the truth about our-selves even if we try for a lifetime.

—YELENA RZHEVSKAYA, SOVIET INTERPRETER, WWII

Seelow, Germany

April 1945

Comrade Bruskina."

Elena started at Lieutenant General Purkayev's crisp voice. "Yes?"

He appeared in front of her chair, a familiar whiff of carbolic soap and tobacco. His tall, wiry frame eclipsed the screen's glow.

She looked up at him, miffed. He'd appeared before the end of the film, before she found out if the couple reunited.

"Come with me," he said.

She felt a dozen pairs of curious eyes on her as she rose, slinging her rifle over her shoulder. Her sniper comrades. What was left of the platoon after the battle of Seelow Heights a week ago. Nine girls had been killed. Including . . . Her mind scudded backwards to that ghastly day. The squall of grenades. The astonishing force that tossed her through the air. The crack of her bone hitting the ground. She shook off the memory but her friends were still gone. Her elbow was still broken. Her shooting days were still over.

Purkayev led her across the hall to the dining room. He had a brusque air that was hard to read.

A thickset bald man, with downturned lips and an extraordinary number of gleaming medals on his uniform, stood by the window. The late-afternoon light emphasized the deep cleft in his chin.

"This is Major Bystrov," said Purkayev.

Major?

"You're being redeployed to a counterintelligence unit," he added. "SMERSH."

As Purkayev's words sank in, a crushing panic came over her. "I don't know anything about spies," she said, referring to SMERSH's motto, "Death to Spies." "Why can't I stay with my platoon?"

Purkayev lowered his gaze.

She spotted her rucksack and canteen on the floor. She eyed him, puzzled.

The tendons in his long neck pulsed. "I have no say in the matter."

"What have I done?"

Impatience flickered across Bystrov's round face, two distinct lines etched between his small, shrewd eyes. "It's not what you've done, it's what you can do for us."

"I'm confused."

"It's a classified mission. I'll explain on the way."

"Where?"

"Meet me in the car in two minutes." Bystrov gave Purkayev a dismissive nod and walked out of the house.

Elena looked at her commander.

He blotted his forehead with a cloth. "You have to go."

"I can't leave like this." She glanced at her splinted arm. "I need to stay until I can shoot. I need to avenge their deaths."

"Revenge won't change anything." He leaned in towards Elena. "What you do with your life, how you honor their memory, that's what matters."

The din of high-spirited female voices surged from the room where the film had been shown. She thought sadly of her fallen comrades.

"I should have protected them," she murmured.

"It all happened too fast. If you'd taken a shot, you might have hit one of them. You'd never be able to forgive yourself."

"But I can't get them out of my head. Their voices——"

"You'll go crazy if you keep thinking about what you could have done. It won't bring them back and you know they wouldn't want you sitting here feeling sorry for yourself."

She swallowed the knot clogging her throat. "Can I at least say goodbye?" she gestured towards her comrades in the sitting room.

"I'm afraid not. The major is waiting in the car."

"Can't you tell me . . . what this is about?"

He pulled her rifle off her shoulder. "We may need this in Berlin."

She bristled at the way he ignored her question. At her bare shoulder. At the loss of the rifle she'd carried since the day her platoon embarked for the front. Four and a half kilograms gone. The weight of a cat.

"Are you sure I can't keep it?"

"With your bad elbow, you can't shoot a rifle. Besides, you still have your pistol."

"Is this what you want?"

He looked squarely at her, as if he were memorizing her features. "This is bigger than you and me. And no, I don't want you to leave."

She felt a tug at her heart. It made no sense, being redeployed, when the end was so near. When she and Purkayev . . . She stopped herself. There was no time for love during war. Romance was for books.

He squeezed her shoulders.

Her skin tingled at the unexpected contact.

He yanked his hands from her, as if her shoulders were on fire.

She felt dizzy. She looked into Purkayev's charcoal eyes to keep steady.

He reached for the doorknob.

"I really liked the film," she blurted.

"Oh? Which part did you like best?"

"The beginning, when they promised to unite after the war."

"That's my favorite part, too." He turned the doorknob. "I'd like to meet someone, when the war ends, on the Bolshoy Bridge."

"You would?"

He opened the door. Nodded. "At six in the evening."

"Six in the evening," she echoed.

"On the Bolshoy Bridge," she heard him say, before the door shut behind her.

3

One day my mother went to work and never came back. The
three of us were left without parents.
—ALLA RAKOVSHCHIK, PRISONER, MINSK GHETTO

Minsk, Belorussia

October 1941

On her way home, Elena Bruskina saw twelve women she'd
presumed were dead reappear. The full dozen. Her breath
hitched. People sent to jail usually vanished. Her thoughts
slid to her father and her older brother, Yakov, arrested months ago
with hundreds of other men from the ghetto. There were no charges.
No trials. No letters from Siberia saying they'd been exiled. No sign
of them whatsoever. In her heart, Elena knew they were gone forever,
but without proof, without bodies, graves, or a funeral, she didn't
know how to mourn. She was frozen in grief.

Elena strained to see the twelve women marching ahead of her,
guarded by German fascists in crisp black uniforms and brimmed
caps. In the drizzling rain, the women were ghostlike with wispy,
hunched silhouettes.

Twilight had set in and Elena was on her way back to the Minsk
ghetto with hundreds of other women after their shift at the Oktyabr
Garment Factory. She appreciated this in-between time, when she
wasn't loading and unloading crates or imprisoned in the ghetto as
if she were a convicted criminal. Walking to and from work was the

only part of her day where she could almost remember what it felt like to be a university student, to be free.

Almost.

There was the Lower Bazaar, a popular department store where her mother had shopped for coats and hats, now hollowed out by a bomb. One block later, balconies hung precariously from the brick veneer of an apartment building. Glass had been blown out of the windows, making them look like black cavities. Up ahead, the Nazi flag, hoisted above the Government House, pulsed in the wind, the black swastika a menacing emblem of, ironically, white pride. On the other side of the street, pillars were the only remnants of another government building. Elena tried to recall Minsk before the Germans invaded in June, but it was getting harder and harder to see the past through the wreckage.

The column of workers turned onto Fruktovaya Street. Aspen trees lay across the muddy road like bones. Elena's feet smarted with fatigue as she stepped through puddles in wide tank treads. Her leather boots, which had come apart at the toes, sloshed with rainwater. She shivered, then looked up at the sky, vast and heavy with grayish-blue clouds that hung so near to the ground, she felt as if they might swallow her whole. This, the sky, the weather, was the only constant in a new and terrifying world rife with uncertainty.

"*Weitergehen!* Don't stop." A soldier lashed a couple of women with a birch rod as if they were cattle.

Elena flinched. She felt Tsila, beside her, go tense. Tsila had a temper that could flare in an instant. This was one of the first things Elena had noticed when they'd met as children at Young Pioneer Camp. Tsila had smacked a boy in the face for making fun of her chubbiness. Seeing a girl stand up to a boy had filled Elena with awe and a touch of envy. She'd wanted to be like Tsila, outspoken and decisive. But here she was, about to turn twenty-two in December and just as quietly tentative as she'd been all those years ago.

Now she could see Tsila's anger in the way her nostrils flared, in the way she drew her small teeth over her bottom lip. Elena squeezed her hand. Tsila crushed her fingers until they were numb.

"*Faule Juden*. Lazy Jews," another soldier shouted.

Elena cringed at the way the words spewed from the guard's tongue. Jagged. Ugly. Mean. Before the war, she'd been in her final year of studying German at university, "the language of civilized people," her father used to say with pride. Until the Germans bombed Minsk. She wondered how something once beautiful and refined could suddenly become crude and heinous. She regretted the years she'd spent learning the enemy's language.

"*Ich habe keine Geduld fur Faulheit.* I have no patience for laziness."

She caught the skull insignia on the guard's cap. In German, it was called *Totenkopf*, death's head.

"Why didn't I see this coming?" she mumbled.

"Nobody knew who Hitler was," Tsila said grimly, "or what he would become."

"True," Elena conceded. Not one word about fascism had been written in any newspaper or discussed on the radio before the German invasion. It seemed as though Hitler had waved a wand and turned rational, law-abiding Germans into Jew-killing nationalists overnight. "But we can't blame one man for corrupting an entire country," she added.

"It had to start somewhere," said Tsila.

Elena looked at her friend through the misty rain. "But why isn't anyone stopping him?"

The rain had ended by the time the column of workers reached the ghetto. The air was dank and smelled of gunpowder and urine. Above the wooden roofs, orange and lavender slivers of light trimmed the evaporating horizon. A policeman with a withering glare stood at the gate. Elena, head down, filed past him into the ghetto. She queued with the rest of the workers at the labor office to be counted and searched. This was the moment she dreaded every day, the moment they might ask about Masha. Her seventeen-year-old sister had escaped the ghetto soon after her father and brother disappeared to volunteer as a nurse for the partisans. Though Elena was fairly certain Masha's name had, by a stroke of luck, gone missing from the list of residents, there were no guarantees. If a guard happened to notice Masha was absent, she and her mother would be shot.

"Pass?" a hefty policeman grunted at Elena.

She showed him her worker's pass.

"Turn out your pockets," he said gruffly. "Open your coat."

She unbuttoned the oversized woolen coat that used to be Yakov's. It was all she had left of him. She tugged the two inside pockets up. One was sticky from Kara-Kum candy wrappers, and there was a gray feather in the other pocket. Elena's heart stirred, remembering how her brother was forever bringing injured animals home, birds mostly, with broken wings, setting them free when they were strong enough to fly.

The policeman roughly probed her thin waist, searching for food. She fought the urge to yank his fleshy hands from her body.

"Go to Yubileynaya, Jubilee Square," he said, after he'd finished groping her.

"The square?" Elena said, piqued by the schedule change. Her routine, though exhausting, held her in place.

"No talking," he barked.

Tsila grabbed her elbow and yanked her forward, onto Opanskaja Street.

Elena pitched at the steely German voices ordering people from their homes. At the sight of a soldier dragging an old woman down the street.

"Where are we going, Mama?" a child's sleepy voice said, in Yiddish.

"Faster," a man barked in German.

Elena prayed her mother hadn't been forced into this chaos.

A baby's cry set off a chorus of wails.

Within minutes, the street was jammed with people on their way to the square that was, in fact, a long, narrow triangle encompassing one hundred square meters, about the size of two ice surfaces used for Bandy, an outdoor game Yakov had played on skates, using a stick to hit a ball into the opposing team's net.

"They must have roused the entire ghetto," Tsila said, astonished.

"Impossible." There were seventy thousand Jews in the ghetto, far too many to fit into the square.

Something hard cuffed Elena's shoulder blade. She jolted upright. A flailing boy, in his mother's arms, had whacked her with his bare foot. She tried to move out of his kicking range but there was nowhere to go. She and Tsila were hemmed in by ghetto residents. She couldn't even move her arms.

Elena's breath quickened as they descended upon Yubileynaya Square, in the center of the ghetto. Frenzied voices rose as the sun fell to the horizon. It all felt so orchestrated, as if she were in an audience waiting for the curtain to rise. From the corner of her eye, she spotted a camera pointed towards a brawny German officer standing still in the middle of the square. She was overcome by a rattling sense of doom.

She gripped Tsila's arm. "I need to get out of here."

"If you sprout wings let me know," Tsila replied, deadpan. "Because unless you can fly, you're stuck. Look." She gestured at the guards surrounding the square. Brandishing their guns like trophies.

Elena curled her fingers around Yakov's feather. It bolstered her spirits, touching it, knowing it meant something to her brother.

"Attention, *Juden*," the officer in the center of the square announced, in a leaden voice.

Armed guards prodded the twelve women into a row behind the officer. The women's arms were tied behind their backs. Signs around their necks claimed they'd refused to work.

Refused to work? Elena reeled with disbelief. Two weeks earlier, the women had been inexplicably dismissed from the factory where she worked. Unemployed, they no longer qualified for rations. The Germans barred children and nonworking adults from receiving food. The women had begged to be reinstated. Instead they were thrown in jail.

"Silence, *Juden*," the officer shouted.

The crowd hushed.

"Before you are twelve women," he continued. "For malingering and refusal to work, they will be shot."

"That's a lie," Tsila burst out.

The officer glared at her.

She met his scowl with unblinking eyes.

Elena was stunned to silence. These women had done nothing wrong. Nothing to warrant a public execution.

An old man with sidelocks and white whiskers was forced at gunpoint to blindfold the women.

Elena's knees went weak. She'd heard hundreds of gunshots in the five months she'd lived in the ghetto. She'd seen bodies sprawled on the ground in pools of blood. But she'd never seen anyone killed. She felt herself sway backwards but there was nowhere to fall. There were too many people behind her, keeping her on her feet.

Three German soldiers aimed machine guns at the women.

There was a collective gasp.

Elena pinched her eyes shut.

Bullets exploded from barrels. Bodies thumped to the ground. In that moment, Elena knew for certain her father and brother were never coming home. In that moment, she knew the extent of Hitler's venom.

"*Juden, geht schnell in eure Häuser!* Jews, get to your homes quickly," a soldier barked.

Elena's gaze fell to the center, to the dead women. They used to be daughters, sisters, mothers, wives. When would the Germans come for her?

"Go home." A fascist soldier loomed over Elena and Tsila.

Elena turned. In her mind, she kicked the bastard in the groin. She shuffled through the crowd pouring from the square onto adjacent streets. The silence was eerie. Not even the flutter of birds overhead.

"See you tomorrow?" she said to Tsila.

"Tomorrow," Tsila replied, with a resolve that centered Elena.

Tsila turned right, towards the other end of the ghetto. Orphaned after her parents were shot, she lived with her grandparents and a handful of cousins.

Elena held the collar of her coat tight around her neck as she walked, head down, against the brisk north wind. Her calloused hands stung. The joints in her fingers were swollen and tender. Her flimsy gloves had been mended so many times she could barely see the original green strands of wool.

The staccato burst of gunfire strafed her mind. Was Masha all right? She hadn't heard from her sister in a few days. Ordinarily, Elena wouldn't be too worried, but after seeing those women executed, all she could think about was Masha looking the wrong way at a member of the Gestapo and . . . it was too horrible to imagine.

The wind propelled her forward, blowing her long, chestnut hair over her broad shoulders. She walked faster, turned onto Flaksa Street, and approached her ramshackle wood house with its caved-in roof, boarded-up windows, and crooked front door.

A child in the neighbor's house let out a plaintive cry. Starving, no doubt.

Elena hesitated before opening her door. The one-room interior reminded her of who she'd become and what she'd lost. She longed to run as far from the ghetto as she could go, but the chances of escaping alive were next to impossible. Besides, she could never abandon her mother, who was increasingly despondent as time went by without a word from Yakov and her father.

Elena leveled her shoulders. She opened the door and nearly crashed into her mother, who was waiting for her with a stricken expression. Her mother's words brought a quick rush of blood to her throat.

"Masha's been arrested."

4

People shoot, kill, bury, rush into the attack, go out into reconnaissance, and that is war. But the starving women with their bags, without proper boots, wandering God knows where with their hungry children, the old people, the refugees, the people burned out of their homes—they are the real horror of war.
—YELENA RZHEVSKAYA, RED ARMY INTERPRETER

Seelow, Germany

April 1945

Major Bystrov was smoking beside an olive-green jeep, slick with dust. Elena turned and took one last look at the red-roofed house, one of the few surviving homes on Gorlsdorfer Street after the fierce three-day battle of Seelow Heights. The gray stucco exterior was mottled with shell pits and there were mounds of debris on both sides of the two-story building.

Elena breathed in the air, warm with the promise of spring. On the other side of the road, a single larch tree dipped over the pavement. A grenade had torn its roots from the ground. Down the street, another tree had fallen across the entire width of the asphalt, blocking automobiles completely.

She strung her well-worn rucksack that contained everything she owned, along with her treasured canteen, over her shoulder. Major Bystrov held the rear door open for her, then got into the front seat. He introduced the driver as Ludis from Siberia.

Ludis, in his mid-twenties, broad-nosed and pockmarked, gave Elena a brief smile, started the engine, and pulled onto the street. She looked back at the house, hoping to see Purkayev through the window, but the lace curtains were drawn. Then it hit her. She didn't even know his given name.

As the jeep moved farther from the house, she felt undone, deserting her platoon before the war's end, leaving the comrades she'd lived and worked with for two years. Leaving Purkayev right after their first meaningful discussion. She slumped in her seat. Snuck a glance at Major Bystrov. She was galled and confused by his stand-offish manner.

"Can you tell me where we're going?" she asked.

"SMERSH headquarters," he answered.

"What are we doing there?"

An elongated pause.

"We need your help interrogating fascist prisoners."

"What?" she said, shaken. "Why me? I'm not an interpreter."

He ran his hand over his shiny head. "This isn't just about translating."

"What do you mean?"

The major pivoted in his seat to face her. "It's about discretion, knowing what to say and how to say it. Knowing how to set sights on a target and expose whatever he's hiding."

"I see," she replied, though she couldn't help but wonder if it was merely a matter of convenience. An interpreter was needed, and she was an injured sniper who happened to speak German.

"Comrade Lieutenant Lobkovskaya told us you've translated German flyers, and talked one of your comrades out of shooting a Fritz who'd surrendered."

"I did but—"

"Your negotiating skills kept a valuable tongue alive. He provided important intel."

Her eyes widened in surprise.

"You've got the right instincts for this position," he explained.

"Oh?"

"You know," he said, thoughtful, "snipers and interpreters aren't that different."

"They're not?"

"A sniper eliminates targets with bullets. An interpreter's weapon is the German language."

She stared at him, unconvinced.

He gave her a look that said their discussion was finished, and turned back to the road.

The jeep started to bounce up and down. The pavement was rutted with shrapnel, cracks, and holes from shells. Elena's mouth was pasty dry. Her stomach grew queasy. She drained her canteen and moved her thumb over the familiar dent, back and forth, to soothe her nerves. She missed her comrades and the burning sense that she was making a real difference in the war.

"Why don't you use the interpreter from my regiment?" Elena pressed.

"She's been sent to a penal battalion for speaking out against collective farms."

She tipped her head like a pensive bird. "Aren't there others?"

"There's been a shortage of interpreters since the fascists invaded. If your regiment commander had known earlier about your fluency in German, we'd have taken you then."

Her heart skipped a beat. Purkayev knew almost right from the day they met that she spoke German. And he must have known about the need for interpreters. She looked down at her lap to hide her smile. In her mind, she replayed their final conversation, heard his steadfast voice say Bolshoy Bridge. Heat rose up the back of her neck. Her head grew heavy. She closed her eyes and felt herself dissolve into the engine's steady rhythm.

5

Masha Bruskina—the schoolgirl of 8th grade in School Number 28 Minsk. She has only good and excellent marks in all subjects.

—PIONEER OF BELORUSSIA (PHOTO CAPTION), DECEMBER 1938

Minsk, Belorussia

October 1941

Arrested? The house receded to a dense fog as the news about Masha plunged into Elena's head.

"Why?" she managed.

Her mother ran her fingers through her hair. Once a sleek, ear-length bob, it was now a tangle of gray that hung like string to her bony shoulders. "Masha was caught helping injured Red Army soldiers escape from the hospital," she went on, her voice breaking.

Elena paled. "How do you know?"

Her mother regarded her with puffy eyes. "One of her friends told me. She saw Masha taken away yesterday."

Elena slumped against the door.

"She . . . she was betrayed. Someone told them Masha was smuggling in clothes and false papers for the soldiers." Her mother clasped her shawl with knobby, arthritic hands that had aged drastically in the five months they'd lived in the ghetto. "Why would she—"

"Who's there?" Mr. Volkhov interrupted, from the wooden slab he used as a bed in the back corner. "Is that you, Vera?"

Elena slouched at his nasal, wistful voice. He had to be at least seventy years old and sounded as if he had pneumonia when he breathed. The years were etched on his face and his skin hung from his bones like dripping candle wax, and though he claimed to be "stone deaf," he had a remarkable knack for hearing private conversations. And for some crazy reason, Mr. Volkhov believed Elena was his dead wife.

"Vera's gone," Elena replied, impatient.

"Gone? For goodness' sake, Vera, I can hear you."

A rustling sound from the opposite corner.

"Hush," said Mrs. Drapkina to her three young daughters, huddled on their wooden bed slab. Mrs. Drapkina, a buxom woman, had a soft, motherly air. Her husband had vanished with Elena's father and brother.

"I shouldn't have let Masha leave," Elena's mother sobbed. "It's all my fault."

"Vera, did you bring the wood? It's cold in here."

"Go back to sleep," Elena told Mr. Volkhov.

She wrapped her arms around her mother. "You begged Masha to stay." She felt the sharp edge of her mother's shoulder blades and held her tighter. "Even after the hospital told her they didn't want Jewish volunteers, Masha dyed her hair blond and said she was Russian, remember?"

Her mother's head bobbed against her chest, and for a second, Elena saw herself as a child, in her mother's arms. Elena clung to the image, reluctant to let go of the past where she was carefree, where her mother took care of her, not the other way around.

"No wonder you're cold," Mrs. Drapkina was saying to Mr. Volkhov. She spoke as though she were talking to a child. "Your blanket is on the ground. Here." She laid the threadbare blanket over the old man.

"You're not Vera," he sputtered.

"She's gone," Mrs. Drapkina replied, kindly. "She died on the way to the ghetto."

"That's a lie. I just heard her voice with my own ears. Where is she? Why are you keeping her from me?"

Elena was crushed by Mr. Volkhov's disoriented grief.

"Close your eyes," Mrs. Drapkina said to him in a soothing tone.

"There's nothing you could have done to stop Masha," Elena went on, softly, to her mother. "And you know she would never refuse anyone in need."

Her mother pulled away and looked at Elena with expectant, honey-brown eyes. "Why haven't they come home yet? Your father and brother are not criminals. They should be here, with us."

The twelve women's cowering faces flickered past Elena's eyes. She shook the image away and clutched Yakov's feather. "I think we both have to realize they're not coming back."

Her mother blanched. "Don't be ridiculous." Her hollow cheeks were wet with tears.

Elena sagged.

"I'm cold," Mr. Volkhov mumbled.

"There's no more wood for the stove," said Mrs. Drapkina.

"Your father and brother will return, and so will Masha," Elena's mother said, obstinate.

"But you can't—"

"Vera?" Mr. Volkhov interrupted. "Is that you?"

Elena's fingers curled into her palms. She was fed up with Mr. Volkhov. She was fed up with her mother's refusal to accept the truth. And she was fed up with having to talk about private matters in front of people she lived with yet barely knew.

"Shhh," said Mrs. Drapkina, to Mr. Volkhov.

"Vera . . . Vera . . ."

His waning voice shifted to fitful snores.

Mrs. Drapkina returned to her girls, cowering on their narrow slab.

"See for yourself." Elena's mother dried her cheeks with her shawl. "Masha's friend gave this to me." She retrieved a paper triangle from the pocket of her long, brown skirt; only letters folded into triangles, making them easy for censors to open, were distributed. She handed it to Elena.

Mama,

I am tormented by the thought that I have caused you great worry. Don't worry. Nothing bad has happened to me. I swear to you that you will have no further unpleasantness because of me. If you can, please send me my dress, my green blouse, and white socks. I want to be dressed decently when I leave here.

Your Masha

"You see?" her mother said, triumphant. "It doesn't sound as if she's afraid, does it?"

She reread the letter, noting her sister's shaky handwriting. Elena admired her sister's courage, defying the Nazis, while she rotted away in the ghetto, following orders like a sheep.

"She's fine, yes?" her mother was saying. "And she'll be home soon."

"We knew there would be risks when Masha joined the partisans," Elena said, tiptoeing around her words to keep from worrying her mother too much, yet trying, at the same time, to be honest.

"She hasn't hurt anyone . . ." her mother said.

"That's not entirely true, Mama. The Red Army soldiers she helped will return to their regiments and shoot fascists again." Elena paused. "And she is Jewish."

"Masha has no time for religion," her mother scoffed. "She is a proud Communist like me."

"It doesn't matter if Masha is religious," Elena said, exasperated. "She's Jewish by blood. Her name is Jewish."

"She is fighting for Stalin, for our homeland," her mother argued.

Elena looked at her mother, vexed by her foolish devotion to Joseph Stalin, their despotic leader and Hitler's equal when it came to murdering innocent civilians. "The Germans see Masha as Jewish. They wouldn't care if Masha wore a cross around her neck. To them, she is a Jew."

Elena's family, like most of the ghetto inhabitants, was far more Soviet than Jewish. She'd rarely set foot in a synagogue, though her father had insisted his children chant Shabbat prayers, light the candles, and observe the High Holidays. And she had fond memories of her late, bearded grandfather, her mother's father, singing her to sleep with Yiddish lullabies.

Her mother brought her shaky fingers to the *lata*, the yellow patch on her blouse, identifying her as a Jew, or a "kike," one of the demeaning terms used by the fascists. Ironic, as she'd supplanted her Judaism for Communism years ago.

These compulsory patches made Elena see, for the first time in her twenty-one years, that being Jewish was more than a hindrance. Before the fascist occupation, all citizens had been considered equal—men and women, Jews and Christians. Religion had been banned; Stalin had shut down all the Yiddish schools, publications, and theaters. People worshipped their Motherland, the Soviet Union, as well as Joseph Stalin. Just as the Germans revered Adolf Hitler. We're caught between two evil regimes, she thought. Even if we're triumphant, we won't gain our freedom, we'll still be Soviet citizens.

"We must see about getting your sister's dress to her after roll call tomorrow."

Roll call? Elena was disturbed by the thought of returning to Yubileynaya Square for the obligatory Sunday meeting, of her mother seeing the women's dead bodies lying in one long row.

"I know the emerald-green blouse Masha wants," her mother chirped on, as if Masha had written from Pioneer Camp. "She looks so pretty in it."

"Maybe you shouldn't expect too much."

"What do you mean?"

Elena racked her brain for the right thing to say. "It's just, I don't think you should get your hopes up."

"But she hasn't hurt anyone," her mother repeated, urgent. "She is a nurse. She helps people."

Elena lowered her gaze. "Yes she does."

"And that green blouse brings out her eyes, don't you think?"

"Yes it does." She brushed tears from her cheeks. She folded her arms across her chest. Elena ached for her father, Yakov, and Masha. In the bleak house, their absence was an emotional squall erupting from her stomach to her throat.

6

Kind, good, happy, gentlemanly, secure people never go Nazi. But those driven by fear, resentment, insecurity, or self-loathing? They would always fall for fascism.

—DOROTHY THOMPSON, "WHO GOES NAZI?," *HARPER'S,* 1941

Müncheberg, Germany

April 1945

Elena's head whacked against the jeep's window. She jerked upright, rubbed her temple, then opened her eyes. It took a moment to remember where she was.

"Have a good sleep, Comrade Bruskina?" Major Bystrov's voice boomed.

"I fell asleep?"

"For a good hour," he responded.

She stifled a yawn and peered out the window. The navy sky glittered with stars. The jeep had come to a stop outside a stone house set back from the road. Two bare apple trees anchored the corners of the front yard like gnarled hands.

"Here we are." Major Bystrov opened his door and stepped out of the vehicle. "Müncheberg."

"This is headquarters?" she said nervously. She was afraid of what lay ahead. What if her German wasn't good enough? She didn't want to disappoint people.

"Temporarily, until we reach Berlin." Major Bystrov opened her door and motioned for her to get out.

She warily followed the major up the stone path to the house. Inside, she was met by the decaying smell of mothballs. She surveyed the expansive interior with its grand staircase and separate rooms in all four corners of the main level. Through an open door on her left, she saw a massive fireplace behind an elaborate wood desk. Two commanders broke off talking when she walked past.

Bystrov led her to the back of the house, into a long and narrow room with a polished oak dining table. Extra chairs lined a wall like the row of an audience. He motioned for her to sit down. He shut the door and sat across from Elena. He drummed his fingers on the table.

Her face tightened with concentration.

His fingers stilled. "What I am about to tell you must not be repeated to anyone," he began, with a slow exactitude.

She sensed the weight of his words. Nodded.

Bystrov clamped his hands over the edge of the table. "Our SMERSH unit has been tasked with a vital covert mission."

Her heart raced as his words sank in.

"We have orders to find Hitler."

"Find Hitler?"

"Stalin wants Hitler captured alive in time for May Day celebrations in Moscow," he finished, in a low and urgent voice.

She shivered at the magnitude of Bystrov's words. She tugged her ear, convinced she was hearing things. You've made a mistake, she wanted to say. I'm just a mediocre sniper from Minsk. At best. "There must be others far more capable," she managed.

"Translators able to hunt like a sniper?" he scoffed.

She was terrified of failing. Of disappointing Bystrov and SMERSH. Then she looked at her useless arm. She thought about her brother's feather, which had accompanied her safely across the

Eastern Front, and felt a rush of strength. She thought about how she coveted revenge for her family. For her fallen comrades. Her doubts sharpened to a budding self-assurance. A Jew stalking Hitler, she thought, her heart pumping in her throat. The irony. The delectable irony.

7

One day, a truck arrived at the orphanage [in the ghetto]. The truck windows were covered up and two pipes came out of the roof. Children were taken from the orphanage, put inside the van and taken away. They never came back. The van was a mobile gas chamber.
—LIDIYA PETROVA, PRISONER, MINSK GHETTO

Minsk, Belorussia

October 1941

Six days after Masha's letter came, there was still no sign of her sister. Elena couldn't take sitting and worrying on her only day off. She had to do something to escape their gloomy flat, where Mrs. Drapkina's daughters were beginning to look like dolls with their glassy eyes and porcelain skin. Where old Mr. Volkhov lay semiconscious in the corner day and night, calling out for Vera in a distraught voice.

"Can you fetch some more water, Elena?" her mother asked.

The wells in the ghetto had been destroyed by the fascists before the Jews moved in. Inhabitants were forced to slip through holes in the ghetto fence to fill containers with water from the Svisloch River that snaked through Minsk.

"We'll need water if Masha comes home today," Elena's mother continued, in a peculiar, jaunty voice. "She probably hasn't had much to eat or drink since she was arrested."

Elena paled. If Masha never returned, her mother would depend on her more than ever. This dismayed Elena. Because she couldn't keep up the encouraging pretense much longer. Because she couldn't bear seeing her mother wither away to nothing. Because she woke every day wondering if it would be her last.

"I assumed Elena would look after my girls while we're at work today, Esther," Mrs. Drapkina said.

"That's right," Elena agreed quickly. She exchanged a nervous glance with Mrs. Drapkina.

Elena's mother puckered her brow. "But there's no water left. Are you going to tell Masha you didn't care enough about her to fetch water?"

Elena's shoulders went stiff. She understood grief. She could handle grief. But her mother's delusions, they were as foreign as the other side of the world. And they were getting worse.

"I'm thirsty," said ten-year-old Dossia, the eldest of Mrs. Drapkina's girls.

Elena glanced at the metal bucket, covered in a cloth to keep the bugs out. She lifted the cloth. "It's empty. I'll go."

"What about my girls?" said Mrs. Drapkina.

"I'll keep an eye on them," Mr. Volkhov interjected, his voice raspy, weak, and surprisingly lucid. "We need water."

Mrs. Drapkina shot Elena an imploring look. Elena's gaze slid to the three frail girls on their slab, nestled together under a tattered blanket. Her eyes lingered on the smallest girl, Perla, with hollow cheeks and open sores on her lips that were not healing. Perla looked as if she were near death.

"I'll be quick," Elena promised.

Mrs. Drapkina sighed. She tucked the blanket tight around her girls and told them not to move or make a sound until Elena returned.

The girls' lethargy upset Elena. If they didn't get a decent meal soon . . . She turned her eyes from them. Worrying wouldn't feed them. Worrying wouldn't bring water to their dehydrated mouths.

"Be back in a while." Elena grabbed the bucket's handle and stepped towards the door.

"You'll never get that bucket past the guards," warned Mr. Volkhov.

Elena started.

He pulled something out from under his blanket. A tin canteen hanging on a rope. His bones cracked as he moved. He held it out to Elena. "Carried this all the way through the Civil War."

Elena took the canteen from his withered hand.

"A bullet grazed it, right there." Mr. Volkhov pointed at a dent on one side of the canteen. "Saved my life."

Elena was surprised. She couldn't reconcile this feeble, old man as a soldier. She thrust the canteen under Yakov's coat and opened the door.

"Be careful, Vera," he said.

She halted. His clarity had vanished as quickly as it had sparked. She opened her mouth to say, I'm not Vera, then heard herself reply, "Thank you. I will be very careful."

It was a warm October morning. Not a cloud in the sky. Not a hint of wind. The lemony sun was low, casting long, thin shadows over Flaksa Street. Elena moved at a brisk pace, winding her way through side streets to avoid guards. She heard women moaning in several houses. Children weeping in others. She brimmed with despair when she passed six women hanging from the gallows, killed that morning because they hadn't worn their yellow patches in the ghetto. She recalled the twelve women executed the previous day and faltered, worn out by the futility of trying to stay alive. Then she felt the air, thick with death, and thought, I can't give up. No matter how bad it gets, I have to keep going.

Elena made her way to a gap in the barbed-wire fence, about three meters from a pacing guard. She dropped to the ground, feigning exhaustion. She planted her gaze on the guard's wafer-thin frame. The instant he turned his back to her, she slipped through the hole in the fence. Her sleeve caught on the wire. She heard the tap of the guard's heels on the sidewalk. She yanked her arm but it didn't budge. The guard's footsteps were getting louder, closer.

With shaky fingers, she found the trapped strand of wool and ran it back and forth to cut it apart with the spiky wire.

"Hey, get back here," the guard bellowed.

The wool split. Elena leapt from the fence onto Kollektornaya Street. She sprinted down the hill.

"Get the kike!" the guard yelled.

Shots fired over her head.

Elena ran towards the remains of a building. She unpinned her yellow patch and stuffed it in her pocket as she ran. She scurried to the side of the ruined building and darted through a window. She cut her cheek on a shard of glass lodged in the window frame. Blood gushed down her face. She spotted a large old desk in the corner and crawled under it. The taste of blood doused her lips.

For hours, it seemed, she hid under the desk. Her cheek throbbed. Outside whistles blew, cars rumbled along the street, and people walked by, their feet tapping the pavement. She was struck by the ordinary sounds of people going about their day. The normalcy that existed right beside the ghetto.

By the time Elena was ready to venture outside, midday sunshine poured through holes in the facade. She crawled out from under the desk. Her joints were sore and she was hungry and thirsty. She peeked through a glassless window. No police officers or Nazis in sight. She made her way onto the street and got her bearings. The river was a few blocks east, a twenty-minute walk.

With an outward confidence that belied her skittish nerves, Elena strolled along the street, dodging shell holes and piles of rubble. She nodded at a trio of young women with babies in arms.

The women looked askance at Elena's face.

She touched her cheek. She felt dried blood, the line of the cut. She covered her cheek with the palm of her hand and kept going. Past a school, a theater, and the university, all gutted by bombs.

A trio of German officers in black uniforms swung around the corner, moving in her direction. Their jackboots clicked against the pavement with a menacing cadence. She leveled her shoulders and looked ahead at the dust churned up by automobiles navigating their way through the fallen city. She held her breath as the Germans brushed past. They ignored her entirely. She was unsettled by the irony of Nazis, who published leaflets with caricatures of Jews—long, crooked noses, dirty faces, and messy beards—walking inches from her without question.

She turned right at the corner. A flurry of voices rose through the air. Heavy feet pummeled the ground. Her knees locked. It sounded as if a crowd was gathering near the river. An irate crowd, judging from the frantic pitch.

German men shouted: "*Haltet euch von den Partisanen fern!* Stay back from the partisans!"

Masha.

On instinct, Elena trailed the voices. People came into view as she approached the bridge that spanned the river. She lurched, seeing so many Russians together. Her anonymity, her safety, depended on their collective belief that she was one of them. She looked over her shoulder. Nothing except a mangy-looking cat. She squatted down and filled the canteen with murky water. She washed the blood from her skin. Guzzled water from her cupped hands. Then she eased into the crowd traipsing over the bridge onto Nizhne-Lyahovskaya Street, lined with factories that puffed black smoke into the limpid sky.

"What's going on?" she asked a middle-aged woman wearing a red and white headscarf.

"They're marching partisans who killed Germans through the streets," the woman replied, nonchalant.

Killed Germans? Elena's pulse quickened. "Did you see them? Are they men or women?"

The woman glanced at Elena. "What happened to your face?"

"It's nothing." Elena brought her hand to her cheek. It was bleeding again. "What did they look like?" she asked the woman. "The partisans?"

"Young. Two of them look like kids. A boy and a girl. And an older man."

Elena thrust her way forward, using her elbows and shoulders to get through the crowd. She saw the backs of German officers and lurched. She'd never pushed boundaries this way. But then, Masha had never been arrested before. She pressed onward and outward to the edge of the street, stretching the distance between herself and the officers. The crowd thinned as she moved sideways. Nobody gave her a second look, but then, why would they? All Jews were either in the ghetto or slaving in factories. Nobody expected to see a Jew walking freely about.

She caught sight of the three partisans, hands tied behind their backs. In the middle, a dyed, sandy-blond frizzy mane with noticeable brown roots. Masha. Tears formed in Elena's eyes. She read the signboard on Masha's chest, written in Russian and German: *We are partisans and have shot at German troops.*

Hate pooled in her mouth.

She pushed her way forward until she was alongside the partisans.

Masha was staring straight ahead, as if she were oblivious to the marchers and officers.

The officers halted the procession in front of Minsk Kristall, a yeast brewery and distillery plant. The hollow-eyed partisans stood under the open factory gates. A terse silence came over the spectators. Elena craned her neck in search of a hero amongst the crowd, someone with the mettle and authority to stop this insanity. But the only people with clout were the slimy fascists.

One of the Germans grabbed a stool from the factory weigher's booth. Another one tossed a rope over the crossbar and made a loop.

Masha's face remained stoic.

Elena had never felt so useless. She wished Masha were different, that she followed rules and didn't break them. That she was back in the ghetto with their mother. Safe.

Masha was led to the rope and shoved onto the stool. She kept her rigid gaze on the fence beside the gates.

"Turn here," a fascist bade Masha in German. He clutched her shoulders and tried to make her face the crowd.

Masha jerked her head to the fence.

"Stubborn bitch," he said, loudly. He thrust her shoulders back towards the crowd.

Again, Masha refused to cooperate. A second fascist intervened, but Masha's stubbornness was tougher than his efforts. He shook his head and moved away from her. Masha stood with her back to the murmuring crowd.

Elena was moved by the way Masha defied her captors with a quiet dignity. Masha wasn't about to let the fascists break her. This gave Elena a smidgeon of peace. Then the guard kicked the stool out from under Masha's feet.

Masha's limbs shook horribly for a couple of seconds. Her head hung at an unwieldy angle. She stilled.

Vomit rose in Elena's throat.

The second partisan was shoved onto the stool. A boy who couldn't have been older than fourteen or fifteen. Masha's body dangled beside him.

Elena darted to the lane beside the adjacent textile factory.

The stool hit the fence. The crowd went silent.

Elena spewed the bile of her stomach. She collapsed on the ground and curled into the fetal position. Her family of five had shrunk to just two. And it was only a matter of time before they came for her and her mother.

8

To believe that Nazism is an exclusively German phenomenon is
to disregard the evidence all about ourselves.

—DOROTHY THOMPSON, REPORTER, *ATLANTIC*, JANUARY 1943

Müncheberg, Germany

April 1945

Elena studied the questions for her first interrogation, all different ways of asking the same two things: What is the Wehrmacht's military position? Where is Hitler?

Hitler. She quivered down to her marrow, seeing the Führer's name in black ink. Realizing that this tongue, or one of the others she would be questioning, might lead her to the monster who started it all.

"Ready?" Bystrov said.

No, she thought. "Yes," she said.

She followed the major down the rickety stairs to the cellar of the Müncheberg house. It stank of feces and urine. The only pieces of furniture were a stool and an iron cot where a German in his thirties lay, his face as gray as his army blanket. A bucket sat beside the cot.

"Take a seat, Comrade Bruskina," said Major Bystrov.

She perched on the stool. Right away, she was caught off guard by the prisoner's molten blue eyes and freckles sprinkled across the bridge of his nose.

"Any time," Bystrov prodded.

She crumpled the list of questions. She was hit by a sense of in-competence, as if she were an imposter in her own life.

"Any time," the major repeated, with an edge to his tone.

"*Wer sind Sie?*" the prisoner muttered. He looked at Elena with a weary flicker in his eyes. "Who are you?"

"*Eine Übersetzerin,*" she replied, anxious. "A translator."

"*Ein Mädchen an der Front,* a girl at the front," he snorted feebly.

His flimsy contempt hit a nerve. She sat up tall. "I'm a sniper. I've killed nineteen of your comrades," she said in German, and then in Russian, for the major's benefit.

The German's mouth dropped open. He looked up at the major, who gave him a smug nod.

"What is Germany's military position?" she asked him pointedly.

"I want . . . a doctor," the prisoner said, his voice faltering. "Then I'll talk."

Elena relayed his request to the major.

The major crossed his arms over his chest, glared at the prisoner and said, "Tell him he gets a doctor after he answers our questions."

Elena repeated this, in German, to the prisoner.

His gaze shifted from Bystrov to Elena and back to Bystrov, as if he were trying to determine whether this was an empty threat or the truth. Elena didn't budge. Bystrov didn't either.

"The situation is grim." He paused to take a breath. The color drained from his face as he spoke, his voice weakening with every word. "The only talk is of how to escape Germany. I've heard cya-nide capsules were distributed amongst the party leaders."

"*Was ist mit Hitler?*" said Elena. "*Hat er Zyanid?* What about Hitler? Does he have cyanide?"

"No idea," the prisoner whispered.

Elena wrote his response in the tablet. She noticed blood on his blanket. She was sure it hadn't been there a minute earlier.

"*Was ist das?*" she pointed at the blood.

The German looked. The stain was growing larger by the second.

"He needs a doctor," she told Bystrov.

He scowled and left the room.

Elena couldn't tear her gaze from the spreading blotch. "*Darf ich?* May I?" She stood and reached for the corner of the blanket.

He nodded.

Gingerly, she raised the blanket and pulled it down. She tensed when she saw the gaping wound in his abdomen. Half of his stomach was missing. Blood drenched the bandages wrapped around his middle, keeping his insides from falling out.

Bystrov returned with a short bespectacled man bearing a red cross on a white armband.

Elena stepped out of the way.

The doctor pulled the blanket off the prisoner, shook his head, then pressed two fingers against the prisoner's neck. "Weak pulse." He probed the wound with his hands, in surgical gloves.

The prisoner groaned in pain.

"He's lost a lot of blood."

"You can stitch him up, can't you?" Elena implored the doctor.

"You are?" he demanded.

"The interpreter."

He gave her an impatient sigh. "It's a bit more complicated. He's bleeding internally. He needed an operation to repair his organs hours ago." He plucked the gloves from his fingers. "It's too late now."

The prisoner gaped at Elena.

Elena looked at Bystrov.

"He's the only doctor who could come," the major replied, defensive. "The others are busy taking care of our soldiers."

"Why do you care?" the doctor asked Elena. "He's not one of us."

The prisoner's face turned ghostly white, as blood seeped from his organs.

His condition dredged up memories of Red Army soldiers'

blood-soaked bodies scattered over the ground as her regiment had plodded west. The vile photo of her own combat partner, captured by the Nazis. She thought, we will never be able to survive amongst fascists. We will never be free as long as fascism is alive. I mustn't think of him as a human being.

"I don't," she said, vehement. "I don't care one bit."

The doctor saluted the major and departed. Bystrov held the door open for Elena. The prisoner started to gag on his own blood as she walked out of the room. She halted. Seized the doorjamb. Exhaled and moved forward.

9

I was all alone. My life was nothing, yet, I wanted to live.
—GERTRUDE BOYARSKI, JEWISH PARTISAN

Prisoner to Partisan

March 1942

Adrenaline fired through Elena's veins as she crawled through the 180-meter tunnel that linked the ghetto to the world outside the barbed wire. The air was thick with a damp, earthy odor, and her knees, fingers, and toes were stiff from the cold. She touched the phony Soviet passports jammed under the waistband of her skirt to make sure they were still there.

Elena had been working towards this moment for five months, since Masha . . . that day . . . Her sister's face barreled into her mind as she recalled the heinous last moments of Masha's life. Her grief had dimmed everything else: fear, hunger, doubt, and most of the time, the aches in her joints that made her feel twice her age.

The tunnel seemed longer going back than it had earlier, when she'd been on her way to meet Tsila. It had been the first time she'd seen her friend in months. Tsila fled the ghetto the day her grandparents were seized by the Nazis and thrown into a *dushegubki*, a van that gassed them and fifty other Jewish souls to death. Elena's stomach churned at the memory of finding their bodies in a ditch in the graveyard, learning what had happened from witnesses who'd seen them forced into the van. Who'd heard the motor running. Screams and pounding against the walls.

"For at least two minutes," one person said.

"No, it was closer to three minutes," said another.

Since then, *dushegubkis* drove through the ghetto almost every night, snatching Jews with the audacity of those who know there will be no consequences, whatever the crime. Staying in the ghetto meant death. Eventually, Elena knew, her turn would come. Her mother's turn would come. This was the reason she'd risked meeting Tsila, who lived in the woods as a partisan. Tsila had been able to get false identity papers that would give her and her mother the best chance of survival outside the ghetto. Still, there were many obstacles in the way, so many things that could go wrong, she thought, as she emerged through a hole in the wood floor. Jewish partisans had dug the tunnel beneath a stove in the bakery, and while most of the ghetto residents knew about it, the fascists had no idea it existed. For now. Elena gave a rueful nod to Pini, the clammy-faced baker, forced to make bread for the enemy.

Pini clutched a mixing bowl and looked away.

"Your turn will come," Elena whispered.

"They watch my family, my children, every day," he said. "If I left them behind . . ."

Elena finished his sentence in her head. Pini's bread was essential for the hungry fascists and for his own family's survival. He was a bear trapped in a pit. She couldn't help him. All she could do was support herself and her mother. She slipped out the back door. A musty sense of abandonment hung over the ghetto. It was unnervingly quiet and still. No scrawny orphans begging for food. No shrunken men in groups, smoking and talking in somber voices. She quickened her pace. She scrunched her coat collar around her neck to keep the cold from sliding down her skin, and turned onto Ratomskaya Street in the center of the ghetto.

"Don't shove sand in our eyes!"

Children's thin wails stopped her cold. Their voices came from the grassy ravine at the end of the street where German soldiers surrounded the area like a human fence. She darted behind a rundown shed. She heard the crunch of shovels and leaned sideways to peep around the corner. Men were shoveling dirt into a long trench. Something poked out of the chasm. An arm? She squinted to get a better view. A Nazi in a black uniform and brimmed cap, a commander, approached the edge of the pit. He reached into his tunic's pockets, then held both hands over the trench. He opened his hands. Pieces of what appeared to be small candies fluttered over the hole like confetti. Small hands writhed from the trench.

She staggered backwards. They were burying children alive.

"Let me out!" a child cried.

Elena was horrified.

"Help!" another child moaned.

She was revolted by the fascists' depravity. By her own uselessness. Again. There she was, witnessing another unthinkable atrocity like Masha's execution, and all she could do was watch.

The clunk of footfalls sounded from the opposite direction. From the ghetto gates. She scrambled left, behind the other side of the shed, and crouched down.

"*Schneller, schneller,*" a German voice barked. Faster, faster.

Elena's heart raced.

"*Beeilt euch.* Hurry."

The German voice was louder. Closer. So were the footsteps.

A commanding figure emerged at the corner, from Opanskovaya Street. Followed by two columns of workers and several Wehrmacht soldiers. They were marching workers towards the pit where the children were being buried.

Elena scooted backwards on her bum until she was around the corner. She scrambled to her feet and ran down Tankovaya Street to Krimskaya, sprinted right for two blocks and turned onto Flaksa Street.

"Please be here," she whispered as her shabby hut came into view. She paused at the door. The hinge at the bottom was broken. There was no lock, no way of stopping monsters. She stepped inside. No sign of the girls. Even Mr. Volkhov's corner was empty.

Elena darted outside to the back door to see if anyone was in the outhouse. The door was wide open. Nobody.

"Elena?"

"Mama?" She twisted her neck.

Tsila appeared in the doorway.

"What are you doing here?"

"I heard what was happening on Ratomskaya." Tsila gestured for Elena to come inside.

Elena reentered her house and shut the makeshift door. Icy air poured through gaps between the pine boards.

"Right after you left," Tsila continued, "one of our contacts radioed us about children being thrown into a pit."

"They . . . they buried them—"

"I know," Tsila cut off Elena. "Our contact also said workers were being taken to the same pit. They are going to be shot."

Elena shook her head with vehemence. "No. They can't." Her voice broke. "My mother is all I have left."

"That's why I'm here."

Elena's throat clogged with tears of grief and fury. "To say you're sorry for me? To say you know what it's like to have nobody?"

"To tell you you're not alone. And to ask you to come with me."

"Come with you?"

"To get *nekumah*, revenge, against the fascists who killed our families. My partisan unit is all Jews. They're my family now."

"Your family?" Elena said, incredulous.

"We live as a family and support each other—"

"Where was Masha's *partisan family* when she was marched to the gallows?"

"You know there is nothing we can do when a partisan is captured."

Elena recalled the gamut of armed soldiers who had accompanied Masha to her execution. "I suppose not—"

A torrent of gunshots cracked in the distance.

Both girls jerked their heads towards the door.

"One of those bullets will be aimed at my mother," Elena cried softly. "Another will hit Mrs. Drapkina. And her children. Mr. Volkhov."

Tsila reached out and placed her hand on Elena's shoulder.

Hot tears pressed against the backs of Elena's eyes. She dragged her gaze to the stove where her mother sat to keep warm. She was overwhelmed by the loss of Masha, her father, and her brother. All gone. Tears streamed down her cheeks.

"Our detachment needs more people," Tsila said.

"My mother is being killed as we speak and you're asking me to be a partisan? What about grief? Don't you think I need a little time to grieve for my mother?"

"There is no time for mourning during war. Imagine how many more of us would be killed if we let down our guard to weep for every murdered Jew."

Elena regarded Tsila amidst the steady thrum of bullets. Her mind leapt to Masha. How her sister and the other two members of the resistance hung from the gallows for three days for people to see. How Masha's execution had toppled her mother.

Now there would not even be a grave for her mother. She would lie forever in a pit filled with innocent victims of fascism. It was impossible to fathom, though she'd heard the mass slaughter with her own ears.

The barrage of gunshots ended.

Tsila was going on about the partisan life, but her voice sounded as if she were talking through a closed door. Elena didn't care what

Tsila said. She didn't care whether Tsila dragged her to the partisans or left her in the ghetto. She didn't care about anything. Her mother was gone. Her entire family was gone.

Suddenly she couldn't stand still. She began pacing from one side of the house to the other. Something caught her eye. A piece of newspaper cut in the shape of a crown on the Drapkinas' bench. Crudely written letters spelled *Esther* on the bottom of the crown. A shadow crossed Elena's face. One of Mrs. Drapkina's daughters had made Esther's crown to commemorate Purim, when girls traditionally dressed up as Queen Esther, who'd risked her life to save Jews from Haman. Elena recalled her father telling her, Masha, and Yakov about Haman, an evil politician who wanted to kill all the Jews.

"We're back where we started from," she mumbled.

Tsila moved to her side.

"It's been thousands of years since Esther saved the Jews, and yet here we are, on the verge of being extinguished by another Haman," Elena went on quietly, "with no Queen Esther in sight."

Tsila bowed her head as if in prayer.

Elena stared at the paper crown in her hands. It was flimsy and strong. Like her feather, still tucked in Yakov's coat pocket.

"Maybe, instead of being saved, we have to save ourselves this time," Tsila suggested.

"Save ourselves?" Elena dried her tears with her coat's sleeve. "What we need is a miracle."

Tsila turned to face Elena. "You haven't seen what we're doing, Elena."

"Yes I have."

Tsila shook her head. "It's more than phony documents and sneaking people out of the ghetto. We're blowing up bridges and laying mines on train tracks to keep the enemy away—"

"Do you have a gun?" Elena said, pointedly.

"No. Not yet."

"But you've been a partisan for months."

"There are other ways to help. Besides I'll have one soon."

Elena nodded, unconvinced. Her thoughts returned to her mother, lying in a ditch as if she were an animal. She folded her knees into her chest and wrapped her arms around them. She sunk her head onto her knees and hugged herself tight to keep from falling apart.

"What's the point of surviving if there's nobody left to care?" she cried softly.

"I care." Tsila leaned her head against Elena's shoulder.

Outside, Elena heard the unmistakable sound of shovels digging into the soil. Fascist scum burying Jews. Her grief boiled to rage. She grabbed old Mr. Volkhov's canteen and slung the strap over her shoulder. "You're right. We need to save ourselves."

10

We dreamed of nothing but the Enlightenment and believed that
the light of reason would illuminate all around it with such power
that delusion and inflamed fanaticism would no longer be able to
be seen.

—MOSES MENDELSSOHN, GERMAN-JEWISH PHILOSOPHER, 1729–1786

On the Reichsstrasse

April 1945

The Reichsstrasse highway was jammed with the 1st Belorussian Front's artillery, tanks, and infantry. Elena, in the
back seat of the jeep, craned her neck, searching for her platoon or any sign of the 3rd Shock Army. But with more than seventy
thousand soldiers on foot, in vehicles, and on tanks, the procession
stretched past the horizon in both directions. Drab shadows, falling
over the convoy like charcoal lines, didn't help.

Disappointed, Elena opened the folder of confiscated enemy
documents Bystrov had given her to translate. The first one—"A
Reminder"—was both chilling and desperate:

*You have no heart, no nerves, they are not needed in war. Kill any Russian,
any Soviet. Do not stop if before you is an old man or a woman, a young
girl or boy. Kill them.*

She couldn't believe how similar the message of indifferent hate was compared to Russian newspaper columns, where writers repeatedly told the Red Army, "Kill the German . . . This is the cry of your Russian earth. Do not waiver. Do not let up. Kill."

How absurd, she mused. The identical command had trickled down from Stalin and Hitler—kill the enemy, even if they're not in uniform, even if they're children. We've lost our ethical compass.

A ruckus from outside caught her attention. A steady stream of German men, women, and children in vehicles and horse-drawn carts, on bicycles and on foot, were moving towards the jeep, fleeing Berlin.

Ludis, ever-stoic, swerved calmly off the road to avoid the refugees.

Elena bounced up and down as the jeep moved over grass, weeds, and debris from incendiaries.

Her broken elbow throbbed from the jerkiness. She clasped her elbow with her other hand, then glanced at the next document. *Berliner Frontblatt.* The Berlin Front Newssheet published by Joseph Goebbels, Gauleiter, leader of propaganda for the Nazi Party. Her stomach heaved at the words jumping in front of her, at the lies she knew were distributed by the newspaper. She slammed the folder shut.

Bystrov glanced back at her. "Already finished?"

"If I keep reading, I'll throw up, and to be honest, my aim isn't nearly as good from my mouth as it is from my pistol."

"No rush," he said, quickly.

Elena looked out the window streaked with dirt. She watched the Germans filing past, deflated. No wonder. They'd finally figured out they couldn't trust Hitler to save Berlin.

Hitler.

How were she and Bystrov supposed to find him? It wasn't as if there would be people on the street directing Russians to his office. There were so many questions she wanted to ask the major, but he wasn't particularly approachable. He made her afraid of doing or saying something stupid.

An hour later, they passed the last refugees and were back on the road. Elena's dry heaves gave way to stomach growls. She rummaged through her backpack and found a sugar cube in her mess tin. She put it on the tip of her tongue and relished the sweetness as it melted. The cold sugar evoked pleasant winter afternoons as a child, hours of sledging with Yakov and Masha on the big hill near her family's apartment. The fresh, icy air was exhilarating as they swooshed down the hill on their sledges, all three of them vying to get to the bottom first. Yakov always won. Until the girls figured out his heavier weight was responsible for his winning streak. Then, Elena recalled with a wistful smile, she and Masha had climbed onto one sledge and flew past an astonished Yakov, landing in a heap at the bottom of the hill. When their fingers and toes were numb, they plodded home and sipped hot tea with sugar from the samovar that had bubbled on the stove all day.

She would have given anything to hear Yakov spin one of his yarns as they huddled around the stove. To see his lopsided grin. To hear her sister's earnest voice cajoling their parents, wearing them down until they gave in. She tried to summon their faces, but they were getting more and more vague, like out-of-focus portraits.

Soviet troops converged on the highway as the sun set, with the darker sky shielding them from German aircraft. There were Studebaker trucks, carts, self-propelled guns, and marching soldiers. *Berlin, here we come* was written on tank turrets. She shared a knowing smile with Bystrov and felt something shift between them, the way a window opens, letting in a breeze of fresh air.

A few minutes later, Ludis turned onto a smaller road that led to Müncheberg. At once, Elena was transfixed by gigantic willow trees encircling a pond. These willows were unlike any others she'd seen, with knobby roots that burst through the ground and twisted branches that spanned at least ninety meters wide. As they neared the willows, Elena's eyebrows rose. Some of the smaller, finer branches drooped from the weight of ashes.

The heat and smell of charred wood leached through the jeep's windows. Elena's armpits pooled with sweat. She started coughing, a dry, hacking cough that made her eyes water. Bystrov fanned the smoggy air with the latest edition of the *Red Star*. Ludis pulled a scarf over his mouth and nose. Elena covered her mouth with her cap.

When they stopped on a hill that overlooked Müncheberg, Elena sprang out of the jeep, choking on the smoke-filled air. She gaped at the halo of fire that was incinerating the town. A church tower, the tallest structure, was engulfed in flames. Like a warning, thought Elena.

"Are we safe here?" she asked Bystrov.

He took a long swig of vodka from a half-empty bottle. He stared at the flames licking the skyline. "For now." He offered the bottle to Elena.

"No thanks." She shook her head.

"You sure?"

"I . . . I had a bad experience with vodka," she stammered. Yurovsky's name was on the tip of her tongue. "So I don't drink it anymore."

"Well," he said, looking at her as if she'd changed from one minute to the next, "that's impressive."

No, she thought. It's a matter of self-preservation.

11

This song is written with our blood, not with lead,
It is not a song of a free bird flying overhead.
—THE PARTISANS' SONG

Kvidnov Forest, outskirts of Minsk

November 1942

Elena was swarmed by hungry children even though it was one o'clock in the morning. To keep the Nazis from finding their hideout, partisans slept during the day and worked at night, under a blanket of darkness. They could never light a fire, even on the coldest nights, for fear of being seen.

Elena cut the loaf of bread she'd stolen from a nearby farm, and gave thin half slices to the children, who stuffed them in their mouths with grimy hands. She felt a tinge of satisfaction. She wished she could do more.

Many of these starving children, some as young as eleven, participated in the resistance, steering Jews from the Minsk ghetto to their camp in the Kvidnov Forest. The contact who'd informed Tsila about the pit on Ratomskaya Street was a twelve-year-old boy, too young to even join the Komsomol, the mandatory Union of Communist Youth, where Elena had learned to shoot. These children have the courage of generals, she thought, impressed and sad at the same time.

"Can you cook the eggs, Elena? Tsila is tending to a couple of wounded men and the other girls are not back from scavenging yet."

Elena spun around and saw Commander Semion, the craggy-faced head of their detachment, looking expectantly at her with his patient, deep-set eyes.

No, I didn't join the partisans to cook, she wanted to say. "Do you think you'll have a rifle for me soon?" she asked. Without a weapon, she couldn't get into an *otryad*, a fighting unit. Without a weapon, she would have to keep scavenging for food, cooking, and dressing wounds.

The veins in his long neck pulsed. "I heard you can read German."

"I studied the language and German literature at Moscow's Institute of Philosophy and Literature."

"We've acquired a German document from a soldier we ensnared. I'd like you to translate it for me."

She nodded, expecting the document to replace her cooking duty.

"Come find me in my hut after you make the eggs." He turned on his heels and marched off.

Elena wanted to wring his skinny neck. He didn't care if she ever got a gun. He didn't see her as a fighter, he saw her as a woman. He would always see her as a woman.

"This is a letter from a German soldier to his wife," Elena said to Commander Semion.

They were standing in the largest earth hut, about two square meters wide, used by the leaders to form resistance plans. It was equipped with two upside-down milk crates used as tables, a few chairs procured from the ghetto, a kerosene lantern that flared on one of the crates, and a bed of pine needles in one corner.

"The soldier talks about the bad food," Elena went on, "the cold that shakes his bones and . . . and he says that locals have eagerly joined the hunt for Jews because of generous rewards from the Nazi Party." Revulsion crossed her face.

"Go on," Commander Semion said quietly.

"For every Jew killed, they receive forty pounds of salt, a liter of kerosene, and twenty boxes of matches."

The commander pressed his chin into his folded hands.

"There's more."

He nodded, keeping his chin in his hands.

"The soldier tells his wife the number of kikes he's killed."

"How many?" Commander Semion raised his chin.

"He lost count at two hundred," she finished.

"Good thing we put him out of commission, permanently," the commander said, wry.

"Yes it is."

He looked at her. "This is vital information for our unit."

"Good."

"And I want you to know I haven't forgotten about the gun," he added.

"Tsila's been here longer than I have, and she still doesn't have one."

"You're both doing valuable work for us."

"I've been a partisan for nine months and all I've done is cook, clean, wash clothes, and scavenge food."

"We're not the Red Army," he countered, with a hint of reproach. "There are seventy people in our detachment, and none of us are equipped or trained for armed combat. We're here to disrupt the fascists any way we can and to keep Jews from being eliminated."

"But I want to shoot the fascists who killed my family," she said, insistent. "I want revenge."

"If you're planning revenge, you better dig two graves."

She tensed. "Things would be different if I were a man. We wouldn't be having this conversation."

He stroked his chin and looked at her. He riffled through a pile of papers on one of the crates. "Aha. Here it is." He unfolded a quarter sheet of paper. "The latest edition of *Voroshilovich*, the newspaper from the front. There's an article that I think will interest you very much."

She took the paper and thanked him, disgruntled. He hadn't listened to a word she'd said. She asked for a gun and he gave her a newspaper. She stuffed it in the pocket of her trousers and spent the next three hours washing rags used as bandages. As the sun peeked over the horizon, she entered the hut she shared with Tsila and lay down on the pine needles. Tsila was already asleep.

Elena was about to close her eyes when she remembered the newspaper in her pocket. She crept from her hut to read under the scant ribbon of daybreak. When she finished, a buoyant smile crossed her face. She rushed into her hut and shook Tsila awake.

"What's wrong?" Tsila moaned.

"I know how we can get revenge against the fascist beasts."

"I'm not leaving," Tsila said.

Elena was stunned by her staunch refusal. "Read the article again. Lyudmila Pavlichenko killed more than three hundred fascists. A woman sniper! She's a hero. Because of her, the Central Committee of the Komsomol is seeking girls to train as snipers. And a sniper school is being organized just for women."

"Not just because of her," Tsila argued. "We lost so many men in the Winter War and Stalingrad, the Red Army has had no choice but to enlist women."

"Perhaps, but Lyudmila has proved that women can shoot as well as men."

"You were a better shot than I was in the Komsomol. It makes sense for you to go, especially if it will make you happy."

"Happy? How can you talk of happiness when the Hitlerites want to exterminate us?" Elena scoffed. "Don't you want to fight the enemy?"

"Existence is resistance," Tsila retorted. "Besides, Herschel is here," she added, referring to her new sweetheart.

"You're going to plan your life, during a war, around a man?"

"If my fate is to die as a partisan, here in the forest, I want to at least enjoy the time I have left." Tsila gave a long sigh. "Maybe if you were in love, you wouldn't be so angry all the time."

"I'm not angry." Elena heard the fury in her own voice.

Tsila chuckled softly. "You'll be a great sniper. I bet you'll kill more fascists than Lyudmila . . . Lyudmila . . ."

"Pavlichenko. And I doubt it. I have months of training ahead of me, if I'm even accepted."

"You've been asking for a gun since the day I brought you here. This is what you're meant to do. That's why Commander Semion gave you this article. He knows it's your destiny to become a sniper."

They stared at one another.

"You've changed," Elena said. "You're not as tough around the edges as you used to be."

"You've changed too. You're like an elastic band pulled as far as it will go. I just hope you don't stretch yourself too thin."

12

My hand didn't even tremble when I killed him. I didn't feel anything. I was pleased; I'd fulfilled my task. I went back inside and had a drink. I was a member of the communist party. Here was a man who might have killed many of my relatives. I'd have cut him up if I'd been asked.

—ZINAIDA PUTKINA, NKVD INTERROGATOR, ORDERED TO "SORT OUT" A PRISONER SO SHE'D HAVE ONE ON HER ACCOUNT

Edge of Müncheberg
April 1945

*W*o ist Hitler?" Elena demanded of the stodgy Nazi officer sitting in front of her.

He regarded her with a blank expression, as if she were speaking Yiddish.

They were in the cellar of another Müncheberg villa, with sentries at the staircase. It was damp and smelled like wet socks, but it was clear of smoke and away from the firestorm at the center of town.

"*Wo ist Hitler?*" she insisted.

The officer's jeering eyes shunted from Elena to Bystrov. "I'm not talking to a Yid."

Elena took in a sharp breath. His insult hurled her back to the Minsk ghetto, where her blood had made her a victim. A pariah.

"She's not a Jew," Bystrov said, adamant, once Elena had repeated the words to him in Russian. "She's a Soviet soldier."

A Jewish Red Army soldier, Elena fumed, though she didn't include this in her translation to the German.

"That's Communist crap." The prisoner glared at Elena. "Once a Yid, always a Yid."

The twelve Jewish women shot in the ghetto's square slammed into her head. She reached for the pistol hanging around her waist. Pointed it at the German's forehead.

He sneered. "Your army must be desperate, handing out guns to Yids."

"Actually, I'm a *zhenshina*-sniper, woman sniper."

He threw his head back. Laughed.

"*Rechte Kniescheibe*, right kneecap." She fired.

The officer grabbed his right knee, fell out of the chair, and cried out in pain.

Elena looked searchingly at Bystrov.

"Not bad," he said, impressed.

She shifted her gaze to the enemy cradling his leg on the floor. She pointed her gun and said: "*Linke Kniescheibe*."

"No, no," the officer pleaded. "I don't know where Hitler is, but the situation is bad."

"How bad?"

"Boys from the Hitler Youth have been sent to defend the Reich."

"Boys?" Elena exclaimed in Russian, stunned.

"What about boys?" said Bystrov.

Elena relayed the officer's words.

"My God! He's sending children to their deaths," Bystrov groaned.

"The Führer has gone mad," the German added.

Elena stared at him. "*Gone* mad? He's always been insane. And so are you if you ever believed killing innocent babies and children was the right thing to do." She turned and ascended the stairs.

Bystrov fell in behind her.

"What about my leg?" the officer called out feebly.

"We'll get you a medic," Elena snapped.

"I didn't know you had it in you," Bystrov said, as they reached the ground floor, before asking a sentry to fetch a medic.

"I didn't know either. I also didn't know what it meant to be Jewish until the Nazis stormed Russia."

"And now?"

"I know that being Jewish isn't the same as being Russian."

"Stalin would disagree. It's not the Communist way."

"I know I can't say I'm a Russian Jew out loud, in public."

"But you're telling me?"

"If you report me, you'll have to get another interpreter."

"I would."

"You said there's a shortage."

"There is."

"Well, then."

13

Lyudmila Pavlichenko's courage and high level of military expertise are inspiring thousands of Red Army snipers—the Stakhanovites of the front—to further feats. Soldiers of the Red Army! Destroy the enemy as mercilessly as Lyudmila Pavlichenko!

—RED ARMY LEAFLET, 1942

Minsk to Moscow

December 1942

Elena sat down in the sledge across from five Siberians, drafted by the Red Army, on their way to the front. The Indigenous men's skin was leathery and dark from working outdoors year-round as farmers, hunters, and reindeer herders. She burrowed her felt boots into the straw, pulled the hood of her white camouflage cape tight over Yakov's coat, and tried not to think about the poor lad who had worn the very same cape. Commander Semion had somehow acquired it for her from a dead soldier.

She hunched her shoulders against the wind blowing sideways across her face. The snowy terrain made it almost impossible to know where the icy tundra ended and the sky began. Her cheeks, the only part of her body exposed, smarted from the unprecedented minus forty degree Celsius temperature.

How on earth will I last 317 versts, she wondered. Then she thought about the German soldiers she'd seen at the side of the road, frozen to death because of their inadequate clothing for a Russian winter, and tugged her shawl over her cheeks.

The pewter-gray horse attached to the sledge gave a ferocious neigh. Its stringy tail rose. A slimy muck emerged through its anus. Elena groaned silently and braced herself for the inevitable stink. Nothing. Her nostrils were numb. She couldn't smell a thing. Thank God! Still, what if this was a sign? What if the horse was trying to warn her of the shit she'd face if she followed through with her plan to become a sniper.

The horse's groom slapped the reins and the sledge lurched forward. Elena's neck snapped back. Her hands slid upwards. Her bottom skidded over the cold, hard wood. The back of her head hit the sledge with a disturbing whack. She felt her brain joggle within her skull as she was thrust forward.

She found herself face-to-face with the tallest Siberian, who had a lantern jaw and a thick neck.

"Timur," he grunted, introducing himself without making eye contact. With his large fur-mitted hands, he pulled her upright as if she were a rag doll.

"*Spaceeba*. Thank you, Timur." Her faint voice was muffled by the wind.

Branches cracked under the sledge's blades. The sky, black with smoke, roared with the menacing hum of low-flying airplanes. It was almost noon and Elena's group was still navigating the glacial swamp that ran alongside the highway to Moscow. The temperature had risen to a balmy minus thirty-two degrees, but they were in German-occupied territory, with no place to take cover.

"*Pashlee!* Let's go!" The groom shouted at the horse. "*Pashlee!*"

The Siberians balanced their rifles on their shoulders and aimed at the raven-black sky, though bullets were no match for bombs. The hum soon turned into a high-pitched wail. It sounded as if the darkness was closing in on them.

The groom leaned forward, thrashing the reins with alarming ferocity. Elena felt the sledge veer from side to side as the horse galloped over the arctic terrain. She curled into a ball with her head tucked between her knees.

"They're approaching from the southwest, Timur," one of the Siberian lads declared, his eyes fixed on the big-mitted man.

"I see them," Timur said.

She looked up just in time to glimpse three Luftwaffe Heinkels, mechanical predators with the red and black Nazi crest embossed on the tail.

"There's a bunch of trees up ahead," the groom yelled.

"No time," said Timur. "Slow the horse. We have to jump."

"Where?"

The air screeched as the planes advanced.

The groom pulled back hard on the reins. The sledge's pace decreased. The horse neighed angrily as its front legs sprang up.

"Now," Timur hollered.

"I'm staying with my horse," the groom shouted.

Elena stared at the ground, still moving. She felt a strong hand grab her shoulder and yank her from the sledge. She tumbled off. She rolled sideways down a snowbank. Heard the clip-clop of the horse's hooves cantering onward.

"Lie on your stomach and put your head down," Timur said. "Dig your boots into the snow. Don't move."

She squished herself into the snow. Icy flakes seeped down her neck, into her nose and eyes.

An explosion lanced Elena's ears. Snow and dirt pelted her body. She lifted her head just as another bomb detonated. She saw a geyser of snow and earth, then closed her eyes again to keep the muck out. She didn't open them until the airplane engines receded to a whir in the distance.

"That was close," said one of the lads.

Elena began to shake off the snow. "What about the groom and horse?"

A long and heavy pause.

"We'll have to go on foot now," Timur said.

A sob wormed its way up her throat. She climbed over the snowbank and squinted in the direction the horse and sledge had been going. Heaps of debris were scattered across the ice-covered swamp. She thought about the horse, innocent and defenseless. She thought about the groom who'd stayed with the horse. His sacrifice was remarkable and terrifying. A standard she didn't think she could ever reach.

After three days of slogging on foot over the subzero taiga, Elena and the Siberians were in Smolensk, on the banks of the Dnieper River, halfway between Minsk and Moscow.

A partisan detachment in Smolensk, one of ten units under the code name Batia, had been expecting Elena and the Siberians; Commander Semion had radioed the unit beforehand, asking for food replenishments and medical care, if needed, before they continued to Moscow. On an airplane.

Elena took in the unexpectedly long strip of land that emerged, once branches used for camouflage were removed. An airstrip. This was real. Her eyes rose to the opening above the trees, an oblong patch of night sky.

A group of partisans began lighting small fires along the airstrip.

"The plane will be ready to go once the fires are lit," said the wiry partisan commander.

"How . . . long is the . . . flight?" Elena stammered.

"First time on a plane?" he asked.

"Yes."

"When was the last time you ate?"

"As soon as we got here. A couple hours ago."

The commander gave her a half smile. "You should be okay."

"What do you mean?"

"Better get to the plane now." He gave her and Timur a quick wave and was off.

"He never answered my question," Elena said.

"Probably because you won't like his reply." Timur shrugged. He headed towards the cargo plane at the end of the airstrip.

Inside the small plane, Elena sat hunched on a freezing metal bench that ran along the aircraft's perimeter. Three Siberian lads were beside her while Timur and the others were seated on an identical bench across from them. The pilot jumped aboard and took his seat at the control panel. Elena's gaze fell on the numerous buttons and lights. She watched the pilot flip a switch and tensed as the propellers roared to life. She hugged her rucksack to her pounding chest. She caught Timur's blinking eyes and realized he was nervous too. This somehow calmed her, knowing she wasn't the only one afraid.

As the plane rose from the ground, Elena glanced over her shoulder, out the window, and was wholly absorbed by the vista expanding below. She saw the forest that harbored the Batia partisan detachment. The Dnieper River meandering through Smolensk. The straight-edged railway tracks laid out like a ruler on the snow. The burning ruins of the city. Smoke billowing from fires. Miniature houses with red roofs poking out from the snow.

Then, when she saw how far they were above the ground, she was hit by a spasm of terror. Her stomach twisted and cramped.

"I need to get off the plane," she mumbled.

A gale-force wind rattled the aircraft. The plane lurched sideways.

"Let me off," she pleaded.

"It's a bit late," Timur said, dryly. He tossed his overcoat to her. "Spread this out beside my comrades and lie down until we land."

The Siberian lads scooted sideways in unison to make room. The lad farthest from her seized the greatcoat and draped it over the metal bench.

She lay on her side and relished the warmth and nearness of their backs. She closed her eyes until the plane touched ground in Moscow with a heart-stopping thump. For a second, she thought the plane had crashed. Then she felt the wheels rolling along the ground and gave a sigh of relief. She gathered her things and was the first person off the aircraft. The ground seemed shaky beneath her feet. It took a good two minutes before she felt steady. She spotted Timur walking away with his comrades.

"Wait!" She sprinted towards them.

Timur stopped. Gestured for the lads to keep going.

"I wanted to say thanks," Elena said.

"For what?"

"For helping me on the plane."

His eyes darted all around. He seemed terribly uncomfortable with her appreciation. "Just remember when you're hunting, if you chase two rabbits, you will not catch either one."

Her heart revved at his not-so-subtle warning. "I don't know if I can do this."

"Neither do I. But what choice do we have."

None, she thought as she watched him catch up to the others. We have no choice.

14

Berlin will remain German! . . . Help is on its way!
—*BERLINER FRONTBLATT*, APRIL 27, 1945

Outskirts of Berlin

April 1945

Elena awoke to a heavy boom. Then heard the scrunching sound of paper.

"Chava?" she said groggily.

She worried she was late, that the rest of the snipers were already in position, that she'd let them down. She threw her blanket off. Newspaper pages scattered everywhere. When her feet hit the wooden floor, she remembered where she was, billeted in a house near the Landsberger railway station, on the eastern flank of Berlin. She was disappointed. She should be with her platoon, sleeping God knows where, hunting officers, eliminating fascists.

An explosion shook the floorboards. She dashed to the window. Katyusha rockets soared through the blue-gray morning sky, streamers of light, followed by a salvo of bullets. A bird flew into the house across the street, smacked against the bricks, then dropped like a stone. Elena looked away, sickened by the collateral damage of war.

She had to pee. She opened her door and padded down the hallway. The floor squeaked beneath her feet.

"That you, Comrade Bruskina?" said Bystrov from his room across the hall.

She groaned silently. "Yes sir."

"Have you finished translating the newspaper?"

The *Berliner Frontblatt*. She'd started to work on it the night before but had promptly fallen asleep. "Almost."

"Finish it up before we head out of here. I want to read your notes on the way."

"When are we leaving?"

"One hour."

I need more time, she wanted to shout. I need more sleep. I need to pee. She wobbled into the bathroom and shut the door. She looked in the mirror and saw newsprint on the right side of her face. She started to laugh at herself and didn't stop until she saw black ink smeared on her cheeks and realized she was crying.

"Reprehensible," said Bystrov.

He was poring over Elena's hastily scribbled translation of the front page of the newspaper, a statement from Hitler. They were in the jeep driving through a chalky mist.

The statement said anyone who "approves of orders that weaken our resolve" would be considered a traitor, ordering them to be "shot or hanged."

"Unbelievable," she agreed. Much like Stalin's order to die rather than retreat, she thought.

Elena was confused and disappointed by Bystrov's unquestioning obedience. How did he not see that Stalin and Hitler were cut from the same cloth? She'd only been a child when Stalin had killed thousands of his own people—generals, those who spoke out against the Party, bourgeoisie—but she remembered, with an astonishing clarity, how this had embittered her father. He'd yelled at the newspaper and the radio. He'd become paranoid, looking over his shoulder whenever he was out of their flat. And when Stalin replaced the church's

Bible and the Jewish Torah with Soviet propaganda, her father became more religious, chanting prayers in the morning and evening,
and telling stories from the Torah to Elena and her siblings, urging
them to put their faith in God, not the government.

"Listen to this from Goebbels," said Bystrov. "He's in Berlin!"

His agitated tone shook Elena from her reverie.

"'I call on you to fight for your city. Fight with everything you have
got. Your arms are defending everything we have ever held dear, and
all the generations that will come after us. Be inventive and cunning.
Your Gauleiter is amongst you. He and his colleagues will remain in
your midst.'" Bystrov paused. "'The battle for Berlin must become
the signal for the whole nation to rise up in battle.'"

"If Goebbels is truly in Berlin," said Elena, thinking aloud, "and
all of his colleagues are here, then Hitler must be here too."

"Exactly." Bystrov drummed his fingers on the dashboard. "But I
must tell you that I want Goebbels as much as I want Hitler, maybe
more."

"Goebbels? Why?"

"I've had it in for him since his 'Total War' speech," the major
explained, referring to the one where he'd galvanized the German
people to "rise up, and storm, break loose!"

"When was this?" Elena asked.

"February 1943."

"I missed it. I was in sniper training school."

"You'd want him as bad as I do if you'd heard what he said about
Jews."

"Oh, I can imagine. I've heard him speak on Radio Moscow." A
chill came over her as she recited one of Goebbels's most repugnant
and incorrect statements: "'Now, for the first time, they will not bleed
other people to death, but for the first time the old Jewish law of an
eye for an eye, a tooth for a tooth, will be applied.'"

"What does that even mean," said Bystrov, "'bleed other people to death'?"

"It's a lie that goes back centuries," Elena explained. "Someone started spreading a rumor that Jews killed Christians for their blood, which is as stupid as it is wrong. Religious Jews actually drain their meat of blood, while Christians eat their meat with the blood intact."

"That's outrageous," Ludis muttered.

Bystrov turned in his seat. "Why would anyone believe such nonsense?"

"Who knows? Goebbels is also mistaken in calling the eye for an eye law Jewish. Jews *and* Christians use this allegory for retributive justice. We're not suggesting people resort to violence, only that the punishment fit the crime."

Bystrov shook his head vehemently. "He's a goddam fanatic, twisting words to rouse Germans with lies and hatred."

"Kind of like——" Elena stopped herself before saying Stalin.

"Like who?" Bystrov pressed.

"Um, nobody . . ." Elena stalled.

The major looked at her with reproof, as if he knew what she'd been about to divulge.

Elena shrank back. She hoped that the end of the war and subsequent defeat of fascism would soften Stalin's rhetoric. Perhaps even lead to the termination of the secret police and the gulag camps in Siberia. She was tired and frustrated, having to watch every single word that came out of her mouth.

Suddenly, a bullet zipped past Elena's head like a hot blast of wind. She ducked, turned in the direction of the shot, and reached for her pistol. She gawked at the sight of a boy in a Hitler Youth uniform, pointing a rifle at the jeep. *Oh my God! I've survived two years of ruthless enemy soldiers firing at me, only to succumb to a young boy's impulsive shooting.*

The boy fired another shot, hitting the jeep's door.

Bystrov leapt from the vehicle and threw himself at the boy, trapping him before he could fire again.

The boy flailed beneath the major's iron grip. Bystrov wrenched the rifle from the boy's grasp and tossed it to Elena.

"Tell him I'm going to let go but will grab him again if he tries to run," Bystrov shouted.

She scrambled out of the car, bent down to the boy's level, and repeated the major's words, in German. Close up, Elena noticed the boy's dark-ringed eyes and dirty skin. His yellow teeth. He was young, just ten or eleven years old.

The boy slumped as he listened to Elena, then nodded.

Major Bystrov peeled himself away from the boy and motioned to a nearby Soviet soldier, on foot, to detain him.

Elena watched the soldier yank the boy by his collar, alongside the road. The boy had been poisoned by Hitler's rhetoric. He'd been willing to die for a heartless dictator. She wondered if his mind could be decontaminated once Hitler was gone, or if it was too late.

15

Every day we were drilled, taught to march and perform the necessary techniques with a rifle. We were supposed to know by heart the Red Army regulations and the ins and outs of firearms—rifles, pistols, and both machine guns and submachine guns.

—YULIA ZHUKOVA, GRADUATE, CENTRAL WOMEN'S SNIPER TRAINING SCHOOL

Veshnyaki, Moscow

January 1943

The Central Women's Sniper Training School was in Veshnyaki, twenty-two versts southeast of Moscow. The school was based in a former silicate plant, a gray three-story building enclosed by a high fence. Sentries were posted at the gates. Girls could only leave with permission. This gave Elena pause; it was eerily similar to conditions in the ghetto. Except here, she'd share a bunk with another cadet, eat three meals a day, and be paid monthly. Seven rubles and fifty kopeks.

Fifty girls were housed in two rooms with double bunks. Each room included clothes stands for greatcoats, as well as two pyramid-shaped rifle racks, two small, square tables, two chests, and two bedside tables. A separate canteen featured a large poster of Stalin on one wall. Cadets would be taken to the bathhouse every ten days; bed sheets would be changed the same day. And the girls' hair had to be cut short before training began.

Elena considered bolting after the first girl walked past the queue, chin trembling, her ebony braids shorn to an unflattering jagged mop. She looked like a boy with her regulation short hair. Elena grabbed a fistful of her own frizzy mane, which was much like her sister's, except Masha's had been dyed a shade lighter. Elena had not expected to be so upset, but now, on the cusp of her new life at the snipers' school, she wanted to keep her hair long because it was part of her past.

"It will grow back, you know."

"What?" Elena jumped at the acerbic voice. She twisted around and saw a coltish girl with sable-red tresses and full lips. With her photogenic smile, she reminded Elena of film stars she'd seen in *Vogue* magazine.

"Your hair," the girl said. "It won't be short forever."

"I know." Elena twisted strands around her finger. "I just don't understand why we can't pull it back and still be snipers."

"It's probably something to do with the helmets."

"Snipers don't wear helmets," Elena retorted.

"Oh." The girl tossed her long red locks over her shoulders with a baffling vanity, considering her nonchalance about short hair. She introduced herself as Zina.

"I'm Elena Bruskina. From Minsk. Where are you from?"

Zina's green eyes flared. "What does it matter?"

Elena was taken aback by Zina's guardedness. "Sorry. I didn't mean to pry."

Zina turned her shoulder to Elena. She fixed her gaze on a soldier who'd just entered the room, stepped out from the queue, and gave him an alluring smile.

Elena was bewildered by Zina's behavior. They were supposed to be snipers, not flirts. How could anyone think of love during war? It was as illogical as Tsila craving happiness.

The soldier with scissors beckoned for Elena. From the corner of her eye, she caught Zina and the soldier getting cozy. Elena hoped Zina would be in a different platoon. Then she sat down and raised her head. She was ready to look like a *zhenshina*-sniper.

The girls were divided, by height, into two platoons. Elena found herself with the taller girls including, to her annoyance, Zina.

"I guess we'll look like men in these uniforms," the trim girl beside Elena quipped in a buttery-smooth voice. With her square jaw and dimpled right cheek, she had the impish smile of someone well acquainted with mischief. A shabby guitar case lay at her feet.

Elena grinned despite her frustration with the uniform, which included jodhpur-style trousers that were four sizes too big, a belted *gimnasterka* (tunic), a white collar liner, and oversized *valenki* (felt boots) with rubber soles. Everything, even the *pogony* (shoulder pads), was intended for men. There were no bras. No sanitary napkins. It was as if women's bodies were supposed to magically transform into men's during the war. She held up the long cotton drawers and wondered how she'd keep the gigantic waist from sliding to her feet.

"Two of me could fit into one leg of these trousers," the girl beside her went on.

"They said they wanted girls, but what they really want are girls pretending to be boys," Elena sighed.

The girl chuckled and extended her slender hand. "Raya."

Elena took her proffered hand and introduced herself. She gestured at the guitar case and said, "Are you bringing your guitar to the front?"

"Why not?" Raya brushed her hand over the curve of the case. "Don't you remember all the singing in the Komsomol?"

Elena stifled a groan. The patriotic and often exaggerated lyrics extolling Lenin, Stalin, and Communism had been sung so often over the years, they were embedded in her brain. She'd thought she'd left those songs behind when she went off to university.

Raya picked up her *ushanka* cap with earflaps and pulled it over her thick ash-blond curls. "This is the only thing that fits properly. I guess this means our heads are the same size as men's."

Elena gave her a wry smile. She tied the waist cord of her wide drawers and put on the long-sleeved undershirt that laced at the throat. She inserted her arms into the sleeves of the wheat-colored tunic, buttoned the front, and hung Mr. Volkhov's canteen over her shoulder. She brushed her thumb over the dent. His voice rose in her head. *Be careful.* Tears welled in her eyes, just thinking of him. How he'd survived the Civil War only to lose his wife and his dignity, before being shot and left to rot in a hole in the ground.

Mr. Volkhov, her mother, Mrs. Drapkina and her precious daughters, her father, brother, and Masha, and all the Jews of Minsk were the reasons she was in men's underwear, with an ugly haircut, thrusting her legs into men's trousers. She wrapped the canvas belt around her waist. Twice. She sunk her feet into her too-large boots. Her feet skated back and forth.

Raya raised one foot and her boot slipped off. They exchanged disappointed looks.

"How are we supposed to be stealthy hunters with clunky boots like these?" Elena said. "This must be a mistake."

"No mistake," Captain Nora Chegodaieva interjected.

Elena turned and saw the head of the snipers' school. With her heart-shaped hairline and kind eyes, it was hard to believe Captain Chegodaieva had seen combat in the Spanish Civil War, receiving the coveted Order of the Red Banner. She'd been summoned from the front to organize the sniper training school.

"The strips of cloth are *portianki*, foot wraps, to keep your feet from blistering," Captain Chegodaieva explained, over her shoulder, as she hastened past them. "There's a diagram in your manual."

Elena snatched the roll of flannelette.

Raya snorted. "I definitely see blisters in our future."

One hour later, her feet stiff and itchy beneath layers of flannelette, Elena joined the rest of the sniper cadets for a brief introduction from Captain Chegodaieva.

"The honor of your uniform, *chest' mundira*, must never be forgotten," the captain began. "Your appearance is a reflection of the Red Army, descended from the Russian military that defeated Napoleon. If your uniform is not worn with the respect it deserves, you could be arrested. You must sew on fresh white undercollars every day, polish your boots until they shine, and make sure your *pogony* are perfectly straight at all times."

Elena squinted at the shoulder tabs with disdain. Not only would they take precious time to maintain, they stunk of nationalism, of a government that wanted to Russify its military by bringing back a distasteful symbol of the Tsarist regime. Even worse, the fascists wore *pogony*.

Captain Chegodaieva began announcing the pairs she'd assigned as bunkmates and shooting partners. Elena glanced sideways at Zina, prattling with another girl as the captain read names aloud. Even short-haired, Zina, with her crimson eyebrows and creamy-white complexion, stood out amongst the rest of the girls. She was a ferocious beauty, like the actress Myrna Loy.

Elena tugged at her own coarse hair. She felt ugly. Without needing a mirror, she knew her head was too big for her neck. Then she took in the other girls, their hair crudely shorn, and was ashamed of her own vanity. There was no room for pride in the maelstrom of war. She wet her lips and forced a smile. She was a true Red Army soldier now.

"Elena Bruskina and Alla Epstein."

Elena's ears perked at her partner's name. Epstein. Jewish. A girl with a distinct overbite and fine, ebony hair that resembled a sleek cap, fell in beside her. They exchanged nervous smiles and joined the formation of paired cadets. They would be spending almost every moment, day and night, together, a prospect that overwhelmed Elena. *Masha should be here in my place,* she brooded. *Masha thrived amongst strangers. More importantly, Masha had been a far better shot.*

"Raya Shkolnik and Zina Gofeld."

More Jews, thought Elena, pleased.

Zina chuckled loudly, as if she wanted to be noticed.

A ripple of distaste flicked across Elena's face. Zina was precisely the sort of girl she'd avoided at university and in the Komsomol, flippant and brash. Zina rushed past Elena, smacking her shoulder.

Elena was miffed, then completely startled when she realized Zina's eyes were wet with tears.

"Let's take those bunks," Raya said.

Elena followed her gaze and took in the pair of upper bunks, directly opposite one another, at the end of the barracks. "Good idea." She looked at Alla's pallid, elfin face. "All right with you?"

"Sure," Alla said quietly.

Elena was uneasy about Alla. She'd barely spoken the entire evening. Not even a word at dinner.

Raya grabbed her guitar and climbed onto her double bunk, kicking her boots off. They landed on the floor with a resounding clunk.

Elena's lips curled up. She liked Raya's confidence. She wished they were partners. She got up on her bunk, two long pieces of wood with sticks nailed across them and a mattress of fir branches.

Zina appeared, a flurry of glamor, even in uniform. She gracefully climbed up to her bunk, swinging her long legs over the wood railing. "There's no room for that," she said, pointing at Raya's guitar.

"I guess you'll have to find another place to sleep, then."

Alla hoisted herself up to join Elena.

Zina lunged at the guitar.

Raya whipped it out of her reach. "Nobody touches my guitar."

"Fine." Zina planted her hands on her tiny waist. "Then you and your guitar can go sleep by the coatrack."

"I'll put it at my feet. You won't even know it's there."

Zina sighed. "Of all the girls I could be partnered with—"

"You don't even know me."

"I can see that you care more about your guitar than anything else."

"If that were true, I wouldn't be here."

From the corner of her eye, Elena caught Alla's face, tight and quivering. Her two front teeth were digging into her bottom lip.

"How about we save our fights for the enemy," Elena suggested.

Zina folded her arms across her chest.

"Sorry," Raya said, after an uncomfortable silence. "I haven't slept the last few nights. My nerves are frayed."

"Me too," Elena admitted. "I keep worrying I made a mistake, coming here."

"*Take?* Really?" Alla said, in Yiddish. "You seem so, so sure of yourself."

"*Mir?*" Elena replied, easily slipping into Yiddish too.

Zina and Raya looked blankly at them.

"You seem so sure of yourself," Alla repeated in choppy Russian, without pronouncing the rolling *r*, a sound that didn't exist in Yiddish.

Alla speaks Yiddish at home, not Russian, Elena realized.

"You're religious?" Zina said.

The hollows of Alla's cheeks went pink. "No I'm not," Alla said, unconvincingly.

"My father taught us Yiddish and we weren't religious," Elena said.

Zina raised her crimson eyebrows.

"Does it matter?" Raya asked Zina.

"I'm just trying to get to know everyone," Zina replied defensively.

"I used to be religious," Alla said softly. "Now I'm not."

Elena was moved by the tremor in Alla's voice. By the way Alla kept tucking the same strand of dark hair behind her ear. By what Alla hadn't said.

Zina reached into her tunic pocket and withdrew a pack of cigarettes and matches. She stuck one in her mouth and offered the pack to the other girls.

"I don't smoke," Elena said.

"Me neither," added Alla.

"What are you doing?" Raya snatched Zina's cigarette from her mouth and crushed it in her hand.

"Don't touch my things," Zina said, her voice churlish.

"You're going to get us all in trouble," Raya said. "No smoking. There was a poster beside the door. Can't you read?"

"You mean the one that showed a female soldier standing in a field of flowers?"

"Yes. Did you read the words at the bottom? *Our girls are clean and tender as flowers in the Caucasus.*"

Elena recalled the poster's contradictory message with disdain. "We're expected to be pure yet deadly," she interjected, "to kill fascists without getting dirty."

"Not one word about smoking," said Zina.

"It's implied," Raya argued.

Zina hopped down from the bunk. "Well, I'm going to wait until a superior tells me not to smoke." She pulled another cigarette from her pack, lit it with a match, and gave Raya a smug look.

"No smoking in the barracks, Zina," Captain Chegodaieva called out.

Zina groaned. She dropped her cigarette and stamped it out with her boot. She climbed onto her bunk and perched at the edge, legs hanging down. She looked at Alla. "It's a good thing you're not religious anymore. Religion and war don't mix well."

Alla drew her lip over her top teeth as if she were trying to hide her overbite.

"You're wrong," Raya said, fervent. She rolled over and sat up. "Religion has everything to do with this war. My family was murdered in the Dvinsk ghetto because they were Jewish." She began to cry. "Hitlerites want to exterminate us."

Elena was surprised by Raya's personal disclosure so soon after they'd all just met. She wasn't sure she'd ever be able to talk about what she'd seen and heard. What she'd lost.

"My parents and brothers were shot in a pit in Bobruisk," Zina replied, "but I'm here because it's my duty to fight for my *Rodina*, my Motherland, to save it from the fascists."

Raya leaned in towards Zina. "It's the same thing. We're here for the same reason, to avenge the Jewish people."

"Stalin says Jews are not a nation," Zina retorted. "Are you going to tell Stalin he's wrong?"

"You need to catch your tongue before it trips your feet," Raya said dryly to Zina.

Elena grimaced. Listening to Raya and Zina reminded her of heated arguments between her mother and father.

"We're all Soviet citizens first and foremost," Zina pressed. "It's our duty to protect our homeland, not our religion."

"Let's just agree to disagree," Elena cut in, the way she'd done for years with her bickering parents. "Politics shouldn't matter here."

"She's right," said Raya. "What's important is we all want to get to the front and shoot the enemy."

"When I read about Lyudmila Pavlichenko, I saw it was possible for women, for me, to be a sniper," Elena said, changing the topic.

"Me too," Raya exclaimed. "That's why I want to go to the front, even if it costs me my life. I'd go tomorrow if they let me."

"That's what I thought too," Alla added. "But what . . ." Her voice trailed off.

"But what?" Elena nudged her.

"What if I'm not good enough?"

Elena bent her head. She knew exactly how Alla felt.

A pall came over the four of them.

"I have no intention of dying," Raya said, breaking the silence. "When this is all over, I'm going to fall in love with a war hero, some-one who kills more fascists than I do, so he doesn't resent me, and we're going to live in a grand house in Moscow."

"Love?" Zina scoffed. "There is no such thing."

"How can you say that?" Raya demanded.

"Because true love is a lie, just like the crazy superstitions my *bubbe* used to go on about."

"Here we go again," Elena whispered to Alla.

"You can't compare love to superstitions," Raya said, indignantly.

"Do you believe in hate?" Elena asked Zina.

Zina opened her palms. "Of course. Hate is in the Fritzes who killed our families. Hate is in the people who collaborated with them. Hate is what brought us here. It's in all of us."

"Then you have to believe in love," Elena continued, "because it's the opposite of hate. You can't have one without the other."

"You're wrong. If you survive, try to find a man who will love you after what you've done in the name of hate. You'll see. Nobody will want us after the war."

"That's ridiculous," Raya scoffed. "In every war men have killed, yet they are welcomed back home as husbands and fathers."

"Look at our uniforms," said Zina. "The Red Army has thrown its doors open to women, yet can't be bothered with female uniforms or even boots that fit. This is a man's world. No matter how short they cut our hair, no matter how many fascists we kill, we'll always be women, judged by men's narrow standards."

Elena recalled her maddening exchange with Commander Semion, how he'd seen her as just a woman, yet gave her an article about Lyudmila Pavlichenko. "Maybe we'll be the exception," she suggested.

"Or maybe we won't," Zina retorted. "Remember what Captain Chegodaieva told us in her lecture before dinner? How we're expected to fill in as medics whenever necessary, because we're women?"

Raya frowned.

Elena's shoulders slumped in defeat.

Raya withdrew her guitar from its case, tuned the strings, and began finger-picking the notes of "Katyusha," a song that had become popular when the Great Patriotic War began. It was about a girl pining for her lover who is in the army, at a faraway outpost.

The noise in the barracks dwindled until all you heard were the guitar strings crooning at Raya's gentle touch.

Elena rolled onto her side to go to sleep. She had no nightclothes. She slept in her uniform, with her greatcoat as a blanket and Yakov's coat as a pillow. She felt the warmth of Alla wedged beside her. She listened to Raya's guitar playing "Katyusha" and found herself gliding on the melody. She wondered what it felt like to be in love. She wondered if she'd ever have the chance to know. If anyone would ever want her after she'd killed. Or if she'd even survive.

16

Motherland rejoice! We are on the streets of Berlin!
—3RD SHOCK ARMY'S NEWSPAPER HEADLINE, APRIL 23, 1945

Pankow, Berlin

April 1945

White sheets hung from windows and posts like flags. In the distance, the tedious beat of Soviet artillery mocked the civilians' pleas to surrender. Ludis was driving Elena and Bystrov through Pankow, a northeast suburb of Berlin. Behind the jeep, Soviet tanks were rolling towards the center of the city. Elena looked back at the soldiers clumped on a tank, rifles ready. She desperately missed her sniper comrades; they'd expected to enter Berlin together, to take the city as a united platoon.

A giant thump.

Ludis slammed on the breaks.

"What the hell . . ." Bystrov roared.

Elena gulped. A Red Army man's face was smashed against the jeep's windshield.

Two chunky hands grabbed the man's ears and yanked him off the jeep, to the side of the road. A German infantryman punched the Soviet in the nose. Blood gushed from his nostrils. He staggered backwards. Regained his balance, then went after the German, both fists up. He pounded his head, his hands clobbering like a machine, left, right, left, right.

"The Germans are desperate," Bystrov explained, "trapped in Berlin, encircled by our army."

The jeep started moving forward again, with Ludis hunched over the steering wheel.

"Our soldier is going to kill him," Elena said, breathless.

"So's he." Bystrov gestured with his head at another brawling pair, on the opposite sidewalk.

"Shouldn't you do something?"

"We can't stop street fighting." He opened his palms. "It's like plucking lice out of your scalp. As soon as you get rid of one, another's there."

"But—"

"They're all drunk and tired and angry the war's lasted so long. They need to take their frustrations out somehow." He turned and looked at her. "Better each other than . . . you know."

Elena pressed her forehead against the jeep's window to keep the unspeakable memories of the past from overpowering her mind. Through her tears she saw white towels and sheets hanging from windows, stark declarations of surrender. She saw old German men and women with blank expressions, as if they'd already left the fray mentally. She saw Hitler posters on advertising pillars and was astonished and annoyed they were still there, poisoning minds with lies born of ignorance.

They were passing an expansive three-story building with a domed tower soaring from the center of the roof. She was surprised by how it seemed completely undamaged by the war, especially compared to nearby buildings without roofs and walls. Strange. She squinted to read the sign posted in the triangular peak below the tower: *The Jewish Hospital?*

That's when Elena recalled the ghetto where the babies . . .

"We need to stop," she said, insistent.

"Why?" said Bystrov.

"There could be people in there who need help." She pointed at the hospital.

"It looks fine," he said.

"On the outside, maybe. But people, children, inside might be in danger."

He scratched his head. "You want to stop here, now, to save Germans?"

"Jews," she said, obstinate.

"You mean Soviet citizens."

She glared at him. "I mean Jews."

The major observed the hospital for a long minute. He gave an impatient sigh. "Pull over."

Ludis swerved sideways, to the curb. He shut off the engine.

Elena stepped out of the jeep and hurried towards the hospital. The closer she got, the more formidable it seemed. She hesitated at the door. She glanced back at the jeep. Ludis was leaning against the vehicle, smoking a cigarette. Unflappable as always.

"What's wrong?" said Bystrov, coming up behind her.

She sagged under his critical gaze. She was afraid of what she'd find and more afraid of how she'd live with herself if she didn't enter. "Nothing."

She pulled the heavy oak door open. The instant reek of urine and feces yanked her back to the Minsk ghetto. She clutched the door-jamb to steady herself. She choked at the sight of hundreds of people crammed together on the floor. Sitting in their own excrement. Skeletons wrapped in skin. Leaden eyes floating in sockets.

"They're alive," Bystrov said, grimly. "Just."

On legs that felt like rubber, Elena ventured towards the group. "How long have you been here?" she asked, in German.

Dozens of pairs of eyes looked at her, impassive.

"Months," a woman answered in a shaky voice.

A man with ears that stuck out from his oblong face stood. He gave Elena a long sheet of paper.

She scanned it. "This form indicates that the Wehrmacht commander saved their lives," she said to Bystrov. "I think they all signed it." She held it up for him to see. "Look at how many signatures there are." She flipped it over. "On the back too."

"Where is the commander now?" Bystrov asked.

"He vanished," the man told Elena after she repeated the question.

"I am a lawyer," he went on. "Was a lawyer. When I heard that the commander had been ordered to kill all of us, I wrote this contract. It saved our lives, and making the commander look like a hero likely saved him from prosecution after the war."

She was impressed by his ingenuity. She conveyed the information to Bystrov.

"How many are here?" Bystrov asked.

"About six hundred." The former lawyer pointed at the ceiling. "The rest are upstairs."

"All Jews?" Elena said.

"*Ja*. Many, like myself, are *Mischlinge*, half-Jews."

Elena's gaze fell on rotting potato peels and beetroot laid out on newspaper. "Is this all you're given to eat?"

"Sometimes there is water soup," he said.

"They're not safe here," Bystrov said, after Elena told him about their meager food supply. "If our soldiers don't torch the place, the Nazis will."

"But they're too weak to go far," Elena said. "That's why they're still here."

She observed elderly people slumped on the floor, jaws open, lips cracked from dehydration. If they were forced to leave, to march for hours to safety, they would die.

"I'll let the medics know," the major said, in a matter-of-fact voice.

"I'll try to have some bread and water sent over, but this is a war zone. I can't make any promises."

"What if we find a nearby cellar for them?"

"For sixty people, maybe, but six hundred?"

"We have to try." She told the former lawyer to stay put, that she and the major were going to look for a safer place for them.

Bystrov glanced at his watch. "We don't have time for this. Headquarters is expecting us. You're here to help interrogate Nazi officers, remember?"

"You have no idea what these people have been through. If we let them die, then we've lost witnesses to terrible crimes. If we save them, they can speak out against the Wehrmacht. They can help bring criminals to justice."

He gave a long sigh. "Does anyone ever say no to you?"

"Only when I'm wrong."

17

At first, I was the worst at shooting. The recoil of the rifle was so strong that my shoulder was constantly bruised.

—KLAVDIYA KALUGINA, FEMALE RED ARMY SNIPER

Veshnyaki, Moscow

April 1943

Elena had been lying underwater in the cold, marshy lagoon, breathing through a reed straw, long enough for her fingertips to shrivel, for her extra-large sopping trousers to hang like mud from her skin, and for her chest to flutter with nerves. There was a foreboding, otherworldly sensation, cut off from life above the water, with a droning silence echoing through her ears.

She inhaled through the straw and got a mouthful of slimy water. Dammit! She'd let the top of the straw slip below the surface. Elena tried to hold her breath, but the muddy water slid down her throat. She was going to suffocate. Her head burst through the lagoon's surface as she struggled for air. A gunshot whizzed over her scalp, so close she felt a burst of wind lift her hair.

"You're dead, Cadet Bruskina," Commander Panchenko barked. He was the short-tempered director of tactics at the Central Women's Sniper Training School. He strode towards her, his face hard with an arrogant fury, his boots squishing through the damp ground.

"Are you tired of your life?" he demanded. "Is that why your head popped up like a target?"

"No," Elena said, contrite. "I didn't mean——"

"You're supposed to be invisible, not obvious," he went on, speaking over Elena. "Camouflage is key to survival."

She clinched her lips. There was no point in telling him she'd inhaled mud through her straw. Excuses were signs of weakness. She'd failed the exercise. She was weak.

"I'm sorry," Elena said.

"Don't be sorry. Be unseen." He steeled his gaze at her. "Again."

Her fingers curled into her palms. She felt her comrades' blistering stares but saw nobody. They were hidden within the terrain. If this were an actual combat mission, she would be dead and they'd be alive. With this sobering thought clanging in her head, Elena unblocked her reed, took in a lungful of air, and sunk into the lagoon with a newfound determination. I will not fail. I cannot fail. For Masha's sake, she vowed, picturing her younger sister's defiant face the day she was executed.

For the next hour, Elena lurked beneath the surface, controlling her breaths as she'd been taught, thinking of herself no longer as a person or as a woman, but as a Red Army soldier. Following in the path of hundreds of thousands killed during the first year of war against Hitler. Expendable.

"Panchenko told me I was dead when I didn't spot the missing treetop the other day, remember?" Raya said to Elena, alluding to one of the most important rules of camouflage—if a tree has been lopped off at the top, the disappeared branches are most likely on the ground, concealing the enemy.

Elena, sulking in her bunk after her camouflage debacle, lifted her eyes from the manual, *Principles of Ballistics*. She was embarrassed and wanted to hide, but there was no place at the school to hole up. She gave Raya a cursory look and said, "I remember." She rolled onto her side and faced Alla, fast asleep. She pored over her manual, hoping to redeem herself, at least partially, in the upcoming written exam.

The murmur of girls' voices hovered in the air. In one corner, a cadet wept over a letter she'd just received. They were on their one-hour break after dinner. At seven thirty, they would reconvene to clean their rifles and march in formation.

Elena flipped a page in her manual.

"Aren't you sick of that?" Raya said.

"Of what?"

"All those calculations. You can take a break. That's what this hour is for, to rest."

Elena rolled over to face Raya. "Aren't you worried about the final exams?"

"I've got it all up here." Raya tapped her head, flippant.

"Good to see you haven't lost your humility," Elena said dryly. "Anyway, you're the best shot here. I don't think anything else matters."

Raya shook her head. "If that were true—"

The barracks door whooshed open, cutting off Raya mid-sentence. A draft of chilly, damp air entered on Zina's heels.

Her artificial leather boots clicked across the wood floor as Zina staggered to the back of the room. She paused at the space between Elena's and Raya's double bunks, exuding the unmistakable scent of bergamot, orange blossom, and cloves. There was only one way to obtain such an expensive and coveted item as Red Moscow perfume. Elena glanced sideways at Zina, struggling to take off her boots. She wondered if the rumors about Zina were true, if she was carrying on with their handsome political instructor.

Zina crawled onto the bunk beside Raya. The bunk creaked as Zina extended her legs to the end.

"Do you think being a good shot is the most important skill of a sniper, Zina?" Raya asked, her animated voice filling the barracks.

Zina shrugged off her overcoat, turned to the wall, and pulled her overcoat up to her chin.

"I said," Raya prodded, "do you think—"

"I heard you the first time," Zina mumbled.

"And?"

A long pause.

"And I don't care what you or anyone else thinks," Zina moaned wearily. "Stop talking. We only have ten minutes left and I'm exhausted. I need to close my eyes."

Raya tossed Elena a mischievous grin. She positioned her left fingers on the neck of her guitar, and strummed a familiar melody, a popular school song they'd all learned as children.

Zina clamped her hands over her ears.

Raya began singing in a soft alto voice, changing the words to fit their less-than-ideal circumstances at the snipers' school, where they dried wet clothes and foot wrappings by sleeping on them:

What a feeling, what a lark!
What a night of rest!
With my damp foot wrappings
Pressed against my chest!

Zina bolted upright and glared at Raya. "You want to know what I think?" she said, incensed.

Raya's face leeched of color.

Elena caught the sheen of a dozen pairs of curious eyes.

"I think the ability to be quiet is the most important skill for a sniper," Zina snapped. "You can have the best accuracy ever, but if you can't dissolve into the terrain, it won't matter. In the end, it won't matter at all."

The room fell silent.

Elena flinched at Zina's harsh yet true words.

"I'm worried I'll make a mistake," Alla whispered into Elena's ear. Elena turned her head and squeezed Alla's clammy hand. "We're all afraid of messing up."

Alla shook her head. "I'm not scared of dying. I'm afraid I'll do something stupid and get one of you killed."

"You can't think that way. If you don't believe in yourself, how are we supposed to trust you?"

"I'm trying," Alla began. "I really am, but I can't get rid of the sadness inside me when I think about . . . you know."

Elena did know and began to quietly cry.

"Sometimes, a lot of the time, I don't feel like a hunter," Alla continued.

She felt the same way as Alla, especially after her botched camouflage exercise. A hot rush of anger rose in Elena's chest like heartburn. She couldn't live with herself if she didn't stick it out.

"You're right where you're supposed to be," she said to Alla, resolute. "So am I."

The corners of Alla's mouth quirked up.

Elena returned to her ballistics manual but couldn't concentrate. What if her ambitions and skills were incompatible? What if she and Alla just didn't have what it took to be snipers?

18

My definition of happiness is fighting for others . . . If I must, for
general happiness, fall, I am ready.
—ROZA SHANINA, RED ARMY SNIPER

Pankow, Berlin

April 1945

Red Army leaflets, dropped from a plane while Elena and
Bystrov were inside the Jewish hospital, were strewn over
the street. Elena plucked one from the ground and rushed to
a deserted patisserie shop, with Bystrov at her heels. She located the
stairs to the cellar in the front corner and thumped down the wooden
steps, hoping it would provide a more secure refuge for the people
stranded in the Jewish hospital. The air was damp and the muted
light made it hard to see.

"Grab hold of the handrail," Bystrov said, tersely.

The words were barely out of his mouth when she missed a step.
Her left foot plunged farther than she'd expected. She lost her balance and pitched forward, landing on a pair of legs. The wind was
knocked right out of her.

"*Was zum . . . ?* What the . . . ?" a man exclaimed in German.

"*Woher kam sie?* Where did she come from?" a woman cried in a
parched voice.

"Who are you?"

Elena's ears rang with the clatter of voices. She inhaled a lungful of stuffy air, moaned at the pain in her chest, and worried she'd fractured a rib. She sidled off the poor woman who'd broken her fall and apologized. She felt a new dent on her canteen from the sharp corner of a wooden step. How ironic. Mr. Volkhov's dent was from a bullet and hers was from a stair tread.

"What do you want?"

"Don't hurt us."

"*Bitte.* Please."

She held her breath and pushed herself up with her good arm. Her shoulder had taken the brunt of the fall. Her broken elbow was miraculously unscathed. But she'd have a nice, big bruise on her shoulder to show for her clumsiness.

"You all right, Comrade Bruskina?"

She inhaled and exhaled to slow her racing heart. "I think so."

"*Russen!*" a man said, aghast.

"Leave us alone," a woman implored Elena and Bystrov.

As Elena's eyes adjusted to the poor light, she saw a jumble of faces. Thirty or forty people. Old and young. Some with towels wrapped around their heads. Children with cheekbones jutting like knives from pale skin. Young men and women with an upsetting gray pallor.

"What is that?" A woman gestured at the leaflet in Elena's hand.

Elena scanned the words. "It's from the Red Army, telling German soldiers it is hopeless to keep fighting."

A bomb detonated somewhere above them. It felt as if the ceiling was about to cave in. Elena ducked down, cradling her head, and waited until the deafening sound receded.

"I'm a member of the German Communist Party. See?" A balding man with round wire spectacles was waving a piece of paper.

Bystrov snatched it from the man's grasp and handed it to Elena.

"It's a Party identification card," she said, skimming the document. "He's been a member since 1923."

"Impossible," Bystrov said. "If he really was a Communist—"

"I'm a member too," said a man with a raspy voice. He produced a crumpled identity card.

Elena gave it a cursory glance.

"If they're Communists, why didn't they rebel against Hitler, against fascism?" Bystrov demanded. "Why aren't they in a partisan unit right now?"

Elena restated his questions in German, unable to keep the scorn from her tone. How dare they call themselves Communists.

"Fight Hitler?" the raspy-voiced man said, astounded.

"I never heard of any partisan groups," the man with spectacles replied. "If they did exist, they wouldn't have lasted long."

"It doesn't make sense," Bystrov was saying, with disdain. "In the Soviet Union, partisan units have become army detachments. People, ordinary working-class citizens are taking up arms to combat fascism. Why aren't German Communists doing the same? Why aren't they rebelling against Hitler?"

"How could you stand by and watch the Wehrmacht kill soldiers fighting to preserve fascism?" Elena goaded the men. "How are we supposed to think you're Communists when you did nothing to stop Hitler?"

Bystrov tore their identity cards to shreds.

The men stared at him, open-mouthed.

"Communists, my ass," Bystrov muttered.

"You two are despicable," a woman with a towel wrapped around her hair said, with venom, to the men posing as Communists. "We're losing our country and all you care about is saving yourselves."

"Wenck's army is going to save us . . ." the spectacled man countered, his voice trailing off.

"The Führer won't let us down," another man crowed. "The final victory will be ours."

Elena spotted the Hitler devotee near the wall on her left, in the midst of a group of very old people. His white-blond hair melded with the gray-faced pensioners. But his bright eyes and unlined skin gave him away. What really gave her pause, though, were his over-sized tunic and clean, round squirrel cheeks. He was in someone else's clothes and, unlike the others, seemed healthy, stronger, well-nourished. He hadn't been down there as long. She glanced over her shoulder at Bystrov. Saw her concern mirrored in his sullen eyes.

"Get their trust," he advised, "then push him."

She turned back to the cellar occupants. She observed a woman with a towel wrapped around her hair. "Why do you have that on your head?"

The woman's hands sprung up to her towel. "It will protect me if the building is bombed," she replied.

"Oh," Elena said, taken aback by the foolishness of the woman's reasoning. "That's very . . . sensible." She racked her brain for some more questions to put them all at ease.

"Do you have any water?" a woman croaked.

"Don't ask for anything from them," the squirrel-cheeked man burst out. "We don't need anything from Russkis."

"Speak for yourself," said an old man with shaggy white eyebrows. "We've been out of water for a day now. We won't last much longer without it."

"I'm hungry," a little boy, his arms around two smaller girls, said quietly.

"We need something to eat, too," the man with shaggy brows added. "All we have left is a loaf of—"

"The Führer knows what we need," the squirrel-cheeked man interrupted. "He will not leave us here to die."

"If you really believe in him," Elena said, "then why have you left the Wehrmacht? Why have you stopped fighting to save Berlin?"

A communal gasp broke out in the cellar.

"Is this true?" the shaggy-browed man asked.

"She's wrong."

"Of course, it's not true."

"Nobody would dare desert the Führer."

"What's going on?" Bystrov said.

"I accused him of deserting the Wehrmacht."

"The one with the fat cheeks?"

"Yes." She paused. "Now the others are not sure whether to be angry at him or me."

"Obviously, you should have waited before publicly denouncing him," he said dryly.

"Obviously."

"You may as well say we need to take him in," he continued.

"What if he says no?"

"Why do you think I wanted a translator who could shoot?"

"Right." Her stomach heaved. With her good arm, she reached for the pistol hanging from her belt. She met the man's icy glare. "We have a few more questions for you. We're bringing you to our headquarters."

"I'm not going anywhere," he said, defiant.

She glanced sideways at Bystrov. He nodded. In one fluid move, she yanked her pistol from her belt and pointed it at him. "You don't have a choice."

"You can't just snatch harmless citizens off the street," a man with a heavily creased brow argued.

"How do you know he's innocent?" she replied. "Do any of you know this man? Have any of you seen him before he appeared in the cellar?"

There was an abrupt silence.

"Isn't he a friend of yours?"

"No. I figured he was your brother."

"Why would you think that?"

"He has the same colored hair."

"Millions of us are blond."

"Isn't he your son?"

"My son is on the front, fighting for Germany."

Elena dug her hand into her tunic pocket. One sugar cube and two stale biscuits. Keeping her pistol on the deserter, she reached out to the boy and two girls huddled together. She handed the sugar to the boy and the biscuits to the girls. Their eyes rounded with astonishment. They crammed the treats into their mouths.

"Order him to remove his tunic," Bystrov said.

She looked at him, confused.

"Trust me."

She turned to the imposter and repeated Bystrov's order.

He speared her with his glare. "Don't be ridiculous."

She raised her gun. "Now."

All eyes fell on him as he unbuttoned the tunic. Slowly pulled one sleeve off, revealing the unmistakable field-gray Wehrmacht uniform. The patina of medals.

"My God!"

"Coward."

"I'd spit at you but I can't," said a woman with an underbite.

"How did you know?" Elena asked Bystrov.

"I saw something sharp under his tunic."

"And it's too large for him," she added.

"Exactly. Now let's get him to headquarters."

"What about the people in the Jewish hospital?"

"I'll send a couple of medics and some food, but that's all we can do for them."

She winced, thinking about all of those Jews counting on her and Bystrov to bring them to safety. If the hospital was shelled or bombed, they'd die. Six hundred more Jews on Hitler's tally. When they were so close to Berlin. This made it worse, somehow, knowing it was almost over, knowing they'd almost survived. Almost.

19

A sniper is obliged . . . in all cases to hit the target without fail and with the first shot . . . To be able to observe the field of battle extensively and thoroughly, to persistently track down the target . . . To be able to operate at night, in bad weather, in broken terrain, amidst obstacles and landmines.

—RED ARMY SNIPER'S NOTEBOOK

Summer tent camp near village of Amerevo, Shelkovsky District

June 1943

Elena marched beside Alla in the darkness, six and a half versts to the shooting range. She felt like a wet rag in her sodden rain poncho, feet swilling in her extra-large *kirza* boots. As the rain stung her face and a miserable dampness settled into her pores, she was daunted by the hours that lay ahead of her.

"Start digging," Commander Panchenko barked, when they reached the vast field sprinkled with clumps of bushes and stands of trees. He moved swiftly across the field until he was a good two hundred meters from the girls. He placed melons as targets amongst the spindly trees and stout bushes, then set up moving targets, helmets in carts that would be pulled by horses.

"I don't know if I have it in me today," Alla said.

"You're stronger than you know," Elena said, as much to herself as to Alla. "Just remember why you're here."

"That's the problem. I can't forget."

Elena couldn't forget either. Every day was a battle to suppress her memory. She took in the dark circles under Alla's eyes. Her ashen pallor. "You have no idea how good you are."

Alla turned away from Elena.

"I mean it," Elena persisted. "It's been six months since we started training together and you definitely have one of the best shots in our platoon, and you're much better at camouflage than I am."

Alla gave a slight nod, her front teeth biting her lower lip.

Elena patted her on the shoulder. She dropped to the ground and began digging. The trench had to be big enough for a squad of eight soldiers, and no more than thirty to forty meters from the next one.

Alla fell to her knees beside Elena. Raya and Zina were digging at opposite ends. Both sets of girls would work their way inwards, meeting at the center.

Elena jabbed the tip of her spade into the heavy, wet soil. She dug, falling into a mind-numbing rhythm that kept her going. Rain pounded her back like nails.

Alla stopped digging. "I don't feel well."

"Maybe you should have gone to the medical unit this morning," Elena suggested.

"I already missed two days last week."

Alla sat back on her knees.

"What are you doing?" Zina hissed at Alla.

"I just need a minute."

"He's coming," Raya said.

"Are you finished, Cadet Epstein?" Commander Panchenko came up from behind Alla. He loomed over her small frame.

"No sir," Alla replied.

"Rain getting to you?" He crouched down so that his head was level with Alla's. "Because if you think this is bad, it will be ten times worse at the front."

Elena sympathized with her, but at the same time wondered if Alla really was up to being a sniper. This wasn't the first time she'd been reprimanded for not following orders. Or the second.

"You're on sentry duty every night for the next two weeks, Cadet Epstein." Commander Panchenko rose.

Elena groaned silently. This was the last thing Alla needed; sentry duty meant just two hours of sleep at a time.

"Yes sir."

"Speak up."

"Yes sir," Alla said, louder. She leaned forward and shoved her spade into the earth.

Commander Panchenko extracted his stopwatch from inside his tunic. "You have one hour to finish, cadets, or you'll all get extra duties for a week."

They burrowed through the earth at a frenzied pace. Alla wheezed as she dug.

"Take it easy, Alla," Raya said. "We'll dig for you if you're not feeling up to it."

"Of course," Zina added. "You sound awful."

Elena's heart melted at her friends' compassion. In the six months they'd lived and trained together, she'd come to realize sisters didn't have to be related by blood.

"Platoon, to arms!" Commander Panchenko shouted when all the trenches were dug. "Shoot from a prone position."

Elena yanked her bolt-action Mosin-Nagant rifle, attached to a strap, over her head. She ran her fingers over her rifle's long wooden stock. It unsettled her with its size and power, with its untold history.

Mosin-Nagants had been issued in Russia for decades though they'd been recently modified with open sights for close-range shooting. She wondered who'd used it before. How many people it had shot. If any soldiers had died with it in their hands.

She opened the ammunition pouch hanging from her belt, took out one cartridge with five bullets that reminded her of lipstick containers, and loaded the chamber. Rain wasn't an issue; from her ballistics class she knew the bullet never got wet because it traveled faster than the speed of sound, which created a protective supersonic shock wave.

She lay on her stomach, placed her rifle on the parapet, the edge of the trench, and pulled the bolt to release a bullet into the chamber. She peered through the eyepiece of the telescopic sight, held her breath, took aim, and pressed the trigger. The butt of the rifle kicked against her right shoulder. A quick flash burst out of the muzzle.

Hitting the target in one shot was crucial. If she missed, the enemy would be able to tell where she was from the trajectory of the bullet. She squinted through her binoculars. Saw the melon shattered into a million tiny pieces. One shot in horrid visibility. Then it occurred to her—in less than four months, she would become just like the people who'd killed her family. She would be a murderer.

The image of Masha's body hanging limp from the gallows rushed into her head. She heard the children's cries from the pit. The shots that killed her mother. She beat back a sob. She felt the loss in the center of her being, an infinite grief she'd have to endure. She focused on the horizon, a future full of uncertainty and potential. And freedom, if she persevered. If she followed Panchenko's motto—"Kill and forget."

The field kitchen arrived with dinner after she'd taken several more shots, none as good as her first. A hot meal would make her feel better. That's what Mama would have said. She longed for her mother, for the strong woman she'd once been, who'd spent hours on the frosty Svisloch River teaching her to skate when she was a child, so that she could join her friends. Her heart tugged at the memory of her mother's sturdy hands under her arms, supporting her as her feet skidded every which way. The gratifying slice of her blades gliding over the ice. Her mother's proud smile.

"Here. Take it."

Elena blinked. Her eyelashes dripped with rain. In place of her mother, she saw the field cook extending a bowl of hot porridge. She accepted the metal bowl and a hunk of bread and sat with Zina, Raya, and Alla beneath an apple tree that hadn't yet budded.

The sticky porridge warmed Elena's insides and kept her from dwelling on what had been.

"Look, the rain stopped!" Alla blurted.

Elena held out her palm. Not a drop.

"Thank God," said Zina. "I thought I was going to float away this morning, it was so soggy."

"And it will help with our shooting . . ." Alla added pensively.

"Technically, yes," Elena said. She wagged her finger at her comrades. "But don't forget what Panchenko says: The harder the training, the—"

"The better prepared we'll be for combat," Raya and Zina chimed in. Alla said nothing.

"You all right?" Raya said. "You're white as chalk."

Alla averted her eyes from Raya's.

Elena leaned in closer to Alla. "You really should've gone to the medical unit this morning."

"I'm not sick. Not in the normal sense, I mean."

"I'm confused," Raya said.

"It's not a stomachache or a sore throat or anything else normal," Alla said, her voice sluggish.

"What is it?"

"It's as if it's always night inside me. I'm constantly on edge, afraid the worst is about to happen."

"You need sleep," Raya said. "When I don't sleep, I'm not myself at all. I feel lazy and don't want to do anything."

"Same with me," Zina agreed.

"I won't be getting much the next two weeks, with sentry duty," Alla responded.

"If you want, I'll take some of your hours so you can rest," Elena offered.

"Me too," Raya said.

"Same for me," said Zina.

"Thanks, but if Panchenko found out . . ."

"Cadets, to arms," Panchenko hollered, as if he knew they'd been talking about him.

"You'll get through this all right," Elena tried to assure Alla. She caught her training partner's glazed-over eyes. A cold shiver ran down her spine. If Alla didn't last the afternoon, her punishment would be far worse than sentry duty.

Shooting practice resumed in earnest, this time from a kneeling position in front of the trench. Elena lodged the rifle butt into the hollow of her shoulder.

"Are you here to shoot or daydream, Cadet Bruskina?" Panchenko ranted from behind her.

Elena stiffened.

"How long should it take to aim?"

"Eight seconds," she replied.

"Maximum. Eight seconds maximum."

"Yes sir."

"Then stop wasting time and start shooting."

Elena aligned the target with the three lines in her rifle's sight, took a big gulp of air, and released the trigger. She exhaled, lost her balance from the recoil, and almost fell over. She'd missed the target. *Because he rushed me.* She braced herself for a reprimand from Panchenko. But she heard nothing except the dry click of triggers and boom of shots.

For hours, Panchenko led the girls in shooting drills where they fired at moving and stationary targets, from lying positions to shooting on the move to standing still. The late-afternoon sun floated over the horizon. Gossamer shadows dappled to the ground. There was an earthy, after-rain smell in the air.

"At ease, platoon," Commander Panchenko announced. "Gather your cartridge cases, then fall into formation."

Elena rolled her tongue in her mouth to get rid of the rotten-egg tang of sulfur. She raised her eye from the scope of her rifle and pried her right hand from the trigger. Her knuckles were swollen and her shoulder was bruised from the kickback. Every muscle in her body ached, she was covered in mud, and she had a seven-kilometer march ahead. Still, her accuracy with moving targets had improved, marginally, enough to give her a cautious sense of accomplishment.

Her knees cracked when she got to her feet. She took a big gulp of water from her canteen, hoisted her rifle over her shoulder, and began picking up her spent cartridge cases. Every single case had to be retrieved so they could be reused. Once she'd collected her cases, she headed to a bush about four meters from the trench and relieved herself. A lone gunshot fired through the air with a resounding crack.

Elena jerked her head towards the sound. Her trench. She yanked up her trousers and turned and ran.

"What was that?" a girl called out.

"Is someone shooting at us?" Raya said.

"Who shot their gun?" Panchenko demanded.

Elena's face went slack when she reached the trench she'd just vacated. Alla lay motionless on her back. Everything faded to a blurry haze when she saw Alla's foot at the trigger of her rifle. The barrel was in her mouth.

"No," Elena sobbed. She sprang into the trench and lifted Alla's bloody head. "Alla! What did you do?"

"My God!" Raya cried.

Zina and Raya jumped into the trench, clutched Elena's arms, and dragged her up and over the parapet.

"Stop your hysterics, Cadet Bruskina," Panchenko barked. "Is this how you'd behave at the front?"

"I spent so much time worrying about my own shooting, I didn't see what was right in front of me," Elena cried. "It's my fault."

"Stop blubbering." Panchenko snatched her from Zina and Raya and heaved her up until she was standing face-to-face with him. "You're supposed to be a soldier, remember? If you can't contain yourself now, how will you cope when your comrades drop like flies during combat?"

A collective gasp surged from the platoon.

"This . . . this is different," Elena managed. "She is . . . was my partner. And I knew she was struggling."

"You think she is the first cadet to commit suicide?"

Elena tottered, then held her arms out for balance.

There was a low murmur from her comrades.

"Many more take their lives at the front." Panchenko's voice softened. "You may face the same decision, with just seconds to act, before being seized by the enemy." He scanned the platoon. "This goes for all of you. Death is preferable to capture. You don't want to know what torture by the Nazis means. Always save a bullet for yourself."

Elena lowered her head. She wondered why Alla had lost the will to go on. She wondered if she was that different from Alla, if she could attain the delicate balance between devoting herself to the fight for the Jewish people while keeping enough of herself to survive.

20

Going into battle, I saw in front of my eyes the train with which
you left Latvia, and I went forth filled with rage to avenge your
murdered mother and you.
— MONIKA MEIKSANE, RED ARMY SNIPER

Pankow, Berlin
April 1945

What is your real name?"

Elena's voice ricocheted in the cavernous area. She, Bystrov, and the phony Communist they'd uncovered in the cellar were in an abandoned tire factory. Rain tapped against the windows and roof.

"Why don't you just shoot me now?" the imposter grumbled. "I'm good as dead when my superiors find out I deserted."

"Tell me your name," Elena demanded.

Lightning cracked, illuminating the room for a fraction of a second, adding a sense of drama to the interrogation.

The man glanced sideways at his medals. "Hans Fischer," he said bitterly. "I'm a Sturmbannführer, assault unit leader, and I decamped when you captured Seelow Heights. Hitler ordered us to fight to the death, but we didn't have enough men or ammunition or food. Besides, we'd lost. I wanted to surrender but that would mean execution by my own troops."

Elena recalled the men hanging with signs identifying them as deserters. Maybe they were, or maybe they'd simply wanted the fighting to end.

"I have a wife and three children to think about." Hans grimaced at Elena and opened his palms. "How can I support them if I'm dead?"

You can't, she thought, recalling Mrs. Drapkina and her three girls.

"Ask him if he knows anything about the new secret weapon," Bystrov prompted her. He was referring to German propaganda about a powerful Nazi special weapon that was predicted to be revealed on Hitler's birthday, April 20. The following day.

Recognition dawned on Hans's face at the question. "I've seen trucks coming and going with tarpaulins covering something big."

"How big? What shape was it?"

"I don't know. Like a big box, I guess."

"That's helpful," the major replied, sarcastic. "What about Hitler's whereabouts?"

"The Führer's in Berlin," said Hans with a certainty that made Elena's mouth fall open.

Bystrov's eyes gleamed at the news.

"Do you know where he is in the capital?" she pressed.

Hans shook his head. "Nobody knows. Hitler's an expert at hiding from everyone, including his own people."

"What about Goebbels?" Bystrov urged. "Ask if he's in Berlin."

Hans's brows snapped together. "Who cares about Goebbels?"

"Do you know where he is?" she asked again.

"Not a clue."

She turned to Bystrov. "He knows nothing about Goebbels, and to be honest, I'm not sure he's telling the truth about Hitler."

"A lie told often enough becomes the truth," he sighed, quoting Vladimir Lenin.

"What now?" Hans asked, his gaze flicking from Elena to Bystrov. Elena hated this part of the interrogation, the ending, when she had to give the false party line: "You'll join the other prisoners. At the end of the war, who knows?"

Hans put his head in his hands. "I'm a dead man."

Elena looked away. Her mind turned to the charred remains of Soviet prisoners of war she'd witnessed on her marches. At least the Red Army wouldn't defile him. They were better than the Wehrmacht. Weren't they?

21

Hey, comrades! Why are you looking so sad? Be brave, fight the
Germans, burn, wipe them out! I'm not afraid to die, comrades. It
is happiness to die for one's people.
—FINAL WORDS OF PARTISAN ZOYA KOSMODEMYANSKAYA, BEFORE
SHE WAS HUNG FOR SETTING FIRE TO GERMAN HOUSES

Podolsk, Moscow Oblast
July 1943

A s children in the Young Pioneers and then the Komsomol,
we pledged allegiance to Soviet leaders and learned that
the Motherland is more important than our own lives and
the lives of our families," said Major Yekaterina Nikiforova, head
of the political department at the Central Women's Sniper Training
School.

Though Elena didn't agree with the relentless propaganda Major Nikiforova touted, she was transfixed by the short-waisted and
busty woman with small blue eyes that squinted when she smiled,
who had already served at the front as a sniper. Curiously, instead of
coming back hardened by her experiences, Major Nikiforova had a
nurturing disposition compared to the rest of their instructors, who
were all men, except for Captain Chegodaieva. Auntie Katya, as the
girls affectionately called Major Nikiforova, intervened on their behalf when they discovered there were no sanitary supplies for their

periods. Elena's lips tugged as she recalled Auntie Katya confronting a red-faced Colonel Kolchak, head of the snipers' school, about the "appalling lack of feminine supplies in an all-women's school."

"Do you remember the Young Pioneer slogan?"

Auntie Katya's insistent voice hauled her back to the lesson in the barracks.

"Prepare to fight for the cause of the Communist Party," Elena chanted reflexively with the rest of her platoon.

"Very good. And now, as Komsomol members, as snipers, and as young women, you have the coveted opportunity to prove you stand behind these words. You have the chance to show Comrade Stalin you can be more than mothers. You can be heroes like Zoya Kosmodemyanskaya," she said, referring to a young girl tortured and hanged four months earlier for setting fire to a German farm.

"Zoya sacrificed her life and her dignity for the Motherland," Auntie Katya went on, "even though she wasn't a trained Red Army soldier, like you. She was a Komsomol member and a partisan. More than that, she was devoted to Stalin and Communism. Zoya is a hero not because she died for our country, she is a hero because she fought the enemy without worrying about the consequences. She put the Soviet Union ahead of herself, which is what all of you must do when given the privilege to fight."

Elena's jaw set. The way Auntie Katya was talking about Zoya, it sounded as if you couldn't be heroic without losing your life, as if heroism and death were inextricably linked. Elena wanted to be a hero, yet at the same time, she didn't want to die. She wanted to be at the front more than anything but wasn't sure she'd be able to put aside fear for her life in the heat of combat.

She glanced left. For a cold moment, she saw Alla sitting beside her. Then Alla's delicate face waned and was replaced by Tanya Baramzina's broad visage. Tanya, with her upturned nose and athletic build, was the polar opposite of Alla inside and out. She was one of five children born into a farming family. In 1930, Tanya's parents had been forced to give their land to the government as part of Stalin's collectivization plan, to combine private properties into state-controlled *Kolkhozes*, farms. One year later, Tanya's father died, leaving her mother to raise the children on her own.

Tanya had initially completed a six-month nursing course in order to get into the Red Army, but when she tried to enlist, she was turned away. Undeterred, Tanya graduated from a sharpshooter's course before she was admitted to the snipers' school. She was, in Elena's opinion, proof that anything could be accomplished if you wanted it badly enough.

"I don't believe it," Zina said, astonished.

The platoon had returned to the barracks after a break, but instead of Auntie Katya, an instantly recognizable woman, with hair cut bluntly to her earlobe and a chest gleaming with medals, stood in front of them.

"Lyudmila Pavlichenko?" Elena said, astounded.

"Comrade Lieutenant Pavlichenko," she corrected Elena.

Elena's face turned red.

Lieutenant Pavlichenko was resplendent in her khaki tunic with red epaulettes and collar tabs. An officer's brimmed cap sat neatly on her head.

"It's you," Zina said, in awe. "It's really you."

Lieutenant Pavlichenko smiled slightly. Close up, her amber eyes were wide and sharp. There was a quiet resignation in her demeanor.

"You don't look like you do in photos," Raya said.

"Not so pretty?" Lieutenant Pavlichenko jested.

"Taller. You look taller in person."

Lieutenant Pavlichenko shrugged as if she'd heard this before.

Elena felt giddy, hearing the lieutenant's crisp, assertive voice for the first time. "How was America?" she said. Her recent tour of the United States and Canada had been the talk of the barracks.

Lieutenant Pavlichenko held Elena's gaze. "Tedious. People were more interested in the length of my skirt and the color of my lipstick than in my shooting."

Elena's smile faded. If a warrior like Lieutenant Pavlichenko couldn't be seen as more than a woman, what chance did any of them have?

"What did you think of Eleanor Roosevelt?" someone asked.

"She is wise, for an American woman."

Voices flooded the lieutenant with questions.

"Did you really kill three hundred and nine Nazis?"

"Were you ever afraid?"

"Are capitalists really terrible?"

Lieutenant Pavlichenko eyed the girls. "Since my travels in America will do you absolutely no good in combat, I suggest we get on with the class I have been asked to give."

A class? Elena could hardly contain herself. A real hero was about to teach her platoon, maybe even share her secrets!

"Grab your notebooks and pencils," Lieutenant Pavlichenko continued, "and follow me in formation." She filed out of the barracks.

Elena scrambled for her notebook. She rushed from the barracks, determined to be as close to the lieutenant as possible, to soak up her aura, to breathe the same air as the greatest woman sniper in the Soviet Union.

"Let's sing for our country!" Raya shouted as they marched past the open-mouthed guards at the school's gates. With the gusto of an opera soloist, Raya broke into "The Sacred War," a patriotic song written just two years earlier when the Germans invaded the Soviet Union. Now, chirping it daily, Elena often found herself waking up to the evocative melody drumming in her head.

The black wings shall not dare
Fly over the Motherland . . .

"Everyone sing, for Stalin!" Raya called out.

Rotten fascist vermin
We will shoot you in the forehead.

Goosebumps rose on Elena's neck as she listened to their con-
joined voices soar overhead with unwavering passion. Even her own
flat tone mingled seamlessly with the rest.

"At least our voices are ready for the front," Raya joked.

Tanya rolled her eyes.

Elena felt a twinge of fear in her gut at the mention of the front.
When she'd started training, nine months had seemed so long. There
had been so much to learn, so much to practice, so much time with
these girls, she considered them as family. And the school, with its
familiar routines and walls, had become a home of sorts. She felt safe
there.

In just a few weeks, however, they would graduate and scatter
across the Soviet Union, deployed wherever they were needed most.
It was a disconcerting prospect, leaving the school's nest. Knowing
they would never be all together again. Knowing many girls would
not survive.

"At ease," Lieutenant Pavlichenko said.

She'd stopped on Lenin Street, at the central square of Podolsk,
almost three versts from their barracks. The city's humid streets
swarmed with mosquitoes and cadets from the Women's Central
Sniper Training School, as well as men from the nearby artillery and
infantry college.

Elena wriggled her toes in her boots. In the boiling heat, her feet were swollen and blistered.

Lieutenant Pavlichenko pointed at a two-story building with a clock tower that was being repaired across the street. "To demonstrate the importance of noticing the slightest details while on reconnaissance, I am offering a valuable lesson one of my instructors gave me. This is the town hall, built in the fourteenth century. As you can see, it has sustained artillery damage."

Elena noted the pitted yellow exterior, broken windows, and caved-in red roof.

"Over the next two hours," Lieutenant Pavlichenko went on, "I want you to record what the workers accomplish, changes on the building itself, and fluctuations in the setting. Then I want you to determine the best shooting position to neutralize the foreman."

"From this distance, Comrade Lieutenant?" asked Irina, a wiry girl with a ready smile.

Lieutenant Pavlichenko lit a cigarette, sucking in her cheeks intensely, before answering, "From this distance and vantage point, Comrade Cadet." She exhaled a veil of smoke and stepped back from the girls.

Elena huddled with Tanya, Raya, and Zina.

"This is so exciting," Zina said.

"I hope she tells us about some of her kills," Tanya said.

Elena cast a sidelong glance at Lieutenant Pavlichenko, huffing on her cigarette with a faraway expression in her eyes. "I think the lieutenant wants to be at the front," she whispered. "She doesn't want to teach. She doesn't want to be here at all."

"Why isn't she at the front?" Raya asked.

"She was injured. Shrapnel. I read about it," Tanya answered.

"She seems fine," Raya said. "If she wants to be at the front so bad, then why is she here with a bunch of cadets?"

"Obviously, she had orders," Zina retorted.

"We don't have time for this," Elena said. "We only have—"

"I would think by now," Lieutenant Pavlichenko interrupted, her voice loud yet even, "you cadets would understand the vital importance of silence while on lookout."

Sweat pooled at the back of Elena's neck. She stared at the town hall, but her eyes kept wandering towards Lieutenant Pavlichenko. It was hard to concentrate in the presence of someone so accomplished, someone whose face had been splashed on magazine covers and the front pages of newspapers for months.

"You must become patient and cunning hunters." Lieutenant Pavlichenko lowered her voice. "Because you get only one shot. If you are distracted, if you miss, you could pay with your life."

Elena poured all her attention into the town hall, jotting down what she saw, from the number of broken windows (three), to the smashed door, to the two workers milling about. She flipped to a clean white page and began sketching the scene, just as she would do under real circumstances, if she were on lookout for a day.

Two hours later, Elena pasted a smile on her face as Lieutenant Pavlichenko praised Raya for choosing the optimum shooting position. Of course it had to be Raya who impressed the lieutenant. It was always Raya and, while Elena adored her, she couldn't help but be a little jealous.

Lieutenant Pavlichenko turned to address the entire platoon. "Before we get into formation and march back to the barracks, I want to give you one last piece of advice."

Elena's ears perked.

"Take one shot and move on. The moment you shoot, you give away your hiding spot. Take one shot and move on."

Elena was startled not by the words, which had been drilled into her head since the first day of training, but by Lieutenant Pavlichenko's melancholy air. It reminded her of Alla's demeanor. She shivered and found herself pining for her training partner for a second chance to reverse the tragic outcome. To save Alla from the despair that had overtaken her soul. To assuage her own guilt for not recognizing Alla's silent cries for help.

As she marched back to the school, Elena wondered if Lieutenant Pavlichenko had witnessed a sniper who'd forgotten to move on and was subsequently shot. Or had Lieutenant Pavlichenko experienced a close call?

This question nagged at Elena long after the lieutenant was gone. Lieutenant Pavlichenko had everything—an impressive tally of kills, fame, and travel to America—yet she seemed unhappy. If victory didn't bring joy to the most accomplished woman sniper, how would the rest of them feel once they started killing fascists?

22

Death is the solution to all problems. No man—no problem.
—JOSEPH STALIN

Berlin
April 1945

A German Focke-Wulf aircraft, nicknamed the *Rama* or Frame in Russian because its twin boom had a distinctive window-frame shape, whirred through the sky. This reconnaissance plane was a blunt reminder of the Wehrmacht's enduring presence, despite the fact that they'd lost most of their own country and were hemorrhaging soldiers, weapons, and ammunition. Even now, flames thrashed over Berlin's city center. The barrage of gunfire was relentless.

Ludis steered the jeep down Kurfürstendamm, one of the few passable streets, though they were crawling forward at a painfully slow four and a half versts an hour. A lemming's pace, thought Elena, agitated. She balanced her pistol on the open window ledge. Electricity coursed through her veins. She was a sniper again. She was back on the front, only this time, the jeep was her foxhole and she was hunting Hitler Youth and Volkssturmer, the militia of teenage boys and old men newly organized by the Nazis to compensate for their dwindling army. This reckless group was armed with Panzerfausts, handheld grenade launchers, and members were known to attack from behind bushes or ruined buildings.

White sheets and towels hung from the windows of countless houses, and a few Volkssturm members were waving white handkerchiefs. Ironic, with their fellow German soldiers, unable or unwilling to accept defeat, firing wildly into the road.

The sound of a horn pierced the air. Elena looked back. A Studebaker was behind them, its fender pressed against the jeep. The truck's driver honked the horn again.

"Does he think I can fly over the cars ahead of us," Ludis muttered.

The truck's horn blew one long squeal. Ludis pressed the heel of his hand on the jeep's horn and held it, searing the air with its wail. Right away, all the horns around them started going off, creating a frenetic energy.

The jeep was approaching a derelict apartment building when a German self-propelled assault gun ahead of them exploded, killing two Red Army soldiers. Elena determined the enemy's shell came from the left side of the street. She inhaled sharply when she saw a boy in a Hitler Youth uniform hopping onto a bicycle. A Panzerfaust was affixed to the handlebar.

He couldn't be more than fourteen or fifteen years old. She dreaded the idea of shooting a boy who hadn't lived long enough to fully understand the consequences of his actions, who didn't yet know it was possible to resist evil. The reek of burning metal seeped through her nostrils. The smell of her comrades' execution. She pulled the trigger. The boy fell sideways from his bicycle.

"Well done, Comrade Bruskina," said Bystrov.

"I feel awful." She slouched in her seat.

"He would have killed again. You had no choice," he assured her. "If you want to blame someone, blame Hitler for sending boys to defend a falling city."

This didn't make her feel better.

An ear-shattering bang shook Elena's nerves. A house had been shelled. Wooden debris soared through the mushrooming, black smoke. German Volkssturmer seeking revenge for the boy's murder clobbered back with badly aimed Panzerfausts, hitting stacks of rubble, abandoned vehicles, and already destroyed buildings. The air thickened with smoke. Still, white sheets and towels emerged through the miasma. And flowers were blooming through spaces in the debris. Dashes of white, yellow, and green amidst black and gray. Dashes of hope.

Ludis steered the jeep right, around a corner onto a narrower street. Elena grimaced at the sight of a German soldier hanging from a tree. There was a placard on his chest with the words *Ich war ein Feigling, I was a coward*, scrawled in black ink. She shut her eyes. She saw Masha being led down the street in Minsk, eyes defiant.

"It would seem Hitler keeps his word," Bystrov said.

His voice melded into the background noise of automobile engines and gunfire. The ominous click of jackboots throttled her head. She heard the clang of the bucket against the ground. Saw Masha's dangling legs. Her body hanging limp.

"Are you all right?" Bystrov's voice reverberated between her ears. Her breaths came short and quick. Masha's absence was a presence.

"Comrade Bruskina?"

"What?" she whispered.

"What's wrong?" His voice sounded far away. "You're white as a ghost."

Elena felt her lungs shrivel. She gagged for air.

"Breathe," said Bystrov. "Slowly. In and out."

She let his modulated voice guide her inhalations. Breathed in. Held the air in her lungs. Exhaled. Inhaled. Exhaled. Her chest opened up. Her breathing slowed.

"Have some water," Bystrov urged.

She unscrewed the lid of her canteen and took a swig.

"What happened?" he asked.

She shoved the memory back into the alcoves of her mind. She considered telling the major, but was afraid of reliving the horror all over again.

"Nothing," she heard herself say.

He regarded her, dubious.

"Really, I'm okay." She turned her gaze to the window. Saw another soldier hanging from a tree. The bile of her stomach rose to her throat. "Stop the car," she cried.

Ludis braked.

She opened the door and retched. The putrid reek of vomit filled her nostrils and mouth. She heaved again, then waited a few seconds to make sure nothing more came up.

"Must have been something I ate." She closed the door and stared out the window, unable to meet Bystrov's eyes.

For the rest of the drive, there was a jagged and shrill silence between them.

23

Eastern Front

August 1943

Shopkeepers waved at the fifty recent graduates of the Central Women's Sniper Training School as they marched down 1st Meshchanskaya Street in Moscow loaded down with duffel bags and gray woolen overcoats, rolled like thick cigars, draped over their left shoulders. Mosin-Nagant rifles were slung over their right shoulders, and Tula-Tokarev pistols, known as TTs, were holstered to their belts.

The snipers' platoon was on its way to the train station, where girls would be divided into two groups and deployed in separate directions. Thirty girls, including Elena, Tanya, Raya, and Zina, had been assigned to the 3rd Shock elite army of the Kalinin Front. Elena's emotions swerved from panic to disbelief. It was all happening too fast.

Up ahead, Auntie Katya, accompanying Elena's platoon to the front, launched into a stirring rendition of "A Farewell to Our Beloved City."

Elena tried to focus on the lyrics, to keep her mind from lurching to the source of her mixed feelings—the graduation certificate in her tunic pocket that ranked her as corporal. One annoying word on her certificate that confirmed she was not one but two rungs below her friends, ranked sergeants. Corporal. The very word left a bad taste on her tongue.

In her head, she reviewed her grades for the tenth time. Practical shooting: good. Firearms mechanics: good. Tactical training: good. Military engineering training: good. Elena frowned. Being rated as merely "good" was a sobering reminder of her inadequacies.

"Why am I even going to the front if I'm just all right?" Elena said. She clamped her mouth shut. She hadn't meant to speak out loud.

Zina, marching in front of Elena, turned her head and raised her brow. "What was that?"

"She doesn't know why she's going to the front," Tanya, who was beside Elena, answered.

Elena gave Tanya a look of annoyance.

"What do you mean?" said Zina.

"I'm not a sergeant. I don't know why they're sending me when I didn't get higher grades."

"All that nonsense about grades, it doesn't mean a thing."

"Don't make it worse by pretending it doesn't matter."

"Zina's right," Raya said, over her left shoulder. "They can't give everyone grades of excellence, or it would look like the school is too easy, so they have to give some cadets lower grades."

"No." Elena shook her head. "That doesn't make sense."

Tanya waved her sniper record book in Elena's face: "Did you get a different book?"

"No, but—"

"We all received identical books to register our kills," Tanya interrupted. "Grades don't matter in combat. Look at Lyudmila with three hundred and nine kills. Does anyone talk about her grades? In the end, it's your tally that matters."

"Get more kills than Lyudmila and you can tell Panchenko to eat your grades," Zina joked.

Elena grinned. Thank goodness for friends. Then she remembered Alla lifeless in the trench. A cold sliver of guilt plunged down her spine.

"Platoon halt!" Auntie Katya shouted.

They'd arrived at Rizhsky station, an impressive building with its lavish seventeenth-century facade, especially the *kokoshniks*, ornate, semicircular details that evoked traditional Russian headdresses.

A hand clinched Elena's wrist. Tanya's hand.

"This is it," Tanya said. "We're really going to the front."

Elena reached for Mr. Volkhov's canteen, strung across her shoulder. Her heart slowed as she felt the solid tin. The indentation from the bullet. Although he'd mistakenly thought Elena was his deceased wife, he'd seen her. He'd listened to her.

"God be with you!" a woman called out to the platoon.

"Hitler, kaput," a child's voice rang out.

Auntie Katya took a step back and addressed the entire platoon: "Stay in formation as we march to the train platform. Remember, we are the first all-female sniper platoon to fight for Mother Russia. We must show Comrade Stalin that he has not made a mistake in sending us to the front."

Elena's hands went cold. There was no going back. She had to hope Tanya was right, that grades wouldn't matter at the front, that she deserved to fight alongside her skilled comrades.

Freight trains that had carried livestock before the war would transport the platoon 337 versts to Rzhev, where they would join the Kalinin Front, a battle unit on the Eastern Front. Thirty female snipers were jammed in a compartment on bunks made of bare boards, without pillows or sheets. The girls folded their overcoats in half lengthwise, lying on one half and using the other half as a cover for the eight-hour journey. Elena had stuffed Yakov's coat in her duffel, though it was against regulations to bring civilian clothing. Just seeing the familiar, ragged wool and brushing her finger over the gossamer plume made her feel safer, as if Yakov was looking out for her.

A cast-iron potbellied stove in the middle of the carriage was used for cooking and boiling water for tea. Meals were largely black rusks instead of bread slices, and salted herring with bones instead of meat. The door had to be kept open to purge the stench from the bucket the girls used to relieve themselves.

Raya, on the bunk below Zina, tuned her guitar and then strummed the melody for "Hey You Steppe, How Vast You Are," a folk song celebrating the Russian grasslands that extended from the coast of the Black Sea to the southern area of western Siberia.

Auntie Katya added her deeper voice, creating a two-part harmony that carried Elena back to Minsk, when her father sang Yiddish songs after dinner. Her favorite one was about the root of a tree, growing in the earth, created by God. Now she had trouble reconciling the simple, trusting child she had been with the cynical woman traveling in the freight train.

Three hours after leaving Moscow, the train approached Vyazma, named after the river on which the town was located. The Red Army had just retaken the town five months ago, in March, from the Wehrmacht, who had been occupying it for a year and a half.

As the train rolled through the town's outskirts, Elena, sitting with Tanya, Raya, and Zina at the open door, was sickened by the reckless devastation. Kilometer after kilometer of ruined buildings. No roofs, doors, or windows. Stone houses gutted as if they'd been made of paper. Debris clogging roads. Cars turned upside down and sideways as if they were toys. Mangled bicycles everywhere.

"It looks like the entire city was bombed," Elena murmured.

"The people," Tanya said, breathless. "What happened to the people who lived here?"

"Probably exterminated," Raya said. "Better to be killed than . . ."

Raya's unsaid words hung heavily in the humid air.

As the annihilated town receded, Zina started talking about the political instructor she'd left behind, and how she was glad to be rid of him because he'd been getting too clingy.

Elena wondered what it felt like, having someone madly in love with you the way men seemed to fall for Zina. Maybe Zina was right to seek romance now, to live in the moment rather than wait for better days that might never come.

As soon as the train stopped, Elena jumped from the car to stretch her legs and get a break from the girls. She loved them all but it drained her, being stuck in one place with them for hours at a time with no breathing room. Her preference for quiet research and writing was the main reason she'd decided to become an academic before this war broke out. The incessant demands of communal living were amongst the biggest challenges at the snipers' school. And now, as the snipers drew closer to the Eastern Front, where they'd be crammed in dugouts to sleep and eat, where they'd spend days and nights with their partners stalking fascists, she knew it would be even more difficult to carve out time alone.

The station was white, pitted with shrapnel, beneath a red roof that was remarkably intact. Women with worn scarves on their heads and raggedy clothing stood on the platform with hopeful expressions, as if they were expecting somebody special.

Elena splashed her face with cold water from a pump near the tracks. She filled her canteen.

"*Dobro pozhalovat'*, welcome," a tiny woman greeted her in Russian. The woman held out a heel of bread. "Please. Eat."

Elena was stirred by the woman's generosity, knowing she probably had hungry children at home. "Thank you, but no. I am well fed."

The woman moved closer and shoved the bread into Elena's hands. "You must take it. Maybe someone will do the same for my boy."

Her boy? Elena's chest swelled with compassion. "Thank you for your kindness."

She took a bite. It was soft and fresh. It reminded her of the challah her father used to bring home for Friday night Shabbat dinners. Her heart stirred, thinking about her family sitting around the candlelit table, tearing chunks of bread and talking. Even her atheist mother hadn't been able to resist challah. She met the woman's gaze. "Delicious."

The woman gave her a toothless smile.

Elena dried her teary eyes with the back of her hand. She searched for her friends to share the bread. She saw them reluctantly accepting gifts of food from other Russian women. She held the bread in her hand and realized she was fighting for more than vengeance.

The train had barely left Vyazma when a shrieking whistle emerged from the sky.

"A German bomber!" Auntie Katya shouted.

Elena's first instinct was to dive for cover, but where?

A bomb exploded a hundred meters in front of the train with a boom that rocked the tracks. Black smoke mushroomed into the air.

The train screeched to a stop.

"Everyone out!" Auntie Katya cried. "Quickly!"

Elena leapt onto a patch of tall, yellow grass. Raya landed beside her, clutching the neck of her guitar.

Elena stared at her, incredulous.

"It was in my hand," Raya said, defensively.

"Take cover," Auntie Katya shouted.

Elena scooted over to a knoll. She curled up, making herself small. Raya pressed beside her.

The guitar poked Elena's tailbone. She frowned. Went rigid at the sound of another German plane sweeping low with an ear-piercing trill. A bomb detonated on the other side of the tracks, searing the earth. Elena breathed in the smoldering air. The acrid smack of metal leached onto her tongue. It was the taste of war.

24

By spreading the claim that Hitler is dead, the German Fascists are clearly hoping to enable him to leave the stage and go underground.

—PRAVDA, MAY 2, 1945

Potsdamer Platz, Berlin

April 1945

From her chair in the cellar, Elena felt the ground vibrate when Soviet bombs attacked nearby Potsdamer Platz. She'd been interrogating prisoners for hours, and was more baffled now than before she'd started. One middle-aged officer said Hitler had escaped and was in Argentina. When Elena had probed him for details as to how he'd managed this feat with Berlin surrounded by Soviet forces, he admitted he had no idea. Another claimed Hitler was on his way to South America by U-boat. He'd smugly refused to divulge any further information.

A German lieutenant said Hitler had escaped in a tank with the head of the Nazi Party Chancellery, Martin Bormann, and that Reichsmarschall Hermann Göring was now in charge of the government. Like his counterparts, however, he was either unwilling or unable to offer more details. Adding to the confusion, the Soviet commandant of Berlin was convinced Hitler had gone into hiding somewhere in Europe. But even he couldn't explain how Hitler (with the most recognizable face in the world) had eluded capture and escaped Germany unnoticed.

"Do you know anything about Hitler?" she asked the young German soldier with two cowlicks standing before her. He couldn't have been older than sixteen. His hands were bound together. "Where he is? What he's doing?"

The soldier answered without hesitation: "My division was protecting Hitler. We were holding out until General Wenck's army came to our rescue."

"Did you really believe General Wenck's army was on the way?" she said, dubious.

His slate-gray eyes flickered with irritation. "Of course. Goebbels himself said so in the latest *Frontblatt*."

"And I suppose Goebbels's word is *heilig*, sacred," Bystrov said, with disdain.

"*Ja, heilig*," the soldier replied after Elena translated Bystrov's remark, with a fervent nod. "I heard Goebbels on the radio. He said Berlin should be defended to the last man. He said men, women, and boys should stand side by side with the Wehrmacht. He said we've been fighting the Bolsheviks for years and that this is not a matter of negotiations, but of life and death."

Her eyebrows rose at the preposterous demand for children to be used as pawns, to face the Red Army without a shred of experience, without weapons, without a chance in hell of surviving. She was conveying the soldier's information to Bystrov when a clatter rose on the stairs.

"*Sie tun mir weh*, you're hurting me," a woman cried. "I promise I won't run."

"*Zamolchi*, shut up," a Red Army soldier snapped.

Heavy footfalls landed on the packed-dirt basement floor. A German nurse in her early twenties appeared, sandwiched between two gangly soldiers. The sleeves of her sky-blue blouse were rolled to her elbows, her white armband was wrinkled and dirty, and her white pinafore was ripped at the hem and soiled.

"This one's head is screwed on backwards," one soldier jeered. "She ran through the line of fire."

"Because I was looking for my mother," the nurse said, her voice breaking.

Close up, Elena saw that her face was stained with soot and tears. And she only had one shoe. "Let go of her," she told the soldiers.

They peered at Bystrov.

A muscle in Elena's jaw twitched in frustration. Her entire uniform could be wrapped in medals and still she wouldn't command the respect of men.

"You heard Comrade Bruskina," Bystrov snapped.

In a huff, they released the nurse's elbows but stayed close.

"Stand back," Elena told them. "Give her some room to catch her breath."

"Whose side are you on?" one soldier hissed.

Elena planted her hands on her hips. "Is she in uniform? Does she have a weapon? Do you feel threatened by her?"

One soldier's chest caved. The other soldier stepped back.

The major gave Elena a nod of approval.

Elena exhaled.

"Ask her why she'd been separated from her mother," Bystrov said, in a steady timbre that calmed Elena's nerves.

Elena posed the question. The nurse raised her wide, icy blue eyes to meet Elena's. "I wasn't with my mother."

"Go on."

"I had orders to escort wounded soldiers from the Vossstrasse to the bomb shelter of the Reich Chancellery."

"Did you get the soldiers to the Chancellery?"

"*Ja*. But when I came out and saw that the shooting had increased, I was worried about my mother. I was on my way to her apartment."

Elena leaned in. "Did anyone talk about Hitler when you were in the Chancellery? Did anybody say where he is?"

The nurse looked back at the soldiers who'd lugged her into the house. She regarded the prisoners standing along the back wall, waiting to be questioned. She touched her hand to her heart. "I overheard soldiers say Hitler was in the underground bunker."

Elena repeated the nurse's words verbatim, to Bystrov.

"Is Goebbels with Hitler?" he asked, his voice clipped.

"I know nothing of Goebbels," the nurse replied.

Elena shook her head.

Bystrov's cheek muscles tightened. "If what she says about Hitler is true, then he's just five hundred meters from the Reichstag. We have to go."

Elena's chest thrummed. She envisioned herself and Bystrov offering the fallen Führer to Stalin like a bottle of the finest champagne, and bolted up the stairs two at a time.

But when she opened the door, she was blocked by a scorching tower of flames.

25

My only desire was to go to the front with a rifle in my hands,
even though I had never hurt a fly until then.

—VERA DANILOVSTEVA, RED ARMY SNIPER

Rzhev, Operation Suvorov

August 1943

Rzhev, a village on the upper Volga River, had been razed by the Wehrmacht and the Red Army, with the Soviets emerging victorious after fourteen months of ruthless combat. Almost all of the shops and buildings had been reduced to piles of bricks, stones, and wood. Elena's skin crawled at the sight of soldiers still lying in battlefields where they'd fallen. Innocent citizens, killed by stray bullets, were splayed on the ground. One young mother had died with her child in her arms. At once, Elena was relieved to be a sniper who killed other armed soldiers, not harmless civilians.

The girls climbed onto the back of an old green truck that didn't look as if it would make it 18 versts, let alone the 243 it needed to go to reach the border of Spas-Demensk, a small town that had been occupied by the Germans for the last two years. There were no seats. The girls had to squeeze onto the steel cargo bed. Still, Elena thought, they were lucky to get a ride at all, with the shortage of trucks. For the remainder of their time at the front, they'd likely be marching hundreds of versts from place to place with other infantry units.

Elena reached into her rucksack for Yakov's coat to use as a seat cushion, but couldn't find it. In a panic, she ferreted through her bag with both hands.

"What's wrong?" Raya asked.

I must have left it on the train, she thought, dejected. "Nothing," she said. How do you tell your armed comrade, on your way to the front, that you depend on an old coat to feel confident, like a baby needs a blanket? You don't dare. Then she remembered putting the feather in her trousers' front pocket. She stuck her hand into the pocket and gave a sigh of relief when she felt the feather's quill. Maybe it was better this way, because nobody would ever notice the feather, nobody would know she needed it. Nobody would know she was weak.

The truck sputtered away from the station. Elena wedged her elbows against the side of the shaky cargo bed to keep steady as they moved through Rzhev. Her stomach pitched. She glanced down at her tunic-clad belly and silently begged it to cooperate. Six hours would feel like a dozen if she had to sit in her own vomit.

She raised her eyes and concentrated on the fleeting scenery to get her mind off her stomach. She saw Russians stooped in front of their destroyed homes, eyes pasted at the ruins, as if they expected something to change. As if they expected a miracle.

"It doesn't seem like a victory," Elena said to Zina, her voice wobbly from the juddering truck.

Zina's brow creased. "What did you expect?"

Elena gestured at the ruined landscape. "Rzhev is gone. We've liberated a village that has been wiped out."

"If the Germans hadn't retreated—"

"I understand why it's a victory," Elena said. "I just don't feel as if we've won, when the people who live here lost everything."

"They still have their land. That's something."

"I suppose," Elena replied, doubtful. Her gaze shifted to the countless Russian bodies lying on the ground. Cannon fodder. Abandoned by their troops as if they were rodents at the side of the road, not humans.

"They'll never be identified," she said.

"Who?" said Tanya.

"All the dead soldiers." Elena paused. "The Bakelite capsules soldiers used to carry, with their name on a slip of paper, were eliminated last year."

"Right," Raya sighed. "I forgot."

"Which means we'll never be identified if we're killed," Tanya pointed out.

"There's nobody left to look for me," Zina said, flatly.

Elena's head dropped. No one would notice if she were killed either. An expression from her favorite Chekhov story, "An Enigmatic Nature," came to mind—"the consciousness of insignificance." Now she knew what Chekhov meant.

"Girls?" Colonel Krupin said, confounded. His whiskered face fell. "They've sent me girl snipers?"

He stood at the door of the two-story wood house near the front where the platoon would be lodged for the night. A shadow from the brim of his cap darkened his eyes.

Auntie Katya stepped forward, saluted the colonel, introduced herself, and said, "Does the enemy see the bullet's shooter before it hits?"

"Of course not," he replied.

"Will a rifle shoot if a girl pulls the trigger?"

"What?"

"I said—"

"I know damn well what you said. Make your point and get on with it, Major Nikiforova," he grumbled.

"I was summoned from the front to oversee the training of these snipers for the last nine months, and I can assure you, they shoot as well as men, some even better."

Elena was afraid for Auntie Katya, standing up to the higher-ranked colonel. She also wanted to hug her.

The colonel clasped his meaty hands behind his back and paced in front of the platoon, shaking his head and muttering, "Girls. Is this some kind of prank? What's next, children?"

"We are Soviet soldiers, not girls," Zina corrected him.

He homed in on Zina with thorny eyes.

Elena was stunned when she saw Zina's bright red hair held off her face with a polka-dot headband.

"Are you unhappy with the Soviet uniform?" he said to Zina.

"Not at all, sir," she replied.

"You realize this is combat, not a dance class."

Zina looked at Colonel Krupin with unflinching eyes. "I hate dancing. I'm here to fight."

Krupin mopped his brow with a handkerchief.

"I'm going to hunt fascists," Raya declared.

"Me too," Tanya added. "And I want people to remember my name, the way people remember Lyudmila Pavlichenko."

"I am fighting for my sister, Masha," Elena heard herself announce for the first time to the whole platoon. She felt liberated, somehow, saying what she wanted, saying her sister's name out loud.

"I am going to kill the fascists who murdered my family," Raya added with great aplomb.

Colonel Krupin looked askance at Raya's guitar, on the ground at her feet.

In one swift movement, without taking her eyes off Colonel Krupin, Raya pulled the strap of her rifle over her head, undid her ammunition pouch, extracted a cartridge, and loaded the magazine.

"See that telegraph pole." She pointed up and to the right.

He flicked his gaze to the pole, ten meters from the house.

"See those loose wires on top," Raya went on.

His eyes followed her outstretched hand.

Raya set the butt of her rifle against her shoulder, peered through the eyepiece, aimed at the wires, and pulled the trigger. Her bullet decimated the wires.

The color drained from the colonel's face.

Raya returned her rifle to her shoulder. She picked up her guitar. "How long until we reach the front?"

Colonel Krupin tugged at the collar of his tunic. "Tomorrow."

He gave a slight nod to Auntie Katya and said, in a conciliatory tone, "Be ready to go at 0340 tomorrow morning."

Elena gazed at Raya with admiration. In the end, she thought, you're distinguished by your actions, not by your words.

Reveille came at 0300 the next morning, far earlier than they'd risen during sniper training. But instead of the usual groans and complaints about the ungodly hour, the girls jumped out of their bunks, already in uniform. They added four leather ammunition pouches to their belts, three grenades, a TT pistol, a knife in a metal sheath, a sapper's spade, a flask of water, binoculars, flashlights with batteries, a flare gun, and a waterproof provisions bag with dry rations for three days, black bread, fatback, and a tin of meat stew.

After washing their hands and faces, the girls devoured bowls of hot buckwheat porridge, a hunk of bread, and tin mugs of sweet tea. The frontline cook had set up six cast-iron ovens on the main level of the house, and her two young subordinates were cutting wood for the ovens, fetching buckets of water, and dragging seventy-kilogram sacks of flour from the outdoor shed into the house. Elena watched the girls toiling in front of the oven, a necessary yet thankless job, and was grateful to be a sniper, even a good-enough corporal.

• • •

Elena clasped her rifle tight while Colonel Krupin went over the frontline rules—don't march in columns; stoop to move, one person at a time; hit the ground if a German Focke-Wulf reconnaissance aircraft was overhead; if you wanted water, go to the nearest shell or bomb crater, as wells were likely poisoned by the Germans.

Her platoon, attached to the 3rd Shock Army's infantry, was on the offensive as part of Operation Suvorov, thrusting the Wehrmacht away from Moscow.

"You need to become all ears and all eyes," Krupin advised the platoon before they set off with an escort to the front. "You're going to start on reconnaissance, to get the lay of the land, but when you begin hunting, remember, one shot only and *always* aim for the head." He brought his lower lip over his upper lip and steeled his gaze. "*Za rodinu, za Stalina!* For the homeland, for Stalin!"

"*Za rodinu, za Stalina!*" Elena echoed, reflexive.

Krupin looked long and hard at the platoon. "Safe return."

"Platoon to arms," Auntie Katya announced.

Elena slipped her thumb under the canvas sling of her rifle and followed a sullen young officer with a hasty gait through the dense pine forest. It was hard to see in the murky darkness, with the half-moon veiled by clouds. The only sound was of their boots scraping the ground.

The officer stopped at a boggy clearing. "We're getting close," he said. "Crawl in pairs from here."

Mud squelched beneath Elena's hands as she crept forward.

There was a whistling noise overhead. Then another. Mortar shells strafed the sky. The girls threw themselves down and covered their heads with their arms.

Shells hit the ground with resounding crashes.

The officer snickered with contempt when the torrent subsided. "Those mortars are nowhere near here."

"What?" Raya raised her head.

"You girls still have a lot to learn," he went on in a patronizing tone. "You need to know how to distinguish, by sound, where mortars are going to land or you'll spend all your time cowering like babies." Raya spat in his direction when he turned around.

"Arrogant windbag," Elena blurted, astonished by her own chutzpah.

The girls chuckled.

The officer halted.

You don't intimidate me, Elena addressed him in her head.

He turned. He rose just enough to see the line of girls. He gave them a look that bristled with revulsion and lust.

Elena swallowed. Very much, she thought. You don't intimidate me very much.

The dugout was built into a grassy hill. A square hole framed with wood marked the entrance. Inside it was larger and more substantial than Elena had expected, about sixteen meters long and more than two high, an underground village with three potbellied stoves, long benches, and walls reinforced by planks. A bathhouse and laundry were located on the far east side; linen was changed regularly to reduce lice infestations. The latrine was in a separate area thirty meters from the dugout.

There was a flagrant reek of dirty laundry, damp wood, and stale smoke. A poster of Stalin hung on a wall at their division's headquarters, in the center of the dugout, where they had gathered to meet their new platoon commander.

A strapping Tatar man with arms too long for his body stood before the girls. A cigarette dangled from the side of his mouth.

"Platoon, this is Comrade Commander Galitsky," Auntie Katya announced. Standing next to Galitsky, she seemed like half a person, not even reaching his shoulder. She turned to him and said with a flourish, "They're all yours."

Galitsky adjusted his cap, then tugged his fleshy earlobe. He spoke in a slow, labored voice that told Elena Russian was not his first language. "We've brought you, along with additional infantry, to the front to help win a summer battle. Since the Germans invaded the Soviet Union, we've never blocked a summer offensive, and they've never blocked us in the winter. It's time to break the stalemate."

Elena, standing at the outer fringe of the group, was overwhelmed by the magnitude of her platoon's mission. She felt like she was in over her head and the dugout was about to collapse around her.

"You have one hour to settle in," the commander went on. "Then you're going on reconnaissance with two scouts, Sergeants Shindel and Konev. For the next couple of days, I want you to study the enemy's defenses, determine their firing points, and identify potential targets. Then locate a secure position to fire from when we begin our offensive."

"Follow Comrade Commander Galitsky to your bunks," Auntie Katya said. "Drop your belongings, clean your rifles, then reconvene back here in one hour, with enough supplies for seventy-two hours."

"One more thing," Galitsky interjected. "When you're out there, stay focused or you'll be dead."

His warning sunk into Elena's bones like frost. She shuffled through a labyrinth of tunnels that branched off from the main path. She felt punchy from hunger and lack of sleep, and the bottom of her left foot ached from blisters because of a wrinkle in her foot wrapping. She trailed the commander as he turned left and continued down a passageway that ended at a fork of new tunnels.

Elena straightened at the sound of a lone male voice. She turned and saw Zina lagging behind the group, chatting with a soldier. She caught Raya's look of exasperation and gave her a sympathetic smile.

"Zina," Raya hissed. "Keep up or you won't know where we're staying."

"Nikolay's a scout," Zina retorted. "It's his job to find people."

"You tell them, sweetheart," the soldier chuckled.

Raya shook her head.

Nikolay whispered in Zina's ear. Her face broke into a smile.

It would be enormously difficult being Zina's partner, Elena thought, forever worrying about what she'd do next, afraid you'd be judged by association.

"What is wrong with you?" Raya said to Zina when they were in their quarters. "You're supposed to be here to fight, not flirt."

"We can't live only for the sake of fighting," Zina argued. "Don't you want to have a little fun now, just in case?"

"Have fun?" Tanya said.

Raya threw her hands up.

Elena didn't like the sound of "just in case." She deposited her overcoat and drawstring rucksack on a birch-slat bunk, sat down, and yanked off her boot.

"You'll change your minds," Zina said. "You'll want your own soldier when you see what Nikolay is going to give me, perfume, real cigarettes, and rose hip tea."

"So now you're for sale," Raya said.

"In combat, everything has a price." Zina's eyes flashed with obstinance. "What if you're killed tomorrow?"

Elena gave a violent shiver, thinking of the dead soldiers strewn across the battlefield in Rzhev. Of Alla. The only certainty in war was uncertainty.

"Maybe Zina has a point," she said, carefully.

"You must be joking," said Raya.

"You don't have to come to my rescue," Zina said to Elena, in a huff. "I'm perfectly capable of handling myself."

"I wasn't—"

"Are you suggesting we all have torrid love affairs with soldiers?" Tanya interrupted.

"No, no," Elena protested. "I just . . . think about Alla, and wonder if she'd still be here if she'd had something to look forward to."

A pall fell over the girls.

Elena's chin dropped. There was no room in the dugout for bitterness. She wanted to make things right between the four of them, but they seemed to have opposite ways of managing the same stress.

"We all have our own ghastly memories," she said finally. "We all have to find ways to manage our pain."

"This is how I cope," Zina said, plainly.

Elena was impressed by Zina's honesty. There was no pretense to her. Zina was who she was. She didn't care what people thought.

Raya's eyes flicked with wariness. "Then be more discreet. Think about the rest of us, not just yourself." She unrolled her overcoat and laid it down on her bunk.

"Forty-five minutes left," Auntie Katya called out from the tunnel.

Elena considered Zina's reasoning as she rewrapped her foot and organized her bunk. She considered why she'd enrolled in the snipers' school in the first place, and had to admit her own rationale was flawed. She'd always claimed it was to avenge the Nazis, but deep down, she knew her decision stemmed from guilt. She was the sole survivor of her family, the last Bruskina. She felt obligated to revolt against the fascists, to do what Masha would have done.

Except I'm not daring like Masha. I so want to be, but I'm not.

26

This afternoon, continuing the fight against Bolshevism to his last breath, our Führer, Adolf Hitler, fell in the battle for Germany at his command post in the Reich Chancellery.
—HAMBURG RADIO STATION BROADCAST, MAY 1, 1945

Potsdamer Platz, Berlin

April 1945

Red Army soldiers swarmed the area, kicking in doors and shooting through windows. The house diagonally across the street was on fire, with flames soaring from the collapsed roof. Elena brought her hands to her face, which was blistering from the heat.

Suddenly the ground rumbled.

"Watch out!" Bystrov grabbed Elena's waist and yanked her back through the doorway of the house where they'd interrogated the nurse.

A Soviet tank on the sidewalk barreled past them. The sidewalk? Gunners on the tank were shooting at the other side of the road.

"On the floor," Bystrov shouted.

Elena dropped to her stomach and cradled her head with her arms. All the prisoners in the cellar would have a decent chance of surviving if the house was bombed. She and Bystrov would most certainly be killed. By their own soldiers. By their own weapons.

Outside, a cannonball hit the ground with a boom, rattling the walls with such force, it felt as if it had landed on the house next door.

When the ground stopped reverberating, Elena lifted her head. She smelled smoke. Bystrov was at the window. She got to her knees and caught Bystrov's eye. He gestured for her to follow him through the door. Keeping low, they made their way along the narrow street. Almost every building was on fire. One crumbled before Elena's eyes, as if it were made of twigs, not thick planks of wood.

A chill came over Elena as they approached a tram that had been shelled. It was eerie, seeing the entire front half-gone. Broken-down cars and mounds of rubble littered the street. Facades stood like black cardboard, ready to fall in a puff of wind. It was like walking through a place that no longer existed. A dead city.

The reek of smoldering wood, metal, and something else Elena couldn't define was overwhelming. And the dust . . . Elena could taste the grit of stones and dirt on her tongue and teeth.

She glanced sideways in the direction of the River Spree, but it was obscured by smoke. She surveyed a pillar splashed with German newspapers. One headline caught her attention: *Russians will never enter Berlin*.

The distinctive roar of a plane's engine took her breath away. She looked up and staggered backwards. A small German plane was rising over the flames and smoke and artillery fire. It flew above the Brandenburg Gate at close to a ninety-degree angle. Soviet spotlights waved back and forth in the sky, illuminating fragments of the plane as it ascended.

"I don't believe it," Elena said.

Her words were overpowered by the hail of gunfire towards the plane, to no avail. The plane deviated left and soared out of the firestorm, disappearing within seconds.

"Hitler," said Bystrov.

Elena lowered her eyes to meet his. "What are you saying?"

"Hitler might have been on that plane."

She returned her gaze to the sky. Spotlights were still shining uselessly, searching for the plane that got away. "The nurse did say he was in the underground bunker, which isn't far from where the plane must have taken off."

"If he was on that plane, it could change everything," Bystrov said, his voice deepening to a hush.

Elena listened to the familiar refrain of clipped gunfire in the distance. She imagined Hitler's evil spreading beyond Germany, beyond Poland, beyond the Soviet Union, infecting the world like the Black Death.

27

My dearest Mum,
I am finally in the front line now. Things are going well. Everyone's
spirit is high. We've been in battle for three days now and we've
won every fight. The Germans run and leave everything behind. I
believe nothing bad is going to happen to me, everything will be okay
in the end.

Kisses, your Natashka

—RED ARMY SNIPER

Edge of Spas-Demensk
August 1943

"Your orders are to advance through no-man's-land and take out the enemy's highest leaders," said Comrade Commander Galitsky, in his languid drawl.

It was 0100 and Galitsky, with his ubiquitous cigarette sagging at the corner of his mouth, was addressing Elena's platoon and six scouts. They'd been on reconnaissance with these scouts for three days and nights, concealed in shell craters and behind dogwood bushes, observing the enemy's various positions and routines. Sentry changes. The location of the headquarters dugout and machine-gun nests. Field kitchen schedules. Officers' habits.

"Don't forget about the medal competition," Deputy Political Instructor Komarov cut in.

In his early thirties, he was scrawny with big teeth and a feverish energy that rankled Elena. But then, she found it hard to like anyone who endorsed the Soviet propaganda machine with such zeal.

"You will receive a medal for eliminating ten enemy soldiers, the Order of the Red Star for twenty, and Hero of the Soviet Union for seventy-five," Komarov explained.

"Lieutenant Lyudmila Pavlichenko killed three hundred and nine fascists, yet she only received a Merit in Battle medal," Zina said dryly.

Komarov glanced sideways at Galitsky, who gestured for the commissar to respond.

Twelve pairs of snipers' eyes ogled Komarov.

"Well, there must be . . ." Komarov replied, his voice detached. "Perhaps Lieutenant Pavlichenko exaggerated her tally—"

"It was published in *Striking the Enemy*, the Red Army newspaper," said a girl called Nedezhda.

"And in *Izvestiya*," Raya added—the newspaper that contained official information from the Soviet Information Bureau.

Elena was pleased by her platoon's show of solidarity.

"If Lieutenant Pavlichenko were a man, somehow I think he would be wearing the Hero of the Soviet Union medal," Zina said.

"That's not true," Komarov sputtered. "You know as well as I do that Article 122 of the 1936 constitution guarantees political, legal, cultural, and economic equality for women."

"In theory," Elena chimed in. "But don't forget about the medal women receive for having ten or more children. This hardly seems fair to men."

The snipers and scouts chuckled.

Komarov's eyes darted around wildly, as if he were looking for an escape.

"I'd prefer women gain the same recognition as men for identical achievements," Elena went on, buoyed by her comrades' encouraging grins.

"Enough," Komarov protested. "You're here to overcome the fascist beast. Not speak with disrespect about our Motherland."

"What about Lieutenant Pavlichenko?" someone asked.

"Why should we care about a medal competition that doesn't award women fairly?" another voice uttered.

Auntie Katya gestured with her hands for everyone to stop talking. "I agree, Lieutenant Pavlichenko has been wronged, but arguing about this with someone"—she glanced over her shoulder at Komarov—"who has no power to do anything about it is a waste of your time and mine."

Komarov's face went scarlet.

"Back to your orders," Galitsky said, firmly. "Stay invisible, get close, and be patient. Only shoot if you're sure you'll hit the target. Then move on." He lowered his voice. "If you make a mistake, it could cost you your life."

Immediately, the banter about the contest was forgotten.

Elena and Tanya were lying on their stomachs in a shell crater three meters from the road, in no-man's-land. It was one thirty in the morning, with ideal conditions for a sniper attack—an overcast sky, the moon's glow obscured, a few stars that gave off just enough light to see yet not enough to draw attention to them, and no wind. The only problems were the stifling humidity and the mosquitoes. It was like breathing sand through a wet cloth.

Elena conducted a visual sweep of the area to see if anything had changed in six hours, a potential sign that fascists were lurking nearby. The field itself was flat and speckled with clumps of dogwood bushes and juniper thickets that would provide good cover for both armies. The lone birch tree at the side of the road appeared to be unchanged, except for the growing puddle of leaves that had fallen to the ground. She focused her binoculars on the tree's canopy. The lowest branch was more than two meters up, too high to climb. Still, you couldn't be too sure. Not when it came to the slimy Germans.

A shrill whistle blew from the enemy's front line.

Bright lights drenched the sky, illuminating no-man's-land. Flares.

"The fascists are saying hello and good evening again," Tanya quipped.

"I wish they weren't so polite," Elena retorted.

A few seconds later, the sky went silent and dark.

"Let's go." Tanya eased herself over the edge of the crater.

Elena heard the rustle of tall grass as other sniper pairs advanced. On their elbows, they moved stealthily towards the enemy's front line, eyes and ears strained for anything unusual. Elena spotted headlights in the distance. She cooed, the sound of a wild dove, the platoon's signal to lay low. A vehicle roared down the road, a jeep from the sound of the engine. Elena waited one minute, then proceeded, knowing the rest of the platoon would follow.

Three minutes later, the enemy set off flares again. Ironically, the instant glow gave Elena and Tanya a superb view of the enemy's frontline trenches. Elena caught the silhouettes of a couple of soldiers standing boldly at the edge of no-man's-land.

"I could get one, then the other," Tanya said. Her rifle was in shooting position. Her eye was pressed against the telescopic sight.

"We're still too far out. We need to get closer."

Tanya plucked her eye from the sight and lowered her rifle. "I know I could get the fascist scum."

Elena wasn't so sure. Although she didn't have Tanya's confidence, she did have a decent memory. And she distinctly recalled, from lectures at the snipers' school, the probability of hitting a person at the distance they were from the enemy's trenches—eight hundred meters—was just one in two.

"We should try to be at least three hundred meters closer," she said. "Your chances of accuracy go up to eighty percent, remember?"

"Those were just estimates," Tanya argued. "It all depends on the shooter."

"And the conditions and the distance."

There was a frigid silence.

"You're right," Tanya sighed. "I just can't wait to start shooting."

"Neither can I," Elena said, apprehensive. She prayed that when the time came, she'd be able to pull the trigger.

During the next respite from flares, Tanya and Elena crept on their stomachs across the road. They moved sideways to the bomb crater they'd discovered the previous night. Elena's hand pressed against something hard and cold. Definitely not a rock. She carefully ran her fingers along the object. She jerked back when her fingertips went over what felt like knuckle bones. It was a hand. A full arm. Attached to a dead German lying on his back. In the dim light, Elena saw that his legs were gone. Her stomach curdled.

She turned away, riven with disgust and compassion. This soldier had died while shooting her comrades. Yet he was a human being. A man fighting for Hitler, who wanted to exterminate Jews. She wanted German soldiers killed but couldn't bear seeing the bodies up close. It became too personal, too difficult to imagine them as the inhuman beasts rendered in Soviet propaganda.

Elena exhaled into the crook of her elbow once they were in the crater. It stunk like rancid meat. Flies buzzed around her irritated scalp. She shooed them away with her hand. She scratched her head. Another cluster appeared. Maybe they were the same flies. Who could tell? She removed her rifle from her shoulder and squinted through the eyepiece of the telescopic sight. She saw threads of smoke spooling from mounds. Dugouts. Wehrmacht soldiers emerging from the largest one. Others going in. A constant stream of soldiers. Headquarters.

"The sentry is pacing back and forth in front of headquarters again tonight," she murmured.

"And the two men coming out right now are officers," Tanya said. "See their chests?"

"Yes." Elena caught sight of their shiny medals. "But we need to move closer."

"The next crater," Tanya agreed.

Just then, a sizzle erupted from the enemy's trenches. A shower of light. Flares.

They pressed themselves against the earth until the sky was black and silent, then slithered over the uneven ground.

"*Denn heute gehört uns Deutschland und morgen die ganze Welt.* For today, Germany is ours and tomorrow the whole world . . ."

Sweat dribbled down Elena's brow at hearing German voices waft through the air like a current. If she was close enough to make out the words, she was close enough to be in their sights. This could be her last night on earth, or the night she opened her tally, she thought as she rolled into the next crater.

"I've got the one on the far right," Tanya was saying.

Elena peered through her sight. She was intimidated by the proximity, by the sudden fear of blowing a man's skull apart, of taking somebody's life.

"Elena? Did you hear me?" Tanya's brash voice cut in.

"I heard you. I've got the one on the left." She adjusted the gun until the horizontal line overlaid her target's head.

"Ready?" asked Tanya.

No, she thought. "Yes."

"On three."

I'm worried I'll make a mistake.

Are you here to shoot or daydream, Cadet Bruskina?

How long should it take to aim?

Eight seconds.

"Three," said Tanya.

SHELLY SANDERS

Elena pulled her trigger. Through her sight, she saw her target turn around. She'd missed.

"I did it," Tanya said, elated.

Elena's heart thudded. "We have to move now."

They scooted right, stopping when they were a couple of meters from their former position. They loaded their rifles and peered through their scopes.

"I'll take the tall one on the left," Tanya said.

"Okay," said Elena.

They counted to three and pulled their triggers.

"I don't believe it," Tanya said. "I got him!"

Elena, discouraged by her own incompetence, couldn't bring herself to congratulate her partner.

"Come on," Tanya said, urgent. "They know where we are. We have to go before they start shooting at us."

Elena nodded and followed Tanya, already slinking back to their front.

Shots whirred overhead. A grenade whistled past Elena's shoulder and exploded a meter away. The ground convulsed, spewing the soil, clay, and stones from below. Elena covered her head with her arms until the storm of debris ended.

"Someone has us in their sights," Tanya said, her voice notched up with fear. "We have to run for it."

"We need to stay low," Elena countered. "Otherwise, when they set off the next flare, we'll be perfect targets."

Tanya looked past Elena, in the direction of the enemy's front line. "All right. But let's move faster."

Elena led Tanya out of the crater. A flare went off. She kept moving. A bullet zoomed over her head with a gale that fluttered her hair. Her heart pumped loud and fast in her ears. They crawled across the road and took cover behind a juniper thicket.

As soon as her feet touched the bottom of their trench, Elena's legs gave way. She collapsed in a heap.

Tanya was hyperventilating. The medic held a paper bag over her mouth and patted her back until her breathing slowed.

"You two put on quite a show."

Elena craned her neck to look up.

Galitsky stood over her, ashes dripping from his cigarette.

"It was Tanya. She opened her tally with three kills."

"Officers," Tanya added.

Galitsky looked at Elena to continue.

"I missed. He moved right when I pulled the trigger."

"It happens. Don't be too hard on yourself. You'll get him next time."

Elena mustered a thin smile. "What if I don't?"

Galitsky didn't answer. He was congratulating Tanya.

28

There is nothing the rabble fears more than intelligence. If they
understood what is truly terrifying, they would fear ignorance.
—JOHANN WOLFGANG VON GOETHE, GERMAN WRITER, 1749–1832

Potsdamer Platz, Berlin
April 1945

Elena was back in the cellar of the Potsdamer Platz house, shouting to be heard over the blare of Red Army tanks demolishing buildings on adjacent streets. Berlin had descended into pandemonium, with civilians huddled underground in subway tunnels, without food and water, while countless Red Army soldiers were looting and raping. Mostly raping. Elena hated herself for looking away. Though she was powerless to stop it, she would live with this regret for the rest of her life.

She and Bystrov still hadn't managed to get anywhere near Hitler's bunker. Lone Wehrmacht soldiers were firing desperately from the Reichstag, and street fighting had spiraled out of control. She was frustrated and exhausted. She'd heard so many conflicting stories about Hitler, she was beginning to wonder if any had a shred of truth.

"The Führer is building a fortress in the Austrian mountains," said the balding soldier in front of her now. "There are bunkers already there and his cars have been sent on too."

"How did you get this information?" Elena asked wearily.

"I overheard the Führer's secretariat on the telephone."

Elena's eyes widened with interest.

After she told Bystrov, he rubbed his chin with his thumb and forefinger and said, "Is Hitler intending to hide out in Austria, or is the purpose to continue fighting?"

The soldier scowled after Elena posed the question. "He was supposed to go on his birthday. With Goebbels. That's what his secretariat said."

Bystrov gave a tight-lipped nod.

"But Hitler's birthday was ten days ago," Elena said to the soldier. "Are he and Goebbels still here or in Austria?"

"I have no idea. I told you everything I know."

"Are you sure?" Elena demanded. "Think back. Is there anything else, any signs of him leaving?"

His eyes glazed over. "I'm just one of the guards. It was only because the secretariat was talking on the phone with his door open that I heard what I did."

Disheartened, she translated the soldier's final information.

"Austria." Bystrov frowned. He gestured for the soldier to be blindfolded, standard protocol, and returned to the makeshift prison, a derelict train station on the other side of the Landwehr Canal.

"At least we know Hitler and Goebbels are traveling together," she said.

"*Could* be together," he corrected her, with reproach. "We can't believe a word that comes out of these tongues. We have to verify everything."

"Of course," Elena replied, chastened. He was right. He was always right.

Bystrov lit a cigarette. He crossed his legs and acted as if he were relaxing at a café.

He's such a hard man to read, Elena thought, exasperated. Purkayev wore his heart on his sleeve, while Bystrov was locked tighter than a bank's safe. The only real thing she knew about him was his extraordinary yearning to capture Goebbels alive. What he planned to do with Hitler's chief propagandist, however, was a mystery.

"We'll have better luck with the next one," Elena said. "It's SS Sturmbannführer Otto Günsche. Hitler's adjutant. He was captured at a brewery in the northeastern part of Berlin yesterday."

Bystrov tapped his cigarette ashes into the glass ashtray on the table.

"This is the first time we've spoken to anyone in Hitler's circle," Elena added.

"He's a glorified secretary," Bystrov scoffed. "He takes notes. He passes on information. He provides security."

"I know but—"

She was interrupted by the door squeaking open. She sat upright and tightened her grip on her pen. Her stomach tensed when she saw Günsche, eyes covered, in handcuffs, being led into the room. Once the rag was removed from his eyes, Elena was disconcerted by his youthful aura, the steadfast eyes that bulged from his long, chiseled face. He could have been one of her fellow university students.

"Let's start." Bystrov nudged Elena with his elbow.

"Right," she began. "Tell me everything you can about Hitler, his plans, where he's hiding, everything you know."

Günsche stared at her with eyes like bullets. "You have to speak up. My eardrums burst a year ago."

She took a deep breath and repeated her questions, loud and firm.

"It's all General Steiner's fault," he sneered.

"What do you mean?"

"My Führer ordered an offensive with General Steiner's army group pushing the Russians back in the south, giving our main army the chance to get to Berlin and organize a new front."

Elena was stunned by Hitler's cruelty. While his own people were cold and starving, while his own soldiers were lying dead on the streets, while boys were being sent into combat on bicycles, Hitler kept throwing soldiers into the fray. It was as if he were trying to plug a leaky dam with paper.

"Preposterous," said Bystrov once she'd translated Günsche's words. "A new front?"

"That's what he says."

"Hitler had to know it was impossible," Bystrov went on, "after we'd crossed the Oder." He glanced sideways at Günsche. "Keep him talking. He knows where Hitler is. I can feel it."

"Why aren't you with Hitler now?" she asked him. "You are his personal adjutant, right?"

Günsche's mouth curled into a haughty smile.

She feared he was stringing them along, saying only what he wanted them to hear. Why wouldn't he lie? Why wouldn't he want to protect Hitler? She planted her forearms on the table. "Tell me the truth."

He leaned forward. "It is impossible to be with Hitler now."

Her nerves pulsed. "Why?"

He looked at her with a contempt that made her want to spit in his face.

"Because Hitler is dead."

29

I thirst, thirst for battle, the heat of battle. I would give everything,
including my life, if only I could satisfy this whim. It torments me.
I can't sleep peacefully.
—ROZA SHANINA, SNIPER WITH FIFTY-NINE KILLS

Spas-Demensk

August 1943

The sun broke through the horizon, casting a lavender-gray
film over the terrain. Red Army bombs rocketed through
the air before falling on the enemy's side with heart-jolting
blasts. The air was scratchy with sulfuric acid and smoke.

Elena and Tanya stood on wooden duckboards in the long, deep
trench, twenty-five meters from the next sniper pair on either side.
Their parapet had been constructed of banked earth, and the rear
edge was elevated to protect soldiers from shells.

Elena held a stick with a helmet above the parapet. A decoy. She
tilted her head so that her ear was just below the parapet and waited.
A German bullet rammed the helmet decoy, knocking it off the stick.
Elena's hand flew backwards. She quickly examined the helmet.
From the sound of the hit and from the location of the bullet, she
calculated the shooter was about eighty meters away at a forty-two-
degree angle. She repositioned herself and peered through her scope.
Spotted a thicket of birch trees with verdant green, sharp-edged

leaves. She narrowed her focus and located the enemy's muzzle at the intersection of two branches. She pulled the trigger. Peered through her scope. The muzzle was still there. Her shoulders tensed with aggravation and embarrassment.

One shot and move on.

She dropped down and edged sideways a couple of meters to change her position. She returned the helmet to the stick and raised it slowly. Waited. And hoped for another chance to prove her worth.

The bombing ended as suddenly as it had begun, followed by an odd and terrifying silence. Elena and Tanya exchanged nervous glances. The lull was short-lived. The fog of smoke hadn't yet dispelled when mortars from the enemy landed in front of the trench. Then came the clatter of bullets. And the unmistakable sound of a tank heaving forward. It was like being in the eye of a storm.

"Weren't we supposed to be on the offensive?" she called out to Tanya. "Weren't our bombs supposed to push the Fritzes back?"

"In theory, yes."

"Fire at the flank of the advancing force," Galitsky announced from the communication passage. "We have to neutralize the machine-gun nests and mortar crews."

A tank emerged through the miasma, spewing bullets towards their trench.

Elena's vision was impaired by the smoke. Which meant the enemy couldn't see her either. She lowered her eyes to determine her shooting line from the iron sights, the gap between the scope and the barrel. Aimed at the tank's eye slots. Held her breath. Pressed the trigger.

The tank kept rolling.

Tanya pulled her trigger. The tank jerked to a stop.

"Another dead fascist," Tanya exclaimed.

Elena tried to summon enthusiasm for her partner but couldn't. She was envious, plain and simple. In her head, she reviewed every step before her shot and concluded that she'd approached the tank the way she faced university exams, with a methodical focus on technique. Not with the hunter's instinct she'd seen in Tanya, Raya, and Zina. Not even with the unharnessed rage she felt towards the fascist parasites who'd murdered her sister.

"God, I wish I was near the enemy's front taking out officers, not stuck in this trench," Tanya muttered. She pulled back the bolt on her rifle to reload.

An incoming mortar shell screeched over their heads. Elena felt the breeze on her forehead before it landed a couple of meters behind them, setting the ground on fire and dousing them with earth and shrapnel. Their comrades in the rear quickly stanched the flames with water.

"Let's drive those Nazis back," Tanya roared, her voice fearless and urgent. "For the Motherland."

The heat of the fire on the back of her neck ignited something inside of Elena. She balanced her rifle on the parapet and looked through her eyepiece. Nothing except whisps of smoke over no-man's-land, barbed wire in front of the Germans' trench, and a few trees and bushes further into enemy territory. Then she caught something in the corner of her eye. A moving bush in no-man's-land. Her heart leapt to her throat. She inhaled. Adjusted her sights. Pulled the trigger. The bush dropped.

"I think I got him," she said, astonished.

"Of course you did." Tanya patted her shoulder. "Now get his credentials."

"But you didn't get any from your kills."

"How could I? They were behind their front line. This one is at our front line. Go. I'll cover you."

Elena hoisted herself up and over the parapet. She pulled back the bolt on her rifle, just in case, and crawled over to the bush, petrified by the relentless chatter of machine guns and rumbling tanks. As she neared the bush, she poked it with her rifle. She caught a branch with the muzzle and dragged it left. The entire bush shifted like a curtain, revealing a dead soldier on his stomach, blood gushing from his neck. Her first kill. A soldier who'd been alive moments ago. A son. Perhaps a husband and father. Her hands held her rifle with a white-knuckled grip. In her mind's eye, she saw Masha writhing from the noose. The agonizing stillness.

She tasted the bile of her stomach in her throat, then forced it back down. She pulled her knife from its sheath, which was attached to her belt. She extracted the soldier's documents from his tunic pocket. She couldn't look at his name or his face. He had to remain anonymous for her to squash the memory into the farthest recess of her brain. She cut off the soldier's epaulette and his Knight's Cross. Finally, she took the soldier's pistol from his holster. In a daze, she returned to the trench and handed the spoils of her kill to Galitsky.

"Congratulations." He examined the documents. "A lieutenant."

"I serve the Soviet Union," she said, reflexive.

Later, as she carved a notch in her rifle to symbolize her first kill, she felt as if she'd crossed a line. She would never be the same. She was overwhelmed by a joy that was steeped in sorrow. She felt untethered.

30

The last time I saw Hitler was at 12 noon on 29 April. I was summoned to the Führer's bunker to fix a malfunctioning ventilator. While doing the job I saw Hitler through the open door of his office.
—WILHELM ZIEHM, TECHNICAL ADMINISTRATOR
OF THE REICH CHANCELLERY

Berlin
April 30, 1945

Hitler is dead.

Günsche's disclosure pealed in Elena's ears like an out-of-tune morning reveille.

"He knows Hitler's location, doesn't he?" said Bystrov.

"Maybe," Elena answered, carefully, "or maybe not."

"What the devil do you mean?"

"How can we be sure he's telling the truth?"

The major threw up his hands. "It's over. Hitler's lost Germany. There's nothing to gain by lying. Hitler can't come after him if he does or says anything against the Party's interest."

She looked at him. "Hitler can't come after anyone anymore."

"What are you talking about?"

"According to Günsche, Hitler is dead."

Bystrov paled. "Why should we trust him?"

"You just said—"

"Ask the question." Bystrov folded his arms over his chest.

"Why should we believe you?" she said to Günsche.

His eyes narrowed to sharp, black points. "Two days ago, my Führer and his wife—"

"What wife?" Elena interrupted. "When did he get married?"

"He wed Eva Braun, his longtime companion, two days ago in the Führerbunker."

"What did he say?" Bystrov demanded.

Elena quickly recapped Günsche's testimony, then asked, "So Hitler got married and then what?"

"They both took their own lives yesterday," Günsche answered, steadfast.

"Both of them? Hitler and Eva?"

"Yes."

"How?"

"My Führer shot himself. His wife took a capsule of cyanide."

She considered his explanation. Was he telling the truth? His aloof demeanor was impossible to gauge. "Did you see them?"

"I did."

"And then?"

"I left."

"You just left?" She was surprised by his total lack of emotion.

"My Führer was gone. There was no reason to stay."

"Where are the bodies?"

"I don't know."

"You expect me to believe you abandoned the Führer's body?"

He stared at her with implacable eyes. "It's the truth."

"What about Goebbels?"

"What about him?"

"Is Goebbels in the Führerbunker?" she pushed, her voice gravelly with exhaustion.

"I am not sure now," Günsche replied, "but he was there with his wife and children."

"My God," Elena said.

Bystrov sat up tall. "What?"

"He claims Goebbels brought his wife and children to the Führerbunker."

"Why does this surprise you?" Bystrov set his elbows down hard on the table. "Goebbels's main concern is for fascism, not family."

Elena mulled this over. "Then you believe Günsche? You believe Hitler is dead and that Goebbels may be in the Führerbunker?"

Bystrov steepled his fingers. "You know we can't take anyone's words at face value. So tell Günsche that as soon as we can get into the Führerbunker, we'll be checking out his story. If we find he's been dishonest, he can expect more time as a guest in one of our prisons. A lot more time."

She repeated Bystrov's warning.

Günsche gave her a malicious smile. She'd never hated anyone more.

31

Wet all through and knee-deep in dirt, we held one another under
the arms not to fall asleep, and, if someone dozed off or fell down,
the comrades walking next to him helped him up.
—NINA LOBKOVSKAYA, RED ARMY SNIPER AND
PLATOON COMMANDER, MEMOIRS

Roslavl Offensive Operation
September 1943

The waxing crescent moon dangled in the black sky like a gold
necklace, elusive and beautiful as peace. And comfort. The
soles of Elena's feet were on fire after marching eighty-nine
versts at a brisk pace. She was pretty sure her shoulder was permanently bruised and dented from the weight of her backpack, which
contained fresh underwear, a gun-cleaning kit, five days of rations,
soap, a toothbrush and tooth powder, and a couple of frontline newspapers. Her platoon was just eleven versts from the Roslavl Front
when they came across the field kitchen, an oven on wheels with hot
pots of pea soup, dry bread, and tea.

Immediately, feverish voices arose.

Elena began to salivate.

"Am I seeing what I think I'm seeing?" Raya said.

"If you see three pots on an oven with wheels, then yes." Elena
stared longingly at the movable kitchen. She was afraid to look away
for fear it would vanish.

"Look at the steam coming from the pots," said Zina.

Elena yanked her canteen over her head and unscrewed the cap. She licked her lips in anticipation of the hot, sweet tea. She was having her monthly, which made her hungrier than usual.

"Fill your mess tins and canteens, then move back into formation," Galitsky announced.

"Why aren't we eating here?" Elena blurted.

Galitsky glared at her. "A full stomach will make you all lazy, too tired to walk the last four versts before the crack of dawn."

"That's ridiculous." She caught Auntie Katya's disapproving gaze and turned away. She was fed up with the military protocol where she had no voice, where orders dictated when she rose, ate, marched, went to the bathroom, and slept.

"Actually, I've heard this theory before," said Tanya.

"That eating makes people sleepy?" Elena said, dubiously.

"Comrade Bruskina," Galitsky began, in a low growl. "It's remarkable how you're never at a loss for words *and* have one of the lowest numbers of kills in the platoon. I wonder if your mouth is getting in the way of your tally."

Her nerves seethed with humiliation. She wanted to disappear.

"Calm yourself," Tanya whispered into her ear.

Elena curled her hands into fists and looked down at her feet.

Tanya grasped Elena's shoulders and steered her towards the queue. "Let's get our rations."

Her comrades were abnormally silent as they filled their mess tins with pea soup and bread, and their canteens with tea. Elena wondered if this was how it would be from then on, an uneasiness around her, the incompetent sniper. She kept her head down so they wouldn't see her tears.

"Galitsky is a bastard," Zina said, as they embarked on the last five-kilometer stretch.

"A fool," Raya exclaimed.

"Thick as two planks," said Tanya.

Elena raised her head.

"An idiot," said a girl called Sheyna.

The insults continued nonstop as the platoon marched up and down the hilly terrain.

Elena's heart filled.

"He's an Ivanushka," said a girl named Anna, using a nickname associated with poor education and sloth-like habits.

"One-and-a-half Ivanushkas," Elena added.

"That's the best one," said Raya, with glee.

"The very best," Zina agreed. "One-and-a-half Ivanushkas."

The pea soup and tea were cold by the time Elena's platoon arrived at the Roslavl Front. A fire couldn't be started to heat the food; that would be tantamount to drawing targets on their heads and inviting a blitz from the Germans. Elena gnawed through her ration of dry bread and drank the liquid from her soup, barely noticing the acrid taste of shrapnel in her food. She saved the solid chunks of her soup for later, though her stomach ached for more.

"You surprise me, Comrade Bruskina."

Elena looked up and saw Auntie Katya. Her beret was pulled back to her hairline and her arched eyebrows made it hard to tell if she was puzzled or mad.

"I've never considered you to be impertinent," Auntie Katya said.

Elena cringed at Auntie Katya's disappointed tone.

"Well?" said Auntie Katya.

"I'm sorry," Elena responded. "I was hungry—"

"Everyone is hungry."

"I know."

"You'll be hungry until the end of this blasted war."

Elena's head drooped.

Auntie Katya knelt down and held Elena's gaze. "It's not just about the food, is it?"

She couldn't respond. She was bloated. Cramps stole her breath with their sharp cuts in her stomach.

"What's wrong?" Auntie Katya asked.

There was a gush of warm blood down her legs; the bandages in her underwear were saturated. They needed to be changed, but there were no fresh bandages left in her platoon, with girls experiencing monthlies almost every day.

"Are you all right?" Auntie Katya pushed.

She closed her eyes and took a deep breath. Exhaled. Another inhale. Another exhale. The pain began to subside.

"Elena?"

"What if I'm not meant to be a sniper?"

"None of us were born to be snipers," Auntie Katya said, reflective. "We are here because our Motherland chose us to stop a brutal dictator from destroying our land and people."

Her explanation bounced uncomfortably in Elena's mind. "I don't believe I was chosen. I'm too slow, I miss too many chances, and—"

"You are a good sniper," Auntie Katya said with reproach. "But you think too much before you shoot."

"That's why I have the lowest tally. You heard Galitsky."

"I did. And while I don't agree with the way he singled you out, I also know it won't do you or your comrades any good if you waste time and energy being angry. You are just one person in a platoon and must respect your comrades with every word you speak and every action you take."

"Which is why I should leave. Let someone better take my place."

"There is no one better." Auntie Katya leaned forward, propping her elbows on her knees. "You are your biggest problem. You have to stop doubting yourself and start recognizing your own value. You need to be more confident."

"You really think I can increase my tally?"

"I know you can. Galitsky knows you can. Do you?"

Elena recalled her missed shots. She knew exactly what she'd done wrong. "Yes. I do."

"Good." Auntie Katya rose. "Without hard work, you won't even get a fish out of a pond."

Elena forced a smile at the well-worn proverb, one of the many sayings ground into children's minds as part of the official school curriculum. She lay on her stomach and began digging with her spade to entrench herself. And even though she didn't like the adage Auntie Katya had uttered, she couldn't keep the words from drowning out all the other notions in her head.

Several hours later, at 0500, the brightening sky cast an incandescent glow over the white birch trunks. Elena peered through her binoculars and saw the German-occupied town of Nevel spread out before her, flat as blini, low-lying clouds black at the bottom edges, as if they'd been charred by gunfire. Skeletal trees, tall and straight, stood at attention.

Elena's platoon, attached to the 3rd Shock Army, had been ordered to attack Nevel, on the western edge of the Soviet Union, to clear the way for upcoming offensive actions in Belorussia and the Baltics. Now, she estimated their distance to the enemy's line. One hundred and seventy-five meters. Give or take. She shifted sideways until she was behind a dense row of soaring birch trees.

"This is as good a spot as any," she said in a low voice.

In answer, Tanya began digging a berm.

Elena, on her stomach, inserted a cartridge into her rifle's chamber and laid it on her right side. With her left hand, she grabbed her spade from her belt and thrust the sharp head into the black earth. She heard the crunch of the spade and was back in the ghetto.

Don't shove sand in our eyes!

Footfalls marching from the gates.

The blast of gunshots.

The ground spun around her. She dropped the spade and clutched her head to stop the spinning.

"You all right?"

Tanya's muffled voice sounded far away.

Don't shove sand in our eyes!

Elena saw the children's hands rising from the pit. The candies falling from the German soldier's hands like sleet.

"What's wrong?"

Hands grabbed her shoulders and shook the memory out of her.

Tanya's worried face emerged. "Where were you?"

"What?" Elena managed.

"All of a sudden you stopped and had a strange look on your face."

"Strange?"

"Like you were someplace else, someplace bad."

The pit flickered before Elena's eyes. She pinched them shut.

"You're shaking," said Tanya.

Elena opened her eyes. She saw her partner. She saw the flat terrain. Her spade on the ground. The partially dug berm. She turned. "Let's finish digging."

"Do you want to talk about it?" Tanya asked, gently.

Elena paused. Though she'd told her comrades about Masha and her family, she'd never spoken about the children and the pit. She kept hoping the images and sounds that plagued her would eventually fade if she buried what she'd seen and heard.

"I need to keep busy," she told Tanya.

Something rustled behind them.

Elena seized her rifle and spun around.

Stay focused or be dead.

Overhead, a birch branch swayed. Her pulse raced. She aimed her rifle at the branch. She put her finger on the trigger. All of a sudden, sparrows winged from the tree. She gasped in relief. Lowered her rifle. Caught Tanya's startled expression.

"Sorry," she said.

"Don't be. You didn't shoot."

But she'd come close.

"Imagine being able to fly away from danger," Tanya said, squinting at the flock of small, identical gray birds overhead.

Elena viewed the sparrows billowing through the sky with an astonishing grace. It was like watching the air breathe in and out.

"My father loved sparrows because they ate the locusts that would have devoured our crops," Tanya went on. "They kept us from starving to death."

"They're small but mighty," said Elena, as the small birds faded quietly into the distance. She heard the chink of a spade breaking up the earth and saw Tanya excavating her foxhole. She resumed digging, while keeping watch on the forest. She scrutinized the area for changes that might indicate hidden enemy soldiers. A shrub in a different place. A mound of leaves in a different shape. Branches on the ground that had moved.

In the distance, she heard a guttural bark.

A German Alsatian?

Another raucous bark.

It sounded more ferocious than a dog, even the wolflike Alsatian. It was getting louder. Closer. She dropped her spade.

Then the squash of feet over fallen, dry leaves.

She pointed the barrel of her rifle in the direction of the bark. Brought her finger to the trigger. Jerked backwards at the sight of a deer loping through the trees. A harmless roe deer that barked like a dog when startled.

She wilted.

"What's wrong?" Tanya asked. "I've never seen you so jittery."

The words dangled from the edge of Elena's tongue. The pit. The children. Masha. The ghetto. But she couldn't bring herself to say them out loud.

"Is this about Galitsky?" Tanya continued. "Because if you're upset about him, don't be. He never should have spoken to you like that, in front of everyone."

Elena heaved a sigh of relief. It would much simpler to blame her bad nerves on Galitsky.

"Nobody takes Galitsky seriously," Tanya went on. "You know that. You know we're all behind you."

"I do," Elena acknowledged. "But he was right. I do need to improve my tally."

Tanya gave her a vague smile and looked off.

She has no faith in me, Elena thought, dismayed. My own partner.

32

This afternoon, continuing the fight against Bolshevism to his last breath, our Führer, Adolf Hitler, fell in the battle for Germany at his command post in the Reich Chancellery.
—GERMAN RADIO BROADCAST, MAY 1

Berlin
May 1, 1945

The red flag waved gloriously over the Reichstag's demolished facade while the Russian national anthem played loudly through adjacent speakers. Chunks of the former government building lay on the road, symbols of the fallen Wehrmacht. White sheets drooped from windows of the few buildings that remained standing. And yet . . . reckless SS regiments kept shooting in the streets and in the Chancellery. Therefore, Soviet rockets continued to fall.

The Germans had offered a ceasefire, but the Soviets wanted an unconditional surrender. And Hitler. Stalin was adamant. In a message sent to Bystrov, he'd made it plain he didn't trust the German propaganda announcing the Führer's suicide.

Elena was in the kitchen in a house by the Anhalter train station. She was going through her notes for the hundredth time, searching for clues, words she might have missed that would offer a clue to Hitler's whereabouts. She put a sugar cube in her mouth and sipped her tea. Her handwritten words had become blurry. She rubbed her tired eyes. Her eyelids fell shut. Her head grew heavy. She felt herself sway back and forth.

"Comrade Bruskina!"

Elena jolted upright at Bystrov's abrasive voice. Her left hand sprang out, knocking over her cup of tea. Her eyes flew open. "Oh no!" Tea spilled all over her notes. She grabbed the pages and waved them in the air to dry them.

"You're a mess," said Bystrov.

Elena glanced down. She had tea all down the front of her tunic, right next to a nasty borscht stain. Embarrassed, she shrouded the spots with her good arm.

"Try to find a clean tunic and meet me in the interrogation room in ten minutes," he went on.

"Why? Do we have someone big?"

"Perhaps." He turned on his heel.

"Who?"

"The mechanic," he called out over his shoulder.

The mechanic? Elena sighed. Another dead end.

Karl Schneider, Hitler's mechanic, appeared to be in his mid-forties and had a double chin that wiggled when he talked. He said he couldn't remember the day he got an important telephone message from Hitler's secretariat. Elena was frustrated. Hitler had been surrounded by officers and administrative staff. Why was it so hard to find one person who knew definitively what had happened to him?

"I don't care if he can't remember the day he got the call," said Bystrov, terse. "He worked in the Chancellery. Let's just see what else he has to say."

Elena's expression dulled. "What did the secretariat tell you?"

"It wasn't the secretariat directly," Schneider explained. "The secretariat told the telephone operator, who told me."

Elena scratched her head. "Okay then, what was the message?"

"He ordered me to bring all the petrol I had to the Führer's bunker."

Elena's eyes sparked with interest. "*Bienzin?*" she said, repeating "petrol" in Russian.

"What about *bienzin?*" said Bystrov.

Keeping one eye on Schneider, Elena told Bystrov what he'd said.

The major leaned forward. "How much *bienzin?*"

She repeated Bystrov's question.

"Eight cans," Schneider said. "And each can has twenty liters of petrol."

"One hundred and sixty liters," Elena told Bystrov.

"A bit later," Schneider added, "the secretariat, I mean the telephone operator, said I needed to send firelighters. So I sent eight."

"And eight firelighters," Elena said to Bystrov.

"Ask if he saw Hitler in the last few days," said the major.

Schneider shook his head, no. "But his chauffeur told me the Führer was dead."

Elena went still. She relayed this news to Bystrov. His eyebrows shot up.

"What do you think?" he asked her.

"I think he may be telling the truth. Why would he make up a story about *bienzin*, or the chauffeur saying Hitler was dead."

"And this morning, right before I was released from my duty, I got another call from the operator, looking for more petrol," the mechanic was saying. "I managed to get another four cans by siphoning it from cars in the Chancellery."

"Someone burned bodies," Bystrov murmured, "of people who didn't want to be identified."

"We need a witness to back up Schneider's statement," Elena said.

"I hope it's not too late," Bystrov said. "I hope there are living witnesses, or that we find some kind of physical evidence."

Elena wasn't optimistic. A hundred and sixty liters of petrol plus another eighty would create a massive fire. There was a very real possibility they'd find nothing but ashes.

33

Nina Lobkovskaya has a sharp eye and a steady hand. Her rifle never misses. Dozens of Nazis have been sent to kingdom come by the fearless lady sniper.

—RED ARMY FRONT NEWSPAPER

Roslavl Offensive Operation

October 1943

The signal to attack—a tawny owl's shrill cry from Lieutenant Nina Lobkovskaya, who had an uncanny knack for making animal sounds—came just before sunrise. All at once, the infantry opened fire. A cacophony of bullets. Submachine gunners emptied magazines with a scathing, urgent tempo. Mortars whooshed through the air, hitting the enemy's trenches with a resounding *ka-ching*.

Elena and Tanya were hiding behind an abandoned Wehrmacht tank that had gotten stuck in the mire. She peered through her scope at the enemy's front line. Glimpsed rows of barbed wire separated by Bruno spirals, coiled wire that expanded like an accordion and stretched over stakes to obstruct the Kalinin Front. But we have to get through, Elena thought, determined. If we don't advance, the Wehrmacht could get dangerously close to Moscow. Beyond these barriers, she spotted two black helmets bobbing over the trench's parapet.

If you chase two rabbits, you will not catch either one.

Timur's words rang in her ears as she plunked her elbows in the cold, muddy ground. She aligned one target's head in the crosshairs of her scope. Inhaled. Pulled the trigger. The soldier's helmet flopped sideways. She trembled violently. Her gut stirred with relief and hunger for another kill. To prove her worth to Galitsky. To show her comrades she wasn't a broken limb in their platoon.

"Over there!" Tanya pointed to a thicket of cedars ten meters on Elena's right.

Elena, keeping low to the ground, led the way. German bullets started flying in their direction, hammering the steel tank. Mortar shells landed, creating tornadoes of smoke. She inhaled the metallic whiff of fiery shells and panicked, realizing she was out in the open and could no longer see the cedars through the burgeoning smoke. *Focus or be dead.* She estimated the location of the cedars and crept forward. Bullets zoomed over her head. A grenade whistled through the air.

"Forward! For the Motherland!" Galitsky shouted from somewhere in the haze.

His deep-timbred voice lifted Elena's spirits. She slunk onward, then plunged headfirst into a shallow bomb crater before gagging on a mouthful of swampy water.

"Whoa!" Tanya cried.

Elena glanced up.

Tanya landed with a splash beside her. Coughed up water. "What happened?" she said, testy.

"I couldn't see," Elena snapped. "It was too—"

The boom of a nearby German mortar cut her off. Elena was thrown against the side of the crater. Time crawled. Her head spun. The noise receded to a dull buzz. She was mesmerized by smoky black particles billowing in the milky gray sky.

"Elena! Elena!"

Tanya's pleading voice tunneled into her ears.

"Let's go!" Tanya shook Elena's shoulders.

Elena felt unstable on her feet.

Tanya's voice rang in her ears: "We have to get out of here."

Elena tasted the muck on her tongue. The crater. She was in the crater. The air had dissipated slightly, enough that she could see the smudge of the cedars. She climbed out and, as bullets volleyed overhead, skimmed the ground on her stomach. She heaved a sigh of relief when they took cover behind the cedars.

Elena scanned the area. From the corner of her right eye, she saw a branch shift. An enemy sniper? She swung around to point her rifle at the branch. The branch wavered. She brought her finger to the trigger. Jerked back at the sight of a girl in her platoon. Chava. A long-limbed eighteen-year-old from Moscow.

"What are you doing?" Elena hissed. "I thought you were the enemy."

"Galitsky was shot," Chava said.

"No," Elena whispered.

"Impossible," said Tanya.

"Is he—"

"Dead." Chava finished Elena's sentence. "He was defending three wounded machine gunners and . . . it happened so fast . . . he was down. A bullet in his chest."

Chava's news staggered Elena. "I just heard him. He ordered us to advance."

"It only takes a second to die," Tanya said, her voice hollow.

"He was a hero," Elena said, distraught. She felt as though she was sinking without Galitsky holding her up, pushing her to work harder, to be better. She'd never get the chance to make him proud of her. She hadn't known, until it was too late, how much she needed him.

"Where's Bella?" Tanya asked.

Anguish crossed Chava's face.

Tears stung Elena's eyes. She hadn't known Chava's partner Bella very well, but they'd been comrades just the same.

"We must get revenge for Galitsky," Tanya said. "Today. Now."

"I'm ready," Elena heard herself say, with resolve.

"For Galitsky," Tanya said.

"And for Bella," Chava added.

"For Bella," Elena said.

"Let's spread out," Tanya suggested, "and try to get a hundred meters from the enemy's front line."

Tanya sidled left on her stomach.

Chava began moving straight ahead.

Elena edged sideways to the right, until she and Chava were about twelve meters apart.

Mortar shells somersaulted through the air. One landed a few meters ahead of Elena, the soil erupting like a volcano. Elena's heart thumped in her ears. She kept going. Another shell blasted a grove of trees on her right. The dirt turned to charred grass as she drew closer to the enemy's frontline trench. The grass crackled as she moved.

She heard Germans speaking in hushed tones. She couldn't make out what they were saying. In one swift motion, she loaded her magazine and positioned the heel of her rifle against her shoulder. Through her scope, she spotted tiny red points that glowed. Cigarettes. Her face tightened with concentration. Contours of faces appeared as the Germans smoked. She centered one in her scope and pulled the trigger. He went down like a stone.

That's for Galitsky.

She loaded another cartridge. Aimed. Fired. Another one down.

For Bella.

She kept loading, aiming, shooting. Three. Four. Five. Six. Nine.

For Masha, Mama, Papa, Yakov, Mr. Volkhov, Mrs. Drapkina, one of her daughters.

The horizon glimmered as the sun poked up. Not much time left.

Daylight is your enemy, Galitsky would say.

I can't stop now, she addressed him in her head. I need two more for Mrs. Drapkina's other daughters. And I need to make up for the ones I've missed. She slathered mud over her face and forage cap. Stuck old leaves and twigs to the mud on her cap and face. Slowly she moved forward until she was just sixty meters from the enemy's front line.

She did a visual sweep of the area through her scope. Saw a shell hit a fascist as he was approaching his trench. He was blown to pieces.

Her rifle shook in her hands.

Masha wouldn't stop now.

Focus or be dead.

She peered through her scope and couldn't believe her eyes when she saw the backs of German soldiers scrambling from the trenches. Retreating. She loaded, aimed, and fired. Right between the shoulders. The soldier dropped instantly. Ten.

For Mrs. Drapkina's middle girl.

As the sky brightened, the second line of trenches grew visible. She caught the unmistakable glint of helmets at the parapet. Dammit. The fascist scum were still fighting back.

A swooshing noise caught her attention. She looked left. A Red Army scout crawled by, pulling a captured Nazi bound in waterproof capes.

A German bullet zinged past Elena's ear. She went flat. She slithered over the ground.

A shell whistled overhead. The crack of an enemy's bullet on her left. A second crack. Then nothing. She took a breath and howled like a wolf, the signal asking comrades to reply with the same sound, to confirm they were safe. Not a peep, except for bursts of gunfire. She tried again, this time a smidge louder. Still no reply. Something was wrong. She crawled sideways on her elbows, bracing herself for the worst. Hesitated when nearby comrades set off a storm of machine-gun fire. The enemy retaliated with a short round of bullets. Then a heavy silence.

"We've pushed them back!" a shrill voice cried in Russian.

"For the Motherland!" shouted another.

"For Stalin!" someone else yelled.

There was the drumming of feet as Elena's comrades ran towards the Germans' empty frontline trenches. Elena took a deep breath and continued moving left until she heard the rattling noise of someone struggling to breathe. She followed the sound, which led her to a clump of bushes. She moved closer with her finger on the trigger. She lowered her rifle when she saw Chava lying on her side, one hand over her bleeding shoulder.

Chava gawped at Elena with frightened eyes. "They caught Tanya."

34

I shuddered, but I was not frightened, and not only because we had seen so many terrible things in four years of war, but rather because those charred remains did not seem human: they seemed satanic.

—YELENA RZHEVSKAYA, RED ARMY INTERPRETER

Berlin
May 1945

Four columns flanking the entrance of the Reich Chancellery loomed in front of Elena and Major Bystrov. They were on foot as the mounds of concrete and metal debris made it impossible to access by vehicle. Black dust motes shadowed the ruined facade like specters. Only the outside walls of the Chancellery had survived, and they were pockmarked from shells and shrapnel. Ironically, the eagle with a swastika in its talons, the ominous symbol of Nazism, still hung above the main double doors, just over five meters tall. Altogether, the exterior was severe and formidable.

Elena and Major Bystrov had been ordered to inspect the Chancellery and the Führerbunker. It was disconcerting, being so close to the place where Hitler had led the Nazis, walking on the same ground as the man who'd planned to eradicate Jews.

They entered the Chancellery garden through the Reichstag, now a veneer of pretension with photographers, journalists, and newsreel reporters talking to soldiers and filming the environs. Elena stepped gingerly through the wreckage, unable to keep her eyes from darting in every direction. She couldn't believe she was actually there, in Hitler's fallen monument to himself. It felt like some bizarre dream. Except for the smashing sound of her feet walking over broken glass. And the buzz of voices. And the flash of cameras.

The gardens, hidden from public view in a brick-walled courtyard, looked as if tanks had rolled through, churning up the soil, grass, trees, and whatever else used to exist in the space. There were deep craters from mortar shells. Scorched branches were strewn underfoot. Random piles of brick, stone, glass, and dirt were scattered on the earth, black with ashes.

More reporters as well as members of the 3rd Shock Army were already in the garden, inspecting the grounds and the underground bunkers where Hitler and his staff could still be hiding. Elena's heart raced with anticipation. What if they found witnesses who knew exactly where Hitler was? Even better, what if they found Hitler alive?

A whistle yanked her mind from what-ifs.

"Got something!" A soldier at the far-right edge of the garden shouted.

Elena rushed over. She heard the click of cameras. Felt her privacy erode when lenses turned on her.

A stocky officer with shiny brown hair combed across the top of his head stood in front of the bodies. He regarded Major Bystrov and quipped, "It's about time."

"It wasn't exactly a drive through the park," Bystrov retorted.

They shook hands with the familiarity of longtime comrades. Elena stepped aside. She felt like an intruder, hearing the two men share accounts of their experiences since their last meeting. She missed the rest of the girls. She wondered if they'd meet up after the war and reminisce. She wondered if they'd ever see one another again.

Bystrov introduced the shiny-haired officer as Colonel Gorbushin.

"The colonel is the third and final member of our counterintelligence group tasked with finding Hitler," Bystrov explained.

Elena bristled under the colonel's intense stare. She saluted him. His patrician nose was skewed, as if it had once been broken, and he was taller than the major, with folds of skin beneath small, leafy green eyes. He pointed at two charred corpses.

Hitler and his wife? Elena plugged her nose to keep out the indescribable whiff of burnt flesh and bitter almonds. The telltale odor of cyanide.

Bystrov stood motionless, his eyes riveted to the bodies. He looked deflated.

"What's wrong?" Elena moved closer to the remains. Her knees wobbled. Her stomach heaved from the stench, even with her nostrils plugged. "Is it Hitler?"

The colonel shook his head. He pointed at the taller corpse's left leg.

Elena spotted a charred metal prosthesis and an orthopedic boot.

"Goebbels," said the major, his voice low and flat.

"Right." Elena remembered that Goebbels had limped.

"And Magda, Goebbels's wife," added the colonel, in a somber tone. He picked up one of the two Walther pistols lying beside her. Held it up and squinted. "Hasn't been fired." He grabbed the other pistol. Looked it over. Shook his head.

Something bright caught Elena's attention. Goebbels's yellow tie, still around his singed neck like a noose. Oddly, it had survived the fire. Her spine went stiff with revulsion. The tie reminded her of the hideous yellow star Jews were forced to wear, the star that Goebbels had created to identify Jews, to brand Jews like cuts of meat in the butcher shop.

". . . wasn't enough *bienzin* to incinerate the bodies," the colonel was saying.

"Not enough *bienzin*?" Elena exclaimed. "Where did it all go?"

"What do you mean?" said the colonel.

Bystrov filled him in with the amount of *bienzin* sent to the Führerbunker, according to the mechanic.

The colonel shaded his eyes with his hand. He surveyed the gardens. "There have to be more bodies here, with that much *bienzin*."

Elena's heart sank. She had a feeling that Hitler's remains were nearby, which meant returning to the Kremlin in defeat.

The major ordered a couple of sentries to load Goebbels's blackened corpse onto a door that had been blasted out of the Chancellery. He beckoned for Elena and the colonel to follow as he escorted the sentries carrying Goebbels from the garden to Wilhelmstrasse.

"If I couldn't capture him alive, at least I can vilify his corpse in public," Bystrov said to Elena.

Newspaper reporters snapped photos of Goebbels and asked the major for comments, which seemed to invigorate his mood. Others shot newsreels of the body and the crowd circling around the corpse.

Elena was struck by the combination of Goebbels's hideous body in front of the desecrated Reich Chancellery, the building Hitler had custom-built, with no expense spared, to showcase Germany's wealth and power. Now Goebbels symbolized the collapse of the Third Reich.

Then she remembered. "What about their children? Goebbels had six children. Where are they?"

35

They also had two soldiers at the machine gun point. They were cleaning something. I shot and he fell down on the machine gun. They pulled him aside by his feet. I despised him for being an enemy . . . but he was also a human . . . I couldn't even eat dinner that night.

—KLAVDIYA KALUGINA, RED ARMY SNIPER

Roslavl

October 1943

They were buried together in the black earth. Galitsky. Bella. Three infantrymen. One machine gunner. Their bodies would lie forever in the ground at the edge of Roslavl. The 3rd Shock Army's infantry honored their sacrifices with a rifle and submachine-gun salute. Officers shot their pistols into the gilded late-afternoon sky. Members of the burial detachment planted wooden crosses in the mounds of dirt.

What about Tanya? How do we pay tribute to our missing comrade?

Elena's gaze lingered over Bella's grave. She was overwhelmed with guilt for being alive. Bella was a much more competent sniper, with thirty-one kills compared to her own tally of eleven. Bella would have continued to kill Nazis at an astonishing rate, had she lived. But she was dead. Like Masha. That was what Elena couldn't reconcile in her mind, why one person lived while another died. If there was a

God, why wouldn't he choose the strongest to live, the ones with the greatest potential to conquer evil?

"Our comrades have not died in vain," said Lieutenant General Purkayev. "In one day, we have increased our salient to twenty-eight versts in width and twelve versts deep. In one day, we have destroyed scores of fascists." He looked over at the snipers. "You women fought valiantly with the men. I am impressed with your courage under fire, your shooting expertise, and your devotion to Stalin and the Mother-land. That's why I am awarding the women's sniper platoon with the Guards Company designation for excellence in battle."

Elena was stunned. Soldiers with Guards Company status received double pay, better clothing, equipment, and food, and best of all, Chava could return to their unit once her shoulder healed. Otherwise, she would be shunted from one unit to another after medical leave. Being part of a Guards unit offered a rare stability within the Red Army, the chance to stay with your comrades until the end of the war.

Purkayev nodded at Auntie Katya, standing behind him. She stepped forward with an ear-to-ear grin. Purkayev cleared his throat and began calling out names. One by one, the snipers saluted him, then stood before Auntie Katya, who pinned the Guards badge on the right side of their tunics, below the epaulette.

"Elena Bruskina."

In a daze, Elena approached Lieutenant General Purkayev. Close up, she noticed his prominent cheekbones and an unruly cowlick where he parted his rust-colored hair, on the left side of his temple. He also had a scar across his chin, an upside-down smile. Reflexively, she touched the bumpy scar on her cheek, from the broken window in Minsk. The last day of Masha's life. Her knees felt weak. From the corner of her eye, she caught Auntie Katya giving her a toughen-up-or-else glare. She braced herself and saluted Purkayev.

"For the Motherland," he said.

She was enthralled by the flatness in his tone. Not a spec of the patriotic zeal that typified commanders.

"You earned this," Auntie Katya whispered. She pinned the coveted badge, a gold wreath with a red star in the center and a red flag on top, on her tunic.

Elena brushed the tip of her finger across the word *Guards* printed in gold on her badge. Her chest simmered with pride. She observed the row of snipers, all displaying the same badge, and was moved by a heady sense of comradeship. For the first time since arriving at the front, she felt equal, as though her lower rank no longer mattered.

"Comrade Commander Galitsky died protecting his soldiers," Purkayev declared, once all the snipers had received their badges. "He died a hero. And Comrade Sergeant Bella Dralyuk killed thirty-one Nazis before giving her life to the Motherland. For their loyalty and courage, both will posthumously receive the Order of the Red Banner."

He'd hardly gotten the words out of his mouth when a tremendous applause burst forth. Elena clapped her hands together vigorously, swept up in the euphoria. Then, as the applause began to ebb, she turned to look at Tanya. Except she wasn't there.

Getting captured was akin to being disloyal to Stalin and the Motherland. Even if she miraculously survived the fascists, Tanya would be executed, without a trial, by her own Red Army as punishment for allegedly revealing military secrets to the enemy.

"Comrade Sergeant Zina Gofeld is also awarded the Order of the Red Banner for her impressive twenty-one kills over two days here," Purkayev continued, "bringing her tally to forty-seven."

A camera's bulb flashed at Zina. A white flare that blinded Elena, standing behind her. For a second, all Elena could see were white spots. Then, as her vision improved, she saw that a gawky reporter with rimless spectacles and round shoulders had squeezed himself in between Zina and Raya. He'd been hanging around more than any of the other journalists lately, watching Zina with barefaced admiration.

Elena gave Raya a knowing look. The Order of the Red Banner and a photo in the newspaper would inflate Zina's already large ego to an unbearable size.

"... Lieutenant Nina Lobkovskaya."

Elena jerked upright at Nina's name and the subsequent applause. "What's going on?" she whispered to Raya.

"Nina is our new platoon commander."

"You mean, she's replacing Galitsky?"

Raya turned her shoulders so that she was clapping in Elena's face. "Is something wrong with your ears?"

"No, it's just . . ." Elena was astonished. A female platoon leader? When the war began, women weren't even allowed to join. Now, two short years later, she was in an all-girl snipers' platoon with a female leader. Tanya would have been so excited. But looking forward, Elena felt only a cold and brutal weariness. She was tired of wet feet, bad food, bugs, and the sight of blood. She was tired of being with people night and day, of putting herself out there, of losing the ones she loved most.

Nina faced the regiment. The whites of her eyes flared. "*Za rodinu, za Stalina!* For the homeland, for Stalin!"

"*Za rodinu, za Stalina!*" Zina cheered, setting off a rowdy ovation from both the men and women.

In an instant, the mood switched from melancholy to joyful. The journalist snapped photos and interviewed Purkayev, then Nina, who seemed uncomfortable with all the attention. Meanwhile, Zina was in her glory, holding court with a number of doe-eyed soldiers.

Elena joined Raya, who was sitting cross-legged on the ground strumming her guitar. Raya began to sing "Meadowlands," about girls pining for their boys off to war.

Elena opened her mouth to join in, but the words were stuck in her throat. She wondered how her comrades could sing so soon after burying one of their own. And what about Tanya?

"You look like you could use this."

Elena spun around.

A lean soldier with bushy whiskers sat down and thrust a tin mug at her. "Vodka?"

She eyeballed him, skeptical. Men in the army went out of their way to be nice to women for one reason.

"Comrade Lieutenant Stepan Yurovsky, 3rd Shock Army."

She spotted three gold chevrons on his sleeve. First lieutenant. Impressive. Intimidating.

"Elena," she managed.

"Elena . . ." he prodded.

"Bruskina." She tensed as his hard eyes fell on the epaulette that branded her as a lowly corporal.

"Here." He held the tin of vodka closer. "It'll calm your nerves."

"Who said my nerves need calming?"

"Your shoulders. They look stiff as iron."

Elena smiled despite her resolve to be aloof. "That's because I have plywood in my *pogony* to keep them from bending." She tapped her left shoulder. "See?"

He looked at her, astonished. "Doesn't it hurt when you're carrying your rifle?"

"My bones are getting used to it," she lied.

"You know it would be a lot more comfortable if you just pressed them every day."

"Who has time to press shoulder pads?"

"Do you enjoy crushing your shoulder bones when you're on a long march?"

"Why do you care about my bones?"

His eyes flickered with amusement. "Who said I cared?"

She couldn't believe how cheeky she was being with a superior officer.

"To bones." Yurovsky took a swig of vodka and handed the cup to Elena.

"To bones," she echoed. "And to becoming a Guards Company."

She took a sip and felt a pleasant tingle of warmth course through her veins. The cup of vodka was heavier than she'd expected. There had to be three hundred grams, at least. A lot more than the daily authorized one hundred grams. "How did you get so much?"

"Friends in high places," he said, his eyes holding her gaze like magnets.

She flashed him a wry smile. "Or the higher the rank, the greater the vodka."

"That too." He grinned.

She relished the slow burn as the vodka spilled down her throat. She drank it all, more than she'd ever had at one time, and soon felt giddy and light and happy.

Yurovsky moved in closer until their shoulders touched. She liked the warmth of him against her. The tobacco scent on his breath. The tickle of his whiskers on her cheek. He draped his arm over her shoulder.

She sagged against his sturdy frame, relieved to have someone to lean on. It had been ages since she'd had anyone to hold on to. Sitting there with him, beneath the vast sky, with Raya's evocative voice resonating through the air, she wanted to cling to the moment.

"Let's go for a walk."

Elena swayed at Yurovsky's breathy voice in her ear. She felt a strange, primeval throbbing sensation within her.

He stood and pulled her up. It felt like the ground was swirling beneath her feet. She stumbled.

"Careful." Yurovsky wrapped his arm around her waist to keep her steady and led her away from the exuberant crowd.

"I feel so good right now," she laughed.

He mumbled.

"What?" She glanced at him. In the buttery twilight, he was out of focus, a smudge of whiskers and eyes that were off center.

"Have some more." He unscrewed the cap of his canteen and gave it to her. "Keeps the demons away."

She took a big gulp. It scalded her mouth like hot vinegar. She gagged.

He gave her a thump between her shoulder blades. "You all right?"

"I thought it was vodka."

"It's not easy to get so much vodka," he chuckled. "This is *sama-gonka*, homemade brandy made of corn." He poured the rest of it down his throat as if it were water.

Elena heard the distant strain of an accordion and Raya's guitar as they rambled through the pitted field. A blast of wind left goosebumps on Elena's neck and arms, yet she wasn't cold. She didn't feel much of anything.

"Here we are." Yurovsky stopped and let go of her hand.

Elena tried to focus on their surroundings, which drifted in and out. A tall oak tree with a broad trunk and crimson leaves blazed in front of the setting sun. An old log house sat beside the tree, with a corrugated tin roof and a front door that had once been painted white. Now most of the color had peeled off.

"Who lives here?" she asked, taken aback by the slur in her words.

"Nobody, anymore. The Fritzes ran them and everyone else off their land."

"Why are we here?"

"Why do you think we're here?"

The low pitch of his voice made her want to throw herself at him. But she also wanted to bolt.

"I think we should get back," she said. "We're starting our march to Smolensk tonight, remember?"

"Not for two more hours. Plenty of time." He tightened his grasp around her. Brushed his lips over her earlobe.

She quivered.

He kicked the door open with long, skinny legs.

All of a sudden, she was on her back on a lumpy mattress, breathing the torpid reek of his sweat. He was on top of her. Heavy. Fiery. Sloppy. His eyes were solid and black, like a locust's. She felt a tug at her waist. He fumbled with her belt. Intuitively, she reached down to stop him. He pushed her hand out of the way.

"No," she said feebly.

He yanked her trousers off.

"No." She writhed under the force of him. She felt him grow hard. Her body pulsed at his touch. She was mortified by her desire.

"Stop," she begged him.

She felt a searing pain between her legs.

She wanted to scream but couldn't find her voice.

He clenched her shoulders and thrust himself into her with an excruciating force.

She cried out in agony.

He arched his back. Shuddered. Fell on her and was still.

She turned her head to the side, unable to look at him. She despised herself for allowing it to happen. If she hadn't been stupid enough to drink so much alcohol . . . She staggered to her feet and pulled her pants up. Hot tears drizzled down her cheeks. It was her fault for leading him on. She had only herself to blame.

36

Ideas are far more powerful than guns. We don't let our people
have guns. Why should we let them have ideas?

—JOSEPH STALIN

The Führerbunker, Berlin

May 1945

The bunker entrance was a nondescript concrete structure
next to a bullet-ridden sentry's pillbox. At first glance, Elena
was put off by the narrow staircase, which was steep, dark,
and gloomy. Major Bystrov handed her a flashlight and headed down
the stairs. Before she descended, Elena pictured Hitler emerging,
hands clasped behind his back, watching mortar shells and artillery
pummeling all that he'd built, then scurrying back to his hole like a
frightened rat.

It took a few minutes to get down to the Führerbunker, almost
nine meters below the Chancellery gardens. As they moved along
the corridor and their eyes grew accustomed to the low light,
they found doors off hinges, smashed chandeliers on the floor,
and charred tables and chairs. The unbelievably damp and thick
air reeked of urine, wet coins, and mold. Elena felt as if she were
breathing in dirty water.

She regarded the bunker with trained sniper's eyes, on the hunt
for a sign of Hitler or any of his accomplices. It was an underground
labyrinth of corridors and rooms that would have been impressive,

except for the sole reason they existed—to protect Hitler and those closest to him.

An image of herself bumping into Hitler popped into her head. There she was, a Jewish woman, a member of the race Hitler had tried to exterminate, hunting for him, in his secret hideaway. Now finding Hitler became personal. She would give anything to look the monster in the face and say, I'm still here. You failed.

In Hitler's office, Elena was hit by a wave of nausea, visualizing the depraved plans concocted within those four walls. The desk was littered with scraps of paper, and a lamp sat useless, without electricity. Ten volumes of Joseph Goebbels's diaries were stacked on a shelf, and logs of Hitler's military conferences were scattered all over the floor. Elena riffled through pages of one of Goebbels's diaries. She wanted to read every word, to get inside the head of a monster, to understand how a human being could become so inhumane.

"What are you doing?" the major snapped. "We don't have time to read."

Elena dropped the diary. "Sorry, Commandant Major."

She followed Bystrov out of the office, miffed. The colonel had told her that all documents found in Hitler's bunker would be taken back to Moscow and locked up, with only highly ranked officers gaining access.

They continued navigating their way through the underground warren, boots crunching broken glass as they moved. Bystrov charged through, as if he were on a deadline, while Elena lagged after him, taking her time. She wanted to absorb every detail, no matter how small.

Then she found herself in what may have been a meeting room, cluttered with overturned tables, broken typewriters, strewn papers, and crates of expensive liqueurs. As she walked out, the major staggered from another room down the corridor.

"You can't go in there," he said, breathless. He closed the solid wood door and hunched in front of it, hands on his knees. His eyes bulged from his waxy gray cheeks.

"Why not?"

"Trust me. You don't want to see."

"See what? Is it Hitler?"

"Just forget it. Go down the next corridor."

"You can't tell me not to look and then expect me to walk away. That's like dangling a chocolate pastry in front of a starving woman and not letting her eat it." She ducked behind him and grabbed the doorknob.

He clamped his hand over hers. "Don't. You'll regret it."

"There's nothing in there that could possibly be worse than what I've seen before."

"Please. Just trust me."

She caught the distress in his eyes and drew back. She had more than her share of atrocious memories implanted in her mind. And yet, she was the only Jew privy to the bunker and the secrets it contained. If she didn't look, she'd regret it later on. She had to bear witness for all those who couldn't. She wrenched his hand from hers, opened the door, and shone her flashlight around the room.

For a second, she thought they were asleep. Then she inhaled the pungent smell of bitter almonds. She saw their pink faces. Her knees buckled. Goebbels's children. All six of them on bunk beds. Five girls and one boy in nightclothes. The littlest couldn't have been more than four or five years old.

"No," she whispered. "How could they?"

Bystrov grasped her shoulders and gently pulled her out of the room. He closed the door again. "I didn't think anything could shock me anymore, but this . . ." His voice waned.

"They're innocent. Those children played no part in the Hitler's atrocities."

"Goebbels didn't want them to know their father was a monster."

"What about their mother? She would have tried to stop him. No mother would kill her own children."

Bystrov turned to face her. "She brought her children here to die."

Elena shivered violently. She saw the small bodies lying there, dressed as if they were simply going to sleep. They'd never grow up. They'd never know their father was a savage who'd brandished words like weapons. They'd never know their own mother had conspired to kill them.

37

We feared capture worse than death; we had seen a number of
times what the Nazis did with captives.
—YULIA ZHUKOVA, RED ARMY SNIPER

Nevel-Gorodok Offensive, Belorussia
October–November 1943

Leaflets flitted to the ground like autumn leaves at dusk. They'd
been dropped by a German plane flying over the Red Army's
soon-to-be-abandoned dugout at the edge of Roslavl. Elena
snatched one that landed near her feet. Her eyes welled up. It was
Tanya. Naked, her torso mangled and broken. Her head bloody. She
dropped the leaflet, and an unsettling moan rose to a primal shriek
from her throat.

Zina sprinted from the dugout, followed by Chava, who'd returned the previous day with a bandaged shoulder.

"What is it?" Chava said.

"Don't look," Elena managed.

Zina caught a leaflet in the air. She cried out: "No!"

Chava's eyes fell on the scattered papers. She stooped over and
plucked one off the ground.

"Let go!" Elena tried to rip it from her hands.

Auntie Katya appeared. She saw the leaflets and broke into a sob.

Chava twisted away from Elena. She glanced at the photo, crumpled it, and threw it to the ground.

Elena collapsed beside her. They held one another tight and wept. Zina sank down and wrapped her long arms around them. Then Raya embraced them. And another girl. And another. And another. She felt part of something bigger than friendship. Bigger than family. Bigger than faith. It felt as though their souls were bound together. Forever. In life and in death.

Auntie Katya's steadfast voice emerged softly with "Retribution," a poem written by the war correspondent Ilya Ehrenburg for the *Krasnaya Zvezda*, the Red Star, the army's newspaper.

We covered her and carried her. The bridge, unsteady,
Appeared to palpitate beneath our precious load.
Our soldiers halted there, in silence stood bare-headed,
Each transformed, acknowledging the debt he owed.

Elena listened to the words as if it were the first time she'd heard them. Coming from Auntie Katya's mouth, the poem sounded more like words of faith that had been so visibly absent at Soviet gravesides.

Then Justice headed westward. Winter was a blessing,
With hatred handled mute, and snows a fiery ridge.
The fate of Germany that murky day was settled
Because of one dead girl, beside a shaky bridge.

The air was still and quiet after Auntie Katya finished.

Justice. The word lodged in Elena's head. Ehrenburg could easily have used *revenge* in place of *justice*. But he didn't. Revenge implied vindictiveness through a personal crusade, while justice denoted vindication through a moral truth. The differences were slight yet formidable.

Lieutenant General Purkayev emerged from the dugout, filling the area with his indomitable presence. Voices went silent as he snatched a leaflet from the ground. He reviewed it with a tight-lipped expression, then scrunched it into a ball. The girls began to separate, their cheeks shiny with tears. From the corner of her eye, Elena saw Auntie Katya collecting the photos with a quiet dignity. It occurred to her that Auntie Katya never spoke of revenge, that she was the personification of fairness and integrity. Justice. Maybe, Elena thought, I'm struggling with my tally, with my conscience, because I'm fixated on the wrong word. Maybe my obsession with revenge is keeping me from seeing what really matters.

Imagine being able to fly away from danger.

Tears dribbled down Elena's cheeks as she recalled Tanya's words.

"It is time to stop crying," Purkayev began, his voice low. "We cannot go back and change things. We cannot give our brave comrade the burial she deserves. But we can remember how the fascist scum treated Junior Sergeant Tanya Baramzina. We can fight on and hit the Wehrmacht harder. We can hold our line without surrendering another soldier. We can stop the Wehrmacht from reaching Moscow by liberating Smolensk. We can keep forcing the Fritzes west so that we take back Belorussia."

A protracted silence.

Elena didn't know how to go on. While Tanya was being tortured, she'd been with Yurovsky. She felt dirty and broken. She was disappointed in herself.

"We must all stay sharp," Komarov was saying in an unctuous tone. "Our fallen comrades have sacrificed their lives for the good of others. You are all true socialists, like them, willing to die for your Motherland. Now it is time to fight harder for Stalin, for the future of Russia. Imagine yourselves with gleaming medals on your tunics, not one or two or even three, but five or six."

"Komarov is certainly in fine form."

Elena jumped at Yurovsky's castor-oil voice over her shoulder.

"I'd rather be a private in the infantry than a windbag like Komarov." Yurovsky lit a cigarette.

She wanted to step back, to distance herself from him, but her feet were rooted to the ground.

"I want to see you when we break formation in the morning," he said.

"I think . . . I should rest before we advance," she stammered.

He twisted his whiskers with his fingers. "I will have salt pork waiting for you, bread, vodka, and a warm blanket."

"I am not for sale," she said, echoing Zina's words.

His eyes flickered with amusement. "This is not a negotiation."

"It was a mistake, what happened between us."

"A mistake?" He dropped his cigarette onto the ground and stamped it out with the toes of his boot. "You certainly seemed eager at the time."

"I changed my mind." Her stomach knotted as she listened to the weak explanation spill from her mouth.

"Elena, we've been looking for you," Zina's voice sliced through the tension between them.

"Come on," said Raya. "We have to get into formation right now."

Raya and Zina each grabbed Elena by an arm and pulled her away from Yurovsky.

"Thank you," Elena said to her comrades.

"We'll continue our discussion later," Yurovsky called out.

"Oh no, you won't," Raya said grimly.

"What the hell did he do to you?" asked Zina. "You look awful."

"I . . . he—"

"You don't have to tell us anything," Raya said. "It's none of our business, right, Zina?"

"It helps to talk about it," Zina insisted.

Elena saw herself in that wooden house, alone with Yurovsky, her trousers bunched at her ankles.

"You like to tell us every word men say to you in private," Raya said to Zina.

"So?"

"So Elena's not like you. She's—"

"What?" Zina demanded.

"She's private," Raya answered.

"She's right here," Elena interrupted. "Don't talk about me as if I'm not here."

Raya and Zina exchanged sheepish glances.

"Sorry," said Raya.

"I'm sorry too," Zina added.

Elena peered over her shoulder. Yurovsky was nowhere to be seen. "It was my fault," she began, tentatively.

"What?" said Zina.

Elena looked at her. "I shouldn't."

"Yes you should."

"Zina," Raya said sharply.

"Maybe she's right," Elena said. "Maybe I will feel better if I tell someone."

Zina gave her a supportive pat on the back.

"I couldn't stop thinking about Bella, how she died so suddenly, and Tanya, who was here one minute, then gone. Then Yurovsky came up to me with vodka, lots of vodka."

"Oh no," Raya whispered.

"The thing is," Elena went on, "I wanted him. At that moment, I really did and, well . . ."

"You did nothing wrong," Zina said, her voice low and urgent. "He plied you with vodka and took advantage of you."

Elena shook her head. "He didn't put a gun to my head. I drank the vodka—"

"He probably planned the whole thing," said Zina. "Find some naive girl, get her drunk, and have his way with her."

"You think I'm naive?" Elena said, taken aback.

"No. Of course not."

Elena looked at Zina, who blushed.

"A little," Zina admitted, "when it comes to men, that is."

"You're the smartest girl in our platoon," Raya said. "Everyone knows that."

"A lot of good that does me here," Elena scoffed. "While my nose was stuffed in books, you and the rest of our comrades were learning how to tell the difference between a man and a weasel."

"You're wrong," Zina replied. "You have no idea how many times I thought I was in love, only to find I was being used."

Elena stared at her, dubious.

"It's true," Zina said, vehement. "There was a man in my village. He said he loved me. I was sure we would be together forever. He was my first. He convinced me to have sex the night before I came to the snipers' school. He told me it would bond us together forever, that it would strengthen our love. I believed him. The next morning, he wouldn't speak to me. He leered at me with such disdain. He . . . he called me a whore," her voice faltered. "I didn't understand how he could say he loved me and then, after I gave myself to him, he loathed me."

Elena recalled Zina's teary eyes the day they'd met. "I'm sorry."

"He was a fool," Raya said. "A horrible fool who will never find love."

Zina puckered her brow. "He's a man. They're all alike."

"Don't be so cynical," Raya said to Zina. "There are good men out there, we just have to keep looking." She glanced at Elena. "What do you think?"

Elena saw their platoon getting into marching formation. They had a fifty-kilometer walk northwest to Smolensk in front of them, in the dark. They had to move invisibly as one unit without making a sound, like sparrows winging through the night sky. "I suppose," she said, "we should all forget about men and love for the time being."

Zina snorted.

"What?" said Elena.

"It's not up to us," Zina said. "It's not our choice. We don't get to choose what happens to us here. Our fate rides on decisions men make for us."

Elena considered Yurovsky, how he'd gotten what he wanted from her and now seemed to think he owned her. Which, in a way, he did, because he was her superior.

"I tried to say no," she said, her voice barely a whisper.

Zina frowned. "It doesn't matter. Whatever you say, however you feel, doesn't matter."

Elena let Zina's words sink in. "Maybe there is no such thing as justice."

38

Hitler may have landed in Argentina or could be hiding in Spain with Franco.
—MOSCOW NEWSPAPER, MAY 8, 1945

SMERSH headquarters, Berlin
May 1945

A dead man was found lying on his back in the Reich Chancellery's vestibule. He was short and thin, like Hitler. He had an ugly slab of a moustache, like Hitler. He had a ruler-straight side part in his hair, like Hitler. Journalists, the only civilians granted access to the body, were all vying for the best shot. The sudden flaring of a camera's flashbulb brought white spots to Elena's eyes. She blinked until her vision cleared.

"I was sure he'd escaped," said a photographer, taking a photo.

"It's really him," a man scribbling madly exclaimed.

"It's not him," Elena said quietly to Bystrov and the colonel. "It's not Hitler."

"A good double, but I agree," the major said.

"So do I," said the colonel.

"Then why?" she asked.

Bystrov motioned for her and the colonel to follow him. They were expecting a telephone call from Stalin at SMERSH headquarters, an old house in the north end of Berlin, in the Buch district.

"The only explanation I can think of is that Hitler escaped," the major said when they were out of earshot. "This man's body is supposed to fool the media and everyone else into thinking Hitler is dead, so that nobody will search for him."

"That's the most ridiculous thing I've ever heard," the colonel scoffed.

"I didn't say it was a good plan, but it's the only reason I can think of for leaving the dead body of a man who resembles Hitler in the Chancellery."

Elena glanced back at the increasing throng of journalists swarming the Hitler look-alike. "Whether it makes sense or not, it seems to be working."

"People are sheep when there's something extraordinary to see," said the colonel. "Even if a few have doubts, they'll go along with the rest, afraid to disagree, afraid of standing alone."

Elena stilled. All of a sudden, she remembered the onlookers' horrified expressions as Masha and the two other "dissidents" were marched down the street. Hundreds of people watched without a word of protest at the obviously false charges. Not one objection. Because they were sheep.

Elena could tell from Bystrov's grim expression that his telephone call with Stalin had not gone well. The colonel, standing a few meters from Elena, lighting one cigarette after the other, sauntered over when Bystrov emerged.

"Stalin is angry that Goebbels's remains were exposed in the media," Bystrov confided. "He's ordered us not to have any contact whatsoever with the press. Everything we find, everything we do, must be conducted in total secrecy."

"Hmph," said the colonel, puffing on his cigarette.

"I'd have thought Stalin would be thrilled, seeing one of Hitler's minions defiled publicly," Elena replied, astounded.

Bystrov regarded her with a severe expression and said, in a voice that left no room for argument: "We must not question our leader's motives."

"Yes Comrade Major." She turned away so he couldn't see the fight in her eyes. She could understand keeping the search for Hitler to themselves, but Goebbels was a triumph for the Red Army and the Russian people. Stalin's order went against all logic.

39

I grew somehow desensitized. I killed—it was supposed to be that
way.
—ANTONINA KOTLIAROVA, RED ARMY SNIPER

Battle of Nevel, Belorussia
October 1943

Hundreds of dead sparrows littered the ground. Elena swatted at flies as she took in the birds cloaked in gauzy late-afternoon shadows. She had a sickening sense they'd died as a result of the poisonous gunpowder that saturated the air. People—the Red Army and the Wehrmacht—had killed them, and she was just as guilty as everyone else.

They kept us from starving to death.

Goosebumps rose on her arms when she remembered how Tanya had praised sparrows for saving her family's crops. She looked at the birds again, identical in their feathery gray and brown uniforms, and thought, if this many sparrows could die at once . . . She foresaw her comrades, lifeless on the battlefield, and she was overwhelmed by despair.

In the distance, cows mooed and dogs barked. She wondered if these animals would also be unintentional victims of war, collateral damage. She gazed at the pockmarked earth, at trees peppered with bullet holes, and wondered what would be left standing after the war.

One day and one night had passed since she and Chava had dug their foxholes and she was beginning to second-guess their location. They were close enough to the Fritzes to smell their burnt gunpowder, to hear their machine guns clatter and study their routine—when food and laundry arrived, their preferred brand of beer, where they congregated to read, smoke, and eat. Yet there hadn't been a sign of any highly ranked officers.

Were the Fritzes better at hiding, or were they looking in the wrong places?

Over the last forty-eight hours, she and Chava had studied every crevice, every bump, every bush and tree. They knew where barbed wire was strung across tree trunks, the locations of machine-gun nests, and the best places to shoot from. Best of all, the Germans had no idea they were being watched. So far.

Elena raised her binoculars and scanned the enemy's trenches. Her ears perked up at a rustling sound. Feet trampling through camel grass. Enemy soldiers. Perhaps four hundred meters away. Too close. She caught the profile of a brownish-green helmet. She adjusted the focus on her scope and glimpsed the contour of a machine gun threading through the tall grass towards Raya and Zina's foxhole. Her adrenaline soared. Another helmet bobbed upwards. And another. Five in total. This was bad. Machine gunners fired constant streams of bullets, while snipers had to reload after every shot. The odds were against the snipers if they came face-to-face.

Instinctively, she shut out the yellow warblers' stuttering call, the barking dogs, and the gurgling stream. She focused on the approaching soldiers. In a heartbeat, her mission had changed from hunting snipers to defending her comrades, which meant she had to get closer. Moving targets were difficult to hit, especially from a distance. She donned her forage cap, still covered in mud and leaves, scrabbled out of her foxhole and, with Chava close behind, crawled in the direction of the gunners. They moved with the agility of cats, keeping low to the ground, using hand gestures to communicate.

She peered through her scope. The lofty wild grass, in one particular spot, swayed noticeably. She glanced over her shoulder and cocked her head at Chava, who scrambled forward on her elbows until she was beside Elena.

Dark shadows stirred through the grasses. The Wehrmacht's field-gray uniform. Elena's heart leapt to her throat. The fascists were getting into shooting positions. She glanced sideways at Chava and gave her a look that said it's now or never.

Chava indicated she'd take the gunner on the far left.

Elena nodded. She calculated the windspeed, shooting angle, and distance in her head. She made the necessary adjustments on her rifle, aimed at a helmet, held her breath, and pulled the trigger. A helmet split the grass as the soldier fell sideways to the ground. A second helmet, from Chava's bullet, crashed through the grass.

One shot and move on.

She rolled three meters sideways, reloaded her magazine, and repositioned her rifle. She took another shot. Chava, now a good ten meters away, released her trigger. Two more machine gunners dropped. One left. Chava sidled over to Elena.

Bullets suddenly whooshed past Elena, a quarter of a meter from her shoulder. The last machine gunner was fighting back. But because of their camouflage, he couldn't pinpoint their exact location.

Chava took aim and fired.

The bullets stopped. The machine gunners were silent.

"We got the whole squad," Chava said.

"Let's wait a minute, to be sure," Elena whispered. "Stay low."

They lay there, guns at the ready, until Elena counted to two hundred in her head. Enough time to ensure there were no more gunners, yet not so much time that the fascists' commander would start wondering where they were. Not a peep from the other side. Still, they were only half finished. They weren't out of danger. They had to prove their kills in order to have them added to their tallies.

This was the part Elena still dreaded. For all she knew, a Nazi could be playing dead, then bolt up as she approached, riddling her body with bullets. If she had her way, she'd forget about tallies altogether. She didn't need or want external validation. But snipers worked in pairs. She had a responsibility to follow orders, for her partner's sake. She skulked forward. She prayed her camouflage and the tall grass would obscure her from the naked eye. Her breaths were quick and shallow, as she lessened the distance between herself and the presumably dead gunners.

Sweat had pooled at the nape of her neck by the time she and Chava reached the machine gunners' nest. Five fascists were sprawled on the ground. Elena removed her knife from her belt and cut off the decorations from one soldier's tunic. She sliced the straps from his field bag, half-full with cigarettes, biscuits, a lighter, and chocolate. She went through his pockets, sticking documents, letters, and photos into the bag. Last, she took his machine gun, the ribbon of ammunition, and binoculars. On to the next fascist.

They moved quickly and thoroughly, not wanting to leave anything useful behind. They seized everything they needed to verify their tally, as well as five machine guns and ammunition looped over their shoulders. They retreated clumsily on their stomachs, laden down with the spoils of their kills.

The girls had gone about four hundred meters when they heard voices shouting from the area where the machine gunners lay dead.

"Goddam Russkis!" a man snarled in German.

The Nazis would track them easily from their trail of flattened grass. They were done for.

Fear ratcheted up to panic.

"Let's drop everything and run," said Elena.

"Not yet." Chava veered sideways off the path, in the direction of the river. "Come on."

Elena dragged what she'd plundered, silently cursing her partner. As they neared the water, the ground became less grassy and muddier, with craters from rim to rim.

Chava stopped at a thicket of bushes that abutted the river. She dumped her rifle and all but one of her machine guns in a shell crater behind the bushes, and gestured for Elena to do the same. From their reconnaissance, Elena knew this area well. She knew exactly what Chava was planning. She cut a few branches from the bushes and covered her loot with them.

They crawled through high grass to a row of towering spruce trees that ran perpendicular to the river. Chava set down the machine gun with half a meter of ammunition at the feed cover. Elena watched, impressed. She'd learned how to shoot German rifles and machine guns at the snipers' school. She'd memorized the instructions the way she'd memorized propaganda. Still, she had more experience shooting her rifle and couldn't get her head around switching from one weapon to another under such pressing circumstances.

A gigantic splash. An enemy grenade exploded in the river. Water spouted into the air. The trees shook. They were going to fall. There was no way roots could survive such a blast. Except they did. Elena and Chava slunk away from the trees, standing tall and defiant as Russian and German bullets whizzed by in both directions. The sky flashed with streaks of light.

Elena thrust the butt of her rifle into her shoulder, loaded the magazine, and peered through her scope. Her ears rang from the hail of mortar fire. Calm down, she told herself. You'll never get a good shot if you're jumpy. She inhaled through her nose and out through her mouth to steady her nerves.

Be patient. Stay low. Aim for the head.

Panchenko's voice arose in her mind: *There is no room for error.* She clung to his words to stay on track.

She could feel a fascist sniper nearby, his beastly eyes searching for Red Army soldiers. She scanned the area. Close up, she saw tendrils of smoke spiraling from the ground, residue from grenades and mortars. In the distance, bare-limbed birch trees swayed from the blizzard of artillery.

She focused on the steppe that rolled gently to the horizon. Golden quills of grass. Rocks with tufts of grass poking through cracks. Rolling violet-gray hills that grazed the cloudy sky. Long shadows that outlined patches of sun. She narrowed in on the dark spots, looking for unusual shapes and sizes.

A wide rock formation caught her attention. A perfect hiding place for a sniper. She adjusted her scope to magnify the area. Her eyes landed on a peculiar silhouette on the wrong side of the rocks, based on the late afternoon sun's position. Other shadows fell to the left of slopes, stretching long and thin. But there was a rounded dark shape on the right side of the rocks. The enemy's profile.

She'd have to expose herself in order to get a good shot. Unless . . . She craned her neck for a good climbing tree. There were a couple of old oak trees just beyond the spruces, with their leaves still intact. The trunks were wide and the lowest branch of one was maybe half a meter off the ground. It would be a challenge to climb without being seen, but it was doable. And it would prove her mettle to the rest of her platoon once and for all.

Elena extended her leg and tapped Chava's foot. She gestured with her head in the direction of the oaks.

Chava looked at the trees and nodded in agreement.

Keeping her ear to the ground, Elena scuttled behind the spruce trees.

Artillery shells whistled overhead. She flattened herself against the terrain. Cowered. Don't stop, she chided herself. She continued, her eyes glued to the oaks. She was afraid to breathe. If the enemy caught even a hint of movement, they'd know precisely where to shoot.

At the base of the tree with the thickest trunk, she rolled onto her back and assessed the branches for climbing. She calculated the angle between the tree and the enemy snipers to determine the best side to climb. If they hadn't noticed any movement in the grass as she made her way to the oak, they might not be looking in this direction. If they had, she'd know soon enough.

Elena set her gun sights to the angle and distance required. She slithered around to the side of the tree where she'd mount. She studied the branches and determined her footing. She lay still and waited for a distraction so that she could climb the tree unnoticed. She wriggled her toes to keep them from getting numb. Yawned.

Suddenly, there was a torrent of mortar fire between the armies. Smoke enveloped the area. Elena grasped the tree's scaly gray bark with both hands and shimmied up. She reached for the lowest branch with her right arm, then her left, and hauled herself up and onto it. Without hesitation, she pulled herself up to the next branch, and the next, until she was about four meters high and totally ensconced in the canopy of leaves. From her perch, she saw two German snipers crouched behind the rock.

She aimed at the first sniper's head. Pulled the trigger and didn't wait to see if she'd hit him. She loaded another bullet, got the second sniper's head in her sights, fired. Her heart pummeled her ribs. Both were down, sprawled on one another. Two snipers who may very well have had Chava or another pair of her comrades in their sights. She had a heady feeling of success.

Then a German *Rama* flew overhead and began circling over the steppe. Menacing iron crosses glared from the bottom of both wings. Shells whistled past the oak tree. Elena was trapped. With her legs straddling a sturdy branch, she pressed her torso against the trunk. She clutched a higher branch with her left hand and held her rifle with the other. The enemy was machine-gunning her platoon and the infantry. Cannonballs were lobbed back and forth with a force that made Elena think the earth was going to crack and devour them all in one gulp. Above her, in the clearing sky, the *Rama* growled as it orbited the front lines at Smolensk.

Elena's hand tightened around her rifle. If I hadn't been so stupid, if I hadn't been so fixated on proving myself, on trying to keep up with everyone else, I wouldn't be in this mess right now, she seethed.

From her branch high above the fray, she had a stupendous and harrowing view of her comrades fanned out across the field. Chava was firing at a machine gunner's nest. Raya and Zina, behind a knoll, took out an officer.

A mortar shell landed right next to a pair of Red Army snipers. They were torn to pieces. The mortar's hot metal splinters soared past Elena. She lost her grip on the branch and wobbled side to side.

This is it, she thought, dazed, before she tumbled from the tree.

40

He will act as Hitler's trump card, creating a hero legend around the Führer's death, while Hitler himself goes underground.
—FREE GERMAN PRESS SERVICE, IN STOCKHOLM, CIRCULATING A RUMOR THAT HITLER'S DOUBLE WAS CALLED TO BERLIN TO BE KILLED INSTEAD OF THE FÜHRER, APRIL 1945

The Führerbunker, Berlin
May 5, 1945

Colonel Gorbushin deposited an oil lamp on the desk in Hitler's bunker office.

"Thank God." Elena rubbed her tired eyes. They stung from reading in such poor light. "This will make a world of difference."

She'd been ordered to translate documents found in the bunker with the goal of learning Hitler's fate.

He peered over her shoulder. "Anything interesting?"

"Yes, as a matter of fact. Martin Bormann, Hitler's private secretary, sent a number of telegrams, all marked secret, to his adjutant, explaining how they were going to move headquarters from Berlin to Berchtesgaden."

"Did they?"

"Definitely not. They were still receiving confidential letters here, up until two days ago." She handed him a folder. "And here are reports from the Allies and us, some as recent as yesterday."

He opened the folder. "Why are the letters so big?"

"That's a mystery," Elena admitted. "It's like reading through my rifle's scope. My hunch is that Hitler's eyesight is poor so a special typewriter with big letters was used, but I won't know for certain until I talk to the person who typed these reports."

"If we can find him. Most of the people closest to Hitler escaped."

"What about the ones we captured in the bunker?"

"None of them were part of his inner circle."

She blew out her cheeks.

He pointed at three wooden boxes containing papers on the floor at Elena's feet. "So, are you going to tell me what's in these documents, or do you want me to guess?"

"Sorry," she said, flustered. "They're Reuters news reports, Moscow broadcasts, and telegrams from major cities around the world."

"Anything worthwhile?"

She bent down and flipped through the papers. "I have found two interesting documents." She handed them to the colonel.

"Go on," he said.

"It's apparent the Nazi Party was aware of their dire situation, from reports written by several leaders."

"Which means they knew damn well they were lying to their people," the colonel remarked, thoughtful.

"Exactly." She rummaged around the desk and handed the colonel a piece of paper with words underlined in blue pencil. "This is a report from a radio station about Mussolini's execution. It looks like someone, Hitler I suspect, underlined the words *Mussolini* and *hung upside down*."

The colonel's gaze flicked from the paper to Elena and back to the paper. "Hitler didn't want anyone parading his body around Berlin, and he certainly didn't want to be hung upside down, like Mussolini."

"That's what I think," Elena agreed.

He looked at her. "Either he's escaped, or he's dead and his body is reduced to ashes."

There was a pensive silence.

"I don't think he got away," Elena said.

A pause.

"Neither do I."

41

No, we're snipers, send us where we're supposed to go.
—BELLA EPSTEIN, RED ARMY SNIPER, 2ND BELORUSSIAN FRONT (RE-
SPONDING TO ORDERS TO STAY AT DIVISION HEADQUARTERS)

Battle of Nevel, Belorussia

October–December 1943

C an you hear me?"

"Is your leg sore? Can you move it?"

A woman's insistent tone buzzed in her ears. Elena opened her eyes and a harsh yellow light shined in her face. She shut her eyes again.

"There she is," a man said.

That pompous voice. Elena shook.

"Turn your head and then open your eyes," the woman suggested.

She twisted her neck right. Pried her eyes open. Found herself face-to-face with Yurovsky. She pinched her eyes shut. Cracked one open. He was still there, beside a dour-faced female medic with a red cross on a white band around her left arm.

"Where am I?" she croaked.

"The regimental first aid section at the rear," Yurovsky replied. "A kilometer from the front."

Elena tried to sit, to prop herself up on her elbows, but dropped back as sharp pains sliced down her side.

"Don't move," the medic cautioned her. "You've got a nasty bruise on your right hip."

"Quite a fall," Yurovsky said. "Good thing I was close by."

"I'll say," the medic added. "Comrade Lieutenant Yurovsky swooped in and carried you to safety."

"I fell from . . . ?"

"From a tree, after destroying two enemy snipers and three machine gunners," Yurovsky said, like a proud father.

She slouched, remembering how she'd climbed the tree to prove herself, to show off. Pride is the mask of one's faults. That's what her father would have said.

"Two," she said, listless.

"What?" Yurovsky leaned in closer.

Her throat constricted. "I only killed two gunners."

He stroked his whiskers. "Chava said you took three out."

"No. Only two. She has better aim."

He looked at her, amused.

"Is she all right?" Elena asked. "Chava?"

"Chava is just fine," Yurovsky assured her in a smarmy voice that churned her stomach. "It's intense out there but we're not giving up. Another day or two and we'll take Smolensk."

Elena reached for her rifle. Sweeping her hand across her bunk, she discovered only a smooth woolen blanket. A real blanket. Something she hadn't had since her home in Minsk.

"Where is it?" Elena asked.

"What?" said Yurovsky.

"My rifle. It's always beside me." Her voice was shrill. "I need it."

"Not here, you don't," the medic interjected.

Ignoring the pain in her hip, Elena propped herself up. "You don't understand. It's part of me. My rifle. I need it."

The medic glanced at Yurovsky. He waved his hand for her to

go look. She pivoted on her feet and walked off, lamenting out loud about "hysterical women giving orders."

"I like the spark in your eyes." Yurovsky squeezed her cheek.

Her skin crawled at his touch.

"Thank God I was there," he said, congratulating himself.

Elena turned her face away.

The medic reappeared with her rifle, gave it to her, and moved on to the next patient.

Elena took the gun eagerly in both hands. She ran her index finger over the edge of the stock and felt the notches she'd carved, symbols of her tally. One, two, three, four . . . "Wait a minute." She frowned. "There's too many. I didn't make all of these."

Yurovsky puffed his chest out. "I took the liberty of carving the newest ones."

Elena stared at the notches he'd made. They were longer and deeper than hers, as though he wanted to prove his dominance. She felt violated, knowing he'd taken a knife to her most sacred possession, her third eye.

Yurovsky bent over her cot and whispered into her ear, "Time for me to leave, but I'll be waiting for you when you return to the front." He kissed her forehead and was gone.

Elena let go of her rifle. She rolled onto her good hip, wrapped her arms around herself, and sobbed.

Later that afternoon, Elena, on her bunk in the first aid tent, came across a photo of Zina in *Frontovay Illyustratsiya* (*Frontline Illustrated*). Zina looked strong and gorgeous, with her hands on her rifle. Her enigmatic gaze followed the angle of her weapon. Behind her shoulder, there was a glimpse of a hand holding binoculars. Raya had been cut from the photo. The entire focus was on Zina.

Elena peeled her gaze from the staged photo that was more propaganda than news. It was also, not surprisingly, one of the few things to read, along with two other publications that oozed with lies—the army newspaper, *Unichtozhim Vraga* (*We Shall Destroy the Enemy*) and the Moscow magazine, *Ogonyok* (*Flame*). Zina's photo was in all three, with glowing tributes to her prowess as a sniper. Nobody else in the platoon was photographed or written about, not even Raya, who had a higher tally.

She read the caption under the photo in *Unichtozhim Vraga*: "Having distinguished herself during an enemy attack, Gofeld has been awarded the medal 'For Valor.' She is an outstanding sniper, says Comrade Commander Galitsky."

Elena's eyes filled with tears when she saw Galitsky's name in print. The photo and caption had been printed the day before he died. She shoved the newspaper to the side of her bunk and lowered her head to her pillow. Lying there in the quiet first aid unit, her life at the front, with its frenzied pace and incessant uproar of combat, seemed almost surreal. The endless uncertainty.

She could sleep all day and nobody would notice. She wished it were possible to accumulate sleep, the way you banked money, then use it in small amounts, over time, when you had to go days without rest.

"Mail," a medic called out gaily.

Her heart stalled.

"Yosif, Oleg, Irina . . ."

Elena curled onto her side and covered her ears with her hands. Every name of a comrade with a family awaiting their return brought a cold rush of grief.

"Daniil, Aleksey, Leonid . . ."

She couldn't keep the medic's voice from her ears. She watched as the man in the bunk across from her accepted a triangular-shaped envelope. She remembered the letter from Masha. She saw the hand-writing as if it were right in front of her. She could recite every one of her sister's last words by heart, even the ones that gave false hope. Especially those ones.

I want to be dressed decently when I leave here.

In her mind, she saw Masha in the jade-green dress she'd naively expected to wear upon her release. It was a special dress. Masha had bought it during a trip to Moscow, and the dress fit as if it had been made specially for her, the way it fell along the contours of her bud-ding figure. Masha had worn it to the theater the evening they went as a family to the ballet—*Romeo and Juliet.* What a night! The mag-nificent clothing and jewelry. The skin-tingling music that rose like magic from the hidden orchestra. The dancers whose feet were so swift and nimble, they never seemed to touch the stage.

Her father had put money aside for months in order to pay for tickets. They'd gone to the ballet for years; it was a subject on which both of her parents had agreed. Food nourishes your body, her father would say, but life is not worth living without art and music. They nourish your soul.

A faint smile crossed her face as she remembered that night. How happy she'd been, seeing her parents walking arm in arm. How proud she'd been to sit next to her brother, handsome in his suit and bow tie, his usually messy hair combed neatly behind his ears. How smug she'd felt as girls' heads had turned when he walked past. It was their last outing as a family before the Nazis invaded Russia. Less than a month later, her father and Yakov had vanished. Her smile faded. She tried to return to the ballet, but once the darkness obscured her mind, there was no going back.

Elena swung her legs over the side of her bunk two days later. Apart from an ugly purple and yellow bruise (which she prayed would repel

Yurovsky), her hip was almost back to normal. There was a bit of pain, but nothing too terrible. It was time to rejoin her comrades, a prospect that was remarkably cheering. Being stuck in bed while her regiment overpowered the Wehrmacht and took Smolensk made her feel horribly useless.

The extra sleep, however, had given her a much-needed fresh attitude. She realized how badly she wanted to be at the front. How much she needed her comrades as well as a solid purpose. She donned her forage cap and tunic, deliced in soap made of lye and fat. She wrapped her feet, pulled on her boots, donned her rucksack, canteen, and defiled rifle, and trekked one kilometer over crunchy snow and ice to the front line.

"You're back!" Raya greeted her with a hug outside the dugout. "Everything is good with your hip?"

"It's good as new." Elena suppressed a grimace of pain. Her hip had stiffened during the last ten minutes of her walk. She embraced Raya and was disconcerted by her comrade's spiky shoulder blades.

"Have you been eating?" Elena asked.

"There's been a shortage of everything. Meat, bread, tobacco, even tea." Raya took Elena's hands and scanned her from head to toe. "You look better. There's more color in your cheeks."

"I've only been gone two days."

"Elena!"

She whirled around at Zina's animated voice.

"I wasn't sure you'd be back for Nevel."

"I had to return to make sure your head didn't swell with all the press you're getting," Elena teased.

Zina gave a dismissive wave of her hand. "Isn't it stupid? I'm only following orders, like everyone else here, but I'm glorified in the newspapers like Klavdiya Shulzhenko," she said.

Elena chortled at her reference to the popular singer.

"Klavdiya Shulzhenko?" Raya said, drolly.

"Who else gets their photo on the front page of every newspaper?"

"Every newspaper?" said Elena.

"Maybe I'm exaggerating a little," Zina acknowledged, her emerald eyes flashing with mirth.

"A lot, I'd say." Raya gave Elena a what-can-you-do look.

"It's good to see nothing's changed here," Elena laughed.

"What are you talking about?"

"Elena!" Chava emerged from the dugout. "Everything's changed," she said. "I increased my tally by five."

Elena was awed and dismayed by Chava's growing tally.

"And now we're on our way to Nevel," Chava finished.

"Except Auntie Katya," Raya interjected with a frown. "She's been sent back to Moscow."

"No. When?" Elena said, taken aback.

"Yesterday morning," said Chava.

"They need her at the training school," Zina added.

"But . . . I didn't get to say goodbye."

"None of us did," Chava said. "She left while we were sleeping."

"Auntie Katya didn't want emotions getting in the way of duty," Comrade Lieutenant Nina Lobkovskaya interjected. She strode towards them, splendid with her chest of medals.

The snipers saluted her.

"At ease." Nina looked squarely at Elena. "You're cleared for combat?"

"It was only a bruise."

"You're up for a two-hundred-kilometer march?"

I hope so. "Yes. Of course."

"I spoke to the medic myself, Lieutenant Lobkovskaya."

Elena quaked at Yurovsky's voice.

Nina's round cheeks flattened. She saluted him.

Elena automatically raised her hand to her forehead.

"Corporal Bruskina is good as new," Yurovsky went on.

Elena boiled under his lusty stare.

"How kind of you, to look out for one of our young women," Nina said, in an icy tone.

Chava squeezed Elena's hand.

"We must take care of one another, don't you agree?" Yurovsky responded, soot-black eyes sharpening on Elena.

Nina grimaced. "Yes."

Elena fought the urge to spit on him.

"I'm sure you must have many soldiers who need your attention," Nina said.

"None so important as my frontline wife." He gave Elena an oily smile. "I will check on you during the march." He turned on his heel and strode off, humming the tune of "The Sacred War."

Elena's body shook with anger. Frontline wife? There was nothing worse for a woman in uniform than being known for having sex with your superior. It was like having *whore* written across your chest. With such a negative reputation, she would never be able to marry. No good man would want a former frontline wife.

"I'm sorry." Nina shook her head. She was ranked lower than Yurovsky, which automatically rendered her moot in terms of influence.

Elena felt her comrades' sympathetic eyes linger on her. She had never felt so alone and so defenseless.

42

SMERSH headquarters, Berlin

May 1945

I was involved in the murder of Goebbels's children," said Dr. Kunz, who'd worked in the Chancellery's hospital. He fidgeted with the sleeves of his SS uniform, rolling them up and down, up and down. He had unkempt whiskers and his cagey eyes had sunk into his gloomy face.

A lump lodged in Elena's throat.

Bystrov listened, spellbound, as Elena translated the doctor's admission.

"Keep going," he urged.

Elena regarded Dr. Kunz. "What happened?"

Dr. Kunz clasped his sallow hands together. "Frau Goebbels approached me in the corridor near the entrance of Hitler's bunker. She said she had to talk to me about an urgent matter and then, without waiting for me to reply, said she needed my help to kill her children."

Elena's thumb and forefinger gripped the pen tighter. His words echoed uncomfortably in her ears.

"I had no choice," Dr. Kunz was saying, his voice hollow and sad. "My duty was to the Führer and the Third Reich. A couple of days later, on the first of May, I met with Frau Goebbels and Goebbels in the Führerbunker. She told me her children had to be killed that night because the Führer was dead. She said—"

"She told you the Führer was dead?" Elena interjected, her voice steeped with urgency.

"Yes."

"Did she say how or when?"

"No. Just that he was dead and that the only way out for her family was to die."

"What did Goebbels say?"

The doctor unclasped and clasped his hands. "He said he would be grateful if I helped his wife put their children to death."

Elena took a couple of deep breaths to ease her cramping stomach. She translated the doctor's statement for Bystrov.

"Jesus," he said.

Dr. Kunz continued in a faraway voice. "I tried to convince them to send the children to the hospital and give the Red Cross guardianship, but Frau Goebbels said no. She said it would be best if they die." He regarded Elena with a remorseful sigh. "It was as if she were telling me her children had fevers and needed medicine."

The hair on the back of Elena's neck rose at the mother's detachment towards her own children. "And Goebbels?" she whispered.

The doctor looked away. "He said . . . he said it would be impossible to let them live because . . . because they were his children."

Elena paused. The major raised his eyebrows, expecting her translation.

She had trouble repeating the doctor's statement out loud to Bystrov. The unthinkable words stuck to the roof of her mouth like tar.

"What did you give the children?" she asked the doctor, once she'd updated Bystrov.

He clasped his head in his hands. "I injected them with morphine to get them to sleep. Frau Goebbels told them . . ." His voice broke. "She told them it was a vaccine that was being given to all German children and soldiers. After I administered the injections, I told Frau Goebbels I wouldn't be able to give the cyanide to the children. She didn't blink. She told me to find Hitler's personal doctor and send him to her."

"So he gave them the cyanide capsules?"

The doctor's face was stiff with sorrow. "Yes. The same capsules Goebbels and his wife took a few minutes later."

"Where did these capsules come from?" Bystrov asked, through Elena.

"Hitler started handing them out at the end of April. That's what General Krebs took," he said, referring to the general who'd been found dead in the courtyard a few hours earlier.

"Do you think that is what Hitler took?" Elena pressed him.

"I don't know. I never saw his body or his wife's."

"So it's true? Hitler married Eva Braun and then they committed suicide?"

"Yes. I overheard Eva correct the children when they called her Tante Braun. She told them to address her as Tante Hitler."

Auntie Hitler. The name bounced in Elena's head like a rock.

"Remarkable," said Bystrov. "Braun must have been crazier than Hitler."

"I think Frau Goebbels is the worst of them all," said Elena.

"She was never a mother," Bystrov replied, disgusted. "She was a Nazi."

43

Men really force themselves. We had a platoon commander
Dugman, who tried to act by giving commands. But I told him
that in this case we are equals, even if I am a corporal and he is a
lieutenant . . . in two days he called me in again and said, if you
don't want to voluntarily, I'll shoot you . . . I scratched and bit and
got away, then I told the Party Organizer. He got five days arrest.
Later, he got back at me. He would send me where the scouts were
to hunt, to places that were mined and shelled more.

—TESTIMONY OF FEMALE RED ARMY SNIPER
DURING MINTS COMMISSION

Battle of Nevel, Belorussia

October–December 1943

The wind smacked the left side of Elena's face as she marched
with her platoon towards Nevel. It was the worst time of
the year, *rasputitsa*, when fall changed to winter. The road
was ankle-deep in mud. Every footstep was an effort. She heaved her
feet from the heavy sludge that famously, in 1812, had prevented
Napoleon's armies from invading Russia. The tall, reddish-yellow
grass had already been trampled by armies who'd come before her
platoon. Remnants of the first snow looked like handfuls of cotton
scattered across the ground. In the distance, trees blurred into the
hazy sky.

Her regiment had to break formation in order to veer around a dead horse. Flies buzzed over the corpse. There were mortar splinters on the horse's thighs. Blood dripped from a bullet hole under its mane.

They'd been marching more than twelve hours. Morning had just broken. Elena, praying they would stop for the day sooner than later, strained to see Nina, ahead. Elena's hip had begun to hurt at around the fifth hour. Now her pain had morphed into a gnawing burn. And she wasn't sure how much energy she had left.

"I'll come find you once we stop for the day," Yurovsky said, with insufferable arrogance as he marched past.

Terror rose in her throat like vomit. Why did he choose her? What did she do wrong? How could she get him to leave her alone?

"Platoon, halt." Nina pointed at a wide and deep trench. "We're going to rest at this *balka* for the next eleven hours." *Balkas* were strange yet natural phenomena on an otherwise flat steppe. They were created by the steppe's crust splitting apart. This one was big enough for their entire battalion of five hundred soldiers and their vehicles.

Elena dropped to the ground and hugged her knees to her chin.

Raya fell beside her. "Want me to take him out?"

"I think I have to leave . . ." Elena answered, her voice dwindling.

"And go where?"

"Another platoon. On the Western Front, as far as I can get from Yurovsky."

"Running won't change things. There will always be another Yurovsky, sometimes more than one."

Hot tears bubbled at the corners of Elena's eyes. "What am I supposed to do, then? Let him have his way with me?"

"You could try making a formal complaint," Raya suggested. "But I know others haven't gotten anywhere by protesting."

Elena bowed her head.

"A couple of girls in our platoon have even been forced to live with their 'frontline husbands,'" Raya continued, derisively. "There's no way out for us. I think the asses in the highest ranks figure this isn't their problem. It is a men's club, after all. As soon as this war ends, we'll be tossed aside like yesterday's news."

Elena considered her comrades' tallies, which were, in some cases, higher than male snipers'. She considered the sacrifices made by girls like Bella and Tanya. She considered the risks she'd already taken, the ones ahead she would undoubtedly face. Yet, in the ladder of military ranks, women were at the bottom, no matter what.

"I'll take my chances," Elena said, startled by her own mettle. "I'm going to Purkayev and I'm not giving up until he listens to me."

Raya exhaled a puff of cigarette smoke. "You know he could make life difficult for you?"

Elena shrugged. "Nothing could be worse than it already is."

Lieutenant General Purkayev was sitting at a table, absorbed in a map of the Eastern Front, when Elena approached him in the middle of the *balka*. She'd come immediately after talking to Raya. Before she lost her nerve. Before Yurovsky came looking for her. Purkayev's freshly pressed uniform set him apart from the soldiers bustling around in rumpled tunics, as he made notations on the map. And his collar was extra-white, not washed-out gray like everyone else's. He was sketching precise lines with deft fingers.

Elena combed the area for a nook where she could speak to Purkayev alone, but *balkas* were, by nature, wide-open spaces where voices echoed from one end to the other. She took a step back. The idea of the soldiers hearing her conversation with Purkayev was enough to make her reconsider entirely.

Come find me once your comrades are settled. Yurovsky's brash voice flooded her senses. She squared her shoulders and stepped forward.

"Comrade Lieutenant General Purkayev," she began in a timid voice.

He didn't look up. He ran his middle finger along the railway tracks on the map. His fingernails were chewed to the quick.

She repeated his name, louder and with more conviction.

He regarded her with close-set eyes ringed with fatigue. He kept his finger on the map.

She saluted him.

"Your cap needs straightening," he said.

She reached up with both hands and adjusted her forage cap. She saw his gaze linger on her wrinkled tunic. Her limp shoulders. She'd forgotten to insert her wooden *pogony*. "Sir, I'd like to talk to you about something."

"Something?"

"A problem."

He withdrew his finger from the map. His arms hung rigid at his sides, as if he were ready to pounce.

She felt the heated stares of nearby soldiers.

"Well, what is it, Comrade Corporal?"

She moved in closer. Noticed that the scar on his chin was inflamed, as if he'd been scratching it. She lowered her voice. "One of your officers is bothering me."

He cocked his head. "Bothering you?"

"He's been forcing himself on me. I want him to leave me alone."

He gave her a searching look.

Behind her, soldiers' voices erupted.

". . . another one . . ."

"I can't believe . . ."

"I bet it's Temkin."

"What do you say, Temkin?"

"Fuck off . . ."

She felt small and insignificant, as if she'd disgraced herself, opening up to Purkayev, letting him and all these soldiers see how far she'd fallen.

"You are certain you did nothing to lead this soldier on?" Purkayev said.

"What?" she replied, aghast. "No."

The vein in Purkayev's neck pulsed.

"This was a mistake." She spun around to leave. "I shouldn't have bothered you."

"Who is this soldier?" he demanded.

"What?"

"The soldier who is pestering you. What is his name?"

She turned around slowly. "Yurovsky."

"I knew it," one of the soldiers burst out.

"That bastard," said another soldier.

Purkayev met Elena's gaze with an air of reproach.

"We'd just buried a comrade and Galitsky," she heard herself say, "and I was upset that my shooting partner was missing, and I was afraid—"

"Comrade Sergeant Baramzina was your partner?"

"Yes." Her thoughts got all muddled upon hearing Tanya's name. It took her a moment to clear her head and continue. "Yurovsky appeared. He started talking to me. He gave me vodka." She made a face. "Too much vodka. He took my mind off . . . things. I liked him. He was kind. At first."

Purkayev heaved his shoulders up and down. Let out a long sigh.

"I tried to stop him. I don't want to be a frontline wife."

He fumbled with a stack of papers beside the map. Scratched his neck. Folded his hands primly and rested his elbows on the table.

"You are a Red Army soldier and your commitment must be to the party and Comrade Stalin first and foremost," he said, remote. "You are supposed to be loyal to the cause, with absolutely no romantic fraternization with your male comrades."

"But . . ." She stared at him, disappointed.

He returned to his map.

She raised her chin and marched off. She managed to hold her shoulders high until she was back at her platoon's section of the *balka*. Then she collapsed in her tent.

"She can't see you. She has her monthly."

Elena, hunched in her tent, smiled through her tears, hearing Zina lie with an astonishing poise. It was an hour after her upsetting conversation with Purkayev. She couldn't believe her comrades were actually going through with their hastily concocted scheme. She was heartened by their loyalty.

"Don't be ridiculous," Yurovsky said.

"Ridiculous?" Raya chimed in. "Have you seen how much blood comes out of a woman during her monthly?"

"It gushes from you-know-where like a faucet," said Zina.

Elena winced. Zina was going too far.

"And do we ever get emotional," Chava added, "bawling like teething babies."

"Out of my way," Yurovsky barked. "That's an order."

Elena shrank back against the canvas. Her comrades and a small tent were the only obstacles between her and Yurovsky. She should have just gone with him, accepted her fate.

"What is going on here?"

Elena's chest stiffened at Purkayev's deep-timbred voice.

"Comrade Lieutenant General," said Yurovsky.

"Comrade Lieutenant General," Elena's comrades echoed, in unison.

Elena crumpled. What now?

"I'm here to check on Comrade Corporal Bruskina," Yurovsky said in a cloying tone. "You may recall I saved her—"

"Yes, yes," Purkayev cut him off. "The entire regiment knows about your gallantry."

Elena tried not to smile at Purkayev's sarcasm.

"I'm afraid Comrade Bruskina is a little under the weather, Comrade Lieutenant General," Raya said.

"Nothing serious?"

"It's her monthly," Zina declared.

"Oh."

Elena cringed. Purkayev would know this was a ruse after she'd practically begged him to intervene.

"Well then, Comrade Lieutenant," Purkayev said, "I would advise you to leave Comrade Bruskina alone."

Elena's face went slack.

"Yes sir," Yurovsky replied, glumly.

"From now on, or you will be shipped off to a penal battalion," Purkayev added. "Is that clear?"

Elena couldn't believe what she was hearing.

"Yes. Sir."

"Your men could use your attention right now, Comrade Lieutenant," he added.

"Yes sir," Yurovsky replied, in a docile voice that was almost unrecognizable.

Elena's nerves eased when she heard him retreat. Then the tent flap rose and she saw Purkayev.

He crouched down to her level and said quietly, "Earlier, when you came to me, I reacted horribly. I'm sorry."

He looked her straight in the eyes. For a moment, it felt like the rank that divided them had vanished.

"This is the first time I've had women in my regiment, the first time . . ." He shook his head, rueful. "The army doesn't condone Yurovsky's behavior. I should have taken what you said more seriously."

"Why didn't you?"

"You're not the first girl to complain about a soldier, or the second or third or tenth. I ordered the offending soldiers away to *shtrafniki*, penal battalions, but they were sent back within a week. Some, two or three days later. And when they returned, they were worse than ever."

She raised her eyebrow. "You mean soldiers can do whatever they want with us?"

The shame on his face was sobering. "Legally, no. Truthfully, yes."

She was riven with anguish and rage. "What about us? What if women can't fight because we've been . . . we're . . . you know?"

He took a deep breath and leveled his gaze at her. "You matter."

Her gut stirred.

He angled himself towards Elena. "All of you women matter."

His nearness made the back of her neck tingle. She was confused by the feelings racing through her.

"I want you to come to me whenever you need help," he continued.

"You just said you can't do anything to stop Yurovsky."

"I said I can't send him away. But I can make his life miserable here."

You can't possibly watch him all the time, she wanted to say. You can't stop him before he grabs me.

"Are you all right?" he said.

"I'm fine," she lied.

He gave her a long, searching look. Then he was gone.

44

I was sure that, in a few days, the whole world would know that
we had found Hitler's corpse.
—YELENA RZHEVSKAYA, RED ARMY INTERPRETER

The Führerbunker, Berlin
May 1945

Elena was back in the underground maze beneath the Reich
Chancellery, in one of Goebbels's rooms, going through the
enormous volume of documents that had to be annotated
before they could be sent to the front headquarters. Two suitcases
contained his diaries, thick notebooks written in heavy, straight lines.
There were even a number of screenplays written by unknown people, and pages of Goebbels's own children's manuscript, "The Little
ABC of the National Socialist." As well, there was another suitcase
that held Magda Goebbels's personal documents, revealing her fas-
tidious nature. She'd inventoried the furnishings in their country
house and their castle in Schwanenwerder.

Elena was enthralled by the level of detail Magda had given to her
family's belongings. Figurines. Ashtrays. Cushions. Handkerchiefs.
Bottles of wine (eighty-seven). Toilet paper holders, for goodness'
sake. All of the children's garments, including underwear. There
was a bizarre document, adorned with the National Socialist German Workers' Party seal, with a fortune teller's prophecies about the
country's future. Elena chuckled, reading about a new aerial weapon

that would destroy the enemy, how Russia would be beaten by Germany in fifteen months. Communism would be crushed. Jews would be eliminated. Another new weapon on German submarines would supposedly destroy Russian and British fleets.

She put the psychic's report aside to show Bystrov and the colonel. It would give them a much-needed laugh. She opened another folder. It contained Martin Bormann's documents. Right on top was a radio-telegram he'd sent to his adjutant on April 22, 1945. *Proposed relocation overseas and south agreed.* It seemed as though Bormann was not only planning to leave Germany, he wanted to get as far away as possible. Interesting, she thought. But it didn't say anything about Hitler. Was he really dead, or did he and Bormann escape together?

"Comrade Bruskina!" Bystrov's voice shouted excitedly from the corridor. "Comrade Bruskina!"

She made her way to the door of Goebbels's room. She leaned sideways and saw the major approaching. "What is it?"

"I'm not sure but it could be important."

"I've got days of work here . . ."

"Leave it for now. Come."

Elena reluctantly set down Bormann's folder. She followed the major up the stairs outside to the former Chancellery garden. It seemed like a junkyard, with a raucous wind flinging broken branches, wood scraps, and empty gasoline cans all over the place. She and Bystrov joined the colonel, standing next to Hitler's personal bomb shelter. In front of them, two guards were digging around a burnt corpse in a shell crater.

A third guard was brushing dirt off another blackened corpse. Smaller than the first. The guards lifted the larger body from the crater and placed it on a gray blanket. Then the smaller one. Both bodies cracked into pieces on the blanket. Both were scorched far more than Goebbels and his wife. There was nothing recognizable about either one. No visible clothing. No badges or medals. Nothing.

"I believe that's a woman," the colonel said, gesturing to the smaller body.

Elena tilted her head and squinted. Apart from the slighter build, she couldn't tell if it was male or female.

"We're going to need a doctor to examine them," Bystrov said quietly to Elena and the colonel.

"We've got something else," one of the guards called out. He was back in the crater, holding the charred remains of a small dog.

This shook Elena.

The other two guards hauled out the corpse of a much larger dog.

"Hitler's dog," the colonel said, with derision. "He killed his goddam dog."

"If that's his dog," said Elena, wound up, "then——"

"We don't know for sure," Bystrov raised his palms. "Let's not get ahead of ourselves."

"You're right," the colonel agreed. He gestured for Elena and Bystrov to move back from the guards.

"What are you thinking?" Bystrov asked him.

"We need to determine if these bodies are Hitler and Braun," the colonel began. "If they are, nobody else can know."

Elena's heart galloped. She wanted Hitler dead, but she also wanted to fulfill her duty to Stalin and capture him alive for the May Day celebrations. She yearned to see him suffer the way her family and comrades had suffered.

"But we have a problem," the colonel was saying.

"What is it?" Elena asked, restless.

"Yesterday, Moscow charged the 5th Shock Army with full control over the Chancellery district. As you know, sentries have been posted at the gates with firm orders not to let anyone in. These bodies were found on the 5th Shock Army's territory, but the three of us are attached to the 3rd Shock Army."

This meant they had no claim to the bodies that were just exhumed.

They had no right to get them examined. They could very well be Hitler and his wife of one day, but their trio might never know.

"There has to be something we can do," said Bystrov, "some way around this ridiculous situation."

The colonel looked at Bystrov and Elena with a conspiratorial glint in his eyes. "I have an idea."

45

On the road even a needle is heavy. A spoon tucked into the boot
top, that's all . . .

SOFYA KRIGGEL, RED ARMY SNIPER, 1ST BELORUSSIAN FRONT

Nevel, Belorussia

November 1943

The old woman hovered over the blackened remains of her
two-story *kolkhoze*, farmhouse. The upper story had been reduced to uneven clumps of bricks, stone, and ash, plastered
in a layer of snow. The windows and doors were gone. A table, a few
chairs, and a dresser stood near the doorway. The retreating Nazis
had set the fields on fire, along with the house and barn. The icy,
smoldering terrain was a barren wasteland. It was just one of hundreds of scorched homes and factories that Elena had seen on the
frosty march to Nevel.

"If there's a hell, it must look like this," Elena said under her
breath.

The reek of melted steel wafted under her nose. They marched
another kilometer and passed a couple of Russian tanks that had
been incinerated to brown heaps.

"Why did they destroy the fields and crops?" Chava said,
flummoxed.

"Spite," Elena answered. "That's what makes it so repulsive."

"Halt," Purkayev shouted. "Entrench yourselves."

Elena turned her head in his direction. He was listening to a couple of scouts, his brow furrowed in concentration. His stalwart posture was still evident in his winter-white camouflage cloak and helmet.

"Don't waste your time," Zina whispered in her ear. "I've tried. He's not interested."

"I'm not," she said, reflexive.

"Then stop gawking at him."

A flush crept up her face.

"We've reached the periphery of Nevel," Purkayev announced. "Our offensive will commence at 0500 hours with reconnaissance-in-force."

Elena clumsily shook the straps of her rucksack off her shoulders. She felt totally inept with the bulky winter cloak over her cotton padded jacket. Her padded trousers, which came up to her chest, were rolled like a tire around her waist. She stabbed the snowy, hard earth with the tip of her spade. She snuck one last glance at Purkayev. He caught her eye. A flush crept up the back of her neck.

"Why aren't you digging?" Chava asked.

Elena turned and began shoveling furiously. One hour later, she leaned her head and neck against the edge of her foxhole and gulped a mouthful of water from her canteen. Shone her flashlight on her watch. 0214. "Almost three whole hours to sleep," she yawned.

"More than enough to attack the fascist vermin, liberate Nevel, and keep going," Chava said. "Who knows? Maybe we can take back Vitebsk tomorrow too!"

"Oh sure, we can easily march another ninety-three versts and attack," Elena replied, dryly. She slumped down to her bottom and shut her eyes. The sepia dreariness made her heart race. She felt Yurovsky holding her down. Her eyes shot open. She stood on her toes and pivoted in a circle, dropping back to the ground when she was satisfied nobody was lurking in the shadows. She drifted off to the soothing murmur of voices as her comrades settled in. The scrape of matches igniting. The erratic hum of breathing. And it occurred to her, as she felt herself sink into the numbing blackness, that she might never be able to sleep alone after the war.

"Orders have come down," the sentry shouted to the snipers' platoon, scattered in foxholes. "We attack in thirty minutes!"

It took a second for Elena to recall where she was amidst the velvety night. She glanced up at the sky, caught the glittering stars, and remembered. Nevel. Her feet tingled with pins and needles. She shook them and curled her toes in and out until the feeling went away. She heaved herself out of her foxhole and ate a piece of fatback from her rucksack.

Chava and several other girls were writing to their families, in case they didn't survive the attack. Beside her, Raya and Zina were watching the letter writers with forlorn expressions. Elena inserted herself between them and wrapped her arms around their waists. Their heads rested on her shoulders. She felt the invisible bond between them strengthen.

Five minutes later, the platoon gathered in the freshly made trench dug by the sappers. Even with the stars overhead, it was like being in a dark, frosty grave.

"Today we've been ordered to liberate the town of Nevel," Nina told Elena's platoon.

"Don't forget about the medal competition," Komarov interrupted. "A tally of seventy-five means you'll be awarded Hero of the Soviet Union."

"If you're a man," Elena mumbled.

Raya snorted.

"Taking Nevel will *also* be advantageous for our advance into Belorussia and the Baltic region," Nina countered, with a scowl at Komarov.

Nina's assertive voice reminded Elena of her sister. Masha had been strong like Nina. Not afraid of anything or anyone.

A fusillade of gunshots and mortar fire lit up the sky. The reconnaissance-in-force had just begun with fifty-four tanks and four infantry battalions.

"Keep a distance of ten to fifteen meters from your comrades and aim at officers," Nina finished. "Don't waste your bullets on soldiers. Stay sharp. Forward!"

"To victory!" The platoon responded with a salute.

"*Bila ne bila*, whatever happens, happens," Zina said, over her shoulder, when they were out of Nina's earshot.

"*Bila ne bila*," Elena and Raya echoed.

"Let's go," said Chava.

In pairs and on their bellies, the snipers fanned out across the open field and wound their way through the icy earth that divided the trenches. There were no trees or bushes to hide behind, just a carpet of white in every direction. With thick clouds of gunfire and tanks obscuring the view, it was impossible to see more than a meter in front of them. Even the town of Nevel, just a few hundred meters ahead, was invisible to the naked eye.

Suddenly there was a whistle of mortar fire from the enemy's side, along with a hail of bullets. Hot mortar splinters skimmed the air and made a fizzing noise when they landed on the snow. The enemy had launched a counterattack.

There were erratic bursts of light from Red Army machine guns. A mortar bomb hit the enemy's side, hurling snow and rocks like a spewing volcano. Tanks rumbled over the ground. Flares hissed from both sides. An enemy's grenade exploded in front of a sniper pair on Elena's left. A primal scream. Two lives gone in an instant.

Blood splattered Elena's face. Her comrades' blood. She cried and wiped it off with her sleeve and kept moving. She was afraid to stop. She was haunted by the fear of being captured.

"This is for our comrades!"

Raya's voice soared above the gunfire.

Elena looked just in time to see her comrade pull the safety pin and toss a grenade. Three and a half seconds later, the grenade detonated. Black smoke burst from the ground. The enemy retaliated with a storm of artillery fire.

An eye for an eye, Elena thought. If we keep going like this, the war will never end. She spotted Chava a couple of meters ahead. She moved faster to catch up with her. It felt as though an entire day had gone by since they'd left the trench, but the sun was just ascending the smooth white horizon.

As artillery volleyed back and forth, Elena grew more anxious about being spotted by the enemy. With nowhere to hide, she felt increasingly vulnerable. The backs of her ears were hot. She had the nagging sense they were being watched.

"Go flat," Elena whispered to Chava.

Both girls pressed their bodies to the ground. The rising sun dusted the snowy area that extended before them. Eighty meters from Elena and Chava, the snow was a shade darker. She looked through her binoculars, painted white to blend in with the wintry landscape, and noted a snowbank in the distance. She gestured for Chava to look.

Chava brought her binoculars to her eyes. "They must've made it themselves."

"That's my guess," Elena agreed.

They lay still as the cast-iron sun rose higher and the shooting around them intensified. The wind picked up. Elena's fingers were getting stiff. She took her finger off the trigger to flex it. She flinched when she saw something poke over the snowbank in her scope. Two black dots. Rifles. Pointed directly at them.

She slowed her breathing and put her finger on the trigger. She pressed her eye socket so hard against the scope it hurt. She pulled the trigger at the same time as Chava.

Only one sniper fell. The one Chava shot.

Elena's heart pounded in her ears. She took another shot. Heard someone cry out. The rifle jiggled but kept pointing at them. *What is wrong with me?* She reloaded but before she could aim, Chava shot the sniper in the head. He went down.

That should have been my bullet, thought Elena, dismayed. "I really messed up," she whispered.

"They're dead. That's all that matters."

Together, the girls scuttled on their bellies towards the dead snipers to retrieve their decorations.

Chava cut the white and red collar patches from one uniform.

"You got both of them. They go on your tally." Elena sliced the other man's shoulder straps.

"You hit one of them twice. That has to count for something."

Elena rummaged through pockets and stuffed documents into her backpack. "My shots weren't good enough. I could have been killed. I put you in danger too."

"You weren't killed. I'm fine." Chava took the rifle of one of the snipers and slung it over her shoulder.

I'm not fine, thought Elena. Under extreme duress, Chava had excelled while she'd failed miserably yet again. She grabbed the other sniper's rifle and hoisted it over her shoulder. Although a Nazi rifle was a coveted find, she took no pleasure in bringing it back to her commander. It was an undeserved victory. She felt hollow inside, as if she'd let down her partner and her platoon. She felt as if her failures always outweighed her successes.

"You're too hard on yourself," Chava said, as they pushed forward, on their stomachs, on the hunt for more enemies.

"That's what my father used to tell me."

"He sounds like an intelligent man."

"Yes, he was," Elena said, wistful.

"Nurse, I need help!" a man cried out feebly, in Russian.

Elena and Chava looked at one another. His voice came from the ditch between the field and the road.

"Nurse, where are you?"

"I'll go," Elena offered.

"I'll wait for you here, do some reconnaissance," Chava said.

Elena removed the German rifle and left it with her partner. She crept in the direction of the wounded soldier, her mind rambling from fears about being in the enemy's sights to anxiety about treating the soldier's injury. She'd had an introduction to first aid at the snipers' school, but that was ages ago and the lesson covered just the bare minimum.

"Help," the soldier called out, weakly.

Elena found him on his back, helmet still on his head. He lay within the muddy ridges of tank treads, clutching his right side with bloody hands. His tunic was covered with blood. His face was ashen. Elena's gaze fell on his abdomen. His right side had been torn open by mortar shrapnel. She was afraid his guts would fall out if she moved him. But if she left him there, he would die. She spotted his rucksack, turned it upside down to get rid of the contents, then placed the empty bag over his gaping wound. She removed her belt, keeping her body close to the ground.

"I'm going to slide my belt under your back, okay?" she said to him.

He nodded.

In the distance, tanks rumbled over the slippery landscape. A Russian "flying tank" soared overhead, showering the enemy with rockets and bombs.

Elena slid her belt beneath the wounded solider, flattening her hand to push it farther. It was like sliding paper under a rock, because he was heavy and motionless. She inhaled and burrowed her fingers under his spine, pushing the belt beneath him. On her stomach, she slunk around his feet and stuck her hand under his waist on the other side, grabbing hold of the belt. Wiggling onto her elbows, she fastened the belt over his backpack, pulling it tight.

He groaned in pain.

"Sorry if I hurt you, but I have to make a tourniquet to stop the bleeding."

"Thank you," he whispered.

She nodded slightly. She felt the enormity of his life in her hands. She took in their surroundings. It was utterly bleak. A shell crater a meter away, on her right. A dead Soviet soldier behind her, one leg missing.

A Stuka dive bomber tore through the sky. Instinctively, Elena ducked, smashing her ear against the ground. She waited until the plane was out of sight and the noise of its engine waned before lifting her head. She considered the injured soldier, who was almost twice her size. She had no idea how get him to the medic. She remembered seeing a comrade dragging a prisoner, using his rain poncho to slide him along the terrain. She pulled hers from her backpack and laid it beside the soldier, on his good side.

"I'm going to have to pull you onto this," she said, apologetic. "I don't know any other way to get you out of here."

He looked at the rain poncho, took a deep breath, and lunged sideways.

"Let's go," he groaned.

Elena rolled onto her side and folded the edges of the poncho, then asked him to hold them together. Next she clutched the poncho beneath his head, pressed her heels into the mud for leverage, and yanked him forward. She slid ahead of him and lugged him farther, a laborious process.

An enemy's tank shell exploded behind them. Splinters poured down like hail. The ground heaved. She clenched her gut. She pictured herself dying while bringing him to safety and panicked. If she had to die, she wanted to go in combat. She gnashed her teeth and hauled the soldier forward with a newfound strength she didn't know she possessed.

"I'll take it from here."

Elena craned her neck and saw a young female medic inching towards her and the injured soldier.

"You're needed at the front," the medic said.

Elena glanced at the soldier still clutching her poncho. "Will he survive?"

The medic inspected the soldier's wound, then regarded Elena. "If he does, it will be thanks to you and your creative tourniquet."

Elena's heart lifted with an emotion she hadn't experienced in a long time—pride.

46

The human remains, disfigured by fire, black and horrible, were
wrapped in grey, soil-stained blankets.
—YELENA RZHEVSKAYA, RED ARMY INTERPRETER

Chancellery Gardens, Berlin
May 1945

Dust permeated the air like fog when Ludis stopped the truck
at the foot of Wilhelmstrasse. The street was piled with rubble from buildings that no longer existed. It was impassable.

Elena was teeming with angst. She was about to raid an area that
was off-limits *and* steal two scorched bodies. The plan was as illogical
as it was dangerous, but she was too far gone to think rationally. She
grabbed a pile of blankets with her good arm and filed out of the
truck with the colonel and Bystrov. All three wore *valenki* felt boots,
though it was warm and dry, as the rubber soles wouldn't make any
noise when they crept across the road.

The street was adjacent to the Chancellery gardens. More importantly, they were directly behind the spot where the two unidentified
bodies lay. The colonel, who'd devised this simple, nerve-racking
plan, led the way. He and Bystrov carried empty sap-green ammunition boxes that resembled suitcases with their handles and rectangular shapes.

Elena stuck close to Bystrov. Her eyes darted side to side, watching
for hints of movement. It almost felt as if she were on the front again,

254

behind enemy lines. Except now she was watching out for members of her own army, comrades who would be livid if they knew they were about to be undermined.

When they reached the two-meter iron fence that separated them from the bodies, the colonel looked askance at her bandaged arm. "You sure about this?"

Her elbow throbbed slightly. No, she thought. "Yes," she said. She'd already lost her chance to exact revenge as a sniper, until the war ended, because of her arm. She wasn't about to let it ruin this all-important mission. Besides, she'd scaled fences higher than this when she was a starving partisan hunting for food. She threw the blankets over the fence, bent her knees, jumped up, and grabbed the top of the railing with her good hand. Tucking her broken elbow against her chest, she heaved her legs over to the other side, then dropped to her feet.

"Well done," the colonel said, impressed.

"Catch." Bystrov tossed his box over the fence, then the colonel's box.

Elena caught them and set them down. The two men scrambled over the fence. In the distance, she heard the click of boots across pavement. Sentries guarding the entrance on the opposite side of the garden.

They crept towards the Führerbunker without a word. They'd gone over the plan a dozen times. The scorched bodies were exactly where they'd been left. Elena began wrapping the two corpses in blankets. She was repelled by the flimsiness, how a human with bones, muscles, and organs could be reduced to light-as-air slivers.

From the corner of her eye, she saw Bystrov and the colonel placing loose bones and fragments in their ammunition boxes. Once the bodies were swathed and all the loose pieces collected, the men positioned themselves at opposite ends of the large corpse and carried it towards the fence. Elena picked up the ammunition boxes. The men retrieved the smaller corpse. She pivoted in a circle to make sure nobody had been watching, then tiptoed behind Bystrov and the colonel.

The fence seemed higher now, with two fragile bodies that had to get to the other side.

"One at a time," said the colonel. "I'll climb over and you two pass them to me."

"Why don't you get Ludis to help?" Elena suggested.

"No!" Bystrov and the colonel said sharply.

"The less he knows the better," Bystrov added.

Elena was ashamed of her lapse in judgment.

The colonel hoisted himself over the fence. He planted his feet and opened his arms to receive the first corpse.

Elena and Bystrov raised the blanket over their heads. The colonel pressed himself against the fence and grabbed hold of Bystrov's end. Bystrov moved to Elena's side and pushed it up. The colonel placed his arms under the body and moved sideways until he was able to catch Elena's end. He stepped back and lowered the body to the ground. They got the second body over the same way. Bystrov passed the boxes to the colonel. He and Elena clambered over the fence.

On the other side, Bystrov and the colonel carried the bodies to the truck, waiting on the street. From there, Ludis drove them back to SMERSH headquarters.

"I can't believe it," said Elena, once the bodies were carefully stored in a secure room. "We might have kidnapped Hitler!"

"It certainly makes for a good story," said the colonel. "Too bad we can't tell anyone."

"Not yet," Elena pointed out. "If we find out they are Hitler and his wife, Stalin will want the entire world to know that the Red Army has identified the remains."

"That would be the most logical assumption," Bystrov said, dryly.

"Hmph," said the colonel, with his ever-present cigarette hanging from the corner of his mouth.

"Now what?" said Elena.

"We wait for the forensic exam," Bystrov answered.

"When will it be?" she said, impatient.

"Soon."

The front page of *Pravda* dashed into her mind, with a bold headline: *Three-member SMERSH Unit Identifies Hitler's Remains!*

"In the meantime," the colonel said abruptly, throttling her daydream, "let's get back to work at the Führerbunker. People are expecting us. If we don't appear, suspicions will arise."

Elena couldn't resist looking back at headquarters as she got into the jeep. While she was still interested in combing through documents in the bunker, the bodies were much more enticing. She didn't know how she'd be able to concentrate. The very idea of holding Hitler's remains made her spine tingle with anticipation.

47

The three of us are from quite different families and have quite different personalities, but something we share is our friendship. It is unshakeable . . . Sasha, Kalya and I are "The Runaway Troika." How will I live without them when the war is over and we all go off in different directions?
—ROZA SHANINA, RED ARMY SNIPER

March to Vitebsk

January 1944

Winter-gray shadows stretched long and thin over Nevel, which was in shambles after the cyclone of artillery. Hunks of thatched roofs were strewn over the cratered town. Building facades had been blown up, revealing stark walls that looked as if they'd collapse in a light breeze. Corpses were scattered over the snowy earth like shale.

Elena, subsisting entirely on adrenaline after hours of grueling combat, got into formation with her platoon. She stood beside Chava and stared at the five captured prisoners roped together and crammed between two armed sentries.

"Onward, march!" Purkayev shouted.

The regiment would follow the retreating Nazis farther south to liberate Vitebsk and then advance into East Prussia.

Elena's gaze lingered on the prisoners. She winced, thinking about what they'd look like after being interrogated. Then the photo of

Tanya charged into her head and she didn't care what happened to them. In fact, she had a sudden, desperate urge to question them herself, to ask why they treated people so heinously. To look them in the eye and see if they showed fear or any emotion at all. To know if they were humans capable of committing barbaric atrocities or beasts without a conscience.

Her regiment approached the railway station at the south edge of Nevel. It was a substantial two-story building, as the town was a main connection to two major cities—Leningrad and Velikiye Luki—and it was curiously intact. But now, there was hardly a town to speak of. Now the train would have no reason to stop at Nevel.

Elena glanced longingly at the snow-covered railway tracks. She had a twenty-hour march to Vitebsk ahead of her. How wonderful it would be to sit back on a train and watch the scenery go by, the way she had going to and from university. Although it had only been a couple of years since she'd been a student, it seemed like another world that was getting harder and harder to recall. She pictured herself in a lecture hall, where her only worries were finishing her essay on Gotthold Lessing's poetry on time or achieving high marks on an exam, and vowed to return to her studies once this unconscionable war was over.

They trampled over snow-covered fields, since there was just one road out of Nevel, which sappers were checking for mines. The regiment was a kilometer from Nevel when Purkayev suddenly ordered them to halt.

"Stay in formation," he bellowed.

Elena and Chava exchanged puzzled expressions.

Purkayev called for the translator, a woman in her thirties with blond hair that stuck out like wings from the sides of her head.

The commander spoke quietly to the translator and gesticulated at something that was out of Elena's vision. She had to know what was important enough to stop the entire regiment *and* consult with the translator. Elena leaned sideways to see what they were looking at. There was a long and wide bulge in the ground with fresh snow on top. She felt as though she'd been punched in the gut. It was grotesquely similar to the pit where her mother lay.

Purkayev and the translator walked towards the prisoners. Elena strained to hear the heated interrogation, with the translator repeating Purkayev's questions in German.

"Tell me," Purkayev demanded, "who is in this grave?"

"I don't know anything," one of the prisoners replied, belligerent.

Another prisoner spat at the translator.

She wiped the spittle off her face and reiterated Purkayev's question in an assertive tone: "Who lies in this grave?"

This time, none of the five men opened their mouths. Purkayev nodded at a guard standing beside the tallest prisoner.

"No," Elena said quietly.

In one swift motion, the guard withdrew his pistol and shot the man in the head. He plunged to the ground.

"Remember what they've done to us," Raya said to her.

"I know. It's just—"

"What?" Chava pressed her.

Elena caught the flare of indignance in her eyes. She turned to look at the remaining four prisoners but, in their place, saw the twelve innocent women murdered in the ghetto's square because they were Jews. She shook her head to get the women out of her mind. She was torn between vengeance and justice. "Killing those prisoners won't change anything."

"Are you crazy?" said Zina. "Killing them will mean five less Nazis pointing machine guns at us."

"Did you forget what they did to Tanya?" Raya said.

"And they set the bodies of our fallen comrades on fire," Chava added.

Elena squirmed beneath the heat of her comrades' glares.

"How can you defend those beasts?" said Zina.

A gunshot pierced the air. A second prisoner collapsed to the ground.

"I'm not defending anyone. But nothing changes if we kill them. The people buried here won't be alive. Tanya won't come back."

"So we tell them to stop shooting at us and just set them free?" Zina snapped.

"No, that's not what I mean." Elena felt as if she were digging herself into a bottomless hole of words she couldn't articulate. "It's just . . . I think shooting them because they won't talk means we're lowering ourselves to their level of depravity."

Zina gave her a scathing smile. "Ethics don't exist in war."

"If that's true, then why does the penal battalion exist?" Elena argued. "And the Geneva Convention, which is supposed to—"

"Kikes," a squat prisoner jeered loudly in German, interrupting Elena mid-sentence. "They're just dirty kikes down there." He gestured with his head at the mass grave.

Elena blanched at the revulsion in his voice. In that moment, she recognized the excessive morality she'd tried to impose on her comrades. She saw herself through their lenses and was ashamed. She thought, if a comrade tried to persuade me to think a certain way, I wouldn't want her as a friend.

"We're standing before a mass grave of Soviet citizens, shot and buried when the fascists invaded Nevel," Purkayev declared, jostling Elena from her reflections.

Soviet citizens? She wilted with a sour disappointment. Purkayev was flogging a revisionist tale. She'd wanted him to be better than other commanders. Perceptive. But he was no different.

"Why won't he admit that the fascists are hunting Jews?" said Zina.

"Why should he?" Chava demanded. "We're all Soviets fighting for Stalin and our Motherland. I hear you talking about Jewish this and Jewish that, and it stinks of nationalism. You need to stop."

Elena was flabbergasted. Chava's attitude felt like a betrayal.

Raya bent towards Chava until they were nose to nose. "You need to understand that this grave is crammed with people killed *because* they were Jewish. My family was killed *because* they were Jewish. So were Elena's and Zina's. The fascists want to exterminate Jews. Not Soviets, not Ukrainians, but Jews. So I think we have a right to be upset."

"You act like you're the only people ever targeted," Chava lashed back. "My father was executed during the purges because he conspired against Stalin. He wasn't Jewish. He was an enemy of the people. He brought shame to our family. That's why I'm here, to make amends for my father."

"By fighting for the man who ordered your father's death?" Elena blurted.

"My father broke the law. He tried to bring capitalism to the Soviet Union."

"And you think he deserved to die, for disagreeing with Stalin?" Zina said.

"Did he even get a trial?" Elena pushed.

Chava's gaze hardened. "My father was killed because he betrayed his country. I will never turn against Stalin. I will never be like my father."

Elena winced at her partner's naive acceptance of Stalin's propaganda and brutality. Chava's father, they all knew, had been one of half a million citizens executed by Stalin from 1936 to 1938, when paranoia drove him to get rid of political rivals as well as people accused of being saboteurs, convicted through sadistic interrogations that led to forced confessions.

"Nobody's suggesting you turn against the Soviet Union," Raya said. "I also believe it's my responsibility to defend my Motherland, but I fight harder because of what the fascists have done to Jews, to my family."

"Jews are not a nation," Chava said, touting Stalin's infamous words. "The people buried there"—she gestured at the mass grave—"are Soviet citizens."

"And they're all Jewish," Elena said, wearily. "Can't you see they were executed because of their faith?"

"Can't you see why our government will never admit fascists are attacking Jews?" Chava persisted. "That would mean supporting Nazi propaganda that declares Jews must be destroyed to overpower the Soviet Union. Nazis believe Jews rule our country. Stalin doesn't want the world to think Jews are in control."

Stalin was worse than Hitler because he hid his anti-Semitism behind his Communism, Elena thought. At least Hitler was open and honest about his hatred.

Chava raised her chin. "Do not divide the dead," she finished, parroting a common Soviet slogan.

Elena exchanged glances of frustration with Raya and Zina. It was no use arguing with Chava; she'd fallen too far down the rabbit hole of Stalin's indoctrination. Besides, Chava was a good person, a loyal partner, despite her misguided opinions.

"All we can do is keep fighting," Zina was saying.

"For what? A future in a country that spreads the extremist anti-Semitic values of the Black Hundreds?" Elena said.

Chava eyed her with righteous indignation. "How can you compare Communism to the Black Hundreds? We're all equal in the Soviet Union."

"That's not true," Zina argued. "The Black Hundreds were organizing pogroms decades ago. Anti-Semitism has always been there, below the surface like electricity, ready to ignite when wires are crossed."

"But I've heard Stalin say, over the radio, that anti-Semitism is dangerous to working people," Chava argued.

"Don't tell me you believe everything that comes out of his mouth," Raya scoffed.

"Of course I do. I'm a Communist."

"You don't think there are Communists who hate Jews?" said Elena.

"It doesn't matter. We're all equal."

"So everyone follows the party line to the letter?" Zina said, with vinegar in her voice.

"Well, yes," said Chava.

Elena raised her brow, exasperated.

"If we're not extinct when the war ends," Raya said, "then Hitler loses and we win. That's what I'm fighting for. Survival."

"Same for me," Zina said.

"And when we trample Hitler and his minions," Chava added, "you'll see that I'm right, that there is no such thing as anti-Semitism in the Soviet Union."

Her words echoed uncomfortably in the fetid air.

Elena glanced sideways at Raya and Zina and thought, none of us are outwardly Jewish, like our parents and grandparents used to be. No wonder people like Chava and Purkayev can easily lump us all into one group, conveniently ignoring the fact that we're being hunted. Because they don't see the differences between us. They don't know what it means to be Jewish because we barely know. Stalin's Communism has already extinguished our culture.

Gunshots cracked through the air.

Elena watched the last three prisoners drop to the ground beside the other two. For the first time since she'd arrived at the front, she felt nothing when she saw dead men lying in their own blood.

48

All that day, so pregnant with the sense of imminent victory, it was decidedly tiresome to be carrying a box about, and to turn cold whenever I thought about the possibility of accidentally leaving it somewhere. It burdened and oppressed me.

—YELENA RZHEVSKAYA, *MEMOIRS OF A SOVIET INTERPRETER*

Surgical Mobile Field Hospital No. 4961, Pankow, Berlin

May 1945

Sweat dribbled from Elena's hairline as she pored over Goebbels's diary in the clammy bunker. What a feast of delusions and lies! "It is essential, no matter what, to continue to spread the rumors: peace with Moscow, Stalin coming to Berlin, the invasion of England in the near future, all in order to cover up every aspect of the situation as it actually is . . . Rumors are our daily bread."

After annotating crucial information that had nothing to do with Hitler's whereabouts and everything to do with hiding the truth from German citizens, she feverishly copied as much as she could into her own notebooks. As soon as the diaries were sent to headquarters, they would become mired in secrecy and she'd never see them again. Her throat was scratchy from the gritty air. She glanced at her watch. She'd been working nonstop for almost three hours. Another few minutes and then she'd take a break outside. Let her lungs unclog before resuming her work.

There was a rustling noise in the corridor. Like the sound of wool trouser legs swishing together. She sat up. Bystrov? No. He and Gorbushin were attending a meeting at headquarters. A guard? Maybe. But in her experience, they made no attempt to arrive anywhere quietly, pounding their feet heavily on the ground as if they wanted to be seen. She held her breath.

Tap, tap, tap. It sounded as if a branch was hitting a window. Except she was underground and there were no windows.

She began to panic. What if it was a Nazi who'd managed to stay hidden during the search of the bunker? A Nazi with a score to settle. A Nazi with nothing to lose. She imagined herself coming face-to-face with an enemy soldier. She grabbed the pistol holstered on her belt. *This can't be how it ends.* She aimed at the doorway.

"Comrade Bruskina?"

Ludis emerged from the darkness.

She jumped in her seat. Pulled the trigger.

The bullet swerved right, hitting the corner of the doorjamb.

He ducked.

"My God!" Elena cried. "I almost shot you! What are you doing sneaking up on me?"

"I didn't mean to," Ludis said, stumbling over his words. "I got confused down here. I wasn't sure where I was going."

"I'm sorry. I'm so sorry." Her entire body was trembling. "Why are you here?"

"Colonel Gorbushin and Major Bystrov sent me. They want you at the field hospital in Pankow right away."

She gathered her notebooks and hurried to the jeep, her mind racing with questions and possibilities.

In the provisional lab at the field hospital, the charred remains were laid out on a table with white sheets. The room had the suffocating pickle smell of formaldehyde. There were jars of human specimens lining shelves on two walls. Elena averted her gaze. She didn't know why anyone would choose pathology as a career.

"Did you find something?" she asked the colonel and Bystrov, standing beside her. "Did the pathologist finish his exam?"

"We're not sure and yes," Bystrov answered.

"What does that mean?"

"Patience," the colonel said. He reached forward to a metal desk and extracted a dark red cigar box from the top drawer. He presented it to Elena as if it were a gift, an expensive gift.

She looked at it, curious and a little afraid. She was obviously the lowest ranked of the three of them. She had a feeling she'd been chosen for a task neither of them wanted. That the box contained something she wasn't going to like.

"Open it," Bystrov said.

She lifted the lid and blanched. A jawbone with yellow decayed teeth was nestled on red satin.

"Are these—"

"We don't know," Gorbushin interjected. "But we're going to find out."

"How?"

"We need to track down Hitler's dentist," Bystrov explained. "Dental records will either prove or refute the origin of these teeth."

"You will translate for us as we try to locate this dentist," the colonel added. "And I am making you responsible for keeping the teeth safe."

"Me?"

"You are the most reliable," said the major, "since you don't drink and are less likely to tell people about them. Or misplace them."

"You must be mute as a fish," the colonel said, vehemently. "We cannot speak about the possibility of Hitler's teeth to anyone."

Hitler's teeth? It was preposterous.

"I understand," Elena replied.

"We will begin tomorrow." The colonel slapped Bystrov's shoulder exuberantly. "But now, we will drink to the death of Goebbels. It would be a pity to let all the liquor we've found go to waste."

The major looked at Elena.

"I'll pour the drinks," she jested.

"Just don't let that box out of your sight," the colonel reminded her, "or heads will roll."

Elena clutched the red cigar box to her chest as she walked out of headquarters, flanked by Bystrov and the colonel.

"By the way, Comrade Bruskina," said Bystrov, "I thought you'd like to know that the doctor who performed the forensic autopsy was a Jewish woman. Dr. Anna Marants."

A Jewish doctor examined Hitler? If it was, in fact, Hitler. She felt the weight of the box in her arms. She could be holding Hitler's teeth. A Jew. This would have driven Hitler crazy. She smiled at the poetic justice.

49

A bullet is a fool; fate is a villain.
We are a feather; a sparrow's feather.
—KLAVDIYA, RED ARMY SNIPER

Operation Bagration, Krustpils, Latvia

August 1944

Our command invites you to come over to our side."
Elena listened with indifference to the German voice crackling from a loudspeaker, concealed somewhere outside their dugout. It was a sultry morning at the beginning of August. She was on her bunk with Raya, Zina, and Chava. Their platoon was south of Lake Lubāns in Latvia. They were all supposed to be asleep in preparation for the offensive that night, but lice embedded in her skin made it impossible to sit still, let alone rest.

"You will receive money, food, a villa . . ." the unseen voice announced in muffled, broken Russian.

Elena took a big gulp of tea made from boiled conifer needles. She made a face. It was far more bitter than the awful dandelion tea her mother used to make when she had cramps with her monthly. She felt a twinge in her stomach, recalling her mother tucking her under warm blankets and speaking to her with an unusual tenderness during those days.

"You will be treated well if you come to our side . . ."

"Why are you forcing that guck down your throat?" said Zina.

"To prevent scurvy." Elena swatted at a cloud of gnats. Her arm was dotted with open sores from where she'd clawed at lice. "You're supposed to be drinking it too."

"You couldn't make me drink that for a thousand rubles."

"A thousand?"

Zina scratched her head vigorously. "Well, maybe a thousand."

Elena looked at the greenish-brown tea in her tin cup. At least one more big, disgusting mouthful.

"There is no way pine needles prevent scurvy," Zina scoffed. "That's as stupid as spitting three times over your shoulder to avoid being cursed," she continued.

"I know," Elena conceded. "But Komarov said it might also cure stomachaches and my—"

"I thought you didn't like Komarov." Raya shrank back from the cloud of gnats that were flitting around her.

"He's a pest. I can't stand him." Elena dragged her fingers over her blotchy neck.

"Then why are you touting his words as if he were Pushkin?" said Chava.

"Don't exaggerate," Elena replied.

Zina folded her arms. "Well?"

"I'll try anything to make my stomach better."

Zina waved her hands in front of her face to get rid of the gnats. "I don't think there's anything wrong with your stomach."

"What? Now *you're* a doctor?"

"You're wound tight as a clock's spring," Zina said.

"You don't know how I feel."

"Anyone with eyes can see through you," said Chava.

"What are you talking about?"

"Whenever you hear Purkayev's voice, you turn red and look at him like he's poisonous chocolate."

"No I don't!"

"Come on. We've all seen you," Raya said.

"We?" Elena's baffled gaze slid over her comrades. "You talk about me?"

"Because we're worried about you," said Chava.

"So you talk about me behind my back?"

"You said you were done with men," Zina said, "after Yurovsky."

"I am," she snapped. She was angry with herself for letting her guard down, for being too obvious. For being attracted to Purkayev. "He's a sheep regurgitating Stalin's lies about Jews——"

"Purkayev doesn't have a choice. You know that," said Raya.

"He doesn't have to flog idiotic propaganda," Elena said.

"You don't have to drink that revolting tea," Chava pointed out.

"You expect too much," Raya went on, gently. "You'll always be disappointed if you hold people to impossibly high standards."

A shooting pain tore through Elena's stomach. She doubled over.

"Are you okay?" Zina said.

"It's just a stomachache. It'll pass." She clutched her abdomen with both hands.

"What if this happens on the front?" Zina said.

"It only happens . . . when I'm off." She exhaled. "When I have time to remember . . . things."

"Remembering is dangerous," Raya said.

"Our command invites you to come over to our side," the recorded German voice started up again.

Elena flapped her hand to get rid of the gnats in front of her face.

"You will receive money, food, a villa . . ."

She slid off her bunk, grabbed her pistol, and left their quarters in the dugout. Perked her ear in the direction of the German voice. She marched towards the pine trees thirty meters away and saw the speaker perched between two branches. She silenced the speaker with one bullet. And when she returned to her quarters, her stomach no longer ached.

Machine-gun fire blasted from both sides at Krustpils, creating a thick haze of smoke. Elena and Chava moved forward, closer to the enemy, taking advantage of the poor visibility. They dropped into a gully as the torrent of bullets diminished and the air cleared. They were just thirty meters from the enemy's trenches. Elena peered through her binoculars and saw the barrel of the fascists' rifles on the rim of their trench.

Chava gestured for her to point her binoculars up and thirty degrees to the left, at a massive oak tree about a hundred meters from them. Elena peered through her lenses. The late afternoon sun backlit the branches and honey-colored leaves. She scanned left to right. Something that didn't belong caught her eye. She squinted and adjusted the focus. Something odd shimmered through branches midway up the tree. A distinctive field-gray hue. A German sniper was perched in the tree, overlooking the Red Army front.

"We didn't spot him earlier because the sun wasn't on him," Chava whispered. "Now, with the sun low in the sky, it's shining right on him."

"Is he alone?" said Elena.

"I haven't seen anyone else."

"We can't let him get away."

"You shoot," said Chava. "I'll stay on lookout."

"No. You're the better shot."

"You shoot," Chava said, firmly.

"Is this about my tally? Because I don't care if mine is—"

"Just shoot," Chava said.

Elena swallowed her apprehension. She loaded her magazine

and assessed the shooting conditions. There was no wind but the air was damp, which would slow the bullet. And she would be shooting upwards.

"Hurry, before the sun dips too far to spot him," Chava said, urgently.

She peered through her scope, aimed at the sniper's head, and made the necessary adjustments. Held her breath and pulled the trigger. Her shoulder kicked back from the recoil. A loud thud. The sniper fell to the ground.

"Another one for your tally," Chava said, as if she were talking about a melon.

The tally. When this godforsaken war was over, Elena never wanted to hear the word *tally* ever again. She scanned the enemy's trench. A German was on her right flank, standing with his arm raised. She caught the flash of a hand grenade. She got his head in the crosshairs of her scope. Pulled the trigger. He went down.

The grenade he'd thrown exploded behind Elena, producing a fiery cloud of dirt and smoke. The blast tossed her into the air and knocked her rifle out of her hands. She landed flat on her stomach, the wind knocked right out of her. She struggled for air. She felt as if she were outside her body, looking down from above. She wondered if she was dead.

The earth trembled. God's anger? Her breathing eased. She wiggled her fingers and her toes in her boots. She drew her knees and elbows into her torso. Her left knee rolled over something hard and lumpy. Cylindrical. Another grenade?

The uproar of combat dwindled to a wasp-buzzing silence. The world began to spin. She closed her eyes and curled her hands into fists. She was ready. If this was her time, she'd go without crying. The path to paradise begins in hell, she thought, soothing herself with a favorite phrase from Dante's *Inferno*.

She waited. And waited. Opened her right eye to see if she was still present, on the Eastern Front. Or if the explosion had happened so fast, she was already gone.

Her knee was still on the object. If it was a grenade that had been stuffed with explosives, she'd be dead. Better an ounce of luck than a pound of gold, she decided, recalling one of her mother's platitudes. She leaned back. Gritted her teeth. Pulled her knee away. She brought both hands to her mouth when she spied the pineapple grenade. The firing pin was pulled out, which meant it had discharged. But the grenade was still intact. It hadn't been filled with gunpowder. Why? The fascists weren't careless.

Tentatively, she moved her hand towards the grenade. She wrapped her fingers around the small device, picked it up, and drew the lever back. A tiny piece of paper fell from the inside, where gunpowder should have been. She plucked the fragment from the ground. The words *We do what we can* sprang up at her like a bold headline. They must have been written by a Russian prisoner of war tasked with filling hand grenades for the Germans. Somehow, he or she had managed to get this one past their guards.

It was *bashert*, fate. Unearthing a grenade armed with words, not explosives. She was supposed to be there. She was supposed to survive. She was there for a reason.

But why?

50

We all picked up our weapons and ran into the street. There were
hugs, tears, laughter and random shooting in the air.

Charité Hospital, Berlin

May 1945

Colonel Gorbushin got into the front of the jeep and instructed Ludis to drive to Charité Hospital. Gorbushin had heard it was the closest hospital to the Führerbunker, which made it a favorable place to begin their search for Hitler's dentist. The problem was, none of them knew their way around Berlin, apart from the route to the Führerbunker.

Ludis unfolded his map of the city.

Elena leaned between the front seats and peered at the map. "Here it is." She pointed at a building on Invalidenstrasse. "By the Kronprinzen Bridge."

Gorbushin stabbed the map with his index finger. "Let's go."

Elena, sitting beside Bystrov, held the red box in her lap with both hands. Today could be the day they verified Hitler's death. Or not. Everything hung on the teeth and the findings of a person who may not even be in Berlin anymore. Who may be one of the thousands of citizens who'd starved to death during the battle for the city. Then what?

The jeep bumped over a scrim of bricks and stones. Through her window, she noticed smoke ascending from piles of debris. She recalled photos of Berlin she'd seen before the war, elaborate buildings with intricately engraved faces and characters, domed roofs and rows of majestic pillars. There was even a bridge with life-sized statues carved on top of the railing. She wondered if any of it remained, or if Hitler's maniacal quest to take over Europe had cost Germans their capital city.

The jeep braked quickly, pitching Elena into Gorbushin's seat.

"Sorry," Ludin said. "This street is blocked. I'll have to back up and go another way."

Elena glanced at the red box. Still intact. No damage done.

Ludis drove backwards, then turned onto another street that was barely passable, with rubble stacked along both sides of the road.

"I don't know where we are," Gorbushin said. "I can't find any street signs."

"They're gone," said Ludis. "So are the lampposts."

"Crushed by tanks," said Bystrov.

"I can't navigate if I don't know what street we're on," Gorbushin said.

Elena squirmed in her seat. This was taking too long.

"Let's ask those kids," said Gorbushin, pointing at a group of boys on a corner. "Bruskina?"

Elena leaned her head out her window. "Excuse me, boys," she called out in German.

They turned their heads towards the car.

"We're looking for Charité Hospital, near the—"

"I know where it is," one of the boys said. He approached the jeep, saw the map in Gorbushin's hands, and stuck his finger on a spot. "You're here. You need to go over to this street, turn left, and take the first right. That'll take you right to the hospital."

"Thank you," said Elena, taken aback by the boy's comfort with a group of Soviet soldiers.

"Here we are," Ludis said.

His voice sounded tinny and far away to Elena, in the midst of sleep. Then she heard two other male voices and her eyes shot open. She saw Bystrov and it all came back to her. She glanced at her watch. Two hours had passed since the boy had given them directions. Two hours to go a few versts. If this wasn't the hospital, they would have ended up spending the entire day in the car going nowhere.

Charité Hospital bordered the River Spree where it curved down to meet the Reichstag and then bent up like an elbow. The brick exterior had been painted with camouflage stripes to avoid air attacks, though portions of the building had still been damaged by bombs. The central part, with its perfectly symmetrical balconies and impressive iron railings, was unharmed.

Ludis turned off the jeep's engine beneath an arched portico. On the right, double black doors marked the entrance.

Elena clasped the red box tight to her chest as she stepped out of the jeep.

"Keep it down," Bystrov said sharply. "The box. You're making it look too important. Hold it at your side."

Elena's arm snapped down. All of a sudden, the task in front of her seemed onerous. The odds of tracking down Hitler's dentist *and* getting hold of his dental records seemed nearly impossible.

The hospital's interior was magnificent, with its soaring foyer, lavish moldings, neoclassical columns, and walls adorned with intricately carved images. Elena paused in front of a rounded niche containing a statue of a bearded man with a kind face and chin-length hair.

"Comrade Bruskina," Gorbushin said, "we need you to talk to this nurse."

She hurried over to Bystrov and Gorbushin. They'd cornered a jittery nurse in a gray smock and white headscarf, embellished with a red cross in the center.

"You want me to ask if Hitler's doctor works here?" Elena said to Bystrov and Gorbushin.

"No, no," said Bystrov, impatiently. "Ask where the ear, nose, and throat department is."

The nurse told Elena it was in the basement. She gestured at a staircase in the far-left corner, then hurried off in the opposite direction.

Elena beckoned for the men to follow her. She led them down the concrete stairs to a dimly lit corridor. A sign indicated the head of the department's name, Doktor von Eicken, and office number, 11.

She found the office and knocked on the door.

"*Eintreten*, enter," came a withered voice.

She turned and gave Gorbushin and Bystrov a this-is-it look. She opened the door.

An old man with stringy long hair sat at a cluttered desk. He greeted them with wary eyes behind wire-rimmed spectacles.

"*Was kann ich für Sie tun?*" he asked. "What can I do for you?"

Elena introduced herself and the men. She apologized for intruding. He waved a veiny, arthritic hand as if it were no bother, though she knew this wasn't the case. Young boys accepting the presence of Russians was one thing; an old man who'd lived under German rule for sixty years was another. She asked if Hitler had ever been treated in the hospital.

"*Ja*," Eicken responded without hesitation. "Reich Chancellor Hitler came to me when he had a bad throat a few years ago. It was 1935, I believe. And after someone tried to kill him, last year, he sought treatment from me for his eardrums. Serious damage was done by the bomb that went off. I thought I might have to operate, but his hearing improved."

Elena conveyed the doctor's words to Bystrov and Gorbushin, her voice quivering with elation.

"I treated Trotsky too." Eicken wobbled out from his desk. "Same problem with his throat. A politician's scourge, I suppose."

Elena could tell that the doctor welcomed the chance to talk. Yet he was so frail, Elena was afraid his bones would break as he shuffled around his desk.

"The chancellor's private doctor used to work here at Charité," he went on, "but he was sent to Berchtesgaden."

Elena's face fell. She recalled documents indicating Hitler's plans to go to his holiday home in the Bavarian Alps.

"What did he say?" Bystrov demanded.

The major scowled when she mentioned the Berghof, Hitler's mountain residence.

"Ask about his dentist," said Gorbushin.

Eicken stroked his neck, pleated with excess skin, before answering. "His other personal doctor was also his dentist."

"Here?" Elena said.

"Yes. But I can't think of his name." He puckered his brow. "Sometimes my memory isn't what it used to be."

Elena nodded as if she understood. "Do you know someone who could help us find this doctor?"

Eicken hobbled to his door and called out a name.

A young man with florid skin appeared. Eicken asked if he knew the name of Hitler's doctor who was also his dentist.

"Dr. Blaschke," the young man replied.

"Very good," said Eicken. He turned to Elena. "This is Helmut, a dentistry student. He can take you to Dr. Blaschke if you like."

"Yes please." She smiled at Eicken. "Thank you for receiving us with such kindness."

"Of course," he said. "It is our tradition."

Tradition?

"I can take you in my car," Helmut said, amiably.

"You mean, Dr. Blaschke is not in the hospital?" Elena said.

"Not today. He is working at his private surgery."

"And you don't mind driving us? Dr. Eicken didn't even ask if you had other things to do."

"I cannot say no." He flashed a cursory smile.

That's it, Elena realized with a sad jolt. The sacrosanct German tradition that oppressed Russians as well. Saying yes when you really mean no. Unquestioning obedience.

51

Having distinguished herself during an enemy counter-attack, Shanina is being awarded the medal "For Valour." She is an outstanding sniper of our sub-unit.

—ARTICLE ABOUT SNIPER ROZA SHANINA, IN *UNICHTOZHIM VRAGA*

Battle of Küstrin, Poland
January–March 1945

G rab hold."

Elena reached for Chava's proffered hand, anchored her other one on the wheel's rim, and hauled herself onto the T-34 tank. Her nose stung at the smack of diesel fuel. The swamp-green tank had been idling for an hour, a necessity to warm the engine in the frosty below-zero temperature. Clutching her rifle in her right hand, she sat on the cylindrical fuel tank between Nina and Chava. Raya and Zina were up front, on the mudguard, with machine gunners from the 3rd Shock Army.

It was almost dusk, on the last day of January, and Elena's regiment had been ordered to launch a surprise attack on Küstrin, a small town on the eastern bank of the Oder River. Küstrin was the final barrier between the Red Army and Germany, but Hitler had just declared Küstrin, with its thirteenth-century castle, to be a fortress city. This meant the Wehrmacht was obligated to defend it until the last man went down.

"If we don't seize Küstrin today, I'm swimming across the Oder," Chava said. "I've had it with this place."

"Me too," Elena replied. After weeks of unsuccessful attempts to capture the bridges across the Oder, she'd pinned all her hopes on this assault.

"Don't you dare speak of failure," Nina retorted. "If you start with a poor attitude, you'll get poor results."

Elena and Chava glanced at one another, startled. Usually, Nina was the essence of composure. That's what made her such a good leader.

"Are you all right?" Elena asked.

Nina took in a sharp breath. "Time is against us. The ice on the river is starting to crack. If we don't take Küstrin before the bridge is destroyed, we could be trapped here for months."

Elena was upended by the enormity of Nina's words. And by the burden of responsibility Nina carried, as their leader.

"We're going in with twelve tanks," Chava began, her voice chirping with optimism. "So we have the element of surprise *and* plenty of ammunition."

"She's right." Elena craned her neck to see the jeep in front of them, transporting Purkayev and several infantry commanders. "We'll be crossing the Oder tomorrow."

Nina leaned forward and gazed at the line of tanks behind them. "I'm just tired. Of course—"

A whistle's trill ended their conversation.

The bullnecked tank commander, perched in the cupola, pumped his fist and blew his whistle again. The tank lurched forward, leading the convoy.

Elena bounced up. She squeezed her thighs against the fuel tank to keep steady.

"*Bystreye*, faster!" the tank commander shouted.

Chilly air slapped Elena's face as the tank picked up speed on a narrow road lined with snow-covered trees.

"I didn't . . . tanks went . . . fast," Elena yelled, her words lost in the wind.

"Me either," Chava hollered. She cleared strands of hair that had blown into her mouth.

The tank raced through the town at an astonishing speed, past columns of houses where civilians stood, late-afternoon shadows falling across their bewildered faces. Elena was infuriated. They should have been evacuated weeks ago, but doing so would have been tantamount to the Germans admitting defeat.

A couple of blocks ahead, a tram was at a standstill. Passengers scurried from the doors and vanished around corners.

The tank closed in on the trolley. Elena, Chava, and Nina exchanged glances of unspoken urgency. They twisted their waists and grabbed onto the bar just below the air louvers with both hands. They sank their heads between their arms, bracing for the inevitable.

With a heart-stopping smash, the tank rammed into the trolley, crumpling it as if it were paper, not steel. Knocking it off the tracks.

Elena's head plunged forward from the impact, hitting the air louvers, then backwards, wrenching her neck. Her fingers began to slip. She curled them around the bar, raking her fingernails into her palms.

Moments later, the tank lurched to a stop in the town's main intersection. Elena was shocked by the sight of civilians with handcarts, horse-drawn wagons, cars, and sledges clogging the streets, desperate to escape. More people intentionally put in harm's way by the Wehrmacht, who hadn't evacuated them sooner.

"What a disaster!" Chava said, frantically.

"Withdraw!" Purkayev shouted from the jeep.

The tank rolled back sluggishly.

Nina cupped her mouth with her hands and yelled: "Snipers, dismount and entrench yourselves, in pairs."

Elena hopped off the tank and, with Chava close behind, pushed her way through the horde. The hysterical voices and the crowds of people squeezed together threw her mind back to the ghetto, when she and Tsila saw the twelve women murdered. She stumbled.

"Elena?" Chava's voice wafted in and out.

Just then, splinters of light zoomed towards their tank. A colossal boom shook the ground. Elena felt the blast through the soles of her feet. The enemy had fired a Panzerfaust, a handheld anti-tank weapon that discharged grenades. Black clouds of smoke engulfed the tank. Then it burst into flames.

Elena watched, horrified, as the blaze consumed the tank. With gunners who'd shared her platoon from the start. The tank commander. The driver.

Soviet machine gunners from the jeep and the second tank retaliated with a salvo of bullets.

More splinters of light. The second tank was on fire. Black smoke devoured the sky.

By dawn, only four tanks remained and dozens of soldiers, including two girls from Elena's platoon, had been killed. Elena and Chava had eliminated two Panzerfaust nests, and their comrades had taken out another five, but still, enemy grenades continued to be launched.

It all seems futile, thought Elena, as she lay down on the floor of an abandoned factory at the edge of town. As if they'd been fighting bullets with slingshots.

It had been two long months since the Panzerfaust assault, two grueling months of daily combat in the sky with dive-bombers and on the ground with artillery. Küstrin was on fire. But this morning was different. This morning, multiple rocket launchers, Katyushas, greeted the enemy with the heaviest flood of explosives yet. Machine gunners and snipers then spent hours bombarding the town with a relentless storm of bullets, mortar bombs, and grenades.

Now crackling flames licked the roofs and walls of buildings. The air was saturated with flecks, like a condensed fog. Küstrin had become an incinerator, a town of cards, and the enemy, down in numbers and weapons, hadn't been able to mount an effective defense. Instead, they surrendered, arms held high.

"It's over . . ." Elena said, exhausted. She and her comrades stood behind a collapsed wall, watching the town burn.

"Berlin, here we come!" Zina combed her fingers through her shoulder-length mahogany tresses.

"Don't get too ahead of yourself," Raya cautioned. "We still have to cross the Oder and get through Seelow Heights."

Zina lit a cigarette and snorted. "After three months here, I'm ready for anything."

"What about Kirill?" Chava teased, gesturing towards Zina's latest conquest, the TASS journalist who'd had his eye on her for months.

Four sets of eyes turned thirty degrees to the bird-thin man snapping photos of the blazing town.

Zina exhaled smoke rings. "He's incredibly talented. You should see his photos of me."

"I'll bet." Elena stole a look at Purkayev, engrossed in a conversation with the 3rd Shock Army commander. She felt a primal stir in her gut that roused and scared her.

"I think he's the one," Zina said.

Elena dragged her gaze from Purkayev.

"Why? What makes him so special?" said Chava.

"Lots of things but mostly . . ." Her voice drifted off.

"Mostly what?" Raya pushed.

"He listens to me. He wants to get to know me. He's not just interested in . . . you know." She giggled self-consciously.

Elena recalled the weight of Yurovsky, the feeling of helplessness, the searing pain. She hugged herself until the bad memory dulled, then said, "There aren't many men like Kirill."

"I know," Zina said, her gaze still pasted on him. "But there he was, right in front of me. I just had to open my eyes."

Elena looked skeptically at Zina. It was hard to believe, after all the duds Zina had complained about over the last two years, after all the men who'd taken advantage of her and then tossed her away, that she was still open to the idea of love. Marriage even. Elena coveted Zina's romanticism but she was happy for her friend. And although she had a niggling sense that Purkayev felt something for her, the prospect of intimacy was terribly frightening.

Zina flicked her glowing cigarette butt on the ground. Elena crushed it with her foot.

That night, the Oder River was silent and calm. The moon was obscured by clouds. It was a perfect night to cross on rafts made from the wreckage of the bridge. Still, Elena watched the German side with trepidation. Wehrmacht soldiers could be lying in wait, concealed by the darkness, ready to pounce the second they landed. They could be loading mortar bombs this very second. Or getting ready to hurl Panzerfaust grenades. The quiet allowed too much room to think.

The devil lies in still waters. Her mother's words came into her head. It's just a dumb saying, she told herself. Devils don't even exist, her father would tell her mother, if he were here.

If they were here.

She looked back at Küstrin as if the answers were there in the smoldering town. But all the light was gone. Küstrin had become a black portrait of war. There were no ambiguous shades of gray. There had been no compromises. There was no way forward, no victory, without total annihilation.

52

I trust no one, not even myself.

—JOSEPH STALIN

City Center, Berlin

May 1945

Helmut drove across the Kronprinzen Bridge into the city center. The roads were still cluttered with debris, yet the number of people on bicycles and on foot had multiplied tenfold. There were children in baskets attached to bicycles, families on sidewalks pushing carts and prams loaded with their belongings. Older people, bent with age, stranded. Adults and children wore the same dazed and bleary expressions.

A few minutes later, they arrived in a neighborhood that was once well-heeled, judging from the grand houses, now blemished with shell marks. A bearded man with a heavily lined face answered the door. He said he was Dr. Bruck. Elena asked if they could see Dr. Blaschke.

"I'm sorry," he replied, "but Dr. Blaschke is in Berchtesgaden."

Elena curled her fingers around the red box. She gave Bystrov and Gorbushin the bad news.

"Find out if he knows any of Blaschke's employees," Gorbushin suggested.

Dr. Bruck gave an enthusiastic nod. "Käthe Heusermann. Her apartment is on this street."

"I can get her," Helmut offered.

288

Dr. Bruck gave him the address, then invited Elena, Bystrov, and Gorbushin to sit with him in the waiting room. Elena sat down and realized they were in the very same chairs that Hitler and his cronies would have sat in while awaiting their appointments. Disgusting, she thought. Then she looked down at the box and a sly smile crossed her face.

"Käthe Heusermann was my student too," Dr. Bruck explained. "And my assistant. Before the Nazis." He lowered his voice and said, "I had to leave. Because I am a Jew."

"I understand," said Elena, sympathetically.

His perceptive eyes roamed from Elena to the box in her hands. "Käthe and her sister shared their rations with me. They helped me disappear."

A whoosh of air and a flash of blue interrupted their conversation. Elena was disappointed. She wanted to talk to Dr. Bruck for a bit longer. She thanked Helmut and told him he could return to Charité. Elena turned her attention to Dr. Blaschke's assistant.

Käthe Heusermann was a willowy girl in a navy-blue coat with a headscarf over long blond hair. Her smile vanished the second she laid eyes on Elena, Bystrov, and Gorbushin.

"Käthchen, it's all right," said Dr. Bruck. "They just want to ask you a few questions."

"About what?" she said, in a thin voice.

"Did you ever work on Hitler's teeth?" said Elena. "We've been told you were Dr. Blaschke's assistant and that he was Hitler's dentist."

"I started working with him in 1937," Käthe answered, guardedly. "I assisted the doctor when he extracted Hitler's teeth."

"She's the one," Elena said to Bystrov and Gorbushin. "She worked on Hitler's teeth."

"Very good," said Gorbushin, "but we still need tangible proof, his dental records and X-rays."

Elena told Käthe what they needed.

"Why?" said Käthe.

"I can't say. It's confidential."

Käthe glanced at Dr. Bruck. He nodded.

"Records are kept in the surgery." She walked into an adjoining room.

Elena, Gorbushin, and Bystrov followed.

Käthe opened a cabinet, took out a box of record cards, and flipped through them with shaky hands.

Elena's gut knotted when she saw records for Himmler, Goebbels, his wife, and their children.

"Found it," Käthe said, with a sigh of relief.

Elena studied the card. "It proves Hitler was a patient, but there are no X-rays and no descriptions of work done, only dates and times," she told Gorbushin and Bystrov.

"We may be able to find X-rays in Blaschke's other surgery," Käthe said to Elena, "but it's in the Reich Chancellery."

Elena reiterated Käthe's words to Bystrov and Gorbushin.

"Let's go," said the colonel.

"*Auf Wiedersehen*, goodbye," Elena said to Dr. Bruck.

He eyed the red box. "I pray you have the truth in your hands."

53

Lads, finish me off quickly.
—ROZA SHANINA, RED ARMY SNIPER, AFTER BEING HIT BY A SHELL
THAT RIPPED HER STOMACH OPEN (SHE DIED SOON AFTER, IN 1945)

East Prussia

April 1945

The first thing Elena noticed in Germany was the stark contrast between the rough scrubland and the tidy farmland. As she marched over a sprawling field, she was taken aback by the rows of ruler-straight lines in front of her, rectangular plots that stretched as far and wide as she could see. The sun peeked over the horizon, casting a pinkish golden beam over the manicured parcels, covered in hoarfrost.

"You wouldn't think there's a war going on here," Elena said.

"These . . . are peasants' farms?" said Chava.

Behind them, soldiers' drunken voices pierced the air. They were hooting and pointing at their slovenly comrade, floundering. He had a glassy-eyed smile that seemed to be more prevalent amongst the men as soon as they'd crossed the Oder.

"Regiment halt!" Purkayev strode towards the staggering man. "Get back into formation now or it's off to the gulag," he roared.

The soldier belched.

Repugnance flicked across Elena's face.

"Excuse me," the soldier wisecracked.

A low snicker rose from the soldiers.

Elena saw a blot of defeat in Purkayev's eyes. He was trying to keep the unruly men in line but couldn't very well send all of them to the gulag. She felt a twinge of sympathy; he wasn't merely a lieutenant general, he was a zookeeper.

Purkayev seized the drunken soldier's canteen. He unscrewed the lid and poured out the last dregs of alcohol.

"Whataya doin'?" the soldier moaned, his words garbled.

"You look like you could use a drink, Commander," another soldier remarked, in a woozy drawl. "Loosen up a bit."

Purkayev tossed the canteen aside. "I don't drink."

"You're joking," said the soldier with the now-empty canteen.

"The only reason I'm still here is because I drink," said the one with a drawl.

"Even if you're lucky enough to survive the end of the war, you'll be dead within months," Purkayev said.

"How do you know?" he scoffed.

Purkayev sucked in his cheeks. "Because I watched my father drink himself to death and you remind me of him."

Elena stared at Purkayev, transfixed by his honesty.

The intoxicated soldier returned to formation.

"Regiment march on!" Purkayev shouted, terse.

For several minutes, the only sound was the crunch of heels on the frosty meadow. Until Purkayev led them from the field onto a paved road.

Elena was astonished by the tidy stretch of asphalt. Back in Russia, there were only dirt roads in the countryside that turned to mud during the spring and fall rain, becoming traps for cars. Here the road that stretched out in front of them was as smooth as city streets in Minsk.

They passed a solid farmhouse made of brick with a tiled red roof that didn't sag like the wooden rooftops on peasants' houses in Russia. And unlike Soviet farms, razed by fire during combat, it was still standing.

"There are no broken windows or pockmarks from shells," she said, glancing around.

"Just look at the yard." Raya pointed at the immaculate front garden with neatly planted fruit trees and trimmed hedges. The bare branches, draped in ice, glittered.

"Who has time to garden during a war?" Zina said, indignant.

"Do you think anyone's still living there?" Raya gestured at a stately farmhouse they were approaching, on the opposite side of the two-lane road. It was even larger than the first and built with stone.

"No sign of a vehicle," Chava answered. "They must have fled."

The long, narrow road unfurled to the horizon like black ribbon. Pristine farmhouses, all with red roofs, lined the road without disruption. Except . . . she caught a glimpse of something white in the middle of the road, about twenty-five meters ahead. As she drew near, she recognized crudely written German words on a placard: *Zittert vor angst faschistisches deutschland der tag der abrechnung ist gekommen.*

"It seems a political contingent got here before us," she remarked.

"What does it say, Elena?" asked Raya.

"'Tremble with fear, fascist Germany, the day of reckoning has come.'"

"Sounds like Komarov, all right," Zina muttered.

"Big-headed fool," said Elena. "We've barely set foot in Germany and—"

"Section halt," Purkayev called out, interrupting their conversation.

"Comrade Lieutenant Lobkovskaya, your platoon will stay here." He gestured at a two-story stone house. "Reconnaissance confirms it's abandoned."

"Yes sir," Nina replied, with a salute. She turned to her platoon with a weary smile.

Elena glanced sideways at Purkayev. He was leading the men through a wooden gate towards a sprawling farm across the road.

"Sleep well, my *dushechkas*, little souls," a slimy voice called out.

Elena cringed at the way the term of endearment sounded like a threat. She looked at the house where they'd sleep, a scant fifty meters from where the men would be staying. Her nerves flared. I'll have to sleep like a rabbit tonight, she thought, with one ear open.

Inside, the farmhouse was full of handsome furniture. An expansive walnut dining table with eight high-back chairs. An elegant couch upholstered in a blue and yellow floral print that matched the wallpaper. A floor-to-ceiling cabinet filled with fine china, crystal wine glasses, and decanters. A grandfather clock standing prominently in the front room, ticking the minutes as if the owners were at home marking time. A sumptuous blue rug that looked as if no dirty feet had ever marred the wool.

"What do they need from us?" Elena said when she opened the larder. She was astounded by the methodical array of tins and bottles, and by the sheer volume of food. Jars of strawberry preserves, sugar, flour. Her mouth watered at the sight of delicacies she hadn't seen or tasted in years. Tins of sardines in oil. Hazelnut paste. Loaves of brown bread. Bowls of eggs. Bottles of milk. Butter. Potatoes.

"This is disgusting," Chava sneered. "Nobody should have this much food for themselves."

"Look," Zina called excitedly from the sitting room.

The girls hurried to see what she'd found.

Zina gestured at a reddish-brown wooden box on a side table. An eagle and swastika were stamped on the front. "A radio." She folded her arms across her chest.

"A *Volksempfänger*," said Elena.

Nineteen pairs of puzzled eyes fell on her.

Her neck reddened. "One of my professors at university had one." She turned it on. A staticky German voice blared through the round speaker: ". . . a historical battle against the Reds we are sure to win."

Elena translated the broadcast for her comrades.

"Don't count on it," Zina declared to the speaker, in a haughty voice.

"You have to see this," one of the girls called out. "Come on up here!"

Elena was torn between listening to the end of the broadcast and joining her fellow snipers to pound up the stairs.

Zina turned the radio off and grabbed her hand. "Let's see what else these Fritzes have been—"

A loud shriek from above interrupted Zina mid-sentence. She hurried up the stairs with Elena close behind. They followed the exuberant voices down a narrow hall into a spacious bedroom, where girls were lounging on the bed, running their dirty hands over crisp white linen. A real bed. Real sheets.

Others were gathered around a large oak wardrobe in the corner of the room. They were pulling out dresses in vibrant shades of pink and blue and green that dazzled Elena. She moved closer. She touched the sleeve of a dress that looked like twilight, with its subtle mauve hue. The silky fabric slipped through her fingers like air.

"So many dresses for one woman?" Elena murmured.

"What do you think?"

Her eyes widened at the sight of Chava twirling in a floral short-sleeved dress with a ruffled front. She couldn't believe how one dress transformed her shooting partner from sniper to woman, how easy it was to discard her military guise. She eyed other girls shedding their trousers and tunics for dresses and was mesmerized by the flowing skirts and beautiful material. Far better quality than they could get in Russia. She wondered again why the Germans had risked so much to invade the Soviet Union.

Elena pulled the mauve dress out of the wardrobe and held it in front of her.

"Take a look." Raya gestured at a tall mirror propped at an angle in the corner.

She hadn't seen herself in almost two years. "I don't know," she balked, turning away.

Raya tilted her head and scrutinized Elena. "You're right. Better not."

"What? Why?" Elena dashed over to the mirror. She planted her feet in front of the glass and was appalled to see the hardened woman looking back at her. "My face . . ." She ran her fingers down the left cheekbone jutting from her skin, a shade darker than usual from the grime and sun. The scar from that day she'd cut her cheek looked like a strand of brown thread on her skin. Her eyes seemed larger and darker in her shrunken face, the way they receded into deep hollows. There were new lines around her mouth and on her fore-head. Even her hair, hanging below her shoulders, looked thinner, as if she'd molted like a cat in the spring. "I look old. I look like my grandmother."

Raya chuckled. She guided Elena's hands, still holding the dress, up until the mauve fabric obscured her uniform. "And now?"

"I realize the Soviet Union isn't the worker's paradise that Stalin claims it is."

"You're right," said Raya. "And I've never seen anything so pretty before." She fiddled with the edges of the puffed sleeves on her blue and white dress, tucked in at the waist with a shiny red belt.

"I'm not taking this dress off until we leave." Chava's buoyant voice cut in.

"I'm going to bring mine in my backpack," said Raya.

"It will never fit," Zina scoffed.

"I'll wear it under my uniform if I have to," Raya argued. "This is coming home with me."

"What a good idea," Chava said. "We've earned them."

"Have you really?" Nina entered the room. "Just like the Germans who looted Soviet houses? Did they earn what they stole?"

There was a gloomy silence. Although Nina was the same age as many of them, her presence had somehow ballooned with her greater authority.

"She's right," said Zina. "We're not thieves like the Fritzes."

"Listen." Nina clamped her hands on her hips. "I didn't say you couldn't wear them in the house. Just leave them here when we go."

Elena clasped the dress tight against her chest.

"And I suggest you get some sleep," Nina continued. "We'll be on the march again in a few short hours."

Elena tore off her uniform and pulled the dress over her head. She felt lighter without the heavy tunic and trousers covering her limbs. Fresher. Exposed. Free. She went back downstairs and joined her comrades gathered around the larder, filling their stomachs with milk, biscuits, bread slathered with jam, sardines, sugar cubes, and sausages. She ate until she felt sick. Some girls vomited, their stomachs unaccustomed to so much food at once.

Elena finished her meal with two generous mouthfuls of Jägermeister liqueur. She savored the numbness that cascaded through her veins, dulling her senses, her memories. Then she realized she was as bad as the men, using alcohol as an escape.

54

The search for truth is more valuable than the certainty gained by
clinging to doctrinaire orthodoxy.
—GOTTHOLD EPHRAIM LESSING, GERMAN AUTHOR

Reich Chancellery, Berlin
May 1945

The sentry guarding the entrance of the Reich Chancellery
refused to let them in. "You need a special permit," he said,
bluntly. "From the Berlin commandant."

"Out of the way," Gorbushin snarled. He withdrew his pistol,
pointed it at the gobsmacked sentry, and shoved him aside. He didn't
explain why they were there because Stalin forbade them from telling
anyone about their mission, even if it put them in danger.

More unquestioning obedience.

Elena could feel Käthe tremble beside her. She glued her eyes on
the sentry's rifle, its butt on the ground. He'd been ordered to shoot
anyone who tried to enter the Chancellery. He could easily have shot
them without any repercussions.

In the assembly hall, chandeliers lay on the ground, smashed into
billions of tiny pieces. Bystrov switched on their only flashlight. He
led the way down the two flights of stairs.

"Where to?" Elena asked Käthe, at the bottom.

"Follow me." She proceeded through the warren with the self-
assurance of a person who had been there many times.

Boisterous laughter punctuated the dank, soggy underground air. An abundance of wine had been left by the German high command, which, Elena knew, Red Army soldiers were enjoying with abandon.

Käthe entered a tiny square room that contained a dentist's chair, a couch, a desk, and a locker. She went right to the desk, removed a key from the top drawer, and opened the locker. She took out a box, much like the one in Dr. Blaschke's other surgery, and skimmed through the cards.

Elena simmered with nervous excitement. All at once, she knew the reason she'd survived as a sniper. This was her destiny, to be part of SMERSH, to find Hitler or identify his remains.

Gorbushin watched, his face shiny with sweat.

Bystrov kept shifting his weight from one foot to the other.

"Found them," said Käthe, triumphant. "Hitler's X-rays and medical records." She set them on the desk.

Gorbushin plucked one of the X-rays off the desk and held it up to his flashlight.

"I also have crowns made for Hitler," Käthe said. She gestured for Elena to open her hand. She dropped three gold crowns in her palm.

Elena gawked at them with repugnance. Hitler's crowns.

"We have to get these records and Käthe to headquarters," said Bystrov. "Now."

Elena assured Käthe they would only need her help for a little while longer, at headquarters in Buch.

Elena saw her reluctance in her skittish face. She tried to put herself in Käthe's shoes, a defeated civilian forced to accompany three enemy soldiers. She couldn't imagine coping well under the strain. She couldn't picture herself alive with three Wehrmacht soldiers.

Outside the bunker, Bystrov managed to find Ludis to drive them.

"I can drive my car," Käthe offered. "Just give me the address. I know almost every street in the city."

"Your car will be safe here," Bystrov said through Elena, though he couldn't guarantee its safety at all. "It will be faster to go in one vehicle."

Elena glanced sideways at him. She wasn't sure why Käthe couldn't take her own car. She wasn't a criminal, for goodness' sake. Quite the opposite. She'd been a huge help. Without her, they wouldn't have located Hitler's dental records.

The jeep broke down within minutes, at the Brandenburg Gate. Ludis opened the hood and shouted that he'd have them up and running in no time. Which meant anywhere from five minutes to five hours. They all got out of the jeep. The colonel paced up and down, peering at Ludis, as if seething looks could speed things up.

Elena gazed up at gate, one of the most photographed symbols of the Nazi Party. She recalled photographs of the flags with menacing swastikas hanging between the columns when Hitler's power was strongest. Now the columns were riddled with bullet holes. Yet there they were, still standing amidst the silent, ruined city, an unnerving reminder of Berlin's monstrous past.

Thirty minutes later, they were on their way again. But they'd only gone a few versts when gunfire erupted.

Elena jolted upright. The Wehrmacht?

"What's happening?" Käthe cried out.

Heavy artillery boomed in the sky.

Käthe is in a Soviet jeep, Elena fretted. If something happens to her because she's with us . . .

"A celebratory salute," Bystrov announced, interrupting Elena's thoughts.

Is it really over? She pressed her hand against her racing heart. Not for her. Combat may be finished, but the war wouldn't be over for her until she was back in Moscow on her native land.

She told Käthe there was nothing to worry about. She watched tracer bullets ignite the sky like strands of pearls and felt a touch of envy for the soldiers firing their weapons with joy.

55

The Russian soldiers were raping every German female from eight
to eighty. It was an army of rapists.
—NATALYA GESSE, SOVIET WAR CORRESPONDENT, 1945

East Prussia

April 1945

A horse's neigh barged in on Elena, still in the grip of her dream.
She opened one eye. The brightness seared her pupil. Her
head throbbed. Her·mouth was cotton-dry. She shivered and
hugged her arms to her chest. Her bare skin was dotted with goosebumps.

Where am I?

A disorienting light-headedness came over her. An overwhelming
dizziness. She remembered when she saw the table. Chairs. Windows.
Her hairy, pale legs outstretched on the rug. The farmhouse.

Outside a car door slammed shut.

"Don't!" a woman screamed in German.

"What was that?" Zina sat upright on the sofa.

Elena stumbled to the window. She gaped in disbelief. A horse-
drawn German cart was being ambushed by the two inebriated soldiers who'd crossed Purkayev. One was dragging a young girl from
the wagon. The other had his paws on a silver-haired woman.

The German horses stomped their hooves and brayed.

"*Hör auf!* Stop it!" the man driving the cart shouted. He threw his
arms around the older woman.

The soldier hit him on the head with the butt of his rifle, knocking him unconscious. He snatched the woman.

Elena opened her mouth but couldn't get enough air to speak.

"My God," said Zina, at the adjacent window with Chava and several other girls.

The earth rumbled with the sound of cantering footsteps. Elena blanched at the sight of an entire Soviet regiment approaching. Thousands of men on horses. Cossacks.

"We have to do something," said Raya, standing beside Elena.

"Like what, ask them to dance?" Chava said. "Look at us."

Elena glanced down. The mauve dress hung loosely from her shoulders. It was wrinkled and stained at her underarms. She was ashamed of her filth. Of her uselessness.

"Please don't hurt me!" The girl's grating wail cut through the air.

Elena clutched her head to keep it from spinning. She vowed to never drink again. "I want to go out there and shoot those bastards."

"You can't kill your own soldiers," Chava retorted.

"So what do we do? Stand here and watch them rape all those women?" Elena cleaved the windowsill with white knuckles. Soldiers held the girl down, spread-eagled, while their comrades got in line as if they were purchasing bread.

"Back from the windows," Nina ordered the girls. "Now."

Elena turned away. Revulsion shot up her throat.

"What are we going to do?" asked Raya.

"Nothing. We are going to do nothing," Nina said.

"But we can't just stand here," Elena disagreed. Nina's decision seemed to her a breach of integrity.

Then they heard a gunshot.

Elena pressed her cheeks to the window. One of the men who'd been restraining the girl tottered sideways. Blood oozed from his chest. She caught sight of Purkayev. With a pistol in his hand. Pointed at the soldier. She felt something like reverence soar in her chest.

"Purkayev could be sent to the gulag," Chava cried.

"He should get a medal," said Elena, awestruck.

The bleeding soldier flopped at the side of the road.

Purkayev aimed his gun at the soldier confining the old woman.

"Are you crazy?" the man said.

"You really want to know?" Purkayev replied.

The soldier let go of the woman and raised his hands.

The girl tugged the older woman to her feet. She wrapped her arm around her waist and led her to the cart.

Purkayev waved his pistol at the herd of wild soldiers. "Get out of here," he bellowed. "All of you. Or I'll keep shooting."

The soldiers awkwardly mounted their horses. They galloped down the road.

The girl helped the woman climb onto the cart, then sat beside her. But they weren't going anywhere. The cart was stuck in the onslaught of mounted Cossacks riding in the opposite direction, towards Berlin. And the driver was still unconscious.

The dead soldier lay at the side of the road like a curse.

"I'm going to report you," a man hollered at Purkayev, from his horse.

"Don't you know vodka and good sense never get along?" Purkayev replied. He fired a shot past the horse's ear.

The horse reared onto its hind legs, hurling the soldier onto the ground with a satisfying thud. He propped himself up on his elbows, then stood on wobbly legs. He leaned against his shaggy horse for a moment before clambering onto the saddle. He kicked his heels against the horse's ribs and was off.

Purkayev wielded his pistol as a never-ending stream of Cossacks passed.

On impulse, Elena ran downstairs, threw her greatcoat over her dress, thrust her feet into her boots, and grabbed her pistol. Outside, the brisk air stank of horse manure. She hunched her shoulders against the cold. She caught Purkayev's astounded gaze and nodded in approval. She aimed her pistol at the Cossacks, resolved to shoot if necessary.

As soon as there was a slight path, the cart driver, who'd gained consciousness, slapped the reins over his horses and continued his exodus from Berlin, followed by a growing stream of anxious Germans.

The chilly afternoon had become an icy twilight by the time the last Cossacks trotted by.

As the road emptied, Elena found herself walking towards Purkayev. He was staring, woeful, at the dead Cossack.

"You did the right thing," she said.

"Did I?"

"You saved two women."

"Two women." He gestured at the farm where soldiers were milling around the property. "We have thousands of pent-up men drinking now. Two women. There will be so many more."

"You helped an entire family," she said.

He stepped closer, pausing when they were an arm's length apart.

Elena trembled at his nearness. "The young girl still has her mother. The older woman didn't lose her daughter. The man has his daughter and granddaughter."

"Elena, come inside," Chava called out from the doorway of the house.

A slight smile broke upon his face. "You should be in politics, the way you can change a bad ending into a good one."

She blushed under his intense gaze. Something was brewing. She could feel it below the surface between them.

"Comrade Bruskina!" Nina's voice intruded. "Unless you plan to march in that dress, you need to get inside now."

Purkayev's gaze dropped to the hem of her dress, just below her bare knees. "I like the color."

"Me too." She racked her brain for something interesting to say, but the icy air and her freezing legs made it hard to think.

"But perhaps you should save the dress for a special occasion," he added.

"I'm not keeping it. None of us are. It was just for fun. To feel like a woman for one night."

"You don't need a fancy dress to look like a woman," he said.

She felt her heart unfurl. She grabbed the collar of her great coat, held it tight, then turned and fled into the house.

Elena was still reeling from her conversation with Purkayev an hour later, when her platoon was marching towards Berlin. She was confident he'd been sincere, and yet at the same time, had doubts. Perhaps he'd been affected by the heat of the moment. Perhaps he'd been overwrought after shooting the Cossack. Perhaps . . . She racked her brain for another reason for his not-so-subtle aside.

The stench of raw meat wrenched Elena from her musings. There was a dead cow at the side of the road with a bullet in its head. The body had been crudely butchered for its meat. Recently. This was the first of several dead cows. There were a couple of oxen as well. And horses that had dropped dead of starvation and overwork.

German farm carts appeared a couple of hours later. Dead refugees hung over the edges, bullets in their heads and chests. Women and girls were sprawled on the snow, half-naked. One couldn't have been older than five. Purkayev's words tumbled into her head: *There will be so many more.*

"Goddam animals," he said now.

"Unbelievable," said Nina.

"My God!" Raya pointed at a dead German woman a few meters off to the side.

She was naked from the waist down. A bottle stuck out from her privates.

A tidal wave of nausea hit Elena. The bile rose into her throat with an awful force. She vomited the entire contents of her stomach. She dropped to her knees. Unscrewed the cap on her canteen and drank it dry.

"I hate those soldiers," Zina said.

"I hate their commanders for letting it happen," said Raya.

"I hate wearing the same uniform," Elena burst out.

Komarov, who always seemed to be around when someone scorned the government, shot daggers at her.

"How can you say such a terrible thing?" said Chava. "It's an honor to wear a Red Army uniform."

Komarov sidled up beside Elena. "Comrade Bruskina regrets her words, doesn't she?"

Masha wouldn't back down, she thought. She glared at him. "Doesn't it bother you, being part of an army that murders innocent people? Children? Out of some kind of misplaced spite?"

"All Germans are bad." He scowled.

"And the soldiers who did this," Elena gestured at the bodies, "make all of us look bad."

"That's not true," Raya argued. "They only make themselves look bad."

"That's enough," Nina cut in.

"Witnesses can't tell the difference between them and us," Elena said, ignoring Nina. "They'll tell people it was the Red Army. That's how we will go down in history, just as the Nazis will be known for the terror they wrought."

"Whose side are you on," Komarov scoffed, "comparing the Red Army with Nazis?"

"It's not about sides," said Elena, her voice choppy with irritation.

"Arguing isn't going to change what happened," Purkayev

interjected. "The only thing we can do is get them off the road. Cover them. At least give them some dignity before moving forward."

Soldiers began picking up the dead German women and carrying them over to a fence set back from the road.

At least, Elena thought. At least.

56

As a sparrow wandering from its nest, so is a person wandering
from his place.
—MISHLEI (PROVERBS), 27:8–9

SMERSH headquarters, Berlin
May 1945

Two days after retrieving the X-rays of Hitler's teeth, Elena
was, to her annoyance, still in Berlin, interpreting a conversation between Käthe and the Red Army's principal forensic
expert, Lieutenant Colonel Shkaravsky. The interviews had dragged
on tirelessly. Käthe hadn't even seen the teeth in the red box that
Elena still diligently guarded.

"Ask her to describe the condition of Hitler's teeth," said Shkaravsky, methodical in appearance and speech.

"I remember his teeth well," Käthe began, "because they were in
such bad condition. His upper denture was a gold bridge. This was
attached to his first tooth on the left with a crown, to the root of the
second left tooth, to the root of the first right tooth."

Käthe explained that the extraction of Hitler's sixth tooth on the
left upper jaw took place in the fall of 1944. She and Dr. Blaschke
had gone to East Prussia to do the procedure. While Dr. Blaschke
sawed through a gold bridge, Käthe had held a mirror in Hitler's
mouth.

Gorbushin and Bystrov compared Käthe's account with dental records, which Elena translated: "'The bridge of upper denture on left behind premolar tooth (four) sawn vertically.'"

The men exchanged satisfied looks.

"Show her the teeth," Gorbushin said to Elena.

"Not so fast," Shkaravsky countered. "I'd like Frau Heusermann to draw Hitler's teeth, including all the dental work, from memory."

Käthe's cheeks pulsed as she began to sketch, under Shkaravsky's watchful eye.

Elena was afraid to look but, at the same time, couldn't tear her gaze away. If Käthe didn't produce an acceptable diagram, she and Bystrov might be reprimanded. Harshly. For some made-up reason like wasting Shkaravsky's time or not finding the dentist himself. Maybe we should have tried harder, she thought. Maybe we should have tracked him down . . . By the time Käthe finished drawing, Elena had convinced herself they were all headed to the gulag, she, Bystrov, and the colonel, for botching up Hitler's identification.

Shkaravsky examined the drawing. He compared it to the X-rays. He reread Elena's notes. He arranged the three exhibits on the table.

"Show her the teeth," he said to Elena.

Holding her breath, Elena opened the lid of the red box.

Käthe let out a loud gasp. She reached out, then jerked her hand back. "May I?"

"By all means," said Elena.

Käthe placed the teeth in the palm of her hand.

"Look closely," Gorbushin said, through Elena. "What can you tell us about them?"

Käthe studied them for a long minute. "These are Adolf Hitler's teeth," she said, decisive.

"Are you sure?" Elena asked.

"I have no doubt." She regarded Elena with steady eyes. "If you want further proof, talk to Blaschke's dental technician, Fritz Echtmann. He made false teeth for Hitler."

Three and a half hours later, Elena and Bystrov arrived back at headquarters with the flustered dental technician, Echtmann, who had a slight build and an anemic complexion. In front of Shkaravsky and the colonel, Echtmann looked as out of place as a lamb at the opera.

In a highly strung voice, he described Hitler's teeth from memory. Then he identified the actual teeth in the red box as Hitler's. Like Käthe, he had no doubt.

"Stalin will have to accept this as proof of Hitler's death," Elena said to Bystrov, once Käthe and Echtmann had been sent home. "There are no more reasons to procrastinate. The world has to know Hitler is dead."

Bystrov regarded her with a thin-lipped smile. "I agree. The question is, does Stalin want the world to know?"

Twelve days later, it became patently obvious that Stalin was intent on delaying the news about Hitler when he sent the head of SMERSH, Lieutenant General Vadis, to Berlin to verify the information.

Once again, Käthe and Echtmann were summoned to headquarters, where Elena translated their interrogations with Vadis, who asked the exact same questions as Shkaravsky. Their answers didn't change. Nor did their unwavering conviction that the teeth were Hitler's.

Vadis, who had drab, gray eyes like stones, took his time in reviewing the material.

Surely his word about Hitler's fate will be final, Elena assumed, as she impatiently watched Vadis sift through the documents with long, deft fingers. There was nobody above him within SMERSH. There was nobody else Stalin could send to stall the news. Soon, Hitler's death would be the headline in every major newspaper around the world.

Vadis pushed the papers to the side. He brushed nonexistent dust from a couple of medals on his chest. He folded his hands on the table. Then he uttered two words that would forever alter the lives of Käthe and Echtmann: "Detain them."

Elena was shocked. "Why? They've cooperated with this investigation entirely."

Bystrov tapped her shoulder. "Don't. You'll make it worse."

She felt Käthe tense beside her.

Vadis gave her an icy stare. "They know too much." He gestured for the guard to take Käthe and Echtmann away.

"What is happening?" Käthe asked Elena, her voice notched to panic.

"Be careful, Bruskina," the colonel hissed.

Elena swallowed the doubts scratching her throat like thorns. While Käthe and Echtmann had provided valuable evidence, they were, after all, Germans. She heaved her chest and told them they were being detained.

"How long?" asked Echtmann, his voice shrill with fear.

Elena shook her head. "Hopefully just until Stalin announces Hitler's death."

Käthe grabbed Elena's wrists. "I'm not a criminal. All I've done is tell the truth."

Echtmann was hyperventilating. He exuded a frenetic quality that made Elena waver.

It's a matter of self-preservation, she reminded herself. She averted her gaze from Käthe and Echtmann. She twisted her wrists from Käthe's grip and watched the guards roughly haul them away.

Self-preservation.

She hated herself for being silent. For not being the person she should have been.

The next morning, Bystrov told Elena that Vadis had sent his report to Stalin in Moscow. He'd confirmed the dentures and teeth were Hitler's.

"Thank God," said Elena. "Then Käthe and Echtmann will be freed soon, once Stalin accepts his death. And we'll finally be on our way to Moscow."

"That's the hope," said Bystrov, who didn't sound at all hopeful.

Only Colonel Gorbushin was summoned to Moscow the next day.

Elena waited anxiously for news, her mind constantly jumping to Käthe and Echtmann. When she wasn't in the bunker, translating documents, she wandered the ruins of Berlin. She saw entire blocks that had been flattened then, curiously, the odd building that remained intact, offering shreds of optimism.

She brought her hand to her heart when she approached the Brandenburg Gate and saw Cyrillic characters, names of Red Army soldiers, written on the columns. *In memory of our fallen comrades.* She circled one column, then another, reading names aloud though nobody was around to listen. Then she withdrew a pen from her tunic pocket and wrote: *You will not be forgotten*, then, the names of her fallen comrades.

Four days later, Gorbushin sent a private radio message: "Comrade Stalin has familiarized himself with the entire course of events and the documents relating to the discovery of Hitler. He considers the matter closed. And he says we shall not make this public. The punishment for breaking this silence will be fifteen years in the gulag."

The following afternoon, Elena, still fuming from Stalin's pronouncement, stood on the train's platform beside Bystrov. After two months of spending every waking hour together, conducting a search that, as far as Stalin was concerned, never took place, they were going their separate ways. The major was staying in Berlin, while Elena was heading to Moscow for her demobilization ceremony. He'd come to see her off, and Elena felt strangely tongue-tied. She hated goodbyes, the formality, the false promises for the future.

"If only we'd been able to get Goebbels alive," he said, interrupting her reverie. "I just wish I could have had five minutes alone with that bastard."

"For me it was Hitler," she said. "I would have liked to see him suffer."

Bystrov lit a cigarette and exhaled. "Well, we both have to move on now. They're gone, which is the main thing."

"I suppose," Elena said, thoughtful. "But the war's not over for Käthe and—"

"Quiet," he hissed. "Do you want to go to the gulag instead of Moscow?"

"Of course not," she said, embarrassed by her gaffe. Still, she couldn't get the two dental assistants out of her mind. They were being transported to Russia's Lubyanka Prison for an indefinite period. She feared that as long as Stalin continued with his charade of Hitler being alive, the two Germans would rot in a cell, simply for knowing the truth.

The train clanged into the station.

"This is it," he said.

"This is it." She saluted him.

He returned her salute. "There were three of us at every stage of this Hitler saga."

"Yes," she agreed, suddenly overcome by the gravity of his words.

"Of those three," he said, "you are the only one who can write about it."

She was moved by the sincerity in his voice. She regarded Bystrov, most likely for the last time, and said, "I will. I promise you, I will write the truth one day."

57

In the Red Army . . . women very energetically proved themselves
as pilots, snipers, submachine gunners [etc.] . . . But they don't
forget their primary duty to nation and state, that of motherhood.
—*PRAVDA*, MARCH 1945, PUBLISHED ON INTERNATIONAL WOMEN'S
DAY

Germany

April 1945

W e're so close to Berlin, I can almost hear Hitler's fanatical voice," Chava whispered.

It was the middle of the night and the girls' platoon was observing the enemy's side from a forest at the edge of a two-lane highway. They'd been ordered to defend the road between two German villages—Rathstock and Manschnow—to stop a Wehrmacht infantry unit from advancing.

"We're not that near," Raya hissed. "It's still more than sixty-five versts."

"When we joined the front line near Moscow, we were almost two thousand versts from the Reich," Chava reasoned. "So I say we're near."

"It doesn't matter," Zina interposed. "As long as we're stuck here, it feels like a thousand versts." She groaned. "I only hope I never hear Hitler squealing over the radio ever again."

"Can we talk about something else?" Elena said. "His name makes my skin crawl."

"Maybe you have lice again?" Chava quipped.

"Again?" Elena scratched her head. "They've never left. I think I have more lice than hair now."

Raya snorted. "You and me both."

"Shhh!" Nina's voice cut in from behind them. "We may as well turn on our flashlights if you keep talking, lead the Fritzes right to us."

Elena shivered at the thought. And the eternal cold. The ground, wet with melting snow, had seeped through her felt boots. They'd been observing the enemy's infantry unit for seven hours so far. And even though an additional nine girls had joined her snipers' platoon, the twenty-nine snipers had no backup. This unnerved Elena, knowing there were no machine guns to cover their movements, no mine-sweeping tanks, no Katyusha rockets to shatter the enemy. There were no planes with the Soviet star on the wings circling overhead, taking in a broader swath, spotting Germans before they closed in on the snipers. There was no Purkayev to keep lewd soldiers away. The sniper platoon was completely alone.

Except for the red beech trees. Elena looked up. Beneath the full moon's glow, the bare branches stretched over her head like a knobby spider's web. These mature trees were their advantage; the other side of the road had only a smattering of bushes. As soon as daylight broke, the Wehrmacht would be exposed. An entire infantry unit. At least a hundred soldiers. This, unfortunately, was the ene-my's advantage—they outnumbered the snipers four to one.

Elena envisioned a dense line of gray uniforms emerging from the other side of the road, bombarding the snipers with machine-gun fire. She checked her position behind an enormous tree, her rifle poised on a branch at shoulder level. Made sure that not even a hair stuck out from behind the broad tree trunk.

The pale sun began to poke over the horizon, emitting a crystalline luster over the highway. The air around her was charged with energy as her comrades readied themselves for combat. Elena pressed her hip against the tree. She tightened her grip on her rifle. She squinted through her scope as the darkness faded. She felt her heart speed up and burn in her chest, an inferno of nerves.

Gray bulges became visible against the snow as the sky lightened. Wehrmacht helmets. Silent and still. Not exposed enough to provide good targets. Yet.

Elena planted her gaze on three helmets directly across from her. Eventually, the Wehrmacht soldiers would have to rise if they wanted to use their machine guns, mounted on tripods.

Come on. Show yourselves. The helmets didn't budge. The quiet was ominous. The tension so thick it left a putrid taste in Elena's mouth. Her foot cramped. She pointed and flexed her toes. She heard a rustling sound from across the road. A helmet bobbed up. One of the snipers on her right fired a shot. The helmet sank like a rock.

All of a sudden, the enemy clobbered her platoon with machine-gun fire. Shots pummeled the snipers' trees. Elena withdrew her rifle and was paralyzed by the squall of bullets zipping past both sides of her face. The hammering sound of nine hundred rounds a minute. And that was just from one machine gun.

The fusillade continued for at least five minutes. Forever, thought Elena, when there's only bark between you and a bullet. She recited one of her favorite Pushkin lines in her head to stay calm: *Don't be sad, don't be angry if life deceives you! Submit to your grief—your time of joy will come, believe me. Don't be sad, don't be angry if life deceives you! Submit to your grief . . .*

Then the enemy's attack ended as suddenly as it had begun. Right away, Elena propped her rifle on a branch and scanned the area with her scope. She caught a flash of something moving in the corner of her left eye. Two bushes seemed out of place on the other side of the road. Too close to the pavement.

"On your left," she hissed at Chava.

"Got the second one in my sights," Chava said.

"On three," Elena responded. "One, two, three."

They pulled their triggers at the same time. The bushes went still.

"Officers at one and two o'clock," Chava said.

Elena swiveled right. Caught a glint of medal between the trees. Aimed. Fired.

An avalanche of machine-gun bullets started up again.

Elena yanked her rifle from the branches and stood straight against the tree. Her heart pounded so hard in her chest she was afraid her ribs would break. She prayed that none of her comrades would be shot. She prayed that she'd be able to stay out of sight. And she prayed that the enemy would run out of ammunition soon.

For the next hour, this David and Goliath sequence continued, with the snipers managing to eliminate several gunners whenever the enemy took a break.

"Comrade Bruskina?" Nina's imposing voice clamored through the blare of machine gunfire.

"Yes?"

"I want you to address the enemy."

"What?" Elena tracked Nina to a nearby tree on her left.

"They must know their position is hopeless," Nina went on, raising her voice to be heard over the racket. "I need you to shout that resistance is useless. Tell them to give up. Lay down their weapons. Those who surrender will be spared."

"But . . . they'll shoot right at me when they hear my voice," Elena protested.

"Stay behind the tree. They've been shooting at all of us for over an hour and haven't hit one sniper. But we're taking them down. They know surrender is the best outcome, and my orders are to capture as many tongues as possible."

Elena drew in a long breath.

"Comrade Bruskina?"

"I'm . . . here," she managed.

"You're the only one who speaks German."

"All right," she said, resigned.

The machine gun assault ended. The smell of carbolic acid hung in the air.

Elena exhaled and called out in a flimsy voice: "*Gebt auf.* Give up. *Widerstand ist zwecklos.* Resistence is useless. *Legt die Waffen nieder.* Lay down your weapons. *Ergebt euch. Rette dein Leben.* Surrender. Save your life."

"Again. Louder," Nina demanded.

Elena repeated the order. She was taken aback by the imposing tone of her own voice.

An eerie silence.

"*Vernichten Sie Ihre Karten und Dokumente*," a German finally announced. "*Bereiten Sie sich auf die Kapitulation vor.*"

"What did he say?" asked Nina.

"He's telling his men to destroy their maps and documents, to prepare for surrender," Elena answered.

"Good. But don't take your eyes off the enemy, comrade snipers," Nina said. "Don't trust a word they say. It's not over until we have their weapons in hand."

Elena was impressed by Nina's composure as a leader. This was the first time Nina had been in charge of the platoon without Purka-yev's vigilant eyes watching her like a fox. A banging sound caught her attention. The Germans were tossing their machine guns onto the road. They were giving up!

Men slowly got to their feet, hands raised. Elena counted twenty-seven Wehrmacht soldiers as they approached the middle of the road, unarmed.

Nina sent a few girls to retrieve the weapons. As the soldiers drew near, snipers emerged from the trees and surrounded them, rifles aimed at their heads. The men's jaws dropped. A giggle wormed its way up Elena's throat.

"*Was ist das?*" one man blurted. "What is this?"

"*Mädchen?*" another said. "Girls? We surrendered to girls?"

Elena translated for her platoon.

Wie kann das sein? How can this be?

The girls laughed at the men's disbelief.

Sie sind keine Frauen. Sie sind Hermaphroditen.

"Did he call us hermaphrodites?" Raya said, incensed.

Elena gave her a tight-lipped nod.

Zina spun on her heel. She pointed her rifle at the jeering soldier.

"Lower your rifle," Nina warned her.

"You think we're freaks?" Zina pulled the bolt on her rifle. Her face was almost as red as her hair.

The soldier shrank back.

Nina grabbed the barrel of her rifle. "Don't let one lousy fascist get the better of you."

Zina wrenched her gun from Nina's grip. "If I'm not normal, you can't expect me to be rational, can you?" She pressed the muzzle of her gun against the soldier's brow.

Sweat poured down the soldier's cheeks.

"Stop, Zina, please," Elena implored her. "You'll only regret it."

Zina squared her shoulders. Adjusted her hold on her gun.

The soldier's chin quivered.

Elena, keeping her rifle pointed at the captured soldiers, edged closer to Zina. "I know you're angry. I'm angry, too. We all are. But killing one stupid fascist isn't going to make you feel better. It won't make any difference. Our families won't come back. The Germans will still hate Jews and women in combat."

Zina started rocking back and forth on the balls of her feet. Her breaths were short and quick.

Elena riveted her gaze on Zina, silently begging her to forget about the soldier.

Zina's head turned towards Elena. Her long-lashed eyes swam with tears.

Elena gave her an encouraging smile.

Zina stepped back from the soldier, the muzzle of her rifle still pointed at him.

Elena extended her arm and gently tugged the barrel down.

Zina jerked her head away. She wiped her eyes with her sleeve.

"*Frauen. Nichts als Schreibaby's*," the soldier said when the muzzle was gone.

"What was that?" Zina said.

Elena hesitated. "'Thank God, that was close,'" she said, surprised by how easily the lie rolled from her tongue.

"Oh."

Elena heaved a silent sigh of relief. If Zina knew what he'd really said, "Women. Nothing but crybabies," she would probably have pulled the trigger, destroying two lives with one bullet.

58

How did the Motherland meet us? . . . The men said nothing but the women . . . They shouted to us, "We know what you did there! You lured our men with your young c———! Army whores . . . Military bitches . . ." They insulted us in all possible ways . . .

—KLAVDIA S., RED ARMY SNIPER

Moscow

July 1945

Elena's train from Berlin pulled into Moscow's Leningradsky station late. The demobilization ceremony at Red Square was in just over an hour. It was a good thing she knew the city's streets from her years as a student in Moscow.

"Army slut," someone hissed over her shoulder.

Elena raised her chin. She shuffled forward, eyes glued to the door.

A young woman with plucked eyebrows was watching her with a sullen glare. Another woman shot her a hostile look.

Elena became rigid. She fought the urge to run as she got off the train. She'd rather trip and fall on her face than give those nasty women the satisfaction of knowing they'd hurt her. She felt their eyes boring into the back of her head as she strode along the platform. To steady her nerves, she caressed the dent in her canteen over and over.

What did you do during the war, she wanted to shout at them. I killed nineteen fascists and found Hitler. She considered the absurdity of her last few weeks. Nobody would believe her even if she were allowed to talk about the odyssey to identify Hitler's teeth.

Outside the station, she glanced over her shoulder and gave a sigh of relief. The women had vanished. Temporarily. There would be more.

Her mind turned to Purkayev as she made her way towards Red Square. She replayed their last conversation, about meeting on the Bolshoy Bridge. He'd know about today's ceremony for her regiment. Her heart tugged, thinking about him. She saw herself standing at the bridge's railing, her shoulder-length hair blowing in the wind, Purkayev coming up behind her. The film popped into her head. The one that gave them the ludicrous idea in the first place.

Don't be silly, she chided herself. Still, she couldn't help but comb the area for Purkayev. She yanked the collar of her tunic and fanned her face with a magazine. Her feet, still in her clunky men's boots, were hot and sweaty. It was not even noon, yet it had to be thirty degrees. And the humidity . . . She couldn't wait to cool off in a real bath with soap that actually smelled nice.

Beads of sweat dripped from her hairline as she wound her way over the Garden Ring, then straight down Myasnitskaya Street, eyes darting every which way in search of the man who dominated her thoughts. She opened her canteen and drank a bit of water, careful to keep some for later. Even though the war had ended, necessities like water were scarce, just like they had been in the ghetto, where her journey had begun.

Her throat filled when she saw Red Army women spilling into Red Square. There they were, her sisters-in-arms.

"We know perfectly well what you were doing out there!"

Elena spun around. Three civilian women were gesturing at the square, clogged with women in uniform.

"You were all sleeping with our husbands," a woman with an upturned nose screamed.

"You're nothing but soldiers' whores," said one in a dress that hung loosely from her skinny frame.

"A slut in uniform," the third woman added.

Elena stared, open-mouthed, at the ignorant troika. After all the newspaper articles about Lyudmila Pavlichenko and Zina, as well as female pilots and machine gunners—heroines of the Red Army—these women condemned Red Army women based on rumors and speculation. They had no idea that Russian men had raped and tortured innocent German women, and that others, like Yurovsky, had taken advantage of Red Army women, that victims like herself would do anything to go back and change what had happened. And these women would never know because Stalin would never acknowledge such ruthless behavior. It would be hidden in the Soviet archives like the identification of Hitler's teeth.

She glanced down at her uniform, which she'd been proud to wear at the beginning of the war. Now, back in the "normal" world, it falsely defined her as a woman who'd done nothing but sleep with married men at the front. A prostitute. She pivoted on her clunky heel and marched away from the women and their venomous words. She couldn't make them see what she'd witnessed. What she'd sacrificed. What she'd lost.

She couldn't wait to get out of her uniform.

59

I experienced being on both the offensive and defensive and fully
knowing the bitterness of retreat and being encircled for many
days at a time.
—YULIA ZHUKOVA, RED ARMY SNIPER

Battle of Seelow Heights
April 1945

"*Willst du meinen Schwanz?*" a German soldier laughed.

Elena caught a glimpse of him, and another Fritz, on their stomachs, rifles poking through a rambling firethorn hedge. At Raya and Zina. Forty meters away. At most.

"Fuck off," Zina retorted, from the other side of the hedge.

"What did he say?" Chava whispered. Her eyes blazed with ferocity.

"He asked if she wanted his cock."

"Bastard," said Chava. "Let's get closer."

They continued slithering along the edge of the meadow, concealed by tall grasses and weeds. Although the hail of artillery had stopped, the musty, sulfuric stench was sharp as a bullet.

Elena stopped when she was about thirty meters from the firethorn, close enough to see that the red berries were dusted with frost. She peered through her binoculars. Nothing but shadows behind the verdant leaves. She didn't know what to do. They'd blow their cover if they went closer. Then all four of them would be dead.

She and Chava stared at one another, helpless.

"One more step and I'll throw it," Raya cried.

Elena's heart ratcheted up her throat.

"They must have run out of ammunition," Chava whispered, taking the words out of Elena's mouth.

Elena pressed her eye against the scope of her rifle. An explosion knocked it out of her hands. She was thrust backwards into the air by the force of the blast. She landed hard. On her right arm. Her bone cracked. She gagged from the smoke. Her eyes watered. Her elbow radiated with pain.

"Grenades," Chava managed. She'd been thrown right beside Elena. "Raya and Zina set off their grenades."

"No," Elena said, frantic. It wasn't possible, what Chava was insinuating. She peered over the bush. A bloody arm poked through the prickly leaves. A man's arm. Blood was spattered everywhere. "They got away. I'm sure they escaped." She lunged towards the bush.

Chava moved faster, flinging her arms over Elena's shoulders. "You don't want to remember them this way."

Elena tried to wrench herself from Chava, but her broken arm screeched in pain when she moved. She sagged. Hot tears ran down her face. "They must have been so scared."

"They're heroes," Chava said. "They waited until those fascist bastards were close enough, then tossed their grenades to kill them too."

Elena held her wounded arm against her side with her other hand to keep it stable. "We're so close to Berlin," she sobbed. "They were supposed to make it. We were all supposed to be together at the end."

There was a long and excruciating silence.

"I'm going to fight for them," Chava declared obstinately. "From now on, every bullet I shoot is for Raya and Zina."

"Me too," said Elena.

Chava's gaze fell to Elena's arm.

Elena looked down. Her elbow was swollen. She couldn't move it without unbearable pain. "How am I going to shoot anyone like this?"

Chava regarded Elena. "You can't."

"What am I going to do?"

"I don't know."

Elena held herself like an injured bird, her elbow throbbing against her ribs. She'd come too far to be discharged with an injury now. This could not be her fate. She had to figure out a way to stay in the Red Army until the very end. To find justice for Zina and Raya without bullets. But how?

60

Warfare is . . . the one human activity from which women, with the most insignificant exceptions, have always and everywhere stood apart . . . Women . . . do not fight . . . and they never, in any military sense, fight men.
—JOHN KEEGAN, *A HISTORY OF WARFARE*, 1994

Moscow

July 1945

Elena waded through the crowd at Red Square, searching for familiar faces. The extraordinary onion domes of St. Basil's Cathedral, overlooking the square, caught her eye. She took in the blue and white striping of one dome, the green and gold of another. After living in shades of black and white for so long, the colors were brilliantly jarring. She expanded her gaze. She was struck by the glaring contrast of scraggy female soldiers in Red Square, beneath the exquisite, curvy domes.

Stalin claims there is no God, Elena mused, yet there is a colossal monument to God right beside the Kremlin. Politics and religion don't just intersect here, they've collided.

She looked towards Spasskaya Tower in Red Square, rising above the rest of the Kremlin towers like Stalin's rhetoric. At the top of the steeple, the red star, heralding Stalin's Communist rule, looked jarringly incandescent in the warm, reddish glow of twilight. Ominous. Like the yellow star she'd worn in the ghetto.

A shudder coursed through her.

"Elena! Elena!"

She spun around.

Chava. She was with the rest of their platoon, in front of an old stone building with two steeples on the roof. Gigantic photos of Lenin and Stalin hung from the facade. Elena grimaced at Stalin's devious face.

Chava threw her arms around Elena. "We made it! Back to where we started."

"We did." She held Chava tight. She remembered her first day at the snipers' training school in Moscow, two years earlier. The day she'd met Zina, Raya, and Alla. Now victory seemed meaningless without them.

"How's your elbow?" Chava asked.

Elena bent her arm in and out. "Good as new."

Nina approached, carrying Raya's battered guitar case.

Elena's eyes welled with tears, remembering how Raya had seized her guitar when their train was bombed. Not her backpack or even her rifle, but her guitar.

"We all decided you should have this." Nina held the case out to Elena.

"Why me?" Elena said, stunned. "I don't even know how to play."

"Raya had no family left," said Chava. "And you were so close, you, Raya, and Zina. We know she'd want you to have it."

In her head, she heard Raya's lyrical voice crooning as she played. Her hand trembled as she took the guitar. "I guess I could learn."

"Of course," said Nina.

"Just get someone else to sing," Chava joked, with an impish grin.

"Thanks a lot," Elena snorted.

The earsplitting drum and brass introduction to "The Sacred War" crashed into their conversation. One by one the girls began adding their alto and soprano voices until they combined, twittering into a crescendo with the orchestra.

Except for Elena. How could she sing about the Motherland, how could she praise Stalin, knowing he was keeping the secret of the century? How could she even feel happy about victory, after seeing the costs of war, the sacrifices made by tens of thousands of soldiers, the women brutalized by soldiers who managed to survive, the earth tormented by manmade weapons?

This is the people's war, a sacred war!
The black wings shall not dare
Fly over the Motherland . . .

She listened to the words emerging from her comrades' mouths, and was afraid of what the future held with Stalin at the wheel. She heard the passion in their voices and felt a tinge of devotion. Is it possible, she wondered, to both love and despise the Motherland?

61

He will cover you with his feathers, and under his wings you will
find refuge. This truth is your shield and armor.

—PSALM 91:4

Moscow

July 1945

President Mikhail Kalinin emerged through the Kremlin's arched entrance when the last note of the anthem faded. He reminded Elena of the expelled revolutionary Lev Trotsky, with his egg-shaped head, wire-framed spectacles, and gray whiskers.

"Comrades! Fellow countrywomen!" he began. "The strenuous work by you women, in the rear and at the front, has not been in vain. Equality for women has existed in our country since the very first day of the October Revolution. But you have won equality for women in yet another sphere: in the defense of your country, arms in hand. You have won equal rights for women in a field in which they hitherto have not taken such a direct part. But allow me, as one grown wise with years, to say to you: do not give yourself airs in your future practical work. Do not talk about the services you rendered, let others do it for you. That will be better."

"This is how they welcome us home?" said Elena, after Kalinin wished them luck amidst a mediocre round of applause. "Thanking us for risking our lives to save our country, then ordering us to shut up about it?"

"It's the Russian way," Chava said.

"That's for sure," said Elena.

"You have it all wrong," said Nina. "President Kalinin doesn't want us to hide, he just doesn't want us getting big heads."

"What about men?" said Elena. "Can they tell people what they did at the front? Isn't Kalinin worried about them getting full of themselves?"

Nina's smile waned. "That's different."

"How is that different?" Elena pressed. "How is a man's tally different than a woman's? Why is a man allowed to discuss the number of his kills, but Chava, for example, can't say proudly that she killed one hundred and nine fascists?"

"It doesn't bother me," Chava interjected. "Honestly, defending my country has been the greatest happiness on earth. I don't need to brag about what I did to feel good."

Elena was thrown by Chava's unwavering patriotism after President Kalinin's speech, by her ready acceptance to pack her accomplishments away with her uniform as if they didn't matter.

She glanced down at her clean and pressed uniform, faded and patched where shrapnel had cut through the fabric. It had become part of her body, a second skin that reflected what she'd endured. Particularly her canteen, now dented in two spots, along with Yakov's feather, her only physical connections to her former life in Minsk.

Elena felt an unexpected burst of pride as a soldier and as a Jewish woman. Giving up her faith and culture was precisely what Stalin expected and the exact opposite of what her father would want. She couldn't let her father down. She couldn't let her family down. And she couldn't let Mr. Volkhov and Mrs. Drapkina and all the murdered Jews down. She ran her fingers over the dents. One day, she promised herself, she'd flaunt her canteen and uniform and tell people how she'd shot fascists *and* was responsible for identifying Hitler's teeth.

"Surely, you know how grateful Stalin is for your service." Nina was gesturing at Chava's hefty backpack. "Just look at what the Red Army has given to help you ease back into your former lives."

They'd been issued food and clothing, just as they'd been allotted supplies when they set out for the front. This time, instead of foot wrappings and oversized, clunky boots, black high-heeled shoes had been distributed amongst the surviving snipers. And instead of uniforms, they'd received two lengths of material, two dresses (winter and summer), and a pair of fashionable trousers. The dispensed food—four kilograms of sugar, four kilograms of flour, oats, and dehydrated fruit—was a not-so-subtle collection of baking ingredients.

Elena held up her high-heeled shoes. "These will come in handy."

"For what?" Chava quipped. "Shopping at the market or cleaning your flat?"

The group broke into a fit of laughter.

"So, where are you all headed?" Nina asked, when the girls had all gone quiet.

"I'm going home," Chava said. "My mother will fatten me up with her stews and pies and my little brother will pester me with questions."

Elena looked away. Chava's mention of family summoned images of her father, Yakov, Masha, and her mother.

"What about you, Elena?" Chava asked. "Are you going back to university?"

Elena was caught off guard by the question. Without family, it didn't seem to matter what she did. She longed to see Purkayev but was afraid she'd built him up in her mind. They'd spent so little time together, really, under the most extreme circumstances. How well did they actually know one another? Her heart had charged whenever they spoke, whenever he looked at her, yet from the day she'd enrolled in the sniper training school, she'd clung to the dream of returning to university. It was what her father would have wanted and it was what she needed, to finish what she'd started, to prove to herself that the Nazis couldn't take everything away from her.

A passage from one of her favorite books, *The Oppermanns*, rose in her head: *It is not your duty to finish the work, but neither are you free to neglect it.*

"Yes," she heard herself say, "I should finish my degree."

Nina nodded in encouragement.

"Sounds like a good way to put off 'practical work' like marriage and motherhood," Chava added.

"For now," Elena said, with a sureness she hadn't felt in a long time.

Chava looked at Elena. "Well . . ."

"I'll miss you."

Chava reached out and embraced her. Elena wrapped her arms around her partner and held on. She didn't want to let go. She didn't want their friendship to change. To end.

"I really have to go." Chava pulled away from Elena.

"At ease, ladies," Nina joked.

Chava gave her a mock salute. "At ease." She and Nina turned and walked towards the train station without looking back.

Elena felt unmoored once her comrades were gone. All of a sudden, she had an urge to go to Minsk to confront the past. To find Tsila. She looked up at the clock on the Spasskaya Tower. Almost seven o'clock. Two hours until sunset. Part of her wanted to jump on a train to Minsk, while the other half wanted to wait a little bit longer, just in case *he* miraculously appeared.

She turned her attention to the demobilized soldiers moving through Red Square, a flurry of tobacco smoke and spirited voices. She enjoyed the warmth of the sun on her cheeks. Then she had the eerie sensation of being watched. Her gaze swung to Gostiny Dvor, a small courtyard that led into the square. A lanky, uniformed man was hobbling on crutches. She blinked, convinced her imagination was playing tricks on her. No, still there. About fifty meters away. Purkayev, his jacket luminous with medals. Forty meters. Thirty. Twenty.

A bewildered expression crossed her face when she saw the empty spot where his left shin and foot used to be. The unoccupied leg of his trousers was neatly folded and pinned just below his knee. Her chest tightened and released into silent sobs.

"Sorry I'm late," he said. His charcoal eyes had become cynical; they were those of a man used to looking at death. And he was dreadfully thin, with his uniform sagging over his haggard frame.

"You're . . . here," she managed.

He studied her a minute, then shifted his weight to his left crutch, reached out, and ran the back of his thumb along her cheekbone.

Something inside her awakened at his touch. She felt dizzy and warm. And scared. There was something unknowable about him. Did he believe Stalin's foolish ideas about nationalism, about Jews being nothing more than Soviet citizens? Could she trust him? Maybe doubt is my fate, she thought. She averted her gaze, confused by her tangle of feelings.

"I didn't know you played." He gestured with his head at the guitar case.

"I don't. It was . . . it was Raya's."

"Ah, yes. I remember her singing."

Her eyes filled at the memory of her comrade. She blinked back tears and looked at the empty space where his leg used to be.

"It happened just after you left, on the way to Berlin. Stray artillery," he said in a tone that didn't invite further questions.

"I'm sorry."

"Don't be. I'm alive. I still have my mind. More or less."

She caught his wry smile and felt something gust between them.

"Let's walk." He pivoted on his right crutch, swung his weight forward with a measured rigidity, and turned left onto Krasnaya Street.

Elena lengthened her stride to keep up with his surprisingly brisk pace as they passed St. Basil's Cathedral. She snuck a glance at his profile and noticed a slight, contemplative tilt to his neck.

"I just realized," she said, thinking aloud, "I don't know your given name."

"Aleksandr," he answered, reticent, as if he wasn't used to saying it out loud.

"Like Pushkin."

"And my uncle," he retorted.

She smiled.

They came to a busy corner where a young woman in a freshly pressed Red Army uniform gestured for them to cross with a group of pedestrians. On the other side, they continued with Zaryadye, the oldest trading neighborhood beyond the Kremlin walls, on their left. Elena had so much she wanted to say, but her thoughts were muddled in her head. She was disappointed in herself for being as interesting as a stick.

"There it is," he said, a few minutes later, "the Bolshoy Bridge."

"There it is," she echoed, with reverence.

They stepped onto the bridge from the embankment. Shiny black automobiles rumbled in both directions across eight lanes, while the pedestrian walkway bustled with families, children skipping ahead in tatty clothes, couples arm in arm, and soldiers walking briskly, chins up, shoulders straight, as if they were still on duty. The Moscow River ran slow and steady, with currents flapping lazily along the mucky shore. Reflections of the Red Square towers in the opaque green water reminded Elena of bullets.

At the center of the bridge, Elena stuck her hand in her coat pocket and pulled out the shabby feather she'd carried thousands of versts through combat. Yakov's feather. She ran the tip of her finger along the downy barbs and thought about how she'd kept it both as a reminder of her brother and as a good luck charm. Now it occurred to her that she'd barely given it a thought since her redeployment to SMERSH. How silly she'd been, thinking a single feather could hold such power. It was time to have faith in herself.

"Did you ever see how that film ended?" Aleksandr was saying. "You know, the one you were watching when you were summoned by Bystrov."

She turned and saw the man who'd convinced Yurovsky to leave her alone, the man who'd shot a Cossack to stop him from raping a young German girl, a reaction that could have gotten him executed. The man who'd said: *You don't need a fancy dress to look like a woman.*

"No," she whispered. "But I'd like to find out."

He leaned in towards her.

I'll be waiting for you when you return to the front.

. . . my frontline wife.

She shrank back, feeling Yurovsky's words like slicks of ice through her veins.

Aleksandr gave her a long, searching look.

She caught the spark of tenderness in his eyes and felt a warm glow spread in her chest. Instantly her qualms dissolved. She tilted her head towards him. He clasped her face with both hands and kissed her eagerly.

Then a sudden chirping refrain overhead made them both pull away and gaze upwards. Sparrows were gathering on the tops of the bridge's lampposts. Dozens of the small, identical birds sweetly chirruping all at once, as if they wanted to be noticed, as if they wanted to be heard. As if they were singing an anthem, like my platoon getting ready to march, thought Elena, with a pang of nostalgia. Then, like an abrupt rush of wind, the sparrows rose together, billowing in the carroty red sunset like a sheet hanging on a line to dry.

She watched the birds soar over the water and disappear at the bend in the river. On instinct, she reached over the railing, held her breath, and released Yakov's feather. Her breath caught in her throat as she watched it swirl in the breeze.

"I know I should be happy the war's over, but I can't stop thinking . . ." She whisked her gaze towards a young family gathered around a worn-out Red Army officer. The three children beamed at their father and vied for his attention, snatching his hands and arms. The youngest was trying to climb his leg as if it was a tree trunk. Tears of happiness rolled down the wife's freckled cheeks.

"Elena?" he nudged.

"Nothing's really changed," she said, carefully. "All around us, people are celebrating, but we're back to the way it was before the war."

"I know." The chords in his long neck pulsed. "I'm already looking over my shoulder because of what I did that morning in Germany."

"The Cossack?"

He nodded, grimly. "One day, someone might tell the wrong person and they'll come looking for me."

She turned to the river, unable to face the truth of his prophecy. She couldn't help but think about Käthe and Echtmann, rotting in a prison cell because they knew the facts behind Stalin's lie. And there was the translator she'd replaced, probably sent to a gulag or prison, because she'd voiced an unacceptable opinion. Liberty was an illusion.

"What was it all for?" she said, flatly. "Was it worth it?"

"Hitler's dead," Aleksandr said, "along with his worst cronies. Don't you think it was worth something to abolish a regime that wanted to exterminate Jews?"

"Yes"—Elena nodded, grateful he hadn't fallen for Stalin's despicable ruse—"although we've already been exterminated on paper. We're not a nation, remember? We're not Jewish, we're Soviet citizens."

"At least you're alive," he responded.

Her heart stirred. She wanted to tell him everything about her time with SMERSH. She wanted him to hold her. At the same time, she was afraid. He didn't belong in her world. He didn't deserve the venom he'd face if they ended up together.

"Stalin thinks he's omniscient after defeating the fascists," she continued, pointedly. "Now he won't allow anyone to oppose him. Now he's going to come after the ones Hitler didn't catch. He's just getting started."

Aleksandr regarded her, thoughtful. "The only thing I know for sure is that we have to live every day as if it's our last. We have no control over our fate. We can never know our future."

She liked his directness, how he didn't shy away from difficult subjects, his truthfulness. She met his unflinching gaze and felt strangely calm. She peered at the river, in search of the feather, but it had vanished with the last splinters of daylight. She looked over her shoulder, then walked beside Aleksandr to the other side of the bridge.

AUTHOR'S NOTE

Spoiler alert: Read after you finish the book!

Yes, I had a mission to make public the secret of the century, that
we had found Hitler's body . . . I myself had no intention of leaving these things hidden away, and my silence weighed heavily on
me, but these facts had been classified a state secret and the price
for disclosing them would have been seven to fifteen years' impris-
onment. Quite a long time. I had to watch history being distorted
without saying anything, confiding in close friends.
            —YELENA RZHEVSKAYA, RED ARMY INTERPRETER

*T*he *Night Sparrow* began to evolve when I discovered the
Central Women's Sniper Training School in Moscow. Immediately, I was enthralled by the idea of an entire school
devoted to training women as snipers during the "Great Patriotic
War," as it was called in the Soviet Union. I pored over photos of the
female cadets, stunned by their youthful faces and charismatic smiles,
devastated by their grim odds of survival. Of the 2,484 female snipers
deployed (about half of whom were graduates from the snipers' training school), only one in five lived to see the end of the war.

I had to write about these courageous women, sorely neglected
within the historical narrative. But first, I had to understand who
they were, what motivated them to become snipers, and how they
endured the brutal conditions on the front.

After a bit more digging, I came upon illicit journals written by sniper girls. I was struck by their candidness, their vulnerability, their diverse backgrounds, and their shared love of music. And I found them to be incredibly relatable, even though almost eighty years had passed since they recorded their thoughts, fears, and experiences. I covered the walls of my office with photos of these girls, and often found myself staring at them, in awe.

Once they'd passed final written exams at the school, a platoon of female snipers was assigned to the elite 3rd Shock Army of the Kalinin Front, part of the Eastern Front. On foot, as the weather became arctic-cold and damp, the girls marched through Roslavl, Latvia, and Spas-Demensk. They took part in the Battle of Smolensk, helped capture Vitebsk, then joined a 1943 offensive that liberated Nevel, a city near the eastern border of Belorussia.

A few, like Roza Shanina (dubbed "the unseen terror of East Prussia"), stood out, not just because of her fierce determination to take down fascists, but because of her insatiable desire to experience all that life had to offer, to live in the moment even if her actions evoked gossip and reprisals. I was so enamored by Roza, she became the inspiration for my character Zina.

I chose Minsk as Elena's hometown after reading Elena Drapkina's interview on the Centropa Jewish Network (centropa.org). Drapkina, from Minsk, courageously escaped the ghetto and became a partisan. She also happened to be a good friend of Masha Bruskina, a seventeen-year-old Jewish girl, publicly executed by the Wehrmacht for helping Soviet soldiers escape. Masha's little-known story had such a visceral impact on me, I took the liberty, as a historical fiction author, to make her Elena's younger sister, whose murder kindles Elena's quest for vengeance.

All of the historical events are true and many of the characters in *The Night Sparrow* are real, including the twelve Jewish women executed in the Minsk ghetto and the workers and children who were shot and buried in a mass grave. However, I did move some accounts from other fronts to Elena's platoon, to intensify the drama and to shine a light on female snipers who showed extraordinary courage. Snipers Natalya Kovshova and Mariya Polivanova, for example, jointly killed more than 300 Germans and demonstrated astonishing valor on the Northwestern Front, on August 14, 1942. Their regiment was unable to resist the German onslaught. One by one, Soviet soldiers were killed until only Natalya and Mariya remained. Both were wounded and both knew being captured was out of the question. Natalya pulled the pin on her grenade. When the Germans reached their trench, she detonated the grenade, killing herself and Mariya, as well as several enemy soldiers. The girls were named as Heroes of the Soviet Union posthumously, the highest award given.

An astonishing half million Jews served in the Red Army, including 303 Jewish generals and admirals and 147 Jewish Heroes of the Soviet Union. Zvi Gitelman, in a paper for the University of Michigan, "Why They Fought and What Soviet Jews Saw and How It Is Remembered," says Jews enlisted for revenge, "to rescue Jewish honour as fighters and resisters," and to "refute stereotypes of Jews as shirkers."

While the motives of Jewish female snipers varied, their actions certainly proved their honor and negated the idea of Jews dodging combat. There was Evgeniya Peretyatko, with an astonishing tally of 148 kills, Bella Epstein, who insisted on going to the front, and Margarite Kotikovskaya, a law student turned sniper. There were also Jewish translators such as Irina Dunaevskaia, Bella Tsukerman, and Yelena Rzhevskaya.

Elena's redeployment is informed by Yelena Rzhevskaya, who worked solely as an interpreter during the war and wrote about her experiences in *Memoirs of a Soviet Interpreter*. In 1945, Rzhevskaya was selected for a SMERSH counterintelligence unit; SMERSH (Death to Spies) was created by Vladimir Lenin to monitor and quell political and domestic dissent. For my character Elena, this unit allowed her to seek vengeance without killing. It gave her a sense of achievement and allowed her to distance herself from the relentless Soviet dogma. Temporarily.

A common thread running between my previous novel, *Daughters of the Occupation*, and *The Night Sparrow* is my quest to understand how ordinary people become killers. Elena, for instance, seeks vengeance, yet at the same time, wrestles with her conscience. Meanwhile, others such as the notorious Lyudmila Pavlichenko, who was on the verge of completing her PhD when the war began, achieved a tally of 309. Tatyana Kostyrina had 120 kills and commanded a battalion in 1943 after her commander was killed. Olga Bordashevskaya had 108 kills, and cherubic-faced Nina Lobkovskaya, with 89 kills, commanded a female platoon in a Berlin offensive, December 31, 1944. Overall, the female snipers' combined tally was 11,280 kills. Still, many girls struggled to pull the trigger.

This was surprisingly common. In his book *On Killing: The Psychological Cost of Learning to Kill in War and Society*, author David Grossman, a former lieutenant colonel in the US Army, says that just 15 to 20 percent of soldiers actually fired their weapons in World War II.

The brazen sexual abuse within the Red Army appears to be erased from the Soviet canon. Women from all ranks were forced into becoming "Front-line wives (PPZh)" or "Mobile Field Wives," which meant living with the officer who'd claimed them.

Remarkably, other female soldiers viewed these "wives" with

disdain for their inappropriate behavior and perceived special privileges because of their relationships with commanders. This attitude is clearly seen in the words of Tatiana Atabek, who wrote, when she was recovering from her wounds in 1945:

> "And that bitch PPZh, awarded by fate, lies on the fifth floor with what [illness] I will not say." (Those who were wounded in honest battle are on the 4th floor of the hospital, while those who are ill with venereal disease are on the fifth floor. Of course they are hostile relations.)

The reprehensible behavior of Red Army male soldiers declined further as soon as they set foot on German soil. In his 2002 essay for the *Guardian*, author Antony Beevor explains how "the subject of the Red Army's mass rapes in Germany has been so repressed in Russia that even today veterans refuse to acknowledge what really happened . . . The Red Army had managed to convince itself that because it had assumed the moral mission to liberate Europe from fascism it could behave entirely as it likes, both personally and politically."

I couldn't get this brutality out of my mind as I traveled to Eastern Europe and drove along the B-1 (also known as Liberation Road Europe), the same narrow, winding road the snipers marched on from the Oder River to Berlin. They'd only gone 20 kilometers (13 miles; 18 versts*) when they found themselves on the outskirts of Seelow, the site of the largest battle of World War II on German soil. The female snipers took part in this bloodbath, where Marshal Georgy Zhukov

---

* Versts are a Russian measurement for distance, with one verst equivalent to 1.1 km and 0.66 mile.

infamously tried to blind the enemy by turning on 143 anti-aircraft searchlights at the front line. Instead, Soviet troops were disoriented by the shadows created by the lights. It took three days for the Red Army, including the snipers, to finally crush the Germans and advance to Berlin, albeit with thousands killed on both sides.

Today, Seelow is home to the Memorial and Museum Seelow Heights, with a vast collection of Soviet artillery including Katyusha rocket launchers. For a historical fiction author, this is like finding gold! I was able to study and photograph actual weapons from every angle, a tremendous advantage when it comes to writing about conflicts like the Battle of Seelow Heights.

By the time Rzhevskaya's SMERSH unit and the snipers' platoon arrived in Berlin in 1945, they'd marched more than 1,600 kilometers from the training school in Moscow. While they didn't take part in the Battle of Berlin, the snipers and Rzhevskaya were there when the city fell. The girls wrote the names of their fallen comrades on the pillars of the Brandenburg Gate, while Rzhevskaya translated interrogations of high-level German officers.

Then a number of bodies, burned beyond recognition, were found in the Chancellery garden, including Goebbels's remains, with his metal prosthesis and orthopedic boot. In an ironic twist, Goebbels, who'd created the yellow star to identify Jews, was spotted by his yellow tie, which had miraculously survived the fire set to his body.

There were two unrecognizable corpses. The only significant remains were one set of teeth. Although many suspected they might be Hitler's, proof was needed. In *Memoirs of a Wartime Interpreter*, Rzhevskaya explains how her SMERSH unit enlisted the help of Hitler's dental assistant, Käthe Heusermann, and dental technician, Fritz Echtmann. Heusermann, who'd stayed in Berlin to await her fiancé's return from the front, had actually assisted Hitler's dentist in extracting his teeth. Echtmann had made a bridge for Hitler's mouth. Little did they know that the straightforward identification of Hitler's teeth would lead to years of detention because of Stalin's inexplicable ploy to hide Hitler's fate from the world.

Since the Chancellery was under the 5th Shock Army's guard, and Rzhevskaya's unit was attached to the 3rd Shock Army, they had to sneak the remains in question out. On May 6, 1945, Rzhevskaya and her two SMERSH comrades managed to get the bodies over the fence and into a truck. Here's another splendid quirk of fate—the doctor who performed the autopsy on Hitler's remains was a Jewish woman, Anna Marants. I love the double irony of a Jewish interpreter (Rzhevskaya) holding Hitler's teeth, which were key to the final identification, and a Jewish doctor examining his charred body!

Hitler's death was conveyed to Stalin, but he suppressed this news from world leaders and the press. The Soviet public was further confused by Hitler doubles who appeared, dead, in the Chancellery, and by relentless rumors that Hitler had been spotted in Argentina or that he'd escaped by air to a secret hideout. For decades rumors persisted, even after North American media unanimously confirmed his death, and you can still find conspiracy theories in modern documentaries about his fate.

Meanwhile, Heusermann and Echtmann were condemned "as witnesses of Hitler's death" in a 1951 resolution of the Special Council of the Ministry of Internal Affairs. Heusermann spent six months in the Lubyanka Prison, followed by six years in solitary confinement in Lefortovo. In December 1951, she was sent to a Siberian labor camp where she almost died of starvation. Echtmann was released in the spring of 1954 and returned to work as a dentist in Berlin.

Käthe Heusermann was finally released in 1955, when Khruschev agreed to return German prisoners. She was forty-five years old. Her family had pronounced her dead in 1950. Her fiancé was married with children. She resumed work as a dental assistant.

Rzhevskaya wrongly assumed Heusermann and Echtmann were living freely in Germany. When she found out they'd been confined for years, she felt terrible. In *Memoirs of a Wartime Interpreter*, she writes: "That burden of guilt will never leave me."

Repression is a recurring theme of *The Night Sparrow*, when you consider how the mass rapes within the Red Army continue to be stifled by the Russian government today, along with the female snipers' accomplishments during the Great Patriotic War and, of course, Hitler's death. At the snipers' 1945 demobilization ceremony in Moscow, President Mikhail Kalinin acknowledged their equality as women and as soldiers who defended their country, before advising them to keep quiet about their tremendous accomplishments in the war: "Do not talk about the services you rendered, let others do it for you. That will be better."

This "don't tell" attitude prevailed, as evidenced by USSR Marshal Timoshenko's address to female veterans in 1966:

> Dear women comrades! It is you who give life, and no one more than you cherishes peace, tranquility and life on earth! . . . As a veteran of the Soviet Armed Forces, I would like to say thank you to the women, to the mothers, who raised strong and courageous sons, brave combatants, defenders of the Homeland.

Thankfully, now that the snipers' journals have been translated into English, their own words are giving voice to all 2,484 of their intrepid comrades. Now we know what they endured and what they achieved during combat. Now there is indisputable proof that historian John Keegan was wrong when he wrote, in his 1994 *History of Warfare*, "Women . . . do not fight . . . and they never, in any military sense, fight men."

I can't let a man have the last word in a book about female snipers. Hence, I'd like to conclude with a quote from Reina Pennington, associate professor of history at Norwich University, whose words in the *Journal of Military History* reveal why I felt compelled to write *The Night Sparrow*: "The history of Soviet women in combat is still a neglected topic. In particular, general histories of the Second World War and the Great Patriotic War say very little about women's participation."

ACKNOWLEDGMENTS

Writing *The Night Sparrow* has been a rewarding experience that I couldn't have accomplished without the support of many dedicated people. I'm incredibly grateful for my editors at HarperCollins—Janice Zawerbny in Canada and Sara Nelson in the United States—for believing in the story and for giving *The Night Sparrow* a home. Their constructive guidance helped me elevate my writing style and the narrative.

While researching *The Night Sparrow*, I watched countless documentaries and films; most notable was *And the Dawns Here Are Quiet*, a Soviet movie about a platoon of female gunners, which was instrumental for learning about Red Army tactics and for seeing the fierce determination of female soldiers. Additional noteworthy films include *War of the Century*, an enlightening documentary about a female interpreter, *On the Road to Berlin*, and *Moscow Strikes Back*.

To immerse myself in the setting and history, I traveled to Eastern Europe with my mostly patient husband, Steven Greer, who drove from Küstrin, Poland, to Berlin so that I could take photos. He didn't complain (too much) when I insisted on trekking to every Berlin location in my novel!

I needed to see an actual rifle in order to write authentically about female snipers. My cousin Dave Sanders (retired sergeant, Toronto Police Services) connected me with a police officer (he prefers to remain anonymous) who has a fascinating collection of sniper rifles. I was able to hold several, experience the jolt of recoil, and see notches carved in the wooden stock, denoting kills. The rifle was heavier than I'd expected, and longer, which boosted my admiration for the female snipers. As well, this officer, who is Jewish and was raised in the Soviet Union, told me fascinating stories about his time in the Pioneers and the Komsomol youth group.

I'm also fortunate to have a friend who grew up in Bulgaria in Soviet times, Maryia Petkova. She and I have spent hours over coffee talking about her childhood under the Soviet regime, and she and her Russian husband, Georgi Shopov, read my manuscript and pointed out language and factual errors that I never would have caught.

Rabbi Stephen Wise, a staunch supporter of my writing, has read all of my manuscripts including *The Night Sparrow*. He gave me valuable suggestions that helped tighten the narrative. Joy Fielding has become a mentor and a friend. I truly appreciate her suggestions and her enthusiasm for my work, especially on those days when it's hard to find the right words.

There would be no book without the unwavering support from my agent, Beverley Slopen, who has an amazing eye for detail. I trust her implicitly and am lucky to have her backing me. As well, I am fortunate to have such a dedicated and professional team at HarperCollins, including production editor Natalie Meditsky, who organized the manuscript's editing process, copyeditor Tilman Lewis, whose scrupulous eye ensured that every detail was correct, and Alan Jones, who designed the galvanizing cover!

A special thank-you to Marianna Evenstein for helping with the German translations.

Finally, I must thank my local coffee shops, Figaro and Aroma, for putting up with my extended writing visits. As a writer with ADHD, I get far more accomplished in cafés, surrounded by the buzz of conversations, than I do in my quiet home office. (There's actually a name for this coping mechanism—body mirroring—which means unintentionally mimicking the behavior of others.) Without such welcoming places to write, and without an absurd number of espressos, I might still be working on this manuscript!

SELECTED BIBLIOGRAPHY

BOOKS

Alexievich, Svetlana, *The Unwomanly Face of War*. London: Penguin Random House, 2017.

Beevor, Antony, *The Fall of Berlin 1945*. New York: Penguin Books, 2020.

Bemporad, Elissa, *Becoming Soviet Jews: The Bolshevik Experiment in Minsk*. Indiana: Indiana University Press, 2013.

Brisard, Jean-Christophe, and Parshina, Lana, *The Death of Hitler: The Final Word*. New York: Da Capo Press, 2018.

Grossman, Vasily, *Life and Fate*. London: Vintage Classics, 2006.

Koschorrek, Gunter K., *Blood Red Snow: The Memoirs of a German Soldier on the Eastern Front*. London: Greenhill Books, 2002.

Le Tissier, Tony, *The Siege of Kustrin, 1945: Gateway to Berlin*. UK: Pen & Sword Military, 2009.

Mogan, A.G., *Stalin's Sniper: The War Diary of Roza Shanina*. A.G. Mogan, 2020.

Obraztsov, Y., and Anders, Maud, *Soviet Women Snipers of the Second World War*. Paris: Histoire & Collections, 2014.

Pavlichenko, Lyudmilla, *Lady Death: The Memoirs of Stalin's Sniper*. London: Greenhill Books, 2015.

Porter, Jack Nusan, *Jewish Partisans of the Soviet Union During World War II*. Boston: Cherry Orchard Books, 2021.

Rzhevskaya, Yelena, *Memoirs of a Wartime Interpreter: From the Battle for Moscow to Hitler's Bunker*. London: Greenhill Books, 2018.

Sakaida, Henry, *Heroines of the Soviet Union*. UK: Osprey Publishing, 2012.

Schechter, Brandon M., *The Stuff of Soldiers: A History of the Red Army in World War II Through Objects*. Ithaca, NY: Cornell University Press, 2019.

Shanina, Roza, *Soviet Sniper: The Memoirs of Roza Shanina*. London: Greenhill Books, 2020.

Snyder, Timothy, *Bloodlands: Europe Between Hitler and Stalin*. New York: Basic Books, 2010.

Vaksberg, Arkady, *Stalin Against the Jews*. New York: Alfred A. Knopf, 1994.

Vinogradova, Lyuba, *Avenging Angels*. London: MacLeHose Press, 2017.

Werth, Alexander and Werth, Nicolas, *Russia at War*. New York: Skyhorse Publishing, 2017.

Zhukova, Yulia, *Girl with a Sniper Rifle: An Eastern Front Memoir*. London: Greenhill Books, 2019.

FILMS

Annaud, Jean-Jacques, dir. *Enemy at the Gates*. France, 2001.

De Concini, Ennio, dir. *Hitler: The Last Ten Days*. UK, 1973.

Hirschbiegel, Oliver, dir. *Downfall*. Germany, 2004.

Mokritskiy, Sergey, dir. *The Battle for Sevastopol*. Russia, 2015.

Popov, Fyodor, dir. *Convoy 48*. Russia, 2019.

Popov, Sergei, dir. *On the Road to Berlin*. Russia, 2015.

Rees, Laurence, dir. *War of the Century*. UK, 1999.

Rostotsky, Stanislav, dir. *The Dawns Here Are Quiet*. Russia, 1972.

Varlamov, Leonid, and Kopalin, Ilia, dirs. *Moscow Strikes Back*. Russia, 1942.

ONLINE RESOURCES

Blavatnik Archive. "Memories of the Front: Soviet Jewish Veterans of WWII." Accessed April 27, 2024. https://www.blavatnikarchive.org/story/memories-front

Centropa. "Alexandra Shifra Melenevskaya Interview." Accessed April 27, 2024. https://www.centropa.org/biography/alexandra-shifra-melenevskaya

Centropa. "Eva Ryzhevskaya Interview." Accessed April 27, 2024. https://www.centropa.org/biography/eva-ryzhevskaya

Centropa. "Marina Sineokaya Interview." Accessed April 27, 2024. https://www.centropa.org/biography/marina-sineokaya

Columbia College. "Weren't We Soldiers Like Everybody Else: Soviet Women in Combat During the Second World War." Accessed May 1, 2024. https://www.academia.edu/43008948/_Werent_we_soldiers_like_everybody_else_Soviet_Women_in_Combat_During_the_Second_World_War

Digital Commons at Buffalo State. "Experiences of Soviet Women Combatants During WWII." Accessed May 1, 2024. https://www.academia.edu/10461938/Soviet_Women_Snipers_Experiences_of_Fire

International Journal of Social Science Studies. "Holocaust and WWII: Jews in the Red Army." Accessed May 1, 2024. https://www.academia.edu/11157526/Holocaust_and_WWII_Jews_in_the_Red_Army

Jewish Chronicle. "Why I Had to Expose the 'Secret' of Hitler." Accessed April 22, 2024. https://www.thejc.com/culture/books/why-i-had-to-expose-the-secret-of-hitler-1.66572

Jewish Women's Archive. "The Shalvi/Hyman Encyclopedia of Jewish Women." Accessed April 27, 2024. https://jwa.org/encyclopedia

Life. "After the Fall: Photos of Hitler's Bunker and the Ruins of Berlin." Accessed April 27, 2024. https://www.life.com/history/after-the-fall-photos-of-hitlers-bunker-and-the-ruins-of-berlin

OpenEdition Journals. "Girls and Women. Love, Sex, Duty and Sexual Harassment in the Ranks of the Red Army 1941–1945." Accessed May 1, 2024. https://journals.openedition.org/pipss/4202

Peripheral Histories. "In the Fight Yet on the Margins: Latvian Jewish Red Army Soldiers." Accessed April 29, 2024.

https://www.peripheralhistories.co.uk/post/in-the-fight-yet-on
-the-margins-latvian-jewish-red-army-soldiers

Politika. "Women at War in the Red Army." Accessed April 27, 2024.
https://www.politika.io/en/notice/women-at-war-in-the-red-army

Sixièmes Journées franco-allemandes. "Soviet Women Snipers—
Experiences of Fire." Accessed May 1, 2024. https://www.academia
.edu/10461938/Soviet_Women_Snipers_Experiences_of_Fire